Simona ARHNSTEDT
ALL IN

piatkus

PIATKUS

First published in Sweden in 2014 by Forum
First published in the US in 2016 by Kensington Books,
by arrangement with Nordin Agency, Sweden
First published in Great Britain in 2016 by Piatkus,
by arrangement with Kensington Books

13 5 7 9 10 8 6 4 2

A CIP catalogue record for this book
is available from the British Library.

ISBN 978-0-349-41376-1

Printed and bound in Great Britain by
Clays Ltd, St Ives plc

Papers used by Piatkus are from well-managed forests
and other responsible sources.

MIX
Paper from
responsible sources
FSC® C104740

Piatkus
An imprint of
Little, Brown Book Group
Carmelite House
50 Victoria Embankment
London EC4Y 0DZ

An Hachette UK Company
www.hachette.co.uk

www.piatkus.co.uk

Simona Ahrnstedt was born in Prague and is a licensed psychologist, a cognitive behavioural therapist, and most importantly, a bestselling author. As her novels have swept bestseller lists in her native Sweden, she has become a spokesperson for books by women, for women, and about women. Her provocative women's fiction has been sold in multiple languages as well as audio format. She lives outside of Stockholm, Sweden, with her two teenagers.

Praise for Simona Ahrnstedt:

'I've been searching for this feeling all year: this book left me absolutely breathless'
New York Times bestselling author Christina Lauren

'*All In* is sexy, smart, and completely unputdownable. Breathtaking, from start to finish. I loved this book, and I can't wait to go whatever Simona Ahrnstedt takes her readers next'
New York Times bestselling author Tessa Dare

'Everything a reader could want!'
New York Times bestselling author Eloisa James

DISCARDED

ALL IN

Wednesday, June 25

David Hammar peered out the domed window of the helicopter. They were a thousand feet over the Swedish countryside and could see about twenty-five miles. He adjusted the headset that let him speak to the other occupants in a normal conversational voice.

"Over there," he said, turning around to face Michel Chamoun, who was sitting in the backseat and also looking out the window. David pointed to the yellow Gyllgarn Castle as it came into view.

The pilot, Tom Lexington, set the course. "How close do you want me to take you?" he asked, his eyes on the destination.

"Not too close, Tom. Just so we can see it a little better." David didn't take his eyes off the castle. "I don't want to attract any unnecessary attention."

Green meadows, glittering lakes, and thick woods spread out before and beneath them like an idyllic pastoral landscape painting. The castle itself was built on an islet in the middle of an unusually wide river. Lively water rushed past on both sides of the islet, forming a natural moat that had at one time provided genuine protection against enemies.

Tom swung the helicopter in a wide arc.

Horses and sheep grazed in the fields below them. An avenue lined with enormous oak trees, several hundred years old, led in from the country road. The well-tended fruit trees and colorful plantings surrounding the beautiful castle were visible even from this height.

It looks like a fucking paradise.

"The realtor I talked to estimated the value of the building alone at over thirty million Swedish kronor," David said.

"That's a lot of money," Michel noted.

"And that's in addition to the forest and pastureland. And the waterways. There's thousands of acres of land and water. That alone is worth over two hundred." David kept listing off the assets. "There's game in the forest and countless smaller buildings that are part of the estate. And then there are the furnishings, of course, the fifteenth-century war trophies, the fancy silver and Russian porcelain, and an art collection that includes pieces from the last three hundred years. All the auction houses in the world will be fighting over them."

David turned around in his seat. Michel studied the yellow castle they were hovering over.

"And it's all owned by the company?" Michel asked incredulously. "Not by the family?"

David nodded in confirmation. "It's unbelievable that they chose to do that," he agreed. "That's what happens when people think they're invincible."

"No one is invincible," said Michel.

"No."

Michel looked out the window. David waited as his friend's dark eyes swept over the fields. "It's a national gem," Michel continued. "If we parcel this up and sell it all off, there'll be a real outcry."

"Not *if*," David said. "When."

Because they were going to do just that, he was sure of it. They would subdivide those fertile fields and sell them off to the highest bidders. People would complain, and no one would scream louder than the current owners. He smiled faintly at the thought of them and gave Michel a questioning look. "Have you seen enough?"

Michel nodded, and David said, "Can you take us back to the city, Tom? We're done here."

Tom nodded. The helicopter made an elegant turn and rose. They left the idyllic scene behind them and headed back to Stockholm. Highways, forests, and factories passed by beneath them.

Fifteen minutes later they entered the capital city's air-control zone, and Tom started talking to the control tower in Bromma. David half-listened to the conversation and the short, standardized phrases.

". . . 1,500 feet, request full stop landing, three persons onboard."
"Approved, straight-in landing, runway three zero . . ."

Tom Lexington was a skillful pilot. He maneuvered the helicopter with calm movements and a watchful eye. In his day job he worked for a private firm that, among other things, managed the security for Hammar Capital. He and David had known each other for a long time. David counted him as one of his best friends, and when David decided to inspect the castle from the air Tom had volunteered his piloting skills and his time.

"I appreciate your flying us," David said.

Tom didn't say anything, just nodded almost imperceptibly to acknowledge he'd heard.

David turned to Michel. "We have plenty of time before the board meeting," he said with a glance at his watch. "Malin called. Everything is ready," he continued, referring to Malin Theselius, their communications director.

Michel adjusted his big, muscular, suit-clad body in the backseat. The rings on his fingers sparkled as he scratched his shaved scalp. "They're going to skin you alive," he said as Stockholm passed a thousand feet below them. "You know that, right?"

"*Us,*" David said.

Michel smiled wryly. "Nah, you. *You're* the cover boy and the evil venture capitalist. I'm just a poor Lebanese immigrant following orders."

Michel was the smartest man David knew and a senior partner in David's firm, Hammar Capital. Soon they would entirely rewrite Sweden's financial map. But Michel was right. David, the founder, who had a reputation for being hard and arrogant, was going to be hung out to dry in the financial press. And he was kind of looking forward to it.

Michel yawned. "When this is over I'm going to take a vacation and sleep for at least a week."

David turned to look back again, peering at the suburbs in the distance. He wasn't tired, quite the contrary. He had been preparing for this fight for half his life, and he didn't want a vacation. He wanted war.

They had been planning this latest battle for almost a year. It was the biggest deal Hammar Capital had ever done, a hostile takeover of an enormous corporation, and the next few weeks would be critical. No one had ever done anything like this.

"What are you thinking?" David said into his headset. He knew Michel inside and out, knew his silence meant something, that Michel's keen mind was working on some legal or financial detail.

"Mostly that it's going to be hard to keep this secret much longer. Someone must have started wondering about the movements on the stock market. It won't be long before someone—a stockbroker maybe—starts leaking to the press."

"Yes," David agreed, because things leaked all the time. "We'll keep it under wraps as long as we can," he said. They'd had this discussion many times. They'd polished their arguments, searched for holes in their logic, grown stronger and more cunning. "We'll keep buying," he said. "But just a little at a time, less than before. I'll talk to my contacts."

"The price of the shares is starting to rise quickly now."

"I saw that," David said. The curve of the share prices looked like a wave. "We'll have to see how long it holds financially."

It was always a balancing act how fast you could proceed. The more aggressively a company's shares were traded, the more the action drove the price up. If word got out that Hammar Capital was the one doing the buying—then the rate would bolt. So far they had been exceedingly cautious. They had bought through reliable dummy companies and only in small quantities, day in and day out. Small transactions that were no more than a ripple on the enormous surface of the stock market. But both he and Michel realized that they were nearing a critical threshold.

"Of course, we knew we were going to be forced to go public with this sooner or later," David said. "Malin has been working on the press release for weeks."

"It's going to be insane," Michel said.

David smiled. "I know. All we can do is hope we can fly under the radar for a little while longer," he said.

Michel nodded. After all, this was what Hammar Capital did. Their team of analysts searched for companies that weren't doing as well as they should be. David and Michel identified the problems—often incompetent leadership—and then vacuumed up shares in order to put together a majority holding.

Then they went in, brutally took over, broke the company into pieces and restructured, sold, and profited. They were better at this than almost anyone else—owning and improving. Sometimes it went smoothly. People cooperated, and Hammar Capital was able to drive its agenda. Sometimes there was a fight.

"I'd still like to get someone from the owning family on our side," David said as southern Stockholm spread out beneath them.

Having one or more of the big shareholders, some of the giant retirement fund managers, for example, on your side was critical for success in a hostile takeover this big. David and Michel had spent a lot of time convincing the managers, attended endless meetings, and run the numbers countless times. But winning over someone from the actual owning family had several advantages. In part, it would be an enormously prestigious symbolic win, especially with this firm, Investum, one of Sweden's biggest and oldest companies. It would also automatically win over a number of other shareholders who would vote in favor of Hammar Capital if David and Michel could show that they had someone from the inner circle on their side. "It would make the process a lot easier," he continued.

"But who?"

"There is one person who actually has gone her own way in that family," said David as Bromma Airport came into view on the horizon.

Michel was quiet for a bit. "You mean the daughter, right?"

"Yes," David said. "She's an unknown but considered to be quite the talent. It's possible that she's dissatisfied with how the men are treating her." Investum wasn't just an old and traditional company. It was patriarchal in a way that would make the 1950s seem modern and enlightened.

"Do you really believe you can win over *anyone* from that family?" Michel asked hesitantly. "You're not exactly popular with them."

David almost laughed at the understatement.

Investum was controlled by the De la Grip family, and the company did billions of kronor worth of business a day. Indirectly Investum, and thus the De la Grip family, controlled close to a tenth of Sweden's GNP and owned the biggest bank in the country. Family members sat on the board of directors of close to every major Swedish company. The De la Grip family was upper-class, traditional, and wealthy. As close to royalty as you could get without actually *being* royal. And with significantly bluer blood than any member of the House of Bernadotte, Sweden's royal family. It would be unlikely for David Hammar, the upstart, to get anyone from the innermost circle—known for their loyalty—to change sides and join him, an infamous venture capitalist and corporate raider.

But he'd done it before, convinced a few family members to join forces with him. That often meant leaving a trail of broken family ties behind him, which he usually regretted, but in this case it would be a welcome bonus.

"I'm going to try," he said.

"That's damn near insane," said Michel. It wasn't the first time in the last year he'd uttered those words.

David nodded briefly. "I already called to set up a lunch meeting with her."

"Of course you did," said Michel as the helicopter started its descent for landing. The flight had taken less than thirty minutes. "And what did she say?"

David thought about the cool voice he'd gotten on the line, not an assistant's but that of Natalia De la Grip herself. She had sounded surprised but hadn't said very much, just thanked him for the invitation, and then had her assistant confirm the lunch appointment by e-mail.

"She said she was looking forward to our meeting."

"She did?"

David laughed, tersely and joylessly. Her voice had been distinctive in that patrician way that almost inevitably triggered his disdain for the upper classes. Natalia De la Grip was one of about a hundred women in Sweden who had been born with the title of countess, the elite of the elite. He hardly had the words to express how little he thought of that kind of person.

"No," he said. "She didn't say that." But then he hadn't expected her to, either.

2

Natalia searched through the stacks of paper on her desk. She pulled out a page of tables and numbers.

"Aha!" she said, waving the piece of paper around. She directed a look of triumph at the platinum-blond woman sitting on the little visitor's chair, which didn't actually fit in the cubbyhole that constituted Natalia's office. Natalia's friend, Åsa Bjelke, peered at the piece of paper with little interest before she went back to examining her pale fingernail polish. Natalia studied the mess on her desk and continued searching. She hated disorder, but it was almost impossible to keep this small workspace tidy.

"How are you *really* doing?" Åsa asked, taking a sip of the coffee she'd picked up on her way over and watching Natalia go back to searching the stacks of paper. "I'm only asking because you seem really unfocused," she continued. "And while you do have a lot of quirks, lack of focus isn't usually one of them. I've never seen you like this."

Natalia furrowed her brow. An important document was gone without a trace. She was going to be forced to ask one of the overworked assistants.

"J-O called from Denmark," Natalia said about her boss. "He wanted me to submit a report, and I just can't find it." She spotted another piece of paper, pulled it out, and read it with weary eyes. She hadn't gotten much sleep the previous night. First, she had worked until the wee hours. The enormous approaching deal was claiming almost all her time. Then a client had called early—very early—in the morning to complain about something that definitely could have waited a couple of hours. She glanced up at Åsa. "What do you mean I have quirks?"

Åsa took a sip from her disposable coffee cup, and then without responding to Natalia's question asked, "What's the problem?"

"Problem*s*," Natalia replied. "My job. My dad. My mom. Everything."

"But what's all this paperwork for? Whatever happened to a paperless society?"

Natalia glanced at Åsa. Her friend looked chipper and well rested, nicely dressed, and neatly manicured. A wave of irritation surged through her.

"Look, not that I don't appreciate your unannounced visits," Natalia said, not entirely sincerely, "but my dad is always complaining about how much money his lawyers make. Shouldn't you be over at Investum working for your salary? I mean, instead of sitting here in my cramped office, swathed in Prada, harassing me?"

"I earn my high salary," Åsa said, waving her hand dismissively. "And you know full well that your father's not going to get rid of me." She gave Natalia a look. "You *know* that."

Natalia nodded. She knew.

"I happened to be in the neighborhood," Åsa continued, "and was just wondering if you wanted to get lunch. If I have to eat one more lunch with any of those other Investum attorneys, I'll kill myself. Actually, if I'd known how extremely boring lawyers are, I don't think I would have gone to law school." She fluffed her blond hair. "Maybe I would have made a good cult leader."

"I can't," Natalia said quickly, a little *too* quickly, she realized, but it was too late. "I'm busy." She cleared her throat. "Sorry," she added unnecessarily. "Like I said, I'm busy." She looked down and started flipping through some papers she'd already flipped through to avoid Åsa's penetrating stare.

"Really?"

"Yes," Natalia said. "That's not so weird, is it?"

Åsa's eyes narrowed. "Considering you have a brain like a supercomputer, you're a terrible liar," she said. "You had time yesterday. You said so yourself. And it's not like you have any other friends. Are you trying to avoid me?"

"No, I *am* busy. And I would never dream of trying to avoid you. You're my best friend. Although I do have other friends, you know. Maybe tomorrow? My treat."

"Busy doing what, if I might ask?" Åsa said, not letting the possibility of a free lunch tomorrow distract her.

Natalia didn't say anything. She looked down at her buried desk. Now would be a good time for one of her phones to ring, or maybe the fire alarm could go off, she thought.

Åsa's eyes widened as if she'd had a realization. "Aha, who is he?"

"Don't be silly. I'm just going to eat lunch."

Åsa's eyes narrowed to two turquoise slits. "But you're acting so weird, even for you. With who?"

Natalia pressed her lips together.

"Natalia, with who?"

Natalia gave up. "With someone from, um, HC."

Åsa furrowed her light eyebrows. "With *who*?" she stubbornly demanded. She might have made a good cult leader, but she also would have made a terrific interrogator, Natalia thought. All that blond bimbo fluff was misleading.

"It's just a business lunch," she said defensively. "With no agenda. He knows J-O," she added as if the fact that her lunch date knew her boss explained everything.

"Who?"

She capitulated. "David Hammar."

Åsa leaned back and beamed at Natalia. "The big guy, huh?" she said. "Mister Venture Capitalist himself. The biggest bad boy in the financial world." She cocked her head. "Promise me you're planning to sleep with him."

"You're crazed," Natalia said. "Sex-crazed. I actually wish I could cancel it. I'm really stressed out. But one of the things I can't find in this mess is my cell phone, which has his number in it," she added. How could you lose a phone in an office that was smaller than forty square feet?

"For God's sake, woman, why don't you get yourself an assistant?"

"I *have* an assistant," Natalia said. "Who, unlike me, has a life. Her kids were sick, so she went home." Natalia glanced at the clock. "Yesterday." With a sigh she sank into her desk chair. She closed her eyes.

She couldn't look anymore. She was really done. It felt like she'd been working nonstop for ages. And there was so much paperwork she was behind on, a report to write, and at least five meetings to schedule. Actually she didn't . . .

"Natalia?"

Åsa's voice made her jump, and Natalia realized she'd been dozing off in her uncomfortable chair.

"What?" she asked.

Åsa looked at her seriously. Her mocking expression was gone.

"Hammar Capital isn't evil, no matter what your dad and your brother think. They're tough, yes, but David Hammar isn't Satan. And he's really hot. You don't need to be ashamed if you think it'll be fun to meet him."

"No," said Natalia. "I know." But she'd been wondering what Hammar Capital's legendary CEO wanted with *her*. And maybe he wasn't Satan, but he had the reputation of being hard and inconsiderate even by financial industry standards. "No, I'm just going to have lunch and get the lay of the land," she said firmly. "If he has business with the bank, he's going to want to deal with J-O, not me."

"But here's the thing. You never know with Hammar Capital," Åsa said, gracefully standing up. "And you're underestimating yourself. Do you know anyone as smart as you? No, exactly." She ran her hand over her completely stain- and wrinkle-free outfit. Even though she was wearing an austere suit (Natalia happened to know that this specific Prada suit had been tailor-made for Åsa), a simple silk blouse, and light-beige pumps, she looked like a glamorous movie star.

Åsa leaned over the desk. "You know very well you shouldn't care so much what your father thinks," she said, as usual putting her finger right on the sore spot and pushing. "You're brilliant, and you're going to go far. You can make your career here." Åsa gestured to the building they were in, the Swedish headquarters of one of the world's biggest banks, the Bank of London. "You don't have to work at the family company to be worth something," Åsa continued. "They have the world's least progressive view of women's rights and you know it. Your dad is hopeless, your brother is an idiot, and the rest of the board wins the male chauvinist pig prize of all time. And I should know, because I work with them." She cocked her head. "You're smarter than all of them put together."

"Maybe."

"So why don't you have a seat on the board?"

"But you work there. You're satisfied, aren't you?" Natalia asked, avoiding the question of why she was not on the Investum board. After all, that was quite the sensitive topic.

"Yes, but I'm only there because of gender quotas," Åsa said. "I was hired by a man who hates having to fill quotas as much as he hates immigrants, feminists, and blue-collar workers. I'm his alibi. He can point to me and say that at least he hires women."

"Dad doesn't hate . . . ," Natalia began, but then stopped. Åsa was right after all.

"Plus your dad feels sorry for me because I'm an orphan," Åsa continued. "And I don't have any ambitions to take over the place and lead the wretched show. My only ambition is to avoid dying of boredom. But you, you could go all the way to the top."

Åsa picked up her fifty-thousand-kronor handbag and started to root around in it. She pulled out a light-colored lipstick and dabbed some on her lips.

"He asked for a discreet meeting," Natalia said. "Actually, I shouldn't have said anything. You won't tell anyone, will you?"

"You weirdo, of course I won't, but what do you think he wants?"

"Must be something about financing. Maybe he's putting together a deal with one of our clients? I don't know. I was up half the night trying to work that out. Or maybe he's just networking?" It wasn't unusual that people wanted to meet with her because of who she was—a De la Grip, a woman with connections and a pedigree. She hated it. But David Hammar had piqued her curiosity. And he hadn't sounded fawning or slick, just courteous. And she had to eat, so . . .

Åsa eyed her thoughtfully. "Actually, I should go with you. Who knows what silly things you'll let slip if you're left to your own devices."

Natalia refrained from pointing out that she was considered one of Sweden's most promising corporate finance talents. Corporate finance was one of the business world's most complex fields, and she was one of the highest-ranked students to have earned a business degree in all of Sweden—ever. In her work with corporate finance, acquisitions, and advising, she managed literally hundreds of millions of Swedish kronor on a daily basis, and she was in the process of executing one of the most complex banking deals ever made in Sweden. Still, Åsa was of course right—who knew what silly things she would let slip today, as unfocused as she was. "I'll call you and tell you how it went," was all she said.

Åsa watched her for a long time. "At least find out what he wants," she finally said. "It can't hurt. A lot of people would do anything for the chance to work with David Hammar. Or to sleep with him."

"You don't think it's too risky to be seen with him, do you?" Natalia asked, hating how unsure her voice sounded.

"Of course it's risky," Åsa said. "He's dangerous, rich, and your father hates him. What more could you want?"

"Should I cancel?"

Åsa shook her head and said, "Of course not. A life without risk is no life at all."

"*That's* today's word to the wise?" Natalia asked. It didn't have much of a ring to it.

Åsa laughed and held out her empty coffee cup. It was white with black lettering. "No, that's just what it says on my coffee," she said. "I suppose I'd better head back to the office and make a couple of calls. Maybe I can fire someone. Lawyers really aren't any fun, huh? Where are you meeting him?"

"On Djurgården Island at the Ulla Winbladh restaurant."

"Could be worse," Åsa said. She couldn't seem to find anything to criticize, despite really trying. She ran her fingers over her scarf. The last time Natalia had seen a silk wrap like that was on a shelf in Nordiska Kompaniet's Hermès department, and the price tag had been considerable.

"You're a snob, you know that?" Natalia said.

"I'm quality-conscious," Åsa said, adjusting the strap of her handbag over her shoulder. "Not everyone can buy mass-produced goods. Surely you can see that." She shivered and then flashed Natalia a brilliant turquoise glance. "Just protect yourself. Who knows who he's slept with."

Natalia made a face. "Apparently mostly princesses, if you believe the rumors," she said. She wasn't above reading gossip on the Web.

"Bah, pretenders and nouveau riches," said Åsa, whose family traced its Swedish roots back to the 1200s. "Just don't do anything I wouldn't do."

Well, that doesn't rule out very much, Natalia thought, but bit her tongue.

"Are you going to wear that?" Åsa asked, looking at Natalia's outfit with a face that suggested there just might be something worse than wearing mass-produced consumer goods. "Where in the world did you find it?"

"It's just a lunch meeting," Natalia said defensively. "And this was actually custom-made, thank you very much."

Åsa surveyed the gray fabric. "Yeah, but in what century?"

"You're really a terrible snob, you know that?" Natalia said as she stood and walked over to the door, opening it for Åsa.

"That is certainly a possibility," Åsa admitted. "But you still know I'm right."

"About what?"

Åsa laughed in that way that usually made men start bragging about their summer homes and offering to buy her drinks. "About everything, darling. About *everything*."

3

David strolled from Hammar Capital's headquarters at Blasiehol-men over to the Ulla Winbladh restaurant on Djurgården Island.

A host led him toward a table where he saw Natalia De la Grip. He glanced at his watch. He was early. It wasn't quite one o'clock yet, but she was even earlier. The other patrons were mostly tourists, but Natalia had still chosen a table at the back of the establishment and was seated so that she was hardly visible. It was clear that she didn't want to be seen with him, but that made sense. He had made the reservation out here instead of at one of the more central restaurants near Stureplan so they wouldn't be recognized.

She spotted him, raised her hand to wave, but then quickly brought it back down as if she'd changed her mind. David started walking toward her.

She was very fair-skinned and looked quite modest, her face serious, her clothes an austere gray. It was hard to believe that she worked as an adviser to one of the world's biggest banks, and for J-O no less. He was one of the most demanding and eccentric bosses David had ever met. But J-O had promoted this drably dressed woman to the top, saying she had the potential to become one of his best corporate finance wizards. "She's bright, alert, and bold," J-O had said. "She can go as far as she wants."

David would have to be careful not to underestimate her.

When he reached the table, Natalia De la Grip stood. She was taller than he'd expected. She held out her hand. It was slender, with short, unpainted nails. She had a firm, professional handshake, and

David couldn't help but glance at her left hand, even though he already knew. No ring.

"Thanks for meeting me at such short notice," he said. "I wasn't so sure you'd make it."

"Really?" she asked skeptically.

David released her hand. The heat from it lingered on his palm, and he smelled a spicy, warm, and vaguely alluring scent. So far she wasn't anything like what he'd been expecting, and that made him more alert.

It had been surprisingly hard to learn anything more than general information about the middle of the three De la Grip siblings. David had skimmed through what had been written online, in articles, and in a few biographies of her family. What he found was mostly about her father and her two brothers, almost nothing about her, not even on Wikipedia, definitely not on the Swedish website Flashback. But then women were traditionally completely invisible in that family, even though the men always married very powerful and well-to-do society women. Natalia's foremothers had all been rich. Her mother was related to Russian grand duchesses and the Swedish financial elite, but the men in the family wielded all the real power—Natalia's father Gustaf, her grandfather Gustaf Senior, and on back through the centuries. Unlike both of her brothers, hereditary prince Count Peter De la Grip and jet-set prince Count Alexander De la Grip, Natalia did not have a particularly high profile in either the business pages or the tabloids. But that fit with the overall picture, of course. She wasn't just shy of the media because of her name and her background. No one presided over as many things behind the scenes as the corporate finance folks, secretly doling out their advice. They ran things from the wings and rarely spoke to the press.

She wore her dark hair up in a fairly severe hairstyle and a strand of pearls around her neck, a mark of upper-class stuffiness that David hated. No, he thought, as he took his seat at the table, in the end Natalia De la Grip looked exactly the way he'd known she would— unmarried, almost thirty, career-focused, well-to-do but utterly ordinary.

Apart from her eyes, that was. He'd never seen anything like them.

"I have to admit I was curious when you called." She gave him a golden look, and David felt something tingle down his spine.

He took the menu from the waiter and quickly perused it. "You must be used to people looking you up," he said with a laugh and a consciously warm, professional smile. A big part of financial sector work came down to networking, and he could hardly remember the last time he'd eaten a lunch that hadn't also been work-related. It was going to take more than a pair of unusually attractive eyes to distract him.

"Well, of course," she said, "billionaires ask me out all the time."

His lip twitched at her wry comment.

She studied her menu and then nodded that she was ready to order.

"I hear you did quite well on the Schibsted deal," he said, to feel her out a little.

"You have good sources," she said, cocking her head slightly. "I don't know if I should feel flattered or alarmed."

"Not alarmed. I did my homework," he said. "You're considered an up-and-coming talent, someone to keep an eye on." She'd been described as tough, cosmopolitan, and serious. There was no reason to doubt that all were true.

"I read that article too," she said. "I suppose time will tell." She laughed. "You know how it is. You're only as good as your last deal. You're either on your way up or your way out."

"And right now?"

"Oh, right now I'm definitely on my way up." She said it without any trace of false modesty. He could count on the fingers of one hand how many members of the Swedish aristocracy he'd met who could talk without wrapping everything they said in false modesty and mock humility.

She ordered fish, and David automatically requested the same. It was elementary psychology to order the same dish as the person you had asked out.

"Did you always want to work at a bank?" he asked once the waiter had left them. "Or were you ever interested in trying something else?" After all, she had been working at the Bank of London for several years now. It wasn't an unreasonable question. The young financial sector elite was a hungry gang, and most of them were always on the lookout for new challenges.

He glanced at her slender, ringless fingers again. She was probably completely dedicated to her job. Just like he was.

"I'm happy at the bank," she said.

"You're the only woman on J-O's team?"

"Yes."

"I'm sure you're an asset," he said neutrally.

"Thanks." Natalia gave him a wry smile. She drank some of her mineral water. "I'm happy at the bank, but if I'm going to be honest, my long-term career plan is to eventually take a position in my family's company. I assume you know which family that is?"

He nodded, feeling that familiar hatred welling up. He smiled, inhaled once, and then nodded encouragingly, as if he was actually interested, not out for blood at all.

"Where I come from, people don't have such a favorable view of your line of work," she continued.

This honesty could be a problem. "That's not a secret," he said, trying to sound neutral, as if he were discussing something abstract, not the fact that the De la Grip family openly detested everything Hammar Capital stood for. Although they wouldn't use the word "detest," nothing so déclassé as that. They just wanted to guard their proud traditions.

She must have sensed something about his attitude because she quickly laughed, a little apologetically. "I know it's conservative and prejudicial. I'm not saying I agree with them."

He raised an eyebrow, because this was the crucial point. Just exactly how much did Natalia's view differ from the rest of her family's? "Oh?" he said.

"I don't think you can just lump together everyone who works in private equity or even venture capitalism. But, that said, my loyalties still rest with my family." She shrugged slightly apologetically and waved her hand dismissively. "Sometimes you have to make sacrifices for family."

David watched her. *Sometimes you have to make sacrifices for family.* She couldn't possibly understand what those words did to him.

But at least he'd learned what he needed to know. He had actually suspected it as soon as he'd seen her—Natalia De la Grip would never act against her family's interests. She wore loyalty and integrity wrapped around herself like an invisible cloak. Lucky for him that she had misconstrued the purpose of this lunch. She thought he was networking and scoping out business opportunities, not trying to get her to sell out her nearest and dearest.

"I understand," he said, while at the same time he couldn't help wondering how the obviously intelligent Natalia justified to herself the fact that she still didn't have a seat on Investum's board, that pretty much *no* women held important positions in any of the companies that Gustaf De la Grip ran. And that her father was known for his chauvinist statements about women in general and gender equality at the workplace in specific. Natalia's love for her family made her blind.

"So, what makes you one of J-O's favorites?" he asked as their food arrived. He added, "Those are J-O's own words. I'm just quoting him."

"Do you know him well?" she asked, placing her napkin in her lap and picking up her silverware. She ate with delicate, silent motions, setting down her utensils between each bite. Boarding school manners.

"Well enough to trust his judgment," he replied. J-O was one of the world's most influential bankers, and they had collaborated several times. "Tell me more."

"Corporate finance is a job that relies a lot on the personal touch, as I'm sure you know, on relationships and building a sense of trust." One of Natalia's shoulders twitched. She set her silverware down again, her back totally straight, without fiddling with her place setting, her glass, or anything else. "I have a lot going for me."

"Yes, I can imagine," he said, realizing with surprise that he was being genuine. There was something reliable about her, almost steadfast. If he weren't too cynical to believe in such a thing, he would have said Natalia seemed like a good person.

"And not just because of my last name," she added, a faint pinkish hue flashing over her cheekbones, subtle as a brushstroke. "I'm good at what I do."

"I'm convinced of that."

Natalia narrowed her eyes. "Why do I feel like you're flattering me?"

"Not at all. I'm just naturally charming," he replied with a smile.

He hadn't expected her to be so appealing that he'd occasionally find himself forgetting her history and her name.

She smiled. Even if this lunch was a waste of time, at least it was pleasant. She was good company and not a snob. Natalia piqued his curiosity. And, actually, he felt a little attracted to her, which was completely unexpected. Her dichotomy was downright sexy: all that cool paleness and at the same time passionate intensity.

"You know," she said, meticulously setting down her silverware yet again. "I *know* I should be grateful for my background—my family, my name, and all that. And I am; anything else would be arrogant. But sometimes I wish I didn't have it all, that I'd done it on my own. I think there must be some satisfaction in accomplishing everything oneself."

"Yes, it is satisfying," David said slowly, studying her expectantly. Not a single upper-class person—neither female nor male—had ever said something like that to him before. "You're lucky you're a woman, then," he added. "At least you've had a bit of a handicap."

"Hmm." She sat in silence, seeming to think.

Few industries were as backward in terms of equality between the sexes as the elite financial sphere. The women were well-educated, but they disappeared as you moved up the ranks. Managing to rise to the kind of position Natalia held was evidence of extreme intelligence. And persistence.

She raised her head and gave him a provocative look. "And what are Hammar Capital's thoughts on gender-equality issues, if I might ask? You're led by two men, right? The field of venture capital isn't exactly known for its high percentage of women. So where do you stand on the issue?"

"My position is exemplary," he responded, picking up a new potato on his fork, salting it, and stuffing it into his mouth.

"But what do you think about the fact that there are so few women serving on Swedish corporate boards?" she continued in a tone that told David she didn't take the subject lightly. "Not to mention the operations side of things. How do things look there?"

"Hammar Capital doesn't hire people based on their sex but rather their expertise," he said.

Natalia scoffed, and David was forced to hide a small smile. When she was passionate about something, she apparently put her heart and soul into it. All her polite blandness was replaced by fire and passion.

"If you do things based on quotas, you run the risk of hiring less-qualified people," he continued, well aware that that argument ought to be like waving a red flag in front of a bull for anyone with a brain. "We hire based on skill."

It was like pouring fuel on a bonfire.

"That is such bullshit," Natalia said, the red patches on her cheeks growing. "Skill isn't the deciding factor," she said, her jaw clenched. "Not if people headhunt the same way they always have—through the same old-boy networks. And they get what they want, the same old men with the same old views. It has nothing to do with merit. That's just window dressing."

"I'm not saying we don't want good women," he said. "But some say they're hard to find."

"With attitudes like that I won't be surprised if you go belly-up soon," she said stiffly. She glanced down at her plate and added a muttered, "I hope so."

"We're doing great," he said. "We have . . ."

"But don't you see . . ." She was looking up again and started waving her hands around. When a woman who could presumably make it through a Nobel Prize banquet without committing a single breech of etiquette starts waving her silverware around, she's got to be pretty worked up.

"Natalia," he interrupted. "You do know that I'm playing devil's advocate, right?"

She paused.

"I've helped hire people for over twenty boards in the last year and a half," he continued calmly. "Fifty-one percent of them are women. And exactly half of the chairmen of the board on boards hired by Hammar Capital are women." He leaned back and watched her breathing calm down. Her chest was moving beneath her blouse. He glanced at her cleavage, at her pearls and pale skin. He flashed her a little smile, maybe the first genuine one he'd given her. He didn't dislike her personally, just what she represented. "Recruiting people with the right expertise is a part of my company's success," he said slowly. "Hammar Capital weathered both the dot-com bubble and the financial crisis, and I'm completely confident that that had to do with the makeup of my staff."

She looked him in the eye, alertly, quietly, and he wondered what was going on beneath that cool exterior. He continued, "An integrated group comes up with different approaches, as I'm sure you know. They dare to say no and are willing to stick up for a divergent point of view. We rode out the crises, unlike many others, precisely because I have the most talented coworkers in the country—both women and men, recent immigrants and native-born Swedes."

Natalia blinked. Long, dark lashes shielded her view for a moment. "Okay," she said calmly. A faint blush across her high cheekbones was all that was left.

"Are you sure?" he asked.

She nodded. "Yes, I let you get to me. That almost never happens." She leaned in over the table. "Plus I feel like a hypocrite."

"How so?" he asked, allowing himself to be drawn in by the twinkle that lingered in her eye. She was flirting with him, maybe without even being aware of it. She wasn't the flirty type, he'd bet his business on that. He permitted himself to play along for a bit. They would soon part ways—what did it matter?

"I'm sitting here talking about gender equality and hiring policies," she said, waving her hand dismissively. "But I know I've had huge advantages simply because of my name and my background. I know it and it embarrasses me." She leaned even farther over the table and lowered her voice, as if she were divulging a big secret. "The fact is that I used my name just the other day. I hate it when people do that."

"And you did it anyway?"

She nodded and looked so guilty that the corner of David's mouth twitched. "How did it go?" he asked.

She eyed him for a bit, her eyes twinkling. "Not very well," she stated dryly.

"What did you do?" he asked, curious despite himself.

"There wasn't even any call for name dropping. I assume you know who Sarah Harvey is?"

David nodded when he heard the name of the woman considered to be one of the best sopranos in the world, with a uniquely clear voice and a tremendous range. He knew who she was and also which circles she traveled in. "What does she have to do with any of this?" he asked.

"She never does tours, but she's coming to Europe this month and is going to give one concert in all of Scandinavia, here in Stockholm. I've idolized her ever since I was a child and really wanted to go."

"Are you saying that you couldn't get a ticket even though you're a De la Grip?"

"Thanks for taking the time to rub salt in my wounds. No, I couldn't, and it still stings. The arrangers weren't impressed by me in the least."

"Did you try bribing them?"

She jutted out her chin. "Maybe."

"Swedes aren't that easy to bribe, if that's any consolation," David said, not entirely truthfully. Anyone could be bribed; it was merely a question of offering the right amount.

"I guess," she said. "I'm a quarter Russian. The Russians, now they're easier to bribe."

"A lot easier," David agreed. He stretched out his legs and leaned back. This lunch had already given him the information he wanted. The smart thing to do now would be to release Natalia De la Grip and move on. She wasn't critical to closing the deal. They didn't need to see each other again. His goal was to destroy her family. He ought to focus on the next step. That would be the smart thing to do. He watched her long fingers as she absentmindedly stroked the side of her glass. She'd taken off her jacket and was wearing a simple, sleeveless blouse underneath. She had beautiful lines, tall and strong. The pictures he'd seen of her had been mostly forgettable, but now he remembered one photo from some evening event, a dinner or a ball at the Villa Pauli Club. Her hair had been up in the same tight bun, but she wore a long red evening gown, and she looked amazing. Strong, powerful. And he convinced himself that he didn't always need to be in such a hurry, that he could sit for another ten minutes with this woman, who really wasn't behaving the way he'd expected.

Natalia noticed David watching her. She wondered what he was thinking as those blue-gray eyes took her in. He hadn't meant for her to notice him checking her out, of course, but she was good at reading people and could tell he was trying to size her up. He was very smooth. When they spoke he gave her his full attention in a way that was completely unsettling. He looked good, attractive in a grown-up, manly way. There was nothing boyish here, just broad-shouldered, full-grown masculinity. Dark, well-cut hair, eyes that were somewhere between blue and gray, chiseled features. Handsome as the devil. He was also charming, polite, and sometimes funny, basically your perfect lunch date.

And yet . . .

Every now and then she caught a glimmer of something in his eyes, something she wasn't meant to see, something hard and cold, which put her on her guard and made her hesitant. David Hammar was a person known for crushing companies and people, a ruthless businessman. Under one picture of him in a business paper the caption had described him as "an ice-cold businessman devoid of pretension." Something warned her not to be seduced by his easygoing charm and intelligent eyes. He was playing some kind of game, she was sure of that. But what?

Secrets, so many secrets.

"What?" he asked with a half laugh, and now there was no frostiness at all. No hardness, no ruthlessness, just attentiveness. As if she were the most interesting person in the world. This must be how he had achieved his almost implausible success. David Hammar *saw* people. He made them feel special, won their trust. *And then he devoured them, flesh, bone, and everything in between.*

"Are you planning to take over any unsuspecting companies in the near future?" she asked.

"Of course I am," he replied. "That's what I do. A venture capitalist never sleeps." His eyes twinkled, and Natalia lost her train of thought. Oh my, that laugh.

Most of the men Natalia worked with, including her father, older brother, and boss, followed the unspoken rules and invisible guidelines that applied to the elite financial world. They were all cast from the same mold. Conforming and often completely devoid of humor, they were all too preoccupied with trying to outdo one another to socialize comfortably, especially with women. But David was completely different, a trailblazing visionary if you could believe his admirers, an unrelenting looter if you listened to his critics. Either way, he was terribly successful, a modern pirate in a custom suit.

And yet . . .

David Hammar hadn't tried to impress her even once. He hadn't bragged or dominated. When they shook hands, his grasp was firm but not unnecessarily hard, as if he was confident of his strength and didn't need to show it off. Talking to him, she realized he made most of the men she met seem hesitant, maniacally domineering, impatient to demonstrate their strength, and not always respectful toward women, to put it diplomatically.

"How did you end up getting into this line of work?" she asked curiously. He seemed like a man who could have been successful at just about anything.

"If you want to become very rich very fast, this is the way. As I'm sure you know."

Natalia nodded. No one could become as rich as a skilled venture capitalist. "And that's what you wanted? To be rich?"

"Yes."

"Has it gone well?" She knew the answer, of course, but she wanted to hear what he would say when given the opportunity to brag.

He studied her for a moment. "Satisfaction is elusive," he said slowly, as if they were discussing something important, not just shooting the breeze. "Strange, isn't it?"

She shook her head. "No, it's the most basic human motivator. For good or ill."

"Is that how you feel too?"

"I guess," she replied, because she recognized the desire in herself, to get ahead, to succeed.

"What?" He leaned forward and studied her attentively. He read her so fast it was frightening.

"Nothing. This has been a very pleasant lunch. I thought you would be more . . ." Her voice faded away.

"Gangster-like? Unscrupulous?"

She laughed. "Maybe."

"The thing is, I like to see results," David said. "A lot of Swedish companies are unbelievably poorly run. Their CEOs and boards are lining their own pockets at their shareholders' expense." He crossed his long legs and ran a hand through his short brown hair. She noted the stainless-steel watch. Patek Philippe, expensive but not garish.

"You have no idea how much shit we see," he continued. "But

when Hammar Capital goes into a board, we aim to make it more efficient and improve the company. And then the shareholders make
money, not someone else."

"Surely you make a little as well," Natalia pointed out dryly. Hammar Capital was valued at close to an unbelievable four billion euros.
Not bad, considering he'd built it himself from the ground up. And
he was young, not even thirty-five if you could believe the Internet.

"That too, of course," he laughed. "Our business is to be contro-
versial. Would you like some coffee?"

She nodded, and he ordered two. The waitress quickly returned
with two cups.

Natalia fingered the chocolate on her saucer. She meant what she'd
said earlier—she admired people who created something of their
own. There were so many people who were born with everything and
then messed it up.

David nodded at her chocolate. "You're not going to eat that?"

She handed it to him, watched him open the thin foil wrapper.
"You travel abroad a lot. How does that work?" she asked.

He raised an eyebrow. "I'm not the only one who did my research,
huh? That's true. I travel the world hunting down financiers. My partner Michel and I both do."

Michel Chamoun. Lebanese, with degrees in finance and law. Yes,
she'd done her research; she was always thorough. "But aren't you
needed here at home?" she asked.

"I have very talented coworkers."

"Women and immigrants?"

"Among others."

Despite the casual small talk, despite the charm that was sometimes difficult to defend against, Natalia couldn't help but think that
there was something that didn't add up. What did this super-attractive
man with the hard eyes want with her? What was David Hammar actually after in inviting her to a "no-strings-attached" lunch? And what
did that phrase even mean? Here he was asking her seemingly ran-
dom follow-up questions and flattering her with his attention. Natalia
glanced at her watch and thought it must be wrong. She furrowed
her brow and saw David tilt his own wrist and check his watch.

He straightened. "How can it be that late?"

"I know. I have to get back to the office," she said.

"I had no idea so much time had passed. I'm sorry I've kept you," he said, gesturing for the check.

"Don't apologize," she said. "But I have a Skype meeting with London that I have to prep for."

He handed the server his credit card.

"Should I have them call you a cab?"

"No, I'm walking," she said, standing and picking up her handbag.

"I'll join you." He stood as well, and pulled her chair back for her.

"Oh, maybe we'd better not," she said apologetically. He was crazy attractive, there was no doubt about that. But she'd done her research. Hammar Capital had gone up against Investum a couple of times in the last few years, and HC had lost both times. She'd mentioned Investum twice today, and both times something had glimmered in his eyes. It was scarcely noticeable, and she would have missed it if she hadn't been studying him so carefully. But she'd seen a coldness that no amount of charm in the world could smooth over, and in many ways she *was* Investum. David Hammar had a bone to pick with her family's company. People said that nothing in the financial world was personal, that money controlled everything. But that was nonsense. A lot of other things always followed in the wake of the money: feelings and impulses, wounded egos and the desire for revenge. So the question was: did David Hammar have some hidden agenda in asking her out?

Natalia studied him closely, her eyes skimming over his unbelievably attractive features, his intense eyes and well-built body.

Probably.

"Thanks," she heard herself say. "Thanks for a lovely lunch."

She shook his hand, let his big, warm palm surround her own, and then walked outside into the broiling heat, not one iota wiser than before she'd come.

4

The lunch with David Hammar had raised more questions in Natalia than it had answered. But at least it had woken her up, she decided as she quickly walked back to her office at Stureplan. She took the elevator up to the fourth floor, nodded to the receptionists, and then shut herself in her office. She decided she needed five minutes for herself before she started working.

During those five minutes she thought about David and the lunch and how she felt confused, fascinated, and, well, attracted to that charismatic but also contradictory venture capitalist.

Natalia leaned back in her desk chair. She actually couldn't figure him out. At times he had been chivalrous and even funny. He had teased her, and she had been drawn into something that felt like a force field of masculine charm.

But apart from that, she had found him to be a person with a very hard core. She knew he'd grown up in some of the toughest areas around Stockholm. It was no secret that he came from a really rough past. But something had happened since then because first he went to boarding school, then the Stockholm School of Economics, and finally Harvard. Probably on a scholarship, but still, talk about pulling yourself up by your bootstraps.

Yes, he was full of contradictions, Natalia thought, and with that her five minutes were over. No matter what she thought about his charisma and appearance, she was sure the lunch was a onetime occurrence. For some reason he had written her off—she had sensed that very clearly. She'd do best to get back to her real life: her work.

Because no matter how, uh, *interesting* lunch with David Hammar had been, it had robbed her of valuable work time.

Natalia devoted several intense afternoon hours to a never-ending stream of paperwork. She and J-O were in the final stage of a really big and, for Natalia personally, prestigious bank deal, and she was pushing herself and her team hard. No one slept more than absolutely necessary. It was all hands on deck. In another few hours when the banks and the stock market opened in the US, this already long workday would keep going, its pace not slowing at all.

Natalia glanced at the time. They were still asleep in Hong Kong, and Los Angeles was three hours behind New York. Somewhere in the world there was always a bank opening or a stock market closing. Trade and business continued around the clock, and her boss drove his employees harder than anyone she'd known.

She wondered if David Hammar worked like this. He was also known for being a hard worker. No one could stay at the absolute top, where he'd been for years, without being indefatigable. Without being unrelenting. That was both the appeal and the downside of finance.

She glanced up when someone knocked on her door frame.

"Do you have a minute?" J-O asked.

"Be right there," Natalia said, glad to be forced to focus on something other than the impression David Hammar had made. Åsa was right. She needed to get out more. Oh, but dating was such an enigma, she thought as she gathered her folders, papers, and iPad. She didn't get it at all. Other women did, Åsa did. They went out with men, slept with men, dated men. But Natalia had never really gotten the hang of what you were supposed to do. There was something about the subtle, modern, essentially un-Swedish rules that she couldn't fathom despite the time she had spent living in New York and London. She was pretty much useless at this stuff with men, as history had shown. On the other hand, she was exceptionally good at her job, she reminded herself as she followed J-O. At least there was that.

Natalia maintained her focus throughout the meeting. There was no room for anyone on J-O's team operating at less than one hundred percent. They were the best of the best. One miss and you were looking for another job. Natalia had been handpicked two years ago by J-O himself when he started the bank's Nordic team. The rest of them, all men, were unique specialists in their fields, just like her. Natalia was an expert on banking and financial institutions. J-O liked to say that he could call Natalia De la Grip in the middle of the night and she would sit up and rattle off the big, listed banks' index rates and their share prices from when the markets closed.

And he wasn't joking.

He'd done it several times.

J-O wrapped up the meeting and thanked those who had participated by phone. Natalia and the rest of them gathered up their things.

"It's almost four o'clock," J-O said to her. "Do you have time for a quick chat before New York opens?"

Natalia nodded, waiting quietly as the conference room emptied.

"Nice work," he said when they were alone.

She smiled at the rare praise. "Thanks."

He drummed one finger on the table. "What are you doing this summer?" he asked.

Natalia tried not to raise her eyebrows, but it was hard. Throughout the finance world, J-O was known for three things: his extremely expensive tastes, his weakness for giving long interviews in glossy magazines, and for never discussing personal matters.

As far as Natalia knew, he had no private life. Not like other mortals. He worked, traveled, and flew so much that people said he spent more time in the air than on the ground.

During the just over two years they'd worked together, first in London and then in Stockholm, they had never discussed anything other than work. What little she knew about J-O she had read in the tabloids or industry papers and since her own family was one of the most widely discussed in Sweden, she assumed that he knew pretty much what everyone else knew about her. At least once a year, whenever her younger brother, Alexander, was caught up in some new scandal, often involving a woman, the tabloids carefully reviewed the details of her family, so it wasn't that hard for people to keep up to date on her. But J-O never said a word about it. J-O hadn't even said anything when her breakup with Jonas hit the papers. He just dispassionately noted her bloodshot eyes and then got down to business as usual. In the middle of all that misery, that had actually been a relief.

"I'm going to keep working until we're done," she said in answer to his question. "Aside from that, I don't have any fixed plans. Aside from maybe Båstad." She managed not to sigh.

Everyone was going to Båstad. Of course her parents had invited her down to the summerhouse—her mother had practically ordered her to come—but Natalia didn't know if she could bear to spend the summer with them. Last year, when her separation from Jonas was still fresh, it had worked, but yet another summer? When she was almost thirty? There were limits to how pathetic a person could be.

Unbidden, her thoughts flitted back to David Hammar again. Was he going to Båstad? If she joined her parents at the villa, would she run into him there?

That bothered her. She had met the man once and she was fantasizing about him already? What was she, twelve or something? At least she hadn't googled him after lunch. Although she was still wondering what he was after. What did she have that he could be interested in? Her father hated him, she knew that. Until today she had never had any particular opinion of David Hammar. They moved in completely different circles. He was a handsome corporate pirate, mingling with American movie stars and British princesses, wreaking havoc on traditional companies. For her part, she was pretty much a bank woman.

"Hello?" J-O said.

"Oh, sorry," she said. "If you need me, I'll be here, of course. I haven't decided on anything. I'll take some vacation when I can."

"I may need you in Båstad."

Natalia nodded neutrally. Of course he would.

J-O stood up from the highly polished conference table. Their office was in a historically listed building, built in the 1800s with period details, high ceilings, crystal chandeliers, and art in gilt frames. He glanced out the window at Stureplan and the roofs surrounding them. "I know you have your own plans for the future," he said slowly.

Natalia's ears perked up. This was about something else, about her. Her most recent annual review had been about her long-term career goal being to eventually work for the family company. She'd always been open about that, that she wanted to build a career on her own merits, but that then she wanted to move on.

"Yes?" she said guardedly.

She admired J-O, but they weren't actually friends. Everyone had their own agenda in this world, and trust was a perishable commodity.

"I heard you met with David Hammar today," he said. "Is there anything you haven't told me?"

"It was just lunch, nothing else," she replied, completely caught off guard.

J-O had a reputation of knowing everything that happened in the gossipy finance world. But still. How the heck did he know this? So quickly? "I hope you're not spying on me," she said, only half kidding.

J-O shook his head. He crossed his arms in front of himself. "This is Stockholm. You can't do anything without everyone knowing about it. What did he want?"

"I don't know," she said honestly. "You know him better than I do."

"He's up to something."

Natalia nodded. "Presumably."

"Keep me posted. And plan on Båstad."

Natalia stood up, still a little taken aback. As she left the room, J-O turned back to the window again. His eyes locked onto some point outside.

They spent the rest of the evening focused on work. Someone fell asleep on the sofa. Someone ordered pizza. The interns, assistants, analysts, and other business folks came and went. Natalia chatted with clients and drew diagrams and yawned when no one was looking.

She took a taxi home late in the evening. She slept for a few hours, showered, changed, and was then back in the office again just after dawn.

J-O came in at 9:30, greeted her with a quick nod, and disappeared into a meeting. Phones rang, an assistant yelled, and her work once again took over Natalia's thoughts.

"Natalia!" one of her colleagues called, and then suddenly the whole workday had passed. "We're starting the conference now!"

She grabbed an apple and a pad of paper. "Coming," she replied.

It was already six o'clock, and they were far from done. It was going to be another long day of work. Just the way she liked it.

5

David leaned back in his desk chair and stretched his neck. Up here on the top floor, he could sense more than hear the noise of the city. He glanced at his designer desk, cluttered with annual reports, quarterly reports, and accounting statements, before his eyes settled on a black oil painting that an enthusiastic interior decorator had billed a fortune for. The décor at Hammar Capital's offices was primarily the product of an expensive and visionary interior design firm that had been given very loose reins. But they often had clients here and occasionally a big party, and all the stainless steel and glass always impressed everyone.

His lunch with Natalia De la Grip yesterday hadn't given him anything. And he was booked up for the whole next week with meetings from morning to night. So he didn't actually have any more time to squander sitting around thinking about her. But every once in a while a memory from their lunch would come to mind and he would dwell on it. A look that stuck with him, a memory of her pale skin and figure.

"Are you still there?"

David nodded, even though, of course, the man on the phone couldn't see the gesture. "Sorry. I'm here," he said.

"Do we need to meet, or is my money in good hands?"

The man on the other end of the line was Gordon Wyndt, one of Hammar Capital's biggest investors and one of David's few really close friends.

Hammar Capital had considerable equity of its own. Against all odds, David had created one of the most powerful venture capital firms in the country, but for really big deals they still depended on leveraging their network of wealthy venture partners. And Gordon Wyndt, a sixty-year-old British-American tycoon, and just like David a self-made man from simple beginnings, was the richest of all and the least risk-averse.

They had met when Gordon was teaching at the Stockholm School of Economics and David was a student. They had e-mailed each other sporadically, and when David studied at Harvard, they had gotten in touch again and stayed in touch over the years. Despite the difference in their ages and their very different personalities, they had become friends as well as business partners. More than once, David had given Gordon tips about stocks or companies worth investing in, and when David started his own business, Gordon had been the first to invest.

"What's actually going on?" Gordon asked. A dog yapped in the background, and David remembered that Gordon's most recent wife was fond of little dogs.

"A big deal. I'm just a little nervous," David responded cagily.

Gordon sniffed. "You don't have a nervous gene in your body, and you love the thrill of the chase. There's something you're not telling me." Gordon disappeared for a little while and David heard him babbling to the dog. David rolled his eyes.

Gordon returned. "It's fine. As long as you know what you're doing. And don't run off with too many of my billions."

"My team is in place in Stockholm," David said. "The Swedish financial crowd will be heading off to their summer places soon. Everyone plays tennis, drinks, and sails. Everything runs at low speed over here."

That was their weakness, taking time off. That would be their downfall—because David never let up.

"I'll meet the last of them in the next few days—brokers, fund managers, a few big shareholders," he continued. "I have a good feeling. The two biggest AP funds are in. And you, of course."

He wondered how many brokers and managers he'd given his presentation to in the last year. Two hundred? At least.

"Did you get anyone from the owning family on board?" Gordon wondered.

"No," David replied. He regretted that he had confided in Gordon that he was going to try to win over one of the De la Grip siblings. He hated admitting he'd failed. "But it doesn't matter," he said curtly. And that was true. He had never been dependent on anyone from the inner circle at Investum, not really. They were game pieces he could do without if he had to. The oldest brother, Peter, had never been discussed for obvious reasons. Alexander De la Grip hadn't taken his calls. And it had become clear during their lunch that Natalia would never go against her family. No, that route was closed.

"My wife wants to buy a castle in Sweden. Apparently all of her friends are doing it," said Gordon. "Where is Skåne anyway? Is there anything for sale there? Y'all have a bunch of castles for sale, right?"

"The nobility in Skåne are as snobby as hell. They're going to hate you. You'll love it."

"Then you'll have to come by and say hello," Gordon said. "We'll throw a big party."

David smiled. He and Gordon had that in common—a total lack of respect for old-money names.

"David?"

"Yes?"

"Was there anything else?"

"Maybe." David had no idea why he was asking. There was no rational reason, but he spoke the word all the same. "I need your help with something," he said slowly.

"More money? Should I talk to my bank?"

"No, it's something else," David said. "You know Sarah Harvey, don't you?"

"The singer? My first wife sang in some choir with her, and we're godparents to Sarah's daughter."

"I need a favor."

Five minutes later David hung up, wondering what he was actually doing. But he shook off the sense of having set something in motion that he couldn't control and instead called out for his assistant, Jesper Lidmark, a young student from the Stockholm School of Economics. Jesper came into the office and gave David a questioning look.

"I want to send something to Mrs. Gordon Wyndt," David said. "It needs to be really exclusive and look expensive. Call Bukowskis and ask them to pick a vase or something else we can send."

Half an hour later, David received a call from Gordon.

"It's arranged."

"Thanks," David said. "Now I owe you a favor in return."

"Can I ask what this is all about?"

David heard the dog yelping in the background, and he could picture Wyndtham Castle: green hills, a steaming pool of Italian marble, party tents and celebrity guests, an extensive renovation that had destroyed centuries of patina and reverberated through the British and American press.

"A deal," he lied.

"Yeah, right," Gordon said dryly and hung up.

6

"Are you going to see him again?" Åsa asked, inspecting the red floral dress on the hanger she'd just pulled out with a critical eye. "You and the pirate?" She glanced inquisitively at Natalia before hanging the dress back on the rack. She was too curvy to get away with a pattern that big.

"Uh, no," replied Natalia, fingering a jacket. Gray, of course. That woman was hopeless when it came to clothes. Åsa wasn't even sure if Natalia owned any clothes that weren't gray, beige, or possibly navy blue. That's what happened when you spent your days competing with testosterone-overloaded finance guys. And when your fashion advice came from a mother who thought anything that looked good on a young woman was vulgar. It killed your taste in clothes.

"But you liked him," Åsa said. Natalia's cheeks turned pink. So, not even super cool Natalia De la Grip could withstand bad boy David Hammar.

Åsa pulled out another dress and scrutinized it carefully. This green color would actually suit her. She glanced over at the clerk hovering nervously in the periphery. "In my size?" she asked curtly. The clerk nodded and hurried off.

"Do you have to sound so unpleasant?" Natalia said, now holding up an insipid jumpsuit and looking like she was about to whip out her gold card.

"Don't you already own one of those?" said Åsa, looking at the jumpsuit with disdain. Natalia visited her mother's tailor in upper Östermalm twice a year and ordered a set of spring outfits or fall outfits, depending. Like clockwork.

"You can never have too many nice outfits," Natalia said, inspecting the brown fabric.

Oh help, not that one, Åsa thought.

Åsa held up a turquoise dress and gestured commandingly. Another clerk obediently scurried off. A fitting room had already been prepared, and the outfits Åsa had selected were all hanging there along with accessories, shoes, and slips. "You have to be authoritative with people; otherwise you don't get good service. They know I'm friends with the owner."

Her second cousin—or third cousin, something distant anyway—who owned the boutique was a supremely gifted seamstress, and Åsa had coerced her into giving Åsa a family discount. Natalia was now studying a beige suit. "Would you stop pulling out brown rags and quit changing the subject. Tell me about the lunch. What did you guys talk about?"

Natalia shrugged one shoulder in a nonchalant gesture that didn't fool Åsa in the slightest.

"Natalia?"

Obediently, Natalia left the ready-to-wear business suits and walked over to a display of new designer garments. Åsa's second or third cousin was very good; a lot of these outfits would be right at home in an international fashion show.

Natalia pulled out a gold dress in a silk satin. It glimmered alluringly, like a living being. "We mostly talked about how unbelievably good I am at my job," she said, holding up the golden dress in front of herself.

Åsa snorted. "Right."

"Weirdly enough, it's true. He didn't say very much about himself."

"You mean you ate lunch with a finance guy who didn't try to get ahead at your expense? He must be one of a kind."

Natalia turned over the price tag and her eyes widened. "I thought he was quite pleasant. He was confident but not stuck up."

"And hot?"

"That too," Natalia admitted, averting her gaze.

Sweet little Natalia. You like him.

"Try it on," Åsa said, nodding to the golden dress in Natalia's hand before slipping into her own changing room, where the outfits she'd selected were hanging. She pushed aside the feeling of meaninglessness that washed over her and decided that she would buy at least two things. Shopping was supposed to cure the blues; it was bound to start working sometime.

"I don't understand why you have to drag me along to shops like this," Natalia complained from the changing room next door to Åsa's. "Everything is so bright and sort of demanding. It makes me nervous. It's too advanced for me. I have no opinion on clothes like these." The changing room went quiet, and only a faint rustling could be heard. "Hmm, I think some of the fabric is missing on this one."

Åsa surveyed the green dress she'd slipped on. Her ample bosom, curvy hips, and stomach made the expensive hand-dyed silk look both glamorous and a tad indecent. This would do. "Was he alone?" she asked, starting to change into the next dress. She studied herself in the mirror: an abundance of white skin, expensive underwear. She smiled. She loved her soft, un-worked-out body.

"Yes, he was alone. What do you mean?"

Åsa adjusted the silvery silk jersey over her breasts. She'd always looked good in silver, a twenty-first-century Marilyn Monroe. "He has a partner," Åsa said, trying to sound nonchalant, as if it didn't really matter how Natalia responded. "I was just wondering if he joined you."

It was quiet in the next dressing room. Åsa could practically hear the gears in Natalia's mind turning. Say what you wanted about the fashion-challenged Natalia, she wasn't dumb.

"And just what do you know about his partner, Åsa?" Natalia asked in her most annoying tone of voice.

Åsa winked slowly at her reflection. If she closed her eyes she could picture him. It didn't matter how long ago it had been or where she was, she could always call up his image.

"What do you think?" she asked breezily.

"You slept with him," Natalia said. Not as a question, not as a value judgment, just as confirmation.

Åsa cocked her head to the side. She *had* slept with a lot of people, so it wasn't so strange that Natalia should draw that conclusion. But the truth was a little more complicated than that.

Ah, Michel.

"Have you slept with David Hammar, too?" Åsa suddenly heard from the next changing room. She smiled. Darling Natalia, was that a bit of a chill she heard in her voice?

"Åsa?" Natalia urged, a little more sharply now.

"Really I didn't," Åsa answered truthfully. "Venture capitalists really aren't my thing." That was *almost* true. She had slept with several, but they had all been terribly wooden. "Besides, your dad is my boss. He and David are archenemies, aren't they?"

She and Natalia stepped out of their changing rooms at the same time. Natalia was wearing the thin, golden evening dress, which caressed her long body and showed more back and skin than it covered. Åsa smiled encouragingly at her.

"I didn't think people had archenemies anymore," Natalia said, stroking her hand over her hip.

Natalia was as slender as a model, and the dress was made for a person who had no chest and a tiny waist but a curvier backside than you would find on any actual model. She looked like she had stepped right out of a photoshopped ad for expensive perfume.

"Buy it," said Åsa.

"But when am I going to wear a dress like this?"

Åsa went to every society party, ball, and wedding she was invited to. She hated to sit around at home, but Natalia said no to anything that wasn't business mingling. One time Natalia had turned down an invitation to dine with the king in favor of reviewing an annual report.

"His partner's name is Michel," Åsa said, surprised at herself for feeling a need to talk about the one man who had rejected her. She passed a pair of high-heeled sandals to Natalia, who seemed to be having a hard time tearing herself away from the dress despite her protests. "Try these with it."

Natalia loved her sensible Bally pumps but obediently put on the sandals and started fastening the thin straps around her ankles. She wiggled her unmanicured toes.

"It wouldn't hurt you to shave your legs once in a while," Åsa commented.

"Yeah yeah yeah. Tell me about Michel."

"Michel and I went to law school together," Åsa began, her voice catching slightly in her throat. She was forced to steady it. "Peter, your brother, knows him too. We took a number of classes together."

But unlike the mediocre Peter De la Grip, Michel had been a star law pupil. He had done his law degree concurrently with a degree in economics from the Stockholm School of Economics while Peter had barely scraped his way through law school. "They didn't like each other."

"No one likes Peter," Natalia said sadly, trying to see her back in the mirror.

Åsa didn't say anything since that was true. The ever-vigilant, evasive Peter De la Grip was extremely hard to like. Not that that had stopped Åsa from sleeping with him, too. She studied the price tag of the dress she had on and wondered if she should look for something even more expensive.

"I haven't actually slept with Alexander yet," Åsa said, since they were talking about the men in Natalia's immediate family. "Where is he these days?"

Natalia's little brother was one of the handsomest men Åsa had ever seen. Speaking purely objectively, he was better looking than either David or Michel. If any man could be said to be beautiful, it would be Alexander De la Grip. Maybe someone like Alexander could cheer her up? Help her shake the awful sense that she just couldn't drag herself through another day?

"My darling little brother is marinating his liver in New York," Natalia said. "You two would kill each other in no time." Natalia shook her head. "And forgive me for saying it, but isn't he a little young for you?"

Alexander was one year younger than Natalia, which made him—Åsa grimaced. She didn't want to think about that.

Natalia's phone rang inside her purse. She apologized and pulled it out. Åsa disappeared back into the changing room again while Natalia took the call.

Åsa contemplated the green, silver, and other outfits. Maybe she should take them all? After all, it wasn't like she couldn't afford them.

Poor little rich girl.

That's what they called her in the tabloids. Better than the Hussy from Östermalm, of course. Even if both epithets were about equally valid.

* * *

Natalia studied herself in the boutique mirror. She glanced down at her feet. The gold sandals were very flattering. She had always liked her feet. She was only half listening, so it took a minute before she really clued in.

"I'm sorry?"

"I said my name is Jesper Lidmark. I'm David Hammar's assistant. I have a message for Natalia De la Grip," she heard the young man with the extremely polite tone repeat. He sounded like a person who believed everything would work out if you were just friendly with everyone and spoke clearly.

"Yes?" Natalia said.

"David asked me to call and tell you that you're on the guest list at Café Opera tomorrow, Saturday. For Sarah Harvey's performance. Just let them know at the door, and you and a friend can go in."

"I'm sorry?" Natalia said, because she felt as if her brain had just taken a detour and she hadn't gone with it. "What did you say?"

Jesper repeated what he'd said, slowly but still politely.

"Sarah Harvey?" Natalia asked stupidly.

"Yes," Jesper replied cheerfully, without showing even the slightest irritation.

"I'm sorry . . . ," Natalia said, but then she broke into an enormous grin as she finally realized what Jesper had been telling her. Sarah Harvey. In Stockholm. Natalia owned every CD and compilation disc the soprano had released. But she had never been to one of her concerts, never, quite simply because Sarah never toured, so when she did all the tickets sold out in a millisecond.

"I do apologize," Natalia said, waving away Åsa, who had come over to the changing room and was making incomprehensible questioning gestures. "I was just so surprised. Thank you." She paused, thinking. "Is David still there by any chance?" she asked impulsively. "Or has he already left for the day?"

There was a moment of silence, and Natalia regretted, regretted, *regretted* that she had said anything, but then the polite assistant replied, "I don't actually know. He was in a meeting a little while ago . . . Could I ask you to hold for a moment?"

She didn't have a chance to say it didn't matter. And then she heard David's voice in her ear.

"Hi. I heard you liked it."

"Thank you, that was so nice of you. I don't know what to say," she said. "I hope I'm not interrupting anything, but I was just so pleased. I had no idea she was going to perform at the Café."

"No, it's a private show," he said. "But I received an invitation. I'm always getting invited to things. When I saw it on my desk, I thought you might like to go."

"You have no idea what this means to me. It was really terribly nice of you." She was about to end the call; his responses were so clipped, she figured she was disturbing him, but then he asked, "Are you still at the office?"

"No, I'm out shopping. How about you? Your assistant said you were in a meeting. I didn't mean to bother you."

"We're done. I was just about to leave."

"Yeah, it's late," she said. She pictured David about to walk out the doors of his office building—the HC building was like a white castle on Blasieholmen, a brash newcomer at one of Sweden's most exclusive addresses. She couldn't help but wonder where he was going, whom he was going to meet. "Well, I just wanted to thank you personally," she said.

"I hope it works out at such short notice. It's tomorrow . . ."

"Yes, it will definitely work out," she said and managed not to blurt out that she didn't have anything planned all weekend. "Thank you." She should really hang up now that she had thanked him. Repeatedly. Surely he was going out with some glamorous, leggy model tonight.

"Natalia?"

"Yes," she said breathlessly.

"You were so quiet," he said. "I was starting to wonder if you'd hung up."

"Sorry," she said. "It's been a long day. I have to go back to the office to check what the market's doing before I head home." She could have bitten her tongue. Why couldn't she have hinted that she was on her way somewhere too?

"Well, then, I hope you have a pleasant evening," he said politely. "Both tonight and tomorrow night."

"You too," she said lamely. "To both." She made a face because she sounded like an idiot. Åsa was staring at her, goggle-eyed.

"Thanks," she added, for what was probably the fifth time, but he had already hung up by then.

She noticed Åsa's raised eyebrows. "What happened? Was that him?"

Natalia nodded. She quietly returned her phone to her purse and pulled out her wallet.

"Nat? What are you thinking?"

Natalia smiled. She was definitely going to buy the golden dress. "I think I just found a reason to shave my legs."

7

David hung up the phone, not completely comfortable with how impulsively he'd acted. But she'd sounded so happy about the tickets—genuinely happy—that he didn't regret having gone to the small trouble. Nor having taken her call.

David spun his desk chair back around. He had forgotten he wasn't alone and found himself looking at a bemused Michel Chamoun. Michel, who was sitting on the low sofa with his feet on the coffee table and his laptop on his knees, raised his eyebrows at David.

"What?" David asked.

"What was that all about?"

"What do you mean?"

"It sounded like you were talking to Natalia De la Grip," Michel said slowly. "A private little conversation with one of the members of the family that owns the company that we're planning to hostilely take over. A deal we've been working on for more than a year. A deal that will define our whole future."

"That was her," he said. "But it was no big deal."

He could be nice to Natalia even though she was a De la Grip. As long as it was no more than a meaningless gesture.

Michel gave him a distrustful glance, as if he hadn't quite bought David's explanation. "I suppose you see that you can't just have your own personal agenda on the side. Didn't you give up on that tangent?"

David felt a flash of anger. He rarely got mad—and definitely not at Michel—so the emotion made no sense. But Michel was right, of course. It was very close to unprofessional. But he had it under control, there was no cause for alarm.

"It's totally harmless," he said, the anger already gone. "It doesn't mean anything. I was just finishing something I started. *She*'s done."

And that was true. Because David knew what he wanted. No one and nothing could make him lose focus on what was most important in his life.

"No distractions now," Michel said, but David saw that Michel had already moved on.

"No risk of that," he replied. No risk at all, he repeated silently to himself.

He couldn't bring himself to hate Natalia De la Grip; she had seemed far too decent for that. But he hated her family. What they stood for, what they'd done . . .

"I don't feel anything for her," he added and knew that was the truth. It didn't matter if she was nice or attractive. Despite that, she was still a typical example of her upper-class, blue-blooded background, born with a silver spoon in her mouth. With her perfect table manners and her well-heeled gentility, she had always been surrounded by the best life had to offer without having to worry about a roof over her head, money, or the future—the things most other people struggled with. She had been fun to talk to, and she was obviously just as fond of the sport of finance as he was, but apart from that they had *nothing* in common.

Michel nodded. David handed him the paper he had been tallying numbers on before the phone call. Michel scratched his bald head as he checked the columns of numbers a second and then a third time.

They had been on an incomparable journey: a poor guy from the wrong side of town and a second-generation immigrant. Together they had challenged the whole Swedish establishment again and again. Hammar Capital's unparalleled success in the field of venture capitalism was due to a number of factors: timing, hard work, and a bold but sound business idea.

But at the same time David would be the first to admit that sheer luck was an important factor in their success. Several of his crucial turning points had been ninety-nine percent luck, a fact that he had never made any secret of.

The media always pointed to his ability to connect with financiers as contributing to his success. Through his network he had access to just about any important global player. But the path here, to becoming a venture capitalist who was on a par with most of his European competitors even though he operated from one of the smaller nations, had been lined with potential catastrophes.

They had gone up against Investum twice before, testing their strength against the Swedish finance world's most venerable family in a battle for board seats, and they had lost. It had cost them appalling amounts of money both times. Some of their financial backers had pulled out, Hammar Capital had bled like wounded prey, and David himself had taken a beating in the press. But they had analyzed their mistakes and started the strenuous work of regaining people's trust.

And now here they were.

Stronger than ever. Ready to do what had never been done before. Hijack Investum.

Some would say it was crazy. But it was basically a sound business plan. They'd run the numbers over and over again. Gordon Wyndt had summarized it for them one night in his office in Manhattan overlooking Central Park: crazy, reckless, but full of possibility. The fact that the De la Grip family would probably go under after the raid was a side effect that Michel accepted as necessary. For David that was the actual motivating factor, the reason he had worked single-mindedly toward this one goal.

Because the downfall of those two men would set him free.

And if a woman who stood at the sidelines was crushed in the process, then that was collateral he knew he was ruthless enough to accept.

8

Peter De la Grip listened to his father's icy monologue. The oxygen in the smallest conference room at Investum was running out. Peter tried to stifle a yawn but didn't succeed and was forced to yawn into the crook of his arm. His father gave him an irritated look and returned to verbally tearing the female chairman of the board to shreds.

Peter glanced at the clock on the wall. It was almost six and the office was emptying out, but when his father got going it could take some time. He wondered if his father did it on purpose, left conversations like these until late on a Friday to really screw up his victim's entire weekend.

Outwardly, his father was in favor of equal rights for women, of course. Anything else would be media suicide. But the small number of female directors at Investum's various subsidiaries didn't usually last long. When Gustaf De la Grip summoned them to headquarters and went off on one of his merciless tirades, they usually resigned voluntarily. His father would then complain in the press about how difficult it was to find women with the right skill set and career focus.

In the sauna and on their fall game-hunting trips, however, he took a different tone. Then the demeaning words about women in the workplace really hit the fan in a way that few outsiders would even believe. Women were scatterbrained, it was that time of the month and it was affecting their logic, they weren't biologically suited to serve on corporate boards. Sometimes it was almost tiresome. But his father didn't believe in having women at the top, and Peter wasn't the type to fight for someone else. People had to fight their own battles. But anyone who claimed that the world of Swedish business was a level playing field had no idea what they were talking about.

He turned in his chair and looked askance at his phone. Louise had texted to say they were having guests over. He'd been to the liquor store and Östermalmshall, but he was going to be late, and he hated to annoy Louise. He quickly texted her that they should start without him. It couldn't be helped.

"I expect your cooperation and loyalty," his father told the director. "I thought you were going to show that you were worth our investment."

Peter was forced to peek at his papers, because suddenly he couldn't even remember her name.

Rima Campbell, age fifty-two. An immigrant, she hadn't had a chance from the beginning.

"But I . . . ," she said, and Peter rolled his eyes. His father hated being interrupted. In the worst of cases, he would begin again. Peter never interrupted his father.

Gustaf continued. "You're not cooperating. You're not loyal. You're questioning the board."

Peter had sat through countless meetings like this. Only women were subjected to such treatment.

Sometimes he agreed with his father—sometimes the victim really was the wrong person for the job. Sometimes, like today, he thought Gustaf was making a mistake.

The woman with the hopelessly un-Swedish name was good at what she did and seemed to be doing a decent job. Simply the fact that she'd made it this far—she was an immigrant, a woman, *and* a single mother—suggested that her skills were above average. Her two sons were probably adults now, but Rima Campbell had built an impressive career for herself while raising two children. She had done it on her own, stayed single, and broken right through most of the glass ceilings. But it didn't matter what Peter thought of her performance. Gustaf did what he wanted. And right now he was intent on breaking the dark-skinned director, whom he'd hired just a few months earlier. He wanted to show that women didn't belong at the top, that they were overly emotional and prone to overreacting. He wanted to show that he was right.

Gustaf continued, "Your colleagues tell me you're not loyal. People are dissatisfied with you."

"Who? Which colleagues?"

"I can't tell you that. But you need to know: no one likes you."

Peter was close to breaking in. Surely this was a little over the top?

Rima was a little pale, but she was holding it together, and Peter didn't say anything. It wouldn't have done any good.

"I can't defend myself against anonymous accusations," Rima said grimly.

Gustaf began anew, attacking her over and over again in a chilling voice. Finally she just sat there in silence, her eyes dry, red splotches on her neck.

"I want you to take the weekend to think about it and consider whether we can work together in the future," Gustaf concluded coldly. "Currently I just don't see it."

Rima swallowed. Peter didn't dare look at either of them; he was practically holding his breath. She stood up. Her hands were shaking. But she hadn't started to cry, and her voice had remained polite throughout. Clearly, she was really tough. But it was over for her, he knew it. On Monday she would resign. He was sure of that.

Before Rima had even left the room, his father said, loudly enough for her to hear, "That's what happens when you hire a jungle bunny."

Peter looked down at the table.

After Rima left, his father asked, "Are you going out to the estate?" as if nothing unusual had happened, as if he hadn't just broken a woman and also been so racist that Peter was ashamed.

But Peter just nodded. It didn't matter; his father never listened to what anyone said. Father always knew best.

"Louise invited some friends over for the weekend," he said.

"Business acquaintances?"

"Yes."

"Good."

Peter bowed his head at the approval, wished his father's praise didn't mean so much to him.

They said good-bye. Gustaf strolled out to the car that his private chauffeur drove up and Peter walked down to the garage. As soon as they parted, he felt some of the relentless pressure lifting. It was almost a physical relief, as if someone had been sitting on his chest and had now gotten off.

He clicked to unlock the car and then opened the door.

Friday. A whole weekend with no other obligations than to possibly play host to one or two well-organized dinners. How wonderful. He drove out of the garage and headed out of the city. As he drove through the Friday evening traffic, his mind turned to the uncomfortable meeting, but he brushed it aside.

He had more than enough of his own problems to deal with. Getting into a conflict with his father was the last thing he needed.

As soon as the speed limit went up, he pushed down on the gas pedal.

But it *had* been a rough meeting. It got rougher every time, but you didn't question Gustaf De la Grip. Not if you wanted a prominent position at Investum. And that, more than anything, was exactly what Peter wanted—a prominent position, the most prominent: CEO.

Sometimes it felt like he'd been fighting his whole life.

He was reminded of that even today. How he started school, worked like an animal, and only heard that he had to put in more effort. How was it possible to fight so hard and still never really get there?

His father, who didn't believe in weakness, psychologists, or other failings, had handled every difficulty by scolding him sporadically. In a family where one was expected to excel at something, where everyone was the best at something, in a family whose motto was "Business is pleasure" he had never been anything more than mediocre.

He stopped at a red light, drumming his fingers on the wheel.

The sense of impotence and frustration had always been like a darkness within him. And his outlet had always been to attack those who were even weaker. Better to bully than to be bullied. Better to hit than to be hit. *That* could have been the De la Grip family motto right there, he thought. Sometimes he dreamed that someone would intervene and speak up, change the story, prevent the catastrophe. But he didn't want to think about it, had devoted so much time to *not* remembering.

Still, it was strange, he thought as he followed the traffic, that at the age of thirty-five he could still be struck by that sense of panic he had experienced as a schoolboy, of never getting it right. It was like one of those nightmares people talked about—you worked like crazy but never got anywhere. That was exactly how it had been.

He had always had to struggle to achieve what had come so easily to Natalia and Alexander. Both of his siblings had earned top grades and gotten into the School of Economics with no problem. After two unsuccessful attempts to get in, he had given up and started a degree at the regular university instead. His father had never said anything, but he hadn't needed to. By that point everyone knew that Peter was and would remain second-rate.

He sighed heavily, wondered why he'd thought of this just now. He hadn't thought about these things for a long time. But something was changing; he sensed it.

Alexander had disgraced himself with his drinking and womanizing. No one was counting on him anymore. And Natalia. Well, she was a woman—it didn't matter how good she was.

Peter looked in the rearview mirror and then passed someone quickly. Natalia seemed to be doing a good job with this new bank deal, he was willing to concede that to himself, even if he would never admit it to his father. But he hoped Natalia would pull it off. It was important to their father, and it was best for everyone that their father get what he wanted.

Peter saw the sign and turned onto the side road to the house. Soon he'd be home. Louise was already waiting for him, the perfect hostess, elegant and refined, content to be a lady of the manor at one of the country's finest estates. As long as Louise got to live out here she would be satisfied, he knew that. Maybe he didn't love her, but he understood her, and that was good enough. They suited each other, and he had never expected love. Didn't even know if he could love or be loved.

He slowed and drove down the long, oak-lined avenue. Some of the trees were several hundred years old. He glanced off to the side, studied the well-tended fields and waterways glimmering in the summer light. The day he'd signed the paperwork and taken over the family seat had been his proudest. It was like receiving the recognition he'd been waiting for his whole life, acknowledgment that in spite of everything, he did deserve his hereditary due. It was an opportunity to finally look ahead toward the long term and not just live from year to year.

He drove in the open iron gates, listened to gravel crunch beneath the tires. Climbed out and stood, gazing up at the yellow façade.

Maybe he should finally let go of the demons that had pursued him for so long. Because when he took over the castle, when he realized his father really was choosing him as his heir and not Alex, not some worthy cousin, but *him*, then it was as if someone had finally let a little light into the perpetual darkness that surrounded him and said, "Now, Peter, you've done the right thing for so long that the statute of limitations is up on what you did in the past."

If that was true, then there was nothing he wouldn't do to keep it that way.

Nothing.

9

It was a magical performance, Natalia thought. She didn't take her eyes off Sarah Harvey for a second. It might have been one of the best evenings of her life. The atmosphere at Café Opera was close and intimate, the experience almost private.

The last note of the final encore ebbed away, and if Natalia had ever felt a spiritual presence, now was the time. There was thunderous applause from the invited guests, and Natalia caught Åsa's attention. They were seated at a table right up next to the stage. She could tell Åsa was so moved that she had tears in her eyes.

The soprano circulated around the tables, greeting friends, and shook both Natalia and Åsa's hands. After that they strolled out into the summer evening. Despite the late hour, it was still light outside, and an almost tropical heat lingered over the city.

"We can't go home now," Natalia said, still filled with the music. "How about one last drink?"

Åsa waved a hand and nodded. "Alright, but somewhere without tourists," she said. "What are all these people doing here?"

Natalia laughed and took a few dancing steps across the cobblestones in her high-heeled golden sandals.

As a child she had danced ballet—long, hard workouts. She had loved the old-fashioned discipline, the pale-pink shoes and simple outfits, but since she wasn't one of the very best in her group, her mother decided it was a waste of time to continue. The next day she began at a school for ballroom dancing instead.

Natalia furrowed her brow. All these choices that had been made for her, which shaped her. If it had been up to her mother, she would never have entered the financial world. "Wasted on a woman." But Natalia had put her foot down on that one.

She wove around an embracing couple. "What did you think?" she asked. "Aren't you glad you came?"

Åsa had grumbled and complained. No normal people stayed in Stockholm at this time of year. And Café Opera wasn't that hip. But she'd still canceled an all-weekend party and come along.

"It was nice," Åsa admitted, but then swore as one of her sky-high heels stuck between two cobblestones. She'd had more to drink than Natalia and was a little wobbly. A curl of blond hair was dangling in front of one eye, and the thin shawl she wore over her shoulders shimmered under the streetlights. She looked like a movie star.

Natalia couldn't stop smiling. The June night was warm and magical. The streets were filled with people, and she felt young and strong, as if the last few years of worry and grief had randomly decided to go off and burden someone else.

"I haven't had such a nice time in ages," she said.

"Not since Jonas," Åsa said, surprising Natalia with her astuteness, because they never talked about the past. Åsa was allergic to pity parties and sadness, so just a few weeks after Natalia's breakup with Jonas, she was already sending clear signals that it was time for Natalia to move on.

Åsa's inclination was always to move on and never look back, but Natalia had taken the breakup hard. And Åsa's limited sympathy had hurt her more than she dared admit. But maybe the tide was finally starting to turn.

"Let's go in here," said Natalia. She pointed at a subdued and very, very expensive bar and its long line and encouraged Åsa: "Get up there and get us in."

Åsa, who personally knew everyone who was anyone in Stockholm nightlife, caught the bouncer's attention. He nodded in recognition, asked the line to step aside, and then they were in.

"You're my idol," Natalia chuckled.

"I'm everyone's idol," Åsa said, clearing the way over to the bar for them. She ordered for them both. "Two vodka tonics, please."

The club was crowded and warm, and the din forced them to stand over by the bar so they could talk.

"I don't know a single person in here," Åsa said.

"Is that good or bad?" Natalia sipped her drink. It was strong and cold, and she was thirsty. She looked around. Well-dressed men and skinny women with long hair laughed, toasted, and flirted.

Lord, when did everyone get to be so young? She tried to remember the last time she'd been out to drink for any reason other than work, but couldn't.

"You know as well as I do that all the civilized people have already started packing for their vacations in Skåne."

"I know," Natalia groaned. The Swedish summer schedule followed a rigidly prescribed pattern. The Royal Swedish Yacht Club's Gotland regatta was this weekend, then all the political speeches during Almedalen week next week, and then the week after that Båstad for a week. Mingle, tennis, sun, and swimming. Year in and year out.

"I'm eternally grateful that you came. And it was something, you have to admit. Better than the same old people you're always hanging around with." She sipped her drink again. "This is good," she said appreciatively.

Åsa shook her head and ordered another drink with a quick hand gesture. She'd finished her first drink in only a couple of minutes. "When are you going to listen to reason and stop rebelling? Okay, I get that you don't want to hang out with your parents, but seriously, Natalia, you can't work all summer. Isn't that how people get burned out?"

"No," Natalia said. "And I'm not rebelling," she lied.

Åsa was right on the mark. She was actually acting like an overgrown teenager, rebelling against everything her parents were used to expecting from her. But she hated the conformity of the Swedish summers she'd grown up with and hated that everyone, absolutely everyone, seemed to think that was the only way to do it. Vacation in the right spot with the right people at the right time. Torekov, Båstad, and Falsterbo in the summer. The Alps in the winter. That's what she'd always done for as long as she could remember.

Wherever they went, they always saw the same people. She'd gone along with it her whole life without even thinking about it. Jonas had done the same. All their acquaintances and *their* parents had done it.

But this year—her first summer on her own—Natalia refused. Thank you very much. It had only taken her half her life to dare to go against the current.

"Although I *am* going to Båstad," she pointed out, taking another sip of her drink. "J-O ordered me to. But I'll mostly be mingling with Danes, so it will be work." She glanced at Åsa. "Are you even listening to me?"

Åsa didn't respond. She was definitely looking for someone or something, and Natalia glanced around for a seat. For a person who loathed any form of physical exertion, Åsa was surprisingly able to stand upright in stiletto heels drinking alcohol for hours on end. But Natalia wasn't used to it.

"My feet hurt," she complained.

"Hmm," Åsa said. She nodded toward a table with a facial expression that Natalia couldn't interpret. "Some people have tables," she said sarcastically. "Maybe you'd like to sit there?"

Natalia looked to see what Åsa was staring at, and when the crowd parted for a moment she saw a table in the corner, with a white tablecloth and shiny glasses: like an oasis amid the noise. The table was surrounded by beautiful young women flipping their hair and batting their eyelashes at the two men who were seated at it. One of them, an enormous man with a shaved, tan head, gold jewelry, and a shiny silk shirt, as if straight out of a gangster movie, was staring at Åsa, who was now openly staring back. Neither of them looked away, and Natalia had the strange sense that some kind of wordless communication was taking place between them in the midst of the crowded bar. The other man at the table—attractive, dark-haired, and exactly the same height with the same broad shoulders, oozing self-confidence—was David Hammar.

David met Natalia's astonished eyes. She nodded, and he nodded back, and it was as if neither of them could look away, their eyes locked. He might have had some idea that Natalia would show up here. If he were being one hundred percent honest, then maybe—*maybe*—he had even been mulling over that very possibility. Stockholm's nightlife for the very rich was fairly limited. The golden triangle that comprised the capital city's financial district during the day was the same small arena for nightlife. There weren't that many exclusive bars, and if a woman like Natalia De la Grip were going to go out after a concert at Café Opera, this was where she would end up.

She was dressed in gold. Her glossy hair was up, and the nape of her neck bare and slender and without jewelry. She stood up straight, poised like a ballerina, and there was something about the lighting in the crowded bar that made her shine.

It took a minute before David noticed the other woman standing next to Natalia, eyeing Michel through narrowed, suspicious eyes. He should have seen her right away, strange that he hadn't. She was in a class all her own, the most beautiful woman in the room, voluptuous and almost surreally sensual.

"Åsa Bjelke," he said, knowing exactly who she was. One of Investum's attorneys and a close friend of Natalia De la Grip. The fact was that David knew almost more about Åsa than Natalia. The press loved to wallow in the details of Åsa's dramatic background, and she was referred to as the Poor Little Rich Girl in the worst of the tabloids. Born with both a silver and a gold spoon in her mouth, she'd gone to all the right schools, was often mentioned as a potential bride for the prince—in the papers anyway, not in real life as far as he knew. And then: the tragedy that had dominated so many of the headlines for weeks.

"She seems to know who you are," David said, looking at Michel, who sat stiff and motionless, and added dryly, "and vice versa. Do you know each other?"

"Yes," Michel said.

"You never mentioned that."

But Stockholm was such a small world, of course Åsa and Michel knew each other. They were both lawyers. David had spotted a stressed-looking Peter De la Grip just yesterday afternoon at Östermalmshall. Peter had walked right by him, his hands full of shopping bags. David could have reached his hand out and touched him.

"There's nothing to say," Michel said, still just as tersely. "We studied together. A few courses. Law school. I can't really say that I *know* her. But we . . ." He paused, took a drink of his mineral water and made a show of *not* looking in Åsa's direction.

David studied the two women. He looked at Michel and then at Åsa again. He had an almost dead-on ability to read people's moods, which was a major asset in his line of work. He didn't even bat an eye now. There was something Michel wasn't telling him. Michel sat there with his water, suddenly more like a sulky teenager than a world-class financial attorney.

David looked at the women again. Or, to be honest, he mostly looked at Natalia.

"I suppose we could go over to them," he surprised himself by saying. He stood up before he had time to reconsider what he already knew was a bad decision and before Michel could oppose it. He could walk over to a woman he was acquainted with without it meaning anything more, he told himself. He could walk over to her and say hello and be polite for two seconds, even though she was a De la Grip. Michel reluctantly rose with him.

"Is that really a good idea?" asked Michel. He ran a hand over his shaved head.

"All ideas are good," said David. He had decided. Because this was about politeness, nothing else. "Come on."

Michel muttered something behind him, and David saw Åsa's face take on a wary expression as they approached.

"Hi," said David as they stepped over to the bar. Natalia blinked with her long eyelashes. She moved forward ever so slightly, and for a fleeting second, David was close to leaning forward and kissing her on the cheek. But she just held out her hand, so he took it and shook it instead.

"Hi," she said.

"Hi," he repeated, holding her hand a moment longer than he needed to. He smelled that scent of something old-fashioned and spicy, a timeless, sensual scent, which he already recognized as hers.

Natalia pulled her hand back. David introduced Michel and saw her slender hand enclosed by Michel's ring-encrusted fist.

"This is my friend Åsa Bjelke," she said. David held out his hand, and a steady, professional handshake reminded him that this silver-clad bombshell with the tipsy eyes was considered to be a very talented corporate attorney.

"We just came from the performance at Café Opera," Natalia said. "Thank you again for the tickets." She was smiling, and something about her eyes made her seem a little inebriated as well. But she looked happy, not drunk, just a little less controlled, a little freer.

The bar was crowded and noisy; someone pushed their way up to the bar and the inevitable happened: they brushed against each other. That scent wafted over to him again; he was captivated by her golden eyes, and even though he had just meant to say hello, he didn't want to go yet. Natalia was taller than he remembered. She was so delicate that you assumed she was petite, but in high heels, she was quite tall. She stood straight, without fidgeting with anything, without fussing with her hair or her clothes, and without chattering away. Normally those boarding-school manners annoyed the hell out of David, but he decided to take a little break from his knee-jerk hatred of the upper class. He smiled, and her eyes twinkled at him.

Åsa raised her glass, drank, and glared over the edge of the glass.

"Michel says you knew each other in law school," David said to her politely.

"Yes, but that must have been over ten years ago," she replied coolly. She gave Michel a quick, hard look. David wondered if this had to do with that same old, tired racism one found among upper-class Swedes. Michel, with his dark skin and foreign background, had suffered his share of prejudice. Åsa Bjelke twisted her mouth into a wicked, but downright sexy smile. "Is he still the same old bore?"

Natalia looked shocked, but David laughed. The woman was drunk, but her grudge against Michel didn't seem to be based on his ethnicity or race. She seemed to not like Michel on a much more personal level, and that made David curious. He hadn't met many women who didn't like Michel.

"More or less," he replied, because Michel *could* be a little dull.

"Luckily no one can accuse you of being boring," Michel said sarcastically, which was completely unlike him. "As I recall, you used to really enjoy yourself back then."

Åsa thrust her chin up in the air, but David was able to read that the comment had stung. That was about as far from Michel's usual behavior as you could get.

"Michel . . . ," he said in a warning tone.

"So lovely to have seen you," Åsa interrupted him acidly. "Pardon me." She left them with angry, clicking footsteps. Natalia watched her go with a look of concern.

"I'm sorry," Michel said gruffly and then he too left.

"Do you know what that was all about?" David asked. "Or am I imagining it?"

"No." She didn't have a chance to say any more before someone bumped into her from behind and she again was quickly pushed into David. He reached out with his hand on her upper arm. She blinked, and suddenly David's thoughts about Michel and Åsa were far, far away. Those two were grown-ups, they would work it out—or not work it out; that was up to them. He looked at his hand resting on her upper arm, and then he looked at her. Her lips were glossy, a little sparkly. A smile played at the corner of her mouth, and David caught himself smiling back, looking deep into her eyes, and stroking her arm with a finger.

She opened her mouth but closed it again without saying anything. He continued to run his finger over her arm, and they looked at each other, not smiling, not flirting, but more questioning. And then she pulled her arm back with an apologetic smile. "They're coming now," she said, and for a moment David had no idea what she was talking about.

"I'm going to head home," he heard Åsa say. And he was glad to be snapped out of it, that strange moment when he was actually dangerously close to flirting with the daughter and sister of the two men he hated most in the world. With the only woman in the whole world he had every reason to keep away from.

"Yeah," Natalia said with a nod. She started to gather her things, the way women always did when they were about to leave.

"Where's Michel?" David asked.

Åsa shrugged. "Maybe he's calling his mother?" she snorted, but despite her scornful tone, David had to agree. Michel did call his mother a lot. He suppressed a disloyal laugh and spotted Michel pushing his way through the crowd of toasting drinkers. It was really crowded in here now, and the normally agile Michel wasn't being particularly careful.

"We should probably be going," Natalia said apologetically, but David heard the ambivalence in her voice, sensed that she would really prefer to stay. And, strangely, so did he.

"Or why not stay for a little bit?" he said. "I'd love to hear more about the concert. Have another drink? Champagne?"

She was on the verge of allowing herself to be convinced, it appeared, and David had already summoned the bartender. A glass of champagne together, what difference would that make?

And then Michel raised his voice behind him. David didn't hear what he said, it wasn't anything particular, but the words were said in a hard tone, and a look of concern flickered through Natalia's eyes.

"We'd better call it a night," she said. "Åsa has to get home." David nodded. He didn't know what was going on between Michel and the beautiful but inebriated blonde, but it sounded as if an argument was about to break out.

"Come, Michel," he said. "It's time to go. You've had enough and it's late."

"I haven't had anything to drink," Michel said.

"I wasn't talking about alcohol," David said. And then in a quieter voice, "Pull yourself together, man."

"Same here," said Natalia with a discreet nod toward her girlfriend. "Åsa?"

Åsa nodded. She swayed a little but seemed to recover. She avoided looking at Michel, and he turned the other way.

Natalia followed closely behind David's and Michel's broad backs as they cut a path through the crowd. The noise was almost deafening, and even though she was concerned that the evening had taken such a sour turn, she was eager for some fresh air. Once they were out on the street, Åsa gave her a quick hug, the briefest of nods to the two men, and sat down in one of the taxis that was waiting outside the bar. Natalia helped shut the door and watched the cab drive away toward Östermalm.

She bit her lip, feeling David's presence behind her. Something had happened between them in the bar, she just didn't know what. "Åsa and I don't live in the same direction," she explained. "I live over there." She pointed in her direction, feeling like an idiot. What did they care where she lived?

Michel Chamoun stood glowering next to David, his brow furrowed. He didn't say anything, and Natalia thought he looked a little scary with his bulging arm muscles, his black suede jacket, and his shaved head. She glanced at David. They were big men. If they hadn't been so well dressed in designer jeans and attractive jackets and if they hadn't had that definitive air of financial men, they could just as easily have been bodyguards or mafiosos.

There was no denying that it was a somewhat uncomfortable situation. Standing at the bar, David had smiled and flirted, and for a second or two she had thought he was about to kiss her. But now he seemed so unyielding, she wondered if she'd just imagined it. But no, she and David *had* clicked in there. And maybe it was the alcohol, maybe it was because she was more dressed up than she had been for ages, but she didn't want to go home, didn't want to part from David, not yet.

"You go ahead," David suddenly said to Michel. It sounded like an order, and he wasn't smiling.

"But . . . ," said Michel and nodded at Natalia.

She squirmed. Clearly Michel didn't think it was a good idea to leave them alone.

David nodded encouragingly at the taxi, looked at Michel, and said, "Go."

Michel said a very stiff good-bye to Natalia and climbed into the cab, and then she and David were left alone on the sidewalk. He still wasn't smiling, just looking at her with an expression she couldn't interpret. It was a warm evening, but she was wearing a thin dress, and suddenly she felt unsure and incredibly aware of how insubstantial her dress was and how little she actually knew about David Hammar.

"I suppose I should probably be heading home too," she said.

"Would you like me to hail you a cab?" he asked tersely, almost impersonally, and she wondered if she'd just imagined everything back in the bar. The situation was making her uncomfortable.

"I'm fully capable of waving over a cab on my own," she replied, suddenly irritated. She hadn't asked him for anything. He could take his weird mood swings and go to . . .

He gave her a long look. "I wasn't questioning your capabilities," he said calmly.

"Sorry," she said. Maybe he was just being considerate. "I didn't mean to sound snappy. It was just so strange." She looked him right in the eye and said honestly, "All of it."

"Yes," he agreed.

"It's such a nice evening. I think I'm going to go for a little walk," she said.

"I'll join you."

Natalia started walking; he matched her speed, and they walked next to each other in silence. She was still confused. And she did not like being confused. She glanced over at him out of the corner of her eye. He'd stuffed his hands into his pockets and was walking along with his brow furrowed. A purely feminine part of her couldn't help but wonder what he would be like as a lover. She was only human, and even if she never admitted it, not even to Åsa—*especially* not to Åsa—she hadn't been with anyone since Jonas. Not because of morality, just because she was pathetically awkward when it came to flirting and dating. She hadn't slept with anyone in over a year. She almost giggled at how shocked Åsa would be if she found out.

"Sarah Harvey was really wonderful," she said once the silence began to become absurd. She glanced over at David's serious face.

"I'm glad," he said and smiled quickly. "I have to admit I've never heard her."

"I really appreciate the tickets," she said, and they both slowed down at the same time. They stopped. In her high heels she came almost up to his face. She looked into his eyes. She blinked slowly. There it was again—that electric charge.

David smiled and raised his hand, as if to caress her. She was just on the verge of closing her eyes to lean in toward him when he said, "It was lovely to see you." And she realized that he wasn't about to stroke her cheek at all. He was saying good night.

"Yes," she said, taking a little step back. She exhaled and tried not to let the disappointment she felt show in her voice. If she'd been someone else, she would have plucked up her courage and asked him if he wanted to come back to her place. That's what people did, right? It wasn't so weird. David was single as far as she knew. She was an independent, free woman. She even had condoms somewhere in one of the drawers in her bedroom. She should be able to do that. Ask if he wanted to come back to her place for a drink.

But a taxi pulled into view, her fragile courage lapsed, and she waved it over.

David opened the door for her. Natalia slid in, felt the cool seat through the thin fabric of her dress. He was still standing there, leaning over the door. She looked up at him, determined to be cool.

David looked as if he were about to say something, but then seemed to change his mind.

"Good night," she said, forcing herself to smile. It didn't matter that much. It wasn't like something had *happened*.

"Natalia?" he said quickly, just as he was about to close the car door.

She felt a shiver down her spine, because her name sounded like a caress in his mouth. "Yes?"

"If you're free tomorrow, I'd love to see you. Can I call you?"

She couldn't think what to say, just nodded mutely.

He nodded too, as if he'd made a decision. The door closed before they had a chance to say anything else. With a soft hum, the taxi drove her the last little way through the summer night. She smiled the whole way home, and she was still smiling when she closed her eyes and went to sleep.

10

Sunday, June 29

The next morning Åsa woke up full of dread. Thank heavens it was Sunday, and thank heavens there was no one next to her in the bed. She was really enormously grateful for that. On far too many mornings she had been forced to kick out a strange man who didn't get that she was serious that sex was okay, but not spending the night.

Nausea washed over her. And then the dread, of course. Oh, how she hated this hangover dread. It was worse than ever today. She couldn't remember how much she'd drunk, and that was never a good sign. She stubbornly tried to keep the thoughts of Michel Chamoun at bay, but it was futile. That man had always found his way into nooks where no one, least of all him, had any business. She flung an arm over her face, fought it as well as she could. She wasn't angry at him, if she were being honest, and she tried to be honest with herself since she lied so much to everyone else. No, she wasn't angry at Michel. She was angry at herself. She groaned into her arm.

Her behavior at the bar had been completely nuts. But she'd been so caught off guard by the effect he had on her—*her*, Åsa Bjelke, who never let anyone get to her. She hadn't had any idea that she still cared. Unbelievable. But he had really hurt her, and when she was at her most fragile. It was over a decade ago; they'd been so young, but it felt like it had just happened. She remembered every look, every word. Every single one . . .

And then Åsa permitted herself to do something she normally never would: to wallow in what never was.

Michel had changed.

The gangly student with the serious eyes and the soft black hair was gone. Åsa had thought Michel was gorgeous back then when they had met at school. But he was much better-looking now, with his shaved head and his grown-up eyes. He didn't wear a wedding ring—she'd checked—but that didn't necessarily mean anything; so many of the finance guys she'd dragged home had a wife and kids in some villa in Djursholm.

Although Michel isn't like that; you know that, Åsa, a voice whispered.

Michel was old-fashioned, proper, and loyal. If he was married to some lovely Lebanese girl and had eight children with her, then he was faithful. That was Michel Chamoun. It was inconceivable that he'd done so well for himself in an industry that was built on deceit and backstabbing

She sat up, flung her legs over the edge of the bed, and groaned. She had to make it through this day. One more day—she ought to be able to handle that. But she hated Sundays with nothing scheduled, and this Sunday she was actually supposed to have been out in the archipelago at that weekend-long party. Surrounded by people who were divinely superficial and didn't try to see into her.

She glanced at her phone with sleep in her eyes. One text message. From Natalia.

Hope you're doing well.

Call if you need to talk.

No more messages.

Åsa set down the phone, irritated at Natalia for no reason.

But if Natalia hadn't gotten those tickets from that arrogant David Hammar, then this would never have happened. She should have been out on an island surrounded by distant friends and even more distant acquaintances, who would help to chat away the Sunday dread and fill the emptiness and silence with sound.

Thank goodness, she had her whole summer vacation ahead of her. A few weeks until she would be with people practically around the clock. There would be parties and sunshine, which would keep away this awful empty feeling that attacked her so quickly when she was alone. And she wouldn't think about Michel even once, she promised herself. Starting now, it would be as if he never existed, as if they'd never seen each other last night in Stockholm, and as if their mutual story had ended, for real, more than ten years before.

She pushed out two headache pills, filled a glass with water, and dropped two rehydration pills into it. She looked at the fizzy, murky liquid.

Suddenly and without warning, she started to cry.

Natalia glanced at the text she eventually got back from Åsa. It was brief, almost dismissive, but she was still relieved that her friend seemed safe and sound.

She and Åsa didn't usually get together on weekends unless they'd scheduled something in particular. They'd been friends since they were kids; their mothers had been friends. They went to the same schools, and after the tragedy, Åsa had lived with them, of course, but they still conducted very different lives. Åsa was an extrovert and kept tabs on everything pertaining to fashion and lifestyle. She had gobs of friends and acquaintances, knew practically everyone who was anyone, was always—almost obsessively—booked up with lunches and parties and drinking, while Natalia worked all the time and was uncomfortable with that circle.

Most of the women Natalia had grown up with lived typical upper-class lives, and very few of them financed their own lifestyle. Many of them were stay-at-home moms with nannies and housecleaners and catered dinners; others took a few fashion or design courses abroad and let their parents provide for them while they waited for a rich husband to turn up.

More than once, this had struck Natalia as a suffocating holdover from another era, from before women's rights. But then she'd always been an odd bird. Not even Åsa, who, to say the least, did a spectacular job at Investum, shared her passion for working. Åsa worked office hours, took long lunches and vacations, and spent her free time doing activities that focused on mingling, shopping, and glamour. It was different for Natalia. Her social life had never really recovered after her separation from Jonas. She and Jonas had socialized mostly with mutual friends, and it was clear now that a single woman simply doesn't get invited to many intimate couples dinners or cozy barbecues. As a matter of fact, none of her and Jonas's friends had invited her over this past year.

At first it stung a lot more than she'd thought, being excluded. But soon she'd gotten used to it. She'd never had many female friends, and now she mostly spent her time working.

Natalia figured she probably shouldn't be anywhere near as satisfied with solitude, but when it got right down to it, she had very little in common with most of the women she knew. Surely life had to be about something more than living at the right address and keeping tabs on who didn't have as much money as they were trying to make it seem they did, right?

Her phone chimed. She glanced at the display, sure that the text was from Åsa again.

Are you awake? —David Hammar

She squeezed the phone hard. He'd asked if he could call and she'd said yes—sure. And yes, maybe she'd hoped he would get in touch at some point during the day. But already, just a few hours after they'd parted, here it was. As if he didn't care at all whether he seemed too eager.

She wrote: *Yes.* Smiled, sent it off, and waited.

Two seconds later the phone rang.

"How are you doing?" he asked.

She smiled so hard her face hurt. "Good. Thanks for calling."

"Did Åsa make it home alright?"

Oh. She melted a little.

"Yes, she just texted me. Thanks."

He didn't say anything, and Natalia thought she ought to say something more. Something that sounded cool and yet charming. Jeez, she was really pitiful at this.

"Do you want to have breakfast with me?" he asked.

Yes! I'd love to! Love, love, love to.

"When?" she asked.

"I'll send a car 'round to pick you up. In about half an hour?"

Natalia exhaled, slowly. She hadn't expected that.

But then, as if what else would a guy do besides send 'round cars to pick her up for breakfast dates, she said, "How nice. Thank you. Then I'll see you soon."

* * *

Exactly half an hour later, Natalia saw a dark car with the Grand Hôtel logo in one of its windows pull onto her street and stop in front of her door. She hadn't given David her address. It hadn't occurred to her. But he'd known where she lived. A young, androgynous person in jeans, a shirt, and vest opened the back door and then shut it again after she'd climbed in. Natalia didn't have time to do anything more than sink down into the soft leather seat before they stopped outside the Grand Hôtel.

One of the doormen came over to her. "Natalia De la Grip?" She nodded, feeling a little like this was straight out of a fairy tale or a movie. "Can you find your way to the Cadier Bar?" he inquired politely.

"Yes, thank you," she said, ascending the carpeted stairs into the hotel, into the realm of the Grand Hôtel's understated opulence.

David was sitting at the far end of the bar, which had been named for the hotel's founder. Sunlight poured in, and the view of the Royal castle and the water were amazing. David stood up, and Natalia was uncertain how to greet him. He gave her a quick smile and held out his hand. She shook it, thinking that she just couldn't figure him out. On the one hand, he was so proper and professional that it was ludicrous to think he had any interest in her. On the other hand, tickets to private performances, Sunday breakfast, and a car to pick her up. If he was trying to confuse her, he'd succeeded.

"I didn't know what you'd like, so I ordered everything," he said, gesturing at the table, which was weighed down with bread baskets, cheeses, cereal, yogurts, marmalades, juices, fruit, and pots of both tea and coffee. "Aside from oatmeal. I can't imagine anyone actually liking oatmeal."

She took a seat and allowed him to pour her a white cup of steaming coffee. "This looks wonderful," she said candidly, setting a heavy cloth napkin on her lap. She buttered a croissant and drizzled raspberry jam over it. She bit into the pastry. Flaky golden crumbs fell onto her plate, and she almost licked her lips. Heaven.

David's gray-blue eyes twinkled. "Good?" he asked.

"I didn't have any food at home, and I was so hungry. Thank you."

He waited while she ate, tossing in a few polite phrases, but letting her eat in peace and quiet. When she glanced over at the newspaper, he handed it to her. "Go ahead and read it," he said. "I'm the same way."

As she scanned through the headlines, he drank his coffee and seemed completely content with their quiet companionship. She closed the newspaper. He poured her more coffee, and she wondered what he actually wanted from her, what he was after.

He wasn't the first venture capitalist she'd had lunch with. Not even the first she'd shared a hotel breakfast with, actually. A big part of her job involved wining and dining potential clients. She was good at it, used to keeping confidences, and an expert at giving concrete advice in complex financial contexts. Natalia knew her famous last name had contributed to J-O recruiting her. Powerful CEOs and influential fund managers were way more impressed than they cared to admit by her high-society name. But she also knew that the reason she was considered one of Sweden's—maybe one of Scandinavia's—best talents now was thanks to her own expertise.

She knew all this about herself.

But it didn't seem as if David wanted to talk business.

"So, what is Sweden's most notorious venture capitalist up to this summer?" she asked casually.

He gave her an impenetrable look. "I'll be working."

"No vacation?"

He set down his coffee cup. He was casually dressed in a short-sleeved shirt and dark jeans. No other man in the restaurant came anywhere close to his charisma. The servers kept their eye on him the whole time; pretty much every single patron had checked them out at some point. David was a force to be reckoned with. And he seemed completely oblivious about it. "I never take a vacation," he said, and she knew he was neither lying nor bragging.

She'd never met anyone like him. Most of the big-finance guys were all cast in the same mold: sunburned and boastful, suave and superficial. David wasn't the least bit sunburned, and it struck her that he wasn't putting on airs. He wasn't a man who lounged around by the Mediterranean or on a Caribbean island. In the pictures she'd seen of him, it was easy to take him for a completely normal, albeit an unusually attractive, finance guy. But here like this, in his immediate presence, there was nothing commonplace about him. He radiated hardness and energy, drawing her in while at the same time putting her on her guard. Imagine having a man like this as your enemy. She shivered.

"You really mean that," she said, resolutely pushing aside her very sinister thoughts. He was just a person, not some evil super villain.

She stabbed a strawberry with her fork and realized he'd probably been sitting here since early this morning working, even though it was Sunday. She glanced at the bag hanging over his chair. Yup, she could see a computer, folders, and several newspapers.

"I work straight through, but I don't have any problem with that," he said.

She smiled into her coffee cup.

"What?"

"I'm just the same," she admitted.

"I know," he said. "I can tell. Aren't you going to take any time off at all?"

"My family is going to Båstad soon, and I'll go down there for a bit too. You know my brother, I think? Peter? You studied together, didn't you?"

"Yes," said David. "At Skogbacka." His voice was so neutral when he said the name of the boarding school that Natalia could tell that he and Peter hadn't gotten along. She wasn't very surprised. Peter could be a real snob. And she'd never heard anyone in her family say a good word about venture capitalists in general or David Hammar in specific. It was the same old, same old: newbies, nouveau riches, blah blah blah.

She set down her fork, leaving the last of the fruit. She was stuffed. It was now or never.

"I have to ask . . . ," she began.

He raised an eyebrow. "Well, if you must . . ."

But she didn't let him frighten her. "I don't really understand why you contacted me." She smiled quickly to take the edge off of how suspicious she sounded. "Not that it hasn't been lovely, but I've really been puzzling over this. I wonder if you have a connection to one of my clients that I missed or some deal you need help with, but honestly I can't think of it. Is this business or—uh—well, something else?"

* * *

David sized Natalia up. She was watching him attentively, straight-forwardly, not backing down. Her direct question hadn't surprised him, not really. Because Natalia didn't seem like a woman playing a game, and she had every right to wonder.

He was the first to admit that his behavior toward her was incon-sistent. And now, in hindsight, sending a car for her had been a little excessive. But the hotel had a chauffeured car service, and it had felt good to send one for her. Maybe as compensation for how last night had ended.

And maybe he was lying to himself, acting as if this were all just professional courtesy. He had never sent a car to pick a woman up be-fore.

"Honestly?" he asked.

Natalia nodded. If she had any ulterior motives she hid them well. He didn't see any trace of hostility in her face or her body language, and he was extremely good at reading people.

"I don't know," he said completely genuinely. "It started out purely as a business meeting. I know your boss, and I try to keep tabs on the most important players in the business. That's what the lunch was about." That was both the truth and a colossal lie. "But then . . ." He fell silent.

Then he had started to behave illogically, and now he was sitting here looking into her intelligent eyes and eating breakfast with a woman who, he had to remind himself over and over again, was ex-tremely off-limits.

"I don't know," he said again. "But it is stimulating to chat with you. Is that enough?"

She blushed a little but didn't break the eye contact. "I was glad you called," she said simply. She glanced at the table, where the re-mainder of their breakfast was being cleared away. "And I was really hungry."

She smiled broadly.

This was a woman born straight into the uppermost elite, he thought. But what was funny was that when he looked at her, sitting there with her hand around her coffee cup and a little smile on her lips, David knew without a doubt that she was every bit as much of an outsider as he was.

He knew all there was to know about being different, about not fitting in, but it had never occurred to him that someone like Natalia could be an outsider. But she was. He saw it.

Small giveaways and the odd word here or there told him that this was a person who'd had to fight for every single one of her choices and that it had made her both stronger and more sensitive.

He shook his head. She sounded like she'd just woken up when he'd called and he suspected that he might have woken her even though it was so late. And yet here she sat, perfectly dressed and with tasteful makeup and a spotless linen dress. Her hair was up in a glossy bun; not a lock of hair was loose. You could probably wake Natalia De la Grip up in the middle of the night and she would sit up, bright-eyed, collected, not a crack in her façade, and give a presentation.

"Did you always know you wanted to be a venture capitalist?" she asked, sounding genuinely interested.

"I wanted to be rich, as I said the other day," he replied.

And I wanted revenge on the people who ruined my life. Which happens to be your family.

"And you've really succeeded," she said.

He didn't hear any insinuations in her voice, no veiled disdain. Just a statement of fact, one that she was mulling over without judgment.

He nodded. But he hadn't actually given her the whole truth, just what he always said.

"I want power," he suddenly heard himself say. He'd never said that out loud before. But it was true. He had wanted the power to control his own life. And only the truly wealthy had that.

She nodded slowly, as if she actually understood. "My family has always had money," she said thoughtfully. "I can't even imagine anything else."

"I was in such a hurry in the beginning," he said, scrupulously ignoring analyzing the fact that he was getting *personal* with her. "I took completely insane risks. Risks I would never take today."

"You were younger," she said with a little smile, as if she too had taken risks before, risks she remembered with a certain pleasure. He wondered what they were, and then felt a surge of excitement at the thought of a risk-taking, impulsive Natalia.

"We worked so unbelievably hard in the beginning," he continued. "Sometimes it felt like I didn't sleep for several years."

"You and Michel? Did you know that he and Åsa, uh, knew each other?"

David shook his head. "I had no idea. They didn't seem to be finished with whatever they had started in the past."

"No," she pondered. "Is Michel married?"

"No. Åsa?"

Natalia shook her head, and their eyes met in mutual understanding. The sun streamed in; her eyes were almost pure gold, and he felt transfixed by them. She picked up her coffee cup and said over it, her cheeks tinged with pink, as if she were embarrassed, "Tell me, completely confidentially of course, what deal you and Michel are working on at the moment."

David smiled. The question was funny in spite of everything—and dangerous—on so many levels. "We're looking at several different things," he responded casually.

"*Ouch*. What a brush-off."

He laughed, couldn't help himself. She laughed too, and something happened between them; it was so palpable that he could almost see it in the air.

His thoughts touched—more than touched—on the possibility that they could see each other again. It was summer, they were adults, and it was totally harmless, after all. He didn't want this to end, not yet.

In some way, time passed with tremendous speed when he was with her. Those clever responses, her quick wits, and that deep laugh—all of it made him lose his sense of time. When he glanced at his watch he couldn't believe it was right. "I'm sorry," he said, catching the server's attention. It had happened again. He had lost track of time. "I have to catch a plane. But the hotel's car will take you wherever you want to go."

"Don't be silly, I can walk."

She didn't ask where he was going, but he told her anyway. "I'm flying to Malmö. But I'd love to see you again," he added. "The logical progression, I think, is lunch, breakfast, and then dinner."

She looked at him. "Yes," she said casually. "That sounds totally logical."

He paid and stood up. She rose as well, her purse over her shoulder. They walked through the hotel together and stepped outside. She looked at him, the sun making her squint, and he leaned in, and his mouth grazed her cheek in an almost kiss.

"Bye," he said softly, cautiously inhaling the scent of her skin in what should have been an impersonal European-style peck on the cheek, but which turned into something else, something much more dangerous.

She stood motionless.

He turned to do the other cheek as well. And when he lingered, it felt like she was holding her breath.

"Good luck in Malmö," she mumbled.

11

Natalia was the first one at work on Monday morning, but J-O arrived just after her.

"I have the new numbers here," she said by way of a greeting.

He took the stack of paper with a nod. Natalia waited while he scanned through the numbers.

"When do you think the deal will go through?" he asked, watching her steadily. J-O was tall and skinny. He could sail, play tennis, and ski like a pro. He'd gone to all the best schools. His parents were Swedish diplomats, and he had the manners of a classic international gentleman. But he was also one of the chilliest and most impersonal men Natalia knew. He had three secretaries who kept track of everything, from which airport he would be at next to which bar he'd spent the wee hours in.

"The Danish CEO is coming to Sweden," she replied, just as impersonally. "I think we should try to meet with him. He needs to talk." A lot of Natalia's work was being a calming influence behind the scenes, holding the hands of nervous CEOs, listening, and being supportive. Giving advice and sealing the deals. She wasn't worried, not about that part of it.

"Yes, and he'll be coming to our party in Båstad. We'll take care of him there." J-O inspected her over his wire frames. Sometime during the last year he'd gone gray. And he had wrinkles at the corners of his eyes she hadn't noticed before. "I need you there," he said. "He likes you."

"Of course. I'll ask my assistant to arrange tickets," she said, realizing there was no chance in hell she would manage to avoid her family if she went to Båstad.

Båstad was where rich, famous, and glamorous Swedes went to play in the summer. Båstad was the reason the capital city was currently devoid of luxury cars, moneymen, and ladies who lunch. Natalia's parents were there, sunbathing and attending the endless string of cocktail parties and champagne minglers.

And, of course, Jonas would be there too.

Damn it all.

Natalia hesitated. There *was* something worrying her. "You don't think this merger is happening too fast?" she asked slowly. A deal of this magnitude often took a year to implement, but now after just a few months, people at Investum were talking about signing the contract this fall. Natalia knew how eager her father was to complete the purchase, but she felt it was being rushed. The prestige of creating a major pan-Nordic bank was clouding their view.

"Why do you think that?"

"I don't know. It's really just a feeling."

"I'll look over the whole deal when I have a chance, but it's normal to start to feel jittery at this stage. That's why there are two of us. Leave it to me."

She nodded and went to leave a note for her assistant to book the trip to Båstad.

Two hours later the office was full of people. Phones were ringing, monitors glowed, and the concentration was almost palpable.

After lunch she received a text from J-O: *I'm in Finland. I'll be in again tomorrow.*

The next time her phone chimed it was three, and Natalia, who hadn't eaten since breakfast, was faint with hunger.

Want to meet up tonight? About to leave Malmö. Sorry for the short notice. Willing to compensate with a picnic and pick up at your door. Pls? —DH

She blinked. She was so lost in her work that it took a moment for it to click that this was a private text. Then she started smiling to herself. She replied: *Picnic seals the deal. Yes, please. P.S. What does pls mean?*

Natalia smiled the whole time she waited. She hadn't had a chance to think about David for more than a few seconds here and there today. But now . . .

She put her feet up on her desk, leaned back in her chair, and kept smiling. It had been such a long time since she'd flirted with anyone. And he'd almost kissed her yesterday. She felt a tingle run through her body at the memory of that quick, warm peck of his lips on her cheek. She glanced to the side, hoping no one would notice that Natalia De la Grip was sitting in her desk chair, getting excited about a peck on the cheek.

Pls = please

The picnic basket and I will pick you up at 7 p.m. —DH (David Hammar)

Natalia took her feet off her desk. She didn't have time to go home in between, but she had a few changes of clothes here at the office, and she had time for a quick shower. It was sunny, and she realized she longed to be outside in the sunshine and fresh air, to be like a normal person, the kind who met men, ate food, and didn't work eighteen hours a day without even living. She typed out a confirmation to David and threw herself back into her work again.

12

"It's just a boat trip, nothing to get all worked up about," David said.

"It's not the *boat* I'm worried about," Michel snapped. "What I'm worried about is whether or not you've gone completely insane. You know you're welcome to borrow my boat and go wherever the hell you want with whomever the hell you want. But with her?" Michel pinched the bridge of his nose. The leather of his desk chair squeaked as he moved his massive body in it.

David walked over to the door and closed it all the way. Hammar Capital's employees were in the next room working, from early in the morning to late at night, busy analyzing companies. They didn't need to hear this conversation.

"You're the one who's always saying people shouldn't mix business and pleasure," Michel continued, sounding angry. "So maybe you'd like to explain what you're up to here. Because I really don't understand why you're suddenly spending so much time with Natalia De la Grip. I thought we'd written her off." Michel looked more concerned than usual. But then he was such a tremendously thorough person, meticulously checking and double-checking everything. There was no one in the entire world David would rather have on his side when it came to work. But that didn't mean he told Michel everything. Not that there was anything to tell, he reminded himself, but still.

"It's nothing serious," he said. Because even the thought that this would be anything more than an extremely short-lived flirtation was downright laughable. Natalia was fun to talk to, time flew by when he was with her, and that impulsive caress on the cheek—for crying out loud, it wasn't even a kiss, just a peck, but it had gotten his body's attention, and he wanted a little more. But it wasn't serious. He knew that better than anyone. "I'm just cultivating a valuable contact."

"Yeah, right," scoffed Michel.

David shook his head. Swapping text messages with Natalia had put him in a good mood; he was practically filled with anticipation, and he had no interest in arguing with Michel. If their roles were reversed, he probably would have reacted too.

Aside from the fact that there was nothing to react to, of course. He needed to eat, she needed to eat, and fresh air was healthy. Besides, it was no fun going out in the boat by yourself. He could think of at least five, maybe ten different reasons that this spontaneous outing was nothing to overreact to. *And* one *very big reason that Michel's reaction made sense.*

"I know what I'm doing," he said placatingly.

"Soon," Michel said, not looking in the least placated. "Soon this takeover is going to be on the front page of every paper. Here, in Europe, and in the US. No one has ever done anything like this before. You've said so yourself, many times. If you have some agenda of your own with that woman, you'd better say so. You're not the only one working on this deal. Don't forget that." Michel had a lot of his own personal money riding on this, just as David did, and he had every right in the world to be worried.

David shoved his hands into his pants pockets and walked over to the window. Michel's office had a view of the Royal Palace and Skeppsbron Quay. He turned around. "I'm just going out for dinner after work on a weekday with an industry colleague," he said. "I don't have any hidden agenda. We're two adults getting together to eat and maybe chat a bit. She's a good contact, she knows everyone, I've worked with her boss. I'm networking."

Michel scoffed again. "Yeah, right."

David gave him a lingering look. Michel wasn't himself. They hadn't talked about what had happened at the bar on Saturday. They were men. They didn't talk about things like that. Maybe that was a mistake. "What's up with you, anyway? If you don't want me to borrow the boat, just say so. Otherwise this is none of your business. She isn't responsible for running Investum. She could be anyone."

Michel flung up his hands as if to say he gave up. "Take the boat. I know you'd never do anything unprofessional," he said. "I just need to get some sleep."

David studied him closely. He actually did look tired. "Does this have anything to do with Åsa Bjelke?" he asked.

Michel clenched his jaw, but just said, "What do you mean?"

"You know what I mean. I've never seen you like that. You were mad at her."

"I was surprised to see her. It was nothing important."

Right.

"Come on," David said decidedly, patting his friend on the shoulder. "I'm going to go buy some picnic food. Come along and I'll buy you a coffee."

Much later, as David stood waiting for Natalia on Stureplan, outside her office, he thought that Michel might be right after all. Maybe he should leave Natalia alone. She seemed to be a genuinely nice person.

The Investum deal was going to explode in the media soon, and the circus would be in full swing. Journalists would be calling like crazy, their columns filled with speculation, and he and Michel could start on the next step.

It was unavoidable that once she discovered the full scope of what he planned, Natalia would hate him. He didn't want that to happen, because he liked her. And if they continued seeing each other, the betrayal would feel personal to her. He would hurt her. That was an uncomfortable thought.

But that chaste peck on the cheek had started something he didn't want to ignore. And she had felt something too. But he couldn't let it go any further, he decided. Picnics, pecks on the cheek—this would have to be enough. Anything more would be sheer lunacy.

And he was many things—hard, inconsiderate, ruthless—but he wasn't crazy.

13

Natalia stepped out onto the street, and the heat hit her. She'd been sitting in her air-conditioned office since morning and hadn't realized how hot it was outside. She'd never been invited on a picnic for a date in her entire life, which was tragic of course, but more importantly, it also made her a little unsure what to wear.

Ultimately, she'd decided on a cap-sleeve silk blouse and thin, light-colored linen pants from the spare outfits she kept at work. Her office was in the Sturegallerian shopping center just off the public square, and as she stepped out, David was waiting for her. When she saw his T-shirt and jeans, she felt absurdly overdressed. He raised his hand, the one with the stainless-steel watch, and waved. Every time she thought of him, she was sure she must be romanticizing how handsome he was, how tall and broad-shouldered he seemed. And every time they actually saw each other she realized that she hadn't exaggerated in the least. It was no surprise that the media went wild over him.

"Hello there," he said with a smile.

"Hi," she replied, gratefully noting that her voice sounded calm and fairly cool.

He put his hand on her shoulder and leaned in toward her cheek with his lips. A quick peck on the cheek. She closed her eyes and breathed in the scent of him. Lord, even that little whiff was enough to arouse her. She pulled away and collected herself, gave him a friendly smile. "Where are we going?"

David surveyed her elegant slacks and nice blouse with bemuse-ment. "I should have known you'd wear something thin and impractical," he said and then looked at her neatly done hair. "And that hairdo is definitely not going to hold up."

He put his hand on her upper arm. "Come on," he said. She didn't have a chance to reflect on how his hand burned her skin before he let go of her again.

They strolled down toward the water, passing through a steady stream of tourists, families with kids, and dog walkers.

"How was Malmö?" she asked.

"You know how they are down there," he replied with a grin.

"I love southern Sweden."

"Yeah, it's nice," David said. He smiled. "And here we are."

Natalia looked around. They had stopped in front of an elegant little place with outdoor seating. Dressed-up waiters were carrying drinks and plates of hors d'oeuvres. Music poured out over the beachside promenade. It looked wonderful to sit out by the sparkling water, and she ignored her discomfort at their being seen together—right here on Strandvägen Boulevard among people who knew who she was. It was only sheer luck that no one had noticed them on the way over here.

"Not there," said David, as if he'd read her mind. "Here." He nodded his head out at the water, and Natalia gasped.

A yacht, gleaming white, was moored at the quay. It was enormous, and with its sleek lines and its chrome railings it looked almost alive, like a shark or a javelin, brimming with energy, raring to go.

"I thought we might not want to be right in the thick of things," David said, giving her a questioning look. "Or would you rather stay onshore?"

"No," Natalia said, admiring the white beast of a boat. She felt a tingle of excitement.

He stepped on board, and Natalia took the hand he offered her. The boat bobbed impatiently under her feet.

"Do you want me to give you the tour first?" he asked.

She shook her head. "I want to get going."

David untied and then began pushing buttons and moving levers. The motor started with a deep rumble. He turned the wheel and backed out.

"Where are we going?" she asked.

"There's a basket of food in the galley. What do you say we just head out to the archipelago and stop in a bay somewhere on the way?"

"That sounds divine."

Soon they had left Stockholm and all the ferries and larger vessels on the busy waters of downtown's Nybroviken behind. They proceeded across Saltsjö Bay and swooshed past the island of Lidingö. Even a ways out into the archipelago on the Baltic, there was a lot of boat traffic, the sun was shining at full force, and the jetties they passed were crowded with people.

After a bit, David steered the boat into a small, secluded bay, pulled down the throttle levers, anchored, and turned to Natalia. "Come on, let me show you what it looks like down below."

They descended a narrow stairway into the cabin, and when Natalia stepped off the last step onto a wood floor, she couldn't help but laugh.

This had to be, hands down, the most ostentatious luxury yacht she'd ever seen in her life. She'd once been invited to the Royal couple's yacht and it didn't come close to this. The whole interior was glossy, varnished wood and white textiles. There was a skylight, porthole windows in the walls overlooking the water, and small recessed spotlights in the ceiling that made the space bright and airy. There was a flat-screen TV hanging on the wall, display cases and shelves full of gleaming Pillivuyt porcelain, and a microwave oven mounted over one cabinet. An enormous wicker basket sat on a table.

David nodded at a cupboard. "Could you get out a couple champagne glasses?"

While Natalia took out two champagne flutes, he opened the refrigerator and pulled out a bottle of champagne. "I bought pink champagne," he said.

"If I didn't know better, I would think you were trying to impress me," she said, stifling a giggle at the expensive-looking bottle.

"You know how we nouveau-riche wannabes are," he said. "It's an eternal struggle, trying to impress all you blue bloods. Tell me if it's working."

"I promise I will."

David took the bottle in one hand, the enormous picnic basket in the other, and disappeared back up the stairs, taking them two at a time. "Come on. We're going to have a picnic," he called over his shoulder.

With the glasses in her hand and a bubbly laugh in her chest, Natalia followed him.

At the stern there was a table and benches coming out of the wall, and they each sat down on their own bench. While David peeled the pink foil off the bottle and then started untwisting the wire, Natalia examined the contents of the basket.

She furrowed her brow. "How many women were you planning to feed with this?" she asked as she started pulling out plates of air-dried prosciutto, salami, bresaola, and various cheeses, plus crocks of olives, roasted vegetables and pesto, and a warm bread basket.

"Just one hungry banker," David said, watching her take out piles of focaccia and still more cheese.

"Wow," she said when she found a butter-stained bag filled with miniature savory pies that smelled heavenly.

"Hmm. Maybe I should have bought red wine," David said, eyeing all the meats and cheeses.

"This will be perfect," Natalia said with a smile. "But this table isn't big enough; there isn't room for all the food."

They ended up each filling a plate and taking it up to the foredeck, where they spread out a blanket. Natalia sat down in lotus position. David handed her a glass, filled his own, and raised it in a toast.

"Tell me more about how you became one of the world's most successful venture capitalists," Natalia said.

"What do you want to know?" he asked. It pleased her that he didn't try to downplay his success, didn't hide behind any false modesty.

"I know why, but I don't know how. And I've never met anyone who's done what you've done," she said between bites. Lord, it was so good. And the champagne went right to her head. "Started from scratch, I mean."

"Mmm," he said. "I've always worked to support myself. When I was in high school and my classmates were going on tropical vacations or ski trips during breaks, I was working, every break, every weekend. That's still how it is."

Natalia took a big bite of tangy taleggio cheese. She was one of the people who'd always gone away on vacation. Although obviously she'd always known on some level that that wasn't a universal, that some people couldn't afford to, she'd still never really reflected on it.

"I saved as much money as I could from my earnings," David continued. "I started buying stocks as soon as I figured out how, and I made some really good picks even back when I was going to Skogbacka."

Natalia wondered what David had thought about the famous—or infamous, depending on how you looked at it—boarding school. Both Peter and Alexander had gone there. And her father was a trustee. You could say that the men in her family had Skogbacka in their blood. She'd gone to one of the other boarding schools, one that was considered milder and gentler, more suitable for the family's women, or *girls*, as her mother called them. But both schools were expensive, and David—the son of a single mother, if she remembered correctly—could only have attended on a scholarship. She wondered how he'd been affected by what must have been a tremendous source of alienation. The elitist boarding school educated the children of the well-to-do, the really rich, people with noble titles, royal pedigrees, and manor houses. As the son of a single mother, David couldn't have had an easy time there.

"I kept that up when I was at the Stockholm School of Economics," David said, and Natalia pushed her other thoughts aside. David Hammar, grinning slightly as he sat across from her, and radiating power and vitality on the bow of a very pricey yacht, was hardly a man to be pitied. "So, all throughout school—as I worked my other side jobs—I kept buying and selling stocks. And I started building a network of contacts." He shrugged. "That's how it started. I studied abroad in London, where I met Gordon Wyndt . . ." He looked to see if she recognized the name.

"I know who that is," she said. The last time she'd checked, Wyndt was number forty-five on the list of the world's richest people. Having a man like that as a mentor was probably exactly what a hungry young student without his own family connections needed.

"Gordon taught me a lot. After the School of Economics I earned a scholarship to Harvard, so I went to the US and studied there. I worked at a restaurant to support myself. And I was a business analyst for an American venture capitalist." He made a face. "I didn't get much sleep during those years."

"But was it fun?"

He nodded. "A lot of fun."

Warmth spread through her chest. She recognized that pleasure, that love of work, and maybe that was why it was so rewarding to talk to him. They were so similar, which was downright crazy. But she saw herself in his passion, in his drive, and the conversation flowed so effortlessly. She felt comfortable with him. A little affected by him, yes; charmed—definitely. But not awkward or self-conscious.

"And then I founded HC," he said with a beaming grin, maybe the first big smile she'd seen on him. "That's when I really got to work."

Natalia laughed, sipped her champagne, and exhaled a deep, contented sigh. This was about as close to the perfect day as you could get.

David looked at Natalia, sitting there on the bow of Michel's boat, sipping champagne, and looking so genuinely content. Somehow she had managed to coax out of him the thing he normally didn't like to talk about: the early years. He wondered how much she actually knew about what had happened at Skogbacka. But then she had carefully guided him through the conversation, and he had babbled on. Now she looked happy and a little giggly, and maybe that should put him on his guard, but he was feeling happy, too.

"What do you see yourself doing in ten years?" she asked.

David took his glass and leaned on one elbow, just like her. "No idea," he said. "Working around the clock, I suppose. Maybe I will have stopped chasing other people's money and just be investing my own."

"Don't you want to have a family?"

David opened his mouth and then shut it again. "No," he clipped. "Not if I can help it."

She cocked her head to the side. "Alrighty then," she said quietly.

God, how wonderful that she just accepted that. He couldn't keep track of how many women stubbornly insisted he would change.

"I've been thinking about you the last few days," he said.

Her eyes started twinkling. "Really?" she said. "I'd almost forgotten about you."

Her lie was so flagrant that David laughed. She sipped her champagne with her eyelashes lowered and a smile at the corner of her lips. He set down his glass, lay down on his back, put his hands behind his head, and thought that he could go back to being his usual calculating self tomorrow, but not now, not here. He couldn't remember when he'd last been this relaxed. And he was just as surprised each time he saw Natalia and ended up having so much *fun*.

"What?" she asked.

He kept watching the sky. The sun was still warm, but the first star was twinkling way up in the east. "I just feel good," he said to the sky.

Seagulls soared high above them. The waves lapped against the hull, and David felt her looking at him, so he turned his head to her. He looked into her big, slightly champagne-tipsy eyes. He'd been right, he thought. Her librarian hairdo hadn't held up very well in the wind out on the water. Loose locks of hair fluttered around her face, and the bun was sagging at her neck.

"I love the archipelago," she said, and he thought her voice sounded breathless.

"When I did my military service a hundred years ago, I spent a lot of time at sea," he replied, looking out over the water. "I love it out here. I'd almost forgotten. I never come out anymore."

"I thought you seemed comfortable on the water," she said. "But this isn't your boat?"

"It's Michel's. He loves flashy things like this. At the moment, I guess I can't blame him."

"No, it's wonderful," she said.

The words hung between them.

David turned his head again. He surveyed the clean, classic features of her face and her strong, slender neck before continuing downward. He caught a glimpse of her small, hard nipples through the almost transparent fabric of her blouse. The sight sent a wave of desire coursing through him before he also noticed that Natalia had goose bumps and realized that she was probably more cold than drowning in desire for him.

He wasn't as smart as he thought, he realized, sitting up.

Natalia watched David get up from their little picnic. With her hand over her eyes, she watched him while he quickly and efficiently gathered up the leftovers.

"Stay here," he said. "I'll be right back." He disappeared into the cabin, and she sat up. She rubbed her arms. It was much colder now.

She heard him rummaging around down there for a bit before he came back up.

He'd put on a thick sweater and held out a similar one to her. "I'm brewing coffee. I hope you saved room for dessert."

Natalia pulled on the sweater, which was much too big, and snuggled into the warmth. "Thank you," she said.

David went back down and returned with a thermos under his arm and two coffee cups and a cooler in his hands. He opened the cooler and looked inside.

"What's that?" Natalia asked.

"I have no idea," he said, pulling out a cup with a lid. "Believe it or not," he continued, his voice full of mirth, "but desserts are one of the exceedingly few realms that I have yet to fully master. I don't remember buying this."

"Give it to me."

Natalia took the cup, opened it, sniffed it, and said, "Tiramisu."

"Is that good?" he asked.

"Very," she said, pleased.

David passed her a spoon and then unscrewed the lid of the thermos. The scent of coffee spread across the deck. She received a plump little mug full of pitch-black coffee and dug into the dessert. "I'm going to get fat if I keep going like this," she said without thinking.

David raised his eyebrows over his coffee cup, and Natalia bit her lip.

David took a spoon and made a satisfied face. "This is good." He took a few more spoonfuls, eating quickly, efficiently. Then he lay down on his side again, stretched out his legs, and cupped his hands around his coffee cup. "So, what do you do when you're not working?" he asked.

Natalia took small sips of the hot coffee while she thought the question over. As a child she'd had dance. And for a long while horseback riding had been everything to her. She still loved to ride, but now . . . She heard David laugh softly and looked at him. "What?" she asked.

"Nothing," he said. "But you always do that when you're asked a question: stop and contemplate."

"I'm not a rash, impulsive person," she replied.

"No," he said. "But that's why you're such a good corporate banker. And I like watching you think."

"Well, like you, I work a lot," she said. "My job is important to me. I'm not particularly interested in fashion or homemaking," she continued. "And I can't even remember the last time I went to the movies." She furrowed her brow. It was pathetic when she thought about it. "I loved horseback riding when I was younger, and I still do," she continued thoughtfully as she tried to remember what her interests actually were. "I'm really fond of handbags and . . ." She stopped herself in time, but David had seen her falter.

"Tsk tsk, Natalia, you have a secret," he teased. "Do tell."

She lay down on her side. With her head propped up on her palm, she buried herself in the sweater. "I'm really stuffed," she said.

"Don't change the topic," he said.

"I'm sure you're an expert at wheedling information out of people that they would prefer not to share."

He nodded smugly.

"I don't usually discuss my, uh, private interests with men." She closed her eyes. "I can't believe I'm considering telling you this, but I collect French underwear. I buy it online. It's very expensive and completely irrational. Most of it isn't even wearable."

She opened her eyes.

David was studying her intently. "Tell me more things that make you blush. You're very attractive, in a non-corporate-finance way, when you're blushing."

Natalia shook her head. She reached for the thermos as an excuse to avoid looking at him. "I think that's enough of a revelation for tonight," she said. "Your turn."

"Hmm, what do you want to know?"

Natalia cocked her head, and they looked at each other over the remains of their picnic. Oh, there was a lot she wanted to know. Why had he asked her out? What wasn't he telling her about his past? What was that coldness she glimpsed in him sometimes all about? And most of all, of course: did he think they would be having sex with each other in the near future?

"What would you have done if you didn't do what you do now?" she asked instead.

"I think I'd sail around the world. Give up the Internet, read books." He laughed. "Maybe learn to cook."

"You can't cook?"

"Can you?" he dared her.

"I opened a jar of pickles the other day. Does that count?"

His eyes twinkled. "I don't think so."

"What did you do during your military service?" she asked. "I have two brothers, but you know, strangely enough, I've never asked them."

"Romp around outdoors, get chewed out, work like a dog," he said. "But I actually liked it. We followed orders, got a lot of exercise, slept well at night." He fell silent.

She listened to the waves lapping. She heard a dog barking somewhere onshore.

He turned to her, raised himself up on his elbows. "Are you still cold?" he asked. "Should I go get a blanket?"

Natalia slowly shook her head.

David looked into her eyes. He reached out his hand and she held her breath. He grazed her pearl necklace with his fingers and she blinked. He fingered the heavy clasp, which had slid to the front. "What kind of pattern is this?" he asked.

She swallowed, trying to sound casual despite his fingers brushing over the base of her throat. A finger caressed her collarbone, almost absentmindedly. "The family crest," she said, her pulse racing under his fingertips. "My brothers each wear it on their signet rings. I wear it on the clasp of my necklace."

"Because you have a title? You're a countess?"

"Yes."

She couldn't interpret the expression on his face. He was staring at the heavy gold clasp as if it meant something. Then he looked at her again, without taking his hand away. He leaned forward but stopped. And Natalia surprised herself. She moved her own hand behind his head, impatient and bold. They came together over the remains of their picnic, and he kissed her lightly, no more than a flutter over her lips. He lingered a second or two, warm and a little rough.

Natalia tried to think clearly, but felt only desire. There was no, *no* reason not to do this. It was as if she'd been waiting her whole life for this, she thought, to be kissed on an ostentatious yacht in the middle of the archipelago by David Hammar, who tasted like tiramisu.

Then he kissed her again, his hand on the collar of her sweater; he spread out his fingers and palm until they covered her breast. She met his tongue eagerly, raised herself up toward him, pressing herself into his hand and mouth and tongue. It had been a long time since she'd felt something like this, this *hunger*, if she ever had.

David moved, and porcelain clanked beneath them. He pulled away from her.

"Not here," he said, shaking his head.

"Should we go down below?" Natalia asked in a hoarse voice, shocking herself.

Nice girls were passive, not active. That's what her mother, her girlfriends, everyone had imprinted on her, but it felt like advice from the nineteenth century. She wanted this so much, wanted to feel his hands on her skin, feel him moving above her, in her. And he seemed at least equally interested. Or had she misread him?

"No, we'll go back," he said.

Rejection. God, how humiliating.

"Believe it or not, I didn't plan on our doing anything more than having a picnic today. This isn't even my boat," he said, smiling apologetically. "I didn't bring any protection. Did you?"

"No," she said, wondering if she could just die of shame on the spot.

"We'll go back before it gets dark." He held out his hand. After a brief hesitation, she slid her hand into his. She followed him in silence, trying not to notice how unbelievably *intimate* it felt to hold his hand.

After David pulled up the anchor, he turned to her, gave her a serious look, and then started the boat with a few quick motions. He turned them out of the bay and let out the gas so the motor roared.

Natalia didn't realize how cold she was until he pulled her into the space between his body and the wheel. She slid into his heat and stopped shivering, stopped anything, just stopped, lost in the sensation of being enveloped by him with the sound of the motor in her ears. He sped up, and with a deafening rumble they bounced over the waves, heading back into Stockholm as twilight sank in around them. Now and then David's cheek brushed her hair, and Natalia wanted to turn around, wanted them to kiss again, but she didn't dare take the lead anymore. She didn't know if she was imagining it or if the mood between them really had changed. She wasn't even sure that she wanted to know.

They pulled up to Nybro Quay. David throttled the engine, hopped ashore, moored the boat, and then held out his hand to her. As soon as she was on solid ground, he let go. They didn't say anything to each other, and the silence was impossible to read.

"I'll take you home," he said tersely, confusing her even more.

They crossed Strandvägen Boulevard in silence. The murmur of voices from all the outdoor restaurant seating faded away as they turned onto her quiet street.

When they stopped outside her front door, Natalia asked, "Did I do something wrong?" Even though she had planned to sound cool and composed, her voice was weak.

Åsa wouldn't stand for this. She would want to know where she stood. But Natalia had never known and didn't have any experience to fall back on.

"Is *that* what you think?" he asked.

Natalia shrugged. The door was just behind her, and she was starting to feel tired and annoyed, as if all the energy had drained out of her. Maybe it was the alcohol, but she just wanted to slip inside, hurry upstairs, and bury her head in a sofa cushion.

David looked at her for a long time.

"What?" she asked testily when the silence started getting on her nerves. Damn it, he was hard to read.

"I was unbelievably self-serving in the beginning," he said suddenly, and it took a moment to realize he was talking about his career, not about them.

"Venture capitalism is not a line of work that values fair play," he continued. "I'm not a gentle or a nice person."

"I grew up with moneymen; I've been in that world since I was a baby. Don't you think I *know* that?" she said. Her father was hard, her brother was hard. She *got* that David was no softy.

David slowly raised his hand and then lightly rested it on her cheek. He stroked her cheekbone with his thumb. And then he kissed her.

How could a kiss, just one kiss, be so different from all other kisses?

She heard a sound, unsure whether it had come from her or him, and then his arm came around her waist, and then there wasn't anything gentle about the kiss, no hesitation, nothing tentative. It was hard and urgent. His leg pressed into her thigh, pushing her backward against the rough façade of the building.

"Would you like to come up?" she whispered.

He stared at her, his chest heaving. Natalia held her breath.

"Yes," he said.

14

He refused to feel sorry about it. He'd warned her, told her who and what he was. She'd asked if he wanted to come up, he'd said yes, and he was *not* going to change his mind.

They stood in silence, looking at each other as the aging, creaking elevator took them to the top floor. Neither of them spoke. He watched Natalia's breasts moving beneath the thick sweater. Her face was serious. The elevator stopped, and David held the door open for her. She took a key out of her purse and unlocked the front door. She stepped to the side and opened her mouth to say something, but David took her face in his hands and kissed her. He had been struggling with himself the whole way. He hadn't been lying when he said he hadn't planned this. It was a weekday. He knew she worked hard and took her work seriously. He had to get up early in the morning himself. He hadn't been lying.

Or had he?

This was an unbelievably bad idea. He was supposed to be breaking his ties with her, not getting to know her better. But the battle within him had already been lost. Maybe he hadn't put up much of a fight. Maybe he'd never wanted anything other than to follow the poised, graceful Natalia De la Grip home and make love to her.

One night, only one night. Surely that wouldn't matter?

He kissed her again, hard, so that she panted against his mouth. He slid a hand behind her head, and closed the door with his other hand. And they stood like that in her dark entryway, him with his hand still in her hair, her with her back and palms pressed against the wall as if she were unsure what she wanted.

She was like a pale shadow in the dark entryway. "Let down your hair," he said hoarsely. Natalia pulled on the pins that were still holding up the loose, windswept knot. One by one she took the hairpins out, and he heard the delicate clink each one made as it fell onto the stone floor. Her hair cascaded down her back as she shook it free. David ran his eyes over her, and then without taking his gaze off her, he ordered: "Take off the pearls."

She obeyed in silence, slowly undoing the necklace, pulling off her earrings, and setting them on top of the hall cabinet. Her neck was slender and white.

"Good," he said.

He put a hand on her hip. Her body trembled and she exhaled heavily. Just the sound of her excited breathing would be enough to make him come. But he wanted to come inside her, dominate that strong body, make her cry out much louder than any of these stifled gasps. He pulled her to him.

"It's been a long time for me, David. I don't know . . ." she said, leaning against his chest. He brought her hips tighter against his. She pushed herself against him. He was so ready.

"Arms up," he said and she obeyed again. He pulled the oversized sweater off her, tossed it onto the floor. With his palms low on her back, he drew her to him again, pushing himself into her, letting her feel how hard he was.

"I've been thinking about this all evening," he said, knowing that was the truth. "You were so sexy on the boat." He moved a hand to the opening of her blouse and spread out his fingers over her breast. The ribs under her thin skin were so slender, so delicate. He tugged on the silk fabric and one button came off. It was covered with fabric and disappeared without a sound. He caressed the side of her neck, curling his fingers lightly around the side of it, let a thumb slide along her jawline. He felt her pulse racing. Her eyes widened, watching him seriously.

He shook his head. "Don't think." With one hand he carefully took hold of her chin, and she gasped as his mouth covered her own. He kissed her. She whimpered and put her hand on his chest, as if to stop him.

He stopped. "What?" he said. Had he misjudged her?

"This is moving so fast. I don't know you, not really." She breathed in short bursts, searching his face. "Who are you?"

"I'm no one, Natalia," he said, slowly bringing his hand to her hair. "Just a man who really wants to make love with you tonight." He hadn't meant to frighten her. "Don't be scared," he murmured quietly, stroking her hair.

Her breathing was audible in the silent apartment. She moved uneasily in his embrace. It was dark in the entryway, and her golden eyes were almost black. He put his hand over hers, the one that was still resting like a gentle restraint against his chest.

"I want you, Natalia," he said. "What do you want?"

Natalia's lip curled slightly and he felt her relax a little.

"I don't usually do this," she said and then grimaced. "Maybe I shouldn't have said that." She smiled. "Even if it's the truth."

"That doesn't matter," David responded with a wink. "Because I do it all the time."

She laughed and then smiled, genuinely and almost boldly. She said, "I invited you up. I want this. And I have, um, protection."

She put both her hands on his chest and slid in against him. David looked at the top of her head, her dark hair as she leaned against his chest, smelled the exotic scent of spices and some kind of wood.

He didn't need to feel guilty, he told himself. Natalia wanted this. They were adults; this was just sex, nothing more. She had said it herself: they didn't know each other. They could share one night without it affecting them on any deeper level. They would both enjoy it. It was completely uncomplicated. In her apartment they were just a man and a woman, nothing more. And he really wanted to make it good for her.

He slowly bent down—giving her a chance to pull away if she wanted. But Natalia tipped her face up and eagerly answered his kiss this time, pressing against him and throwing her arms around his neck. If she'd been afraid before, that had subsided now, he thought, meeting her hungry mouth, her bold kisses. She was a passionate woman, animated in his embrace.

He ran his fingers through her dark hair. It was as soft as mink fur and long, much longer than he'd thought. He gathered up a fistful and gently pulled her head back. She moaned, a muffled sound well back in her throat, and his body responded reflexively and intensely. With his hand still buried in her hair, he scanned the enormous entry hall. He preferred to think of himself as somewhat more sophisticated than a man who had sex with a woman just inside her front door. "Show me the rest of the place," he said.

Natalia looked at him, her eyes smoldering, her lips slightly swollen. Then she took his hand in her own cool one. She led him down the hall, and he smiled at how easily she took charge. She was used to deciding, to being in control. It was going to be an interesting night.

They passed doors, paintings, and mirrors. And more doors.

"How big *is* this place?" he asked, stifling a laugh.

She turned a corner and then stepped out into an enormous living room. Extremely tall, open French doors led onto a balcony. This room was just as dark as the rest of the apartment, and cool air poured in.

"I can close the doors," Natalia offered.

"No," he said. "I want to see the view."

They stepped out onto the balcony together.

She had a view of both Djurgården, the vast green area belonging to the king, and the Djurgårdsbrunn Canal down by Strandvägen Boulevard. When she shivered, he pulled her toward him. He caressed one breast through her thin blouse. She had small, sensitive breasts, and with a shudder, she closed her eyes. He kissed her again while he started unbuttoning her slacks. When he pulled the zipper down, her breathing sped up. He slid his hand over the gentle dome of her stomach and she pushed herself against him. He ran his finger along the thin edge of her panties. Her panties were so sheer that he could have easily torn them. He caressed her through the lace. She was warm and damp. She was wet. He pulled away the cloth, slid in a finger. She wasn't waxed, which he liked. "You're so hot," he whispered and playfully bit her earlobe.

Natalia moaned at his touch and pushed herself against his hand.

"Where do you keep them?" he asked.

"I'll get them," she said. "Wait here."

He stepped back into the living room. Her two sofas were long and deep, her décor tasteful and antique, surely inherited.

She came back, her slender body glowing inside her half-open silk blouse. She had taken off her slacks, and her legs were powerful and extremely pale. She held out her hand and passed him the thin box with an embarrassed smile. He studied it. It hardly looked like it had been opened. Apparently she really meant it that she didn't do this very often. He wondered if she'd been with anyone since her fiancé. He tried to remember how long it had been since that relationship ended. A year ago? The information he'd read about her hadn't mentioned any new love interests.

They cooperated to undo the last of the fabric-covered buttons on her blouse before he swept it off her. She was wearing a lacy bra underneath, a glossy little number that he thought must be one of the expensive ones she collected.

"You undo it," he said, afraid he would damage the thin fabric if he tried to do it.

Natalia brought her hands behind her back and undid the hooks. She watched him hesitantly, her hands over the fabric and her breasts. But he was impatient now. Her coyness set his blood racing.

"I want to see," he commanded. "Move your hands."

Slowly she complied. She had small but perfectly rounded breasts, with small, dark nipples. "You're unbelievably beautiful," he said hoarsely. When he placed his hand over one small breast, his palm covered it completely. He moved his hand, caressing her, and she moaned hoarsely. God, how he loved women with sensitive breasts.

She started untucking his T-shirt and they took it off together. He placed his hands on her upper arms while she ran her hands over his torso. Her hands were delicate, and he closed his eyes as she explored his body.

It seemed to happen so fast, he was caught off guard when she leaned forward and ran her hands around behind his back. He didn't have a chance to stop her, and now he didn't want to make a big deal about it. But he stiffened under her touch, steeling himself. He never let anyone touch him there.

Natalia's brow wrinkled. She ran her hand questioningly over the roughness on his back, and he could feel her trying to make sense of what her fingertips were feeling. But he didn't say anything, didn't want her to understand. He pulled away. "Not now," he said, fending off her questions.

She gave him a curious look. "But David, you . . ."

He held onto her shoulders and cautiously pushed her back. "Not now."

Natalia blinked. "Okay," she said quietly.

He studied her, standing there. She was a fascinating mix of modesty and sensuality. She was slim, but still curvy with her rounded belly, her narrow waist, and her soft hips.

He undressed himself until he was naked. Her eyes widened, and then she quickly pulled off her panties and stepped into his arms.

Her skin was smooth, like polished ivory, soft as silk. He held her head and kissed her. She pushed against him, and he lifted her one leg and placed it around his hip. Somehow they ended up on the sofa, him half lying on his back, her astride him. He found the condom package, opened it, and quickly slid one on.

They looked into each other's eyes, and then he lifted her up by the hips, grasped her, and took her in a single motion. Natalia fell forward onto his chest with a shout, inhaling in a gasp. Her dark hair fell around him like a scented silk curtain.

David lifted her head and looked into her foggy eyes. "Is this alright?" he asked with difficulty. He'd almost come. She was hot and wet, but she was small and tight, and the friction and the sight were almost overwhelming.

Natalia nodded. "Just let me get used to it," she said faintly. "It's really been a while."

David took hold of her buttocks, one hand around each cheek, and lifted her carefully upward. She put a hand on his chest, the other on his thigh behind her. Slowly, with his eyes locked on hers, he let her slide down again, seeing in her eyes how he filled her. She was breathing heavily, and he repeated the motion until she too adopted the rhythm.

"Wonderful," he said, his voice muffled, seeing that she was far away. She slowly closed her eyes and let her head fall back until her dark hair grazed his legs. Up and down, with slippery, wet sounds, moans and whimpers.

David came.

Without style or consideration, he exploded. It happened so fast, and he wasn't able to stop himself, so instead he took a firm hold of her hips—she would have marks from his fingers, he thought foggily—and held her down until he filled her and held her there and just came in wave after pulsing wave. He closed his eyes and collapsed back onto the sofa.

When he opened his eyes again, the living room was still dark. His eyes had adjusted, though, and he saw her clearly. With her long hair and those big eyes, she looked young and vulnerable. And sexy as hell. She moved her legs, and he realized she was still on top of him, that he was still inside her. It had been totally amazing for him, but he had left her unsatisfied.

He grimaced. "I'm sorry," he said.

"For what?" she asked.

But David knew that she hadn't experienced the same climax he had. So much for pleasuring *her*. He stroked her thigh. "Normally, I'm able to control myself better," he said, sounding pained. "I don't know what happened."

She started squirming. "It doesn't matter," she said half-heartedly.

David shook his head.

He lifted her off and gently laid her down on the soft sofa. He took a pillow and placed it under her head. He brushed her hair to the side, leaned down, and kissed her, tenderly this time. Chilly air was still streaming in from the French doors, so he retrieved a throw from an armchair, kissed both her nipples, and then spread it over her.

"What are you doing?" she mumbled, studying him through her long, dark eyelashes.

"I'm pampering you," he said. "Would you like anything to drink?"

"Not really," she replied. "But there's vodka in the freezer if you want some."

"Vodka," he said with a smile. "What else? Stay here."

David went out to the kitchen, and Natalia squirmed on the sofa. She was unsatisfied. Not that she normally came with particularly impressive frequency, but she'd been close and now it was over. She closed her eyes. She supposed she wasn't exactly disappointed; it had been really amazing, but . . . Yes—*but*.

"Natalia?"

He stood in the doorway with a frosty bottle of Stolichnaya and two plain glasses in his hand. He sat down next to her on the sofa, poured the vodka, and handed her one glass. "Cheers," he said.

"*Nah zdarovya*," she replied, and then they drank in silence. The liquor was viscously cold. She rarely drank vodka—her brother Alex had forgotten the bottle at her place at some point—but she liked the burning sensation in her stomach.

She studied David over the rim of her glass. She had never met a man who could sit naked on a sofa and yet still seem like he was in total command of the room.

He set down his glass. Slowly he ran his hand over her leg, brushing the soft throw aside. Natalia closed her eyes and let herself be swept away by the sensation. He had such incredible hands, strong and sure. He massaged her feet, her calves.

"So soft," he murmured.

Natalia heard a sound, like a purr, and realized it must have come from her. His hands searched their way up her calves, and she heard her breathing change. She hadn't come, and endorphins and adrenaline were coursing around in her blood now. His touch aroused her, made her soft, pliable, short of breath, and very, very excited.

"I like your legs," he said, pulling away the blanket so she lay completely naked before him. "Spread your legs, Natalia," he said softly.

She swallowed.

Okay.

She did as he said, opening her legs.

"Farther," he ordered.

Natalia's pulse galloped and her heart pounded as she slowly spread her legs under his gaze, opening herself to him. She had never done anything like this before.

"Good," he said. "Now I can see you." As he spoke, he caressed the inside of her thigh, higher and higher, and Natalia shuddered.

"So sensitive," he murmured and pinched her, not hard, but not softly either. She moaned.

"I want you to enjoy this too." He pinched her again, higher this time, and Natalia's breathing quickened. She was so turned on she was having a hard time lying still.

David lay down next to her on the sofa, moving so that she was between him and the back of the sofa. He took one of her nipples between his thumb and index finger and studied her intently as he squeezed, quite hard. *Oh God.*

He slid his hand down her stomach, stroking his finger along the dark hair that began there.

"Please . . . ," she moaned softly.

He cupped his hand over her and finally, finally began to stroke her. He was so incredibly attentive, found a rhythm that was frighteningly right. She only needed to pant, nod, or close her eyes, and he adjusted his pace. It was magic. He leaned over and kissed her deeply, continuing his stroking all the while.

Natalia started to tremble.

He murmured words that would normally have made her blush, hot, arousing words between kisses and caresses, and she passed the limit where she knew she was going to come now. She pushed herself against his body, against his hand, against his mouth, and she—who was always analyzing, considering, and reasoning—quit thinking, stopped doing anything. She just was, dissolving under his hand, and then she came.

This can't be happening, she thought, and realized she was sobbing. Afterward she lay heavily on the sofa. She couldn't move a limb. David slid his arm under her and cradled her against him.

"So *this* is what everyone is always talking about," she said, her voice sounding lazy. "I had no idea it could be like *that*, no idea." Her eyelids closed. She'd never felt so relaxed in her life.

"Yes, it was different for me too," David said into her hair. He slowly stroked her arms and captured her legs between his own. "Better. We're a good fit," he said. "Sexually, I mean."

His voice sank to a low murmur. His mouth moved against her hair while he cautiously stroked her oversensitized skin. Natalia drifted off. It was impossible to stay awake, as if days of tension, hours of concentration, had disappeared. Her eyelids closed and she was asleep.

David's snoring in her ear woke her up. It had been a long time—too long—since she'd had a man here. Cautiously she started to disentangle herself from the sofa.

"What are you doing?" he murmured, moving an arm over her in protest.

"Lighting some candles," she replied, managing to slip off the sofa.

"Don't be gone too long," he said. "You're very nice to lie next to."

While Natalia found some candles and a lighter, she heard David's breathing deepen as he fell asleep again. She padded around, lighting every candle she could find. Then she stopped by the sofa and watched him. He was basically made of muscles, his lines all masculine. The candles cast flickering shadows over him, and her eyes lingered longingly on his chest, his legs, his . . . well. He was magnificent. She couldn't find any words. The fleeting thought of whatever she'd felt on his back came to mind, but she shook it off. He hadn't wanted to talk about it, and it was none of her business.

She took a thin blanket off the other sofa and padded out onto the balcony.

She had bought this apartment with her own money, not her family's, but with her own salary and through a realtor who wasn't her father's. She rarely invited anyone over. She'd only had Jonas up here before, at least in this sense, and that had been quite some time ago.

She pulled the blanket more tightly around her, the soles of her feet adjusting to the cool balcony. She loved her apartment, and most of all she loved her balcony. It wasn't particularly wide, but it was long, and she had set out pots along the iron railing with easy-to-tend shrubs. She had added big hurricane lamps, which she now lit while she was at it, and then she leaned her forearms on the railing and looked out. She was surrounded by technology, electronic devices, and ringing phones every day. She needed this oasis.

"What are you doing?"

David's voice made her jump, and just as she did his arm slid around her from behind.

"Just enjoying myself," she replied.

David laughed quietly against the nape of her neck. "You're good at enjoying yourself," he said. "I can't remember the last time I heard a woman enjoy herself so loudly."

"Thanks for reminding me," she replied. "All my neighbors probably heard me."

"Heard us," he said. "That was amazing. *You* are amazing." His hands slid up and cupped her breasts. Natalia pressed back against him while jutting her breasts forward into his hands. The blanket started to slide off her.

"Maybe we ought to go back inside," she said as his hands found their way between her thighs. The iron railing was thin, and if anyone down on the street looked up, they would be seen. She trembled as his finger slid into her, stroking her just the right way. How could he already know so much about what she liked?

"David . . ."

"Shh," he said. "You're disturbing my concentration. Put your hands on the railing."

She should have hesitated or protested but instead she did what he said, spellbound and seduced. *Chemistry, it's just chemistry,* she convinced herself as she closed her eyes and squeezed the iron railing.

David ran his hand down Natalia's spine. He pulled her curvy buttocks to him and enjoyed the feeling of having her so close. He pushed himself against her, caressing the silky cheeks.

"David," Natalia gasped over her shoulder.

"Do you want to go inside?" he asked with a smile.

"Don't you?"

"No."

He wanted her here, out on her balcony with her hands on the railing. He quickly fetched a condom and ripped open the package. He entered her slowly, enjoying the view. Natalia made a soft, delightful sound. Then she started moving against him.

Perfectly, she fit perfectly. He leaned forward and held a sensitive nipple between his thumb and index finger in the way he'd already learned she liked. He felt her muscles tighten around him and then she made another sound, an almost animal sound that echoed over the street below.

David pinned her to the railing. He held her so hard that she could hardly move as he took her in slow, deep thrusts. He leaned into her back, cupped one hand over her sex, and separated her heat. "I want you to come for me again, Natalia," he whispered.

"David," she panted against the railing.

"Let go," he urged her, thrusting into her, harder and deeper.

Natalia came just as intensely as the first time and stifled a scream that made the railing reverberate. David kept pumping into her until he too detonated. His orgasm was so powerful that he literally lost his footing for a moment. Gasping for breath, he leaned against her, rubbing his chin against her back, burying his nose in her hair.

"Well, that does it," Natalia said. "Now I'm going to have to move."
He laughed.

Afterward they sat entwined on one of her enormous sofas.

They watched the candles burning, listened to Sarah Harvey, talked, and sipped vodka.

Then, when the sun started to rise, they made love again. Slowly and sincerely, which made Natalia shed a tear that she quickly wiped away. Because she knew, she just knew he wasn't going to stay, that it was over. And sure enough, even though it was only two or maybe three in the morning, it was already getting light in the eastern sky when David gathered up his clothing, quickly got dressed, and said good-bye.

Natalia heard his footsteps fading away in the stairwell, and she refused to feel anything but pleasure, pleasure for the experience, pleasure for having gotten to feel so beautiful and attractive, and happiness, despite his not having said anything about their seeing each other again.

She walked into the kitchen and opened the fridge. It was almost totally empty, just a jar of gherkins and one of cocktail onions. After a moment's hesitation she opted for the gherkins. She poured herself a splash of vodka and took the jar and her glass out to the balcony.

The sun was already at full strength. It was going to be another broiling day, and she heard the paperboy coming down the street. She was only human, just a woman, she thought, fishing out a gherkin with her fingers. And David was so very much a man. She took small sips of the vodka and pulled the blanket tighter around herself. The smell of him was still everywhere, and she breathed in the scent of his aftershave, of salt, and of their lovemaking as she let her mind wander.

She had grown up with animals. She had taken care of horses her whole life, from her first pony to her chestnut Lovely, whom she still rode as often as she could.

As a teenager she'd tagged along with various veterinarians who worked with abused racehorses. Once she'd gone along with a veterinarian on a call to treat a stallion whose owner had whipped him. The animal recovered tolerably, but the scars never went away.

She stuffed the last gherkin into her mouth meditatively. True, she had never worked at a hospital or other doctor's office, but she was guessing that scar tissue looked about the same in people and animals. She set down the jar and swallowed the rest of the vodka. She rested her chin on her knees and pulled the blanket over her.

So the question was—who had whipped David Hammar's back so horrifically?

15

Tuesday, July 1

A few hours later that same morning, David stepped off the plane that had taken him back to Malmö again. He glanced at his watch, which said it was 9:30, squinted into the sunlight, and stretched slightly to wake himself up.

During the last year, as he and Michel had literally flown around the world looking for financial backers, he occasionally realized that he hadn't been in the same country for more than a day at a time for several weeks. It was hard work, he thought, walking down the staircase that had been rolled over to the little domestic plane, but it was necessary.

Their financial backers were all over the globe. Banks and funds, the biggest of the big, had their offices in Moscow and Beijing, in London, New York, and Singapore. So they'd flown there, given their pitch, presented their plan, and then moved on to the next one. Always on the go, twenty-four hours a day. They had compiled all the information, formulated their strategy, and then done the same thing all over again. And again. They slept on the plane they'd chartered, each in his own airplane seat.

Outwardly, in interviews and articles, David always maintained that he liked to fly, that he lived for this. And that was partially true. You couldn't work like this if you didn't have a deep conviction that it was meaningful. But the truth, David thought as he strolled across the tarmac toward the terminal, was that the travel wore on him. And he'd been doing it for so long.

He had been about twenty when he started his first business. The first few years it was pretty much all about survival. In the following years it had been about going from an upstart to a superstar without losing focus.

David walked through the gate and out onto the street, flagged a cab, and gave the driver the address of the man he was going to meet. He leaned back in the seat and watched the familiar buildings and streets pass by. How many times had he been here? Twenty? Thirty?

He knew he was good at what he did, maybe one of the ten best in the world. Of course he had failed sometimes. Especially in the beginning, when he was inexperienced and compensated for that by being excessively ruthless.

The first time Hammar Capital had wound up in the spotlight was when he'd pulled off a really brazen coup against one of the most venerable companies in Sweden, a medium-size company with a good reputation among the conservatives, but one that he'd known he could make more efficient. It had been lunacy from beginning to end. With an extremely large loan, he'd made an aggressive move. It had failed, which earned him a lot of bad press. The Investum-owned evening paper, in particular, had hung him out to dry, called him a butcher, a pirate. It had been tough, but it had also made him stronger. Because the abuse he took in the press—sometimes deservedly so, sometimes completely undeservedly—taught him to take a beating. If there was anything his childhood had demonstrated, it was the importance of being able to handle a real thrashing. He'd always endeavored to learn from his failures and bring that experience to his next deal.

Twice Hammar Capital had struck at Investum directly. Twice, they had fought for dominion of a company they both wanted to control. And both times, the bigger and stronger Investum had emerged victorious.

The first time, David had been almost bankrupt. Hammar Capital had been up to its ears in debt again, and David had only managed to save the business by a hair's breadth. The second time, a few years after the dot-com bubble, which had weakened Investum but made HC strong, the battle for a position on the board of a software company had been more evenly matched, but HC had still lost. They had

had to back out, injured and humiliated in the press, but largely intact.

After that David had decided that he needed to stay away from Investum for a while. He realized he needed to plan better, that he needed to rely more on a cool head and logic, and act less out of emotion and hatred. He had started over, taking on Michel, whom he'd known from both his military service and the Stockholm School of Economics, as his partner. And that strategy had paid off. In recent years, Hammar Capital had gone from being an admired but very small venture capital firm to one of the biggest and most respected in Europe.

Now David didn't have any trouble getting meetings with the foremost representatives of superbanks and superfunds the world over. Everyone knew that HC delivered, and today, whatever money David Hammar asked for, they gave him. His team of analysts was talented, his whole organization was as efficient as well-oiled machinery. They had never been stronger. He belonged to a new generation of finance men without old-school loyalties but with global contacts, and if he wanted to he could take over any big company.

David watched out the cab window. The thing was, he needed to think about where he was going next. For almost so many years he had dreamed of what he and Michel were about to do in a few weeks: a hostile takeover of Investum. Take it over and break the company up, crush it and crush Gustaf and Peter.

And Natalia.

God. Natalia. The woman with the golden eyes and the silky soft skin. What had he gotten himself tangled up in?

As David greeted the Russian he had come here to meet, as he summarized all the details, as he invited the man to lunch, as he flattered and convinced him, as he packed up after the successful meeting and took the afternoon flight back to Stockholm, he must have thought of Natalia a hundred times. As he walked into his office at Blasieholmen, he thought about how she was just a short walk away, so close over there at Stureplan. As he sat in his desk chair, he thought of her.

Was she also both tired and upbeat at the same time?

When was the last time he'd made love to a woman three times in the same night? He had no idea. She'd felt it too. He didn't need to wonder. He knew that she'd felt what he'd felt, the intensity.

It had been unparalleled.

He let out a heavy sigh. There was a huge problem here. It was supposed to have been a one-time occurrence, making love to Natalia De la Grip. In principal, he reminded himself with a grimace, it shouldn't even have been that, of course. But then when he'd agreed to go in, against *all* better judgment, he'd known that it could only be one night, nothing more. He hadn't exactly been promiscuous in his life, but he'd never had any difficulty moving on from meaningless, casual dalliances.

David stretched, started his computer, and then just sat there, his eyes glazed over. He knew what he had to do, what he should have done from the beginning, before things had gone this far.

Break things off with Natalia for good.

He had to put it behind him. Not dwell on thoughts of the best sexual experience he'd ever had, not fantasize about seeing her again, not suspect that sex could never be meaningless or even casual to her.

He gazed out the window, wondering absentmindedly where Michel was. He'd forgotten to call Michel. Forgotten to call his closest and most important colleague, his best friend, while at the same time he'd thought about calling Natalia a hundred times.

He opened a couple of documents on the computer to do what he needed to do, focus on what was important. They had everything they needed now. Signed confidentiality agreements from everyone in question. *Nothing* could get out. Access to four billion euros. Brokers at the ready. In a week, when Båstad week began, the financial elite would all be off at their summer homes. Stockholm would empty out; all the alert systems would be running at half speed. They had chosen the timing with care. By this time next week pretty much every Swedish banker and moneyman would be in Båstad or Torekov, or on a boat in the Mediterranean. Summer, sun, and vacation would take over. And then they would strike.

David took a deep breath and decided to get to it.

Ten minutes later he hadn't done a thing.

His mind kept turning to Natalia the whole time, replaying little movies in his head of how her skin glowed when she was aroused, how her eyes had shone in the dawn when they made love that last time, how she sounded when he kissed her, the taste of her tongue and mouth. He could hardly bear the thought that it wouldn't happen again.

He abruptly stood up, walked over to the window, and looked out over the water. Actually it would be completely insane to deprive himself of a sequel. This had nothing to do with deepening the relationship, he convinced himself. He just questioned why it had to end so abruptly.

The more David thought about it, the more sensible he thought it seemed. Nothing was keeping him from seeing Natalia one more time. Of course he could call her if he wanted to, invite her out for a real dinner. Natalia was a sophisticated woman, an adult, her own person. They could have another night of sex. David ignored the alarms going off in some remote part of his brain. *Of course* he could call her.

"How did it go?"

David was snapped out of his reverie as Michel walked in, studying him with a puzzled expression on his face.

"I didn't hear you come in," David said.

Michel looked at him with concern. "Is everything okay?"

"It went well in Malmö," David said. "The Russian is in. Now we have what we need."

Michel nodded. "Good. And how did it go with the boat?"

"The boat?"

"David, are you alright? You seem really distracted. Are you sure it went alright in Malmö?"

"Sorry. It went well in Malmö with the Russian. And with your boat," he added. "Thanks for letting me use it."

"How is she?"

"The boat?"

Michel rolled his eyes. "Not the boat."

"She's decent. Not like the other members of her family. Different from all the bank women I've met. Not typically upper class. A nice person," he concluded lamely.

Michel gave him an odd look.

David hadn't planned to say so much, but he needed to express it out loud, put what he was thinking into words. Natalia was unique. And fun. And genuinely good-hearted, he was convinced of that.

Somehow she managed to be a rock-solid finance woman—David knew very well what J-O demanded of his staff—and yet she was profoundly human, almost fragile when they were together.

"You know that I would never intrude into your personal affairs," Michel began in a somber voice, and David knew he *really* didn't want to hear this. Michel scratched his scalp. "But, David, what the fuck is going on between you two? Do you know what you're doing? Are you going to see each other again?"

"Nothing happened," David said tersely, without blinking. He didn't like lying to his best friend, but he couldn't talk about sex with him. Although, he thought uneasily, of course that wasn't the worst thing he was keeping from Michel. "She's working on something that has to do with Investum's bank," he said. "A big acquisition of some kind. She has insight into Svenska Banken." That much was true. J-O had said it, and there had been rumors, the way there always were in this industry. It was a massive deal, a gigantic merger, and it would make Investum vulnerable precisely at the right time, as if he'd ordered it. "If I keep tabs on Natalia, then I'll find out if she suspects anything."

As excuses went, it was pretty lame.

Michel shook his head as if he saw right through it. "Just try not to ruin us. That's all I'm asking."

"You know how important this is to me; you don't need to worry."

"I know." Michel was quiet, shifting from one foot to the other. "So what did you guys talk about?" he asked nonchalantly.

"What or *who*?"

"Nah, it's not like I care." Michel twisted one of his thick, gold rings. "We were never a couple," he said. "I didn't even think she'd remember me." He started poking at a pen on the desk. "I don't think she likes me anymore. We were friends, but then something happened, and now I don't think she likes me at all. And why should she? You've met her. She could have anyone in the world she wants."

David tried to keep a straight face, but he'd never seen Michel like this, like a twelve-year-old who wanted to ask out the most popular girl in class. "She looks good," David said neutrally. "I assume we're talking about Åsa Bjelke now, right?"

"She works for Investum," Michel pointed out. "So she's off-limits anyway."

"But she's not responsible for their operations," David said. "Try not to mention that we're planning to do a hostile takeover of her company and destroy her boss, and I'm sure it'll be fine. Call her."

Michel shook his head. "That woman is trouble. One hundred percent." He gave David a wry smile. "We would do best, both of us, to keep away from the Investum women."

"You're right," David said, his voice lacking conviction.

Because he wasn't sure he could do that.

Keep away from Natalia De la Grip.

16

After David had left her, Natalia had slept for a few hours, which meant she hadn't gotten to work until ten, which had caused a few raised eyebrows. It was actually crazy that everyone was so used to her always being the first to arrive and the last to leave.

J-O called her at eleven.

"Where are you?" Natalia asked.

"In Moscow. I'm having lunch with the minister of industry and trade."

They coordinated, and then the day proceeded with an unrelenting stream of calls to sift through, documents to read, and analytical reports to write. She realized she hadn't looked up from her desk for several hours when, at two o'clock, she overheard a conversation in English. The office space outside of her own was open-plan, with standing desks where a sea of people were constantly moving around. A group of men from the main office in London stood around one of the desks, all with their laptops on, having an argument. She didn't know them, but that wasn't unusual; there were always people from different parts of the world here. So she stretched, got up, got herself some coffee, and then went back to work.

A few hours after a late lunch, Natalia asked her assistant to screen her calls and only bother her with the most important, which gave her a few relatively quiet hours. The deal Natalia was working on was one of the biggest the Bank of London's Nordic team had ever been involved in and her own first solo project. Investum's bank, Svenska Banken, was acquiring a chain of Danish banks. It was an unbelievably complicated deal, and Svenska Banken had chosen the corpo-

rate finance section at Bank of London as advisers. There were a myr-
iad of possible pitfalls, and it was Natalia's responsibility to identify
them all and to give solid financial advice throughout the process.
Everything looked good on paper, but Natalia still couldn't shake the
sense that it was being rushed through, that it was being driven by the
desire for prestige—her father's dream of creating a Nordic super
bank—and that more careful scrutiny of the whole thing would be a
good idea. Investum, which was a major owner of Svenska Banken,
was putting up a huge amount of capital.

J-O called again around four.

"How was lunch?" she asked.

"Warm vodka and caviar," he said. "I hate that. I'm heading to
Helsinki soon."

"When will you be back in Sweden?"

"Next week, Stockholm. Then I fly down to Båstad."

J-O was hosting one of the two biggest parties in Båstad during tennis week. The Bank of London party was the party that *everyone*—
politicians, celebrities, tennis pros, and the financial elite—wanted to
be invited to. Five hundred invitations had gone out, and no one had
RSVPed no. Traditionally the party was always held on Thursday at
J-O's massive mansion, the day after Natalia's parents held their
own—just as traditional and just as large—barbecue at the De la Grip
mansion. That's how it had always been, and that's how it always
would be.

"I'll call tonight," J-O said and hung up.

Natalia browsed the material she was going to report to the representatives of both banks, two men whose interpersonal chemistry
wasn't the best.

The next time she and J-O spoke, early that evening when their
Stureplan offices were beginning to empty out, he was already in
Helsinki.

"I'm almost ready," she said. "But I'm still thinking about talking
to Dad," she added hesitantly.

"I read the paperwork you gave me. Several times. I don't see anything for you to worry about. Could it just be that you're nervous?"

Was he right? Or should she listen to her gut? "I don't know," she
said uncertainly.

"My dearest Natalia," he said in his occasionally awkward Swedish, which broadcast the fact that he spoke any and every language perfectly, the result of boarding schools on two continents and constant travel. "It's your nerves getting to you, right?" She could hear from his voice that J-O was there, really there. That he was focused, that he was filtering out everything except what was most important. He was eccentric and liked to hear himself talk, but he was a good boss.

"I'm sure you're right," she said.

They didn't say it out loud, either of them, but they both knew that this deal was the one Natalia hoped would make her father appreciate what she could do. This deal would be her leverage to get herself onto Investum's board. There was no room for error.

"I've got your back," J-O said calmly.

And Natalia knew he meant it. In this industry, where you were never better than your last deal, where even senior-level corporate finance types could be fired with an hour's notice, J-O would protect her. As long as she didn't screw up too much.

"I think I'm going to stay here," he said. "I like Helsinki. Have you been here?" Natalia thought she heard laughter and glasses clinking in the background.

"It's a beautiful city," she agreed. "I went to the Presidential Palace Ball there once."

"I talked to David Hammar," J-O said suddenly.

Natalia's heart skipped a beat. She had managed not to think about David for at least ten minutes, and now this. She waited impatiently while J-O covered the receiver and spoke to someone. It sounded like a woman.

"Are you still there?" he asked.

"Yes," said Natalia. Each time she floated away on a meandering tangent related to David Hammar in some way—his smile, his body, their nonexistent future—she had to rein herself back in. She refused to be a woman who neglected her work and sat around daydreaming about a man. Simply refused. She was better than that. But J-O's comment caught her off guard.

"He's up to something," J-O said, and Natalia thought this sounded like gossip. She pictured J-O at one of those trendy, fashionable restaurants he was so fond of, maybe with a chilled bottle of champagne in a bucket, maybe with a beautiful woman next to him, maybe two.

"Everyone's up to something," Natalia said vaguely. That's how it

was in this business: gossip, rumors. The trick was being able to analyze and sort out what was true and what was false.

"This is something big," J-O said. More laughter and clinking in
the background.

"I'm on my way out," Natalia said. "Can we talk tomorrow?"

"Is anyone left in the office?"

Natalia looked around. The place was almost empty. "Most people
are off on their summer vacations," she said.

"It's impossible to get things done while everyone's gone. I think
I'm going to go to St. Tropez this year. Have you been there?"

"It's nice." She pictured palm trees and white sand. "But I don't
tolerate sun for very long."

"I'll go through your paperwork one more time, okay?"

"Thanks."

Toward evening, when the last of the London guys had gone out
on the town and all the assistants had been replaced by the night
shift, Natalia called Åsa.

"How are you?"

"My therapist says I'm depressed, but I don't know. I'm thinking
about buying shoes. Or a new condo. What are you doing?"

"I'm thinking."

"About work?"

"Partially. I've got such a funny feeling about this bank deal. J-O
says I'm nervous because I've never done anything like this. But I
don't know." Natalia paused. "I think I have to talk to Dad." She made
a face to herself. "And Peter, I guess." She hated having to report to
her older brother. She waited for a second and then added: "Oh, and
I slept with David Hammar."

"J-O might be right, you know. He's been doing this for a while.
And you've always been a worrywart. Or should we call it neurotic?
Or maybe you're depressed, like me? Lord knows if I'd been with
Jonas as long as you were, I'd be depressed."

"Are you drunk?"

"Does the pope wear a funny hat?"

Natalia scratched the back of her head. "Did you hear what I said?
About David?"

Åsa scoffed loudly. "Well, the way you two were looking at each other and the way you look every time someone mentions his name, I can't say I'm surprised. How was he?"

"I don't know if I can talk about such things," Natalia protested, although it felt like the only thing she wanted to talk about. About David. About the magical sex. She looked around her office and lowered her voice even though she was practically the only one around. "This was totally on a scale of its own. Not good or bad if you know what I mean, but completely off the charts. Have you ever experienced anything like that?"

"Sweetie, I'm afraid you're going to have to be a little more specific than 'like that.' We have different frames of reference. I sleep with people all the time. You do it, like, basically never."

"I slept with Jonas," Natalia pointed out. They'd been together for four years and had a completely normal sex life. Not crazy, scream-out-loud sex, but normal.

Åsa made another scoffing sound. "You do know that Jonas is the most boring man in the world, so we can't include him in this discussion?"

"How can you know that Jonas is boring in bed?" Natalia protested, and then a thought struck her. "Did you sleep with him?"

"Nah, I don't think so," said Åsa, sounding as if she had to think about it for a minute. "Quit trying to change the subject."

"I think it was just a one-time event," Natalia said, finally allowing herself to do what she'd been avoiding all day: analyze her relationship with David Hammar. "I'm almost sure it has to be—we haven't been in touch since."

And Natalia realized that this was exactly what people did. They were attracted to each other, slept together, then parted ways, and moved on. Why did it feel so unfinished?

She had never been party to anything like what had happened between her and David. She'd been a late bloomer, and maybe or very definitely she'd been a little inhibited sexually, marked by her old-fashioned upbringing, which she'd never managed to shake off. She'd slept with guys in London, finance guys who were just as focused on their careers as she was. And then with Jonas, who had also been a late bloomer, inhibited by *his* upbringing and some weird Madonna/whore issue. But they *had* done well in a caring, cautious way. Nothing out of the ordinary, just nice, normal vanilla sex. But

David . . . Natalia suspected there was no limit to how wild she could get with that man. Just the memory of what they'd done and how he'd touched her made her . . .

"Did he say anything about seeing you again?" Åsa asked.

"No. And neither did I. I don't expect anything else."

"You'll just end up sorry if you get too attached."

"I know," Natalia said sharply. This was exactly the reason she refused to open herself up. "I'm not dumb," she said. "And he is so incredibly hot, it's almost annoying."

"You're hot, too, Nat. You just don't know it," Åsa said, her voice taking an unusually serious tone. "I think Jonas really wasn't good for you. You two weren't good for each other. And what he did to you . . . No, you have to move on."

"Yeah right, because I'm such a catch," Natalia said dryly, hating how self-pitying she felt.

"Enough of that," Åsa said. "So, are there any down sides to David? Sexy, rich, and good in bed."

"I don't know. He can be really hard. And he's quite good at manipulating people. And everything that's been written about him can't have been made up." She remembered the articles about competitors who'd been ruined unscrupulously, infidelities and marriages that fell apart, noble houses leveled to the ground. It couldn't all be exaggerated, could it?

"What else did you do? I mean, aside from the amazing sex. What did you talk about?" Åsa sounded indifferent, but Natalia wasn't fooled.

"If you're wondering if we discussed anything in specific, ask me, would you? Just what is it you want to know?"

"Damn it, Natalia, I hate it when you do that. There must be something wrong with you. This is super hard for me."

"Michel isn't married," Natalia said. "And clearly he feels something for you."

"Did David say that? What does he feel?"

"No idea. I was busy having fantastic sex."

"Michel's family wanted him to marry a pretty Lebanese girl, and he always did what his family wanted. You know: honor, morality, responsibility, and all that crap. He always had a lot of opinions about right and wrong, black and white, even back in college. Good qualities in a lawyer or an economist, maybe even for a coworker or an adviser to Super David, but kind of tiresome. He was a typical patriarch."

"While you were more of a typical tramp?"

"I was sure he was going to have kids by this time, chubby Lebanese kids, eight of them."

"I don't think he has any kids, either chubby or otherwise. In terms of David . . ."

"I don't like kids," Åsa interrupted. She sounded almost panic-stricken. As if someone were standing over her demanding that she start reproducing immediately. "I don't understand how anyone can want kids. I don't get it."

Well, to each his own.

"Sorry, fuck. I know how it was for you," Åsa said. "Sorry."

"No biggie," Natalia said, but she wasn't up to talking about kids. Not now, not so soon. It was only a year ago; she wasn't over it, no matter what Åsa thought, not that they ever discussed it. If Åsa had any kind of slogan, it was: Never look back. Followed closely by: Never get attached to another person. They'd both been hurt by their experiences, although in totally different ways.

"Are you interested in him?"

"Not really," Åsa scoffed. "He had his chance. He blew it."

Natalia shook her head. Åsa had a habit of dumping men as soon as she found the least little thing to criticize.

"Because you *seem* interested."

"Not in the least. He bugs me, that's all."

They sat in silence, each on her own end of the line.

"I want to talk to Dad," Natalia finally said.

"About David?"

"Right. I'm going to call my father and say I slept with his archenemy. No, about this deal. It's just rubbing me the wrong way."

"But haven't you already talked to him? And J-O?"

"Yeah."

It was quiet on Åsa's end. Then she said, "J-O is actually really hot."

"I think he likes group sex," Natalia said.

"Who doesn't like group sex?" Åsa said. "Okay, I have to get going. I think I promised I'd go to Riche. I have a date. He's only twenty-four. When you get tired of David, you should try a younger guy. They don't want anything, don't need anything. Hey, you . . . ?"

"Yeah?"

"This is the twenty-first century. *You* could actually call *him*, you know. Sooner or later you're going to have to stop listening to your mother's worthless relationship advice about keeping your knees together and waiting. You can't sit home pining away."

"I'm not sitting home pining away. I'm sitting at work, managing a billion-kronor business deal."

"Call him, that's all I'm saying." Åsa laughed. "Maybe ask him if he likes group sex. That ought to get him talking."

"You're disturbed."

"Now you're really starting to sound a lot like my therapist. I gotta dash. Bye."

17

David had already left his office by seven that evening. He was restless and anxious to get going. The heat wave wasn't over yet. The evening was warm as he strolled downtown.

He should go home.

He should call Michel.

He should work out until he was sweaty and then go to bed early.

He should do anything other than what he was doing now: heading toward Stureplan. He quickly passed Nybro Bay, strolled past the Royal Dramatic Theater and Restaurant Riche, squeezed between tourists and regular Stockholm folks, and stopped outside Sturegallerian—the hub of Stockholm's golden financial triangle.

He glanced up at the façade of Sturegallerian, the shopping mall and office complex, knowing exactly where the windows of her bank's offices were on the fourth floor. It was almost seven-thirty. Surely she wasn't still there. And yet there he stood, trying not to feel too much like a stalker. *Now what?* he wondered, touching the phone in his pocket.

"David?"

He blinked. Natalia had materialized in the entrance to the building, and at first he thought he might be imagining her. But it was her.

"Hi," he said.

She looked as if she couldn't believe her eyes. "What are you doing here?"

"I'm not really sure," he answered honestly. "Were you working until now?"

"Yes," she nodded. "It was a really hectic day."

"It's a beautiful evening. Would you like to take a walk? With me?"

Her eyes widened, but she didn't say anything, just nodded.

They strolled down to the water, toward Nybroplan and Strandvägen Boulevard. She walked close to him, but they didn't touch each other.

"How are you?" he asked. It had been so many hours since they'd parted. He regretted not contacting her during the day, not showing more consideration. She deserved so much better.

She smiled at the question, but just said, "I'm fine. How about you?"

"It's been a long day," he said, realizing that he shouldn't mention where he'd been today. *Be careful what you say, remember who she is. Think, David.*

He nodded to the hot dog stand in Berzelii Park. "Would you like one? They're really good here."

She blinked slowly. The sun was low, and the golden light made her dark hair shine. Her eyes glowed. "I've never had a hot dog before," she said.

"You're kidding, right?"

"No, my mother says it's vulgar to eat street food. She's very preoccupied with what's vulgar." She laughed suggestively. "And *who*'s vulgar, of course. That's just the way she is. But yes, please, I'd love one."

He bought them each a spicy hot dog with lots of mustard, and they sat by the water and ate in silence, her with her back straight without spilling even a crumb.

Afterward she fastidiously folded up the paper wrapper, wiped the corners of her mouth with her napkin, and then folded her hands over her purse on her lap. He handed her the can of mineral water he'd bought, and after a brief hesitation, she took it and drank.

"Don't tell me drinking water in public isn't done either?"

"It's so silly, I realize that," she said, and his eyes locked in on her mouth, those light-pink lips. He would give quite a lot to feel those lips again. On his mouth. On his skin. On his . . .

"Your childhood was different, I assume," she continued, and David forced himself to focus on the conversation.

"I don't think about that very often," she continued, and a little wrinkle appeared on her forehead. "About how different people's lives are." She ran her finger thoughtfully over the can of sparkling water. "I always think I'm so liberal, but then I see myself from the outside, through someone else's eyes, and it isn't always flattering."

"It's hard to reflect on yourself," he said. "But, yeah, I'm guessing my childhood was a little different from yours. My mom was a single mother. She had me when she was nineteen, and she never went to college. She supported us with odd jobs. She had no one. We lived in a really tough neighborhood."

"And your father?"

"He was never in the picture. He's been dead for a long time now."

"That sounds rough. Both for you and for her."

"I didn't make it any easier. I was a lot of trouble as a kid."

She held up her hand to shield herself from the sun and looked at him. Her eyes were filled with warmth. She didn't offer any of the usual clichés, nothing about how all kids were a lot of trouble, that he shouldn't blame himself, nothing. She just watched him somberly.

"We moved a lot," he heard himself say. Had he ever talked to anyone about this, about his childhood, which had actually shaped him more than he was comfortable with?

"Why?"

She was so seductively easy to talk to, but he got control of himself. "For various reasons," he replied simply, cagily. "When I was sixteen I started at Skogbacka. My mom got me in on a scholarship."

A couple of students were admitted every year basically for free. As long as they never actually forgot their place, as long as they never forgot to be grateful. "That's where things turned around," he said.

Eventually.

"It's hard to be different," she said slowly. "Especially at a school like that. So many of the students there are so similar to each other. People talk about how nice the place is, how many people they got to know there, but the price is conformity. It's complicated."

"Were you different?" he asked.

"Yes."

That one word told him so much. That's why it was so easy to be with her. She was an anomaly in her privileged world. And he was an outcast in his. From the outside Natalia seemed so comfortable with who she was, but she must have fought her own battles. Her father was known for his rude and sexist statements about women working in finance. Natalia must have grown up with that talk, day in and day out, absorbing it at the kitchen table. In many ways it would obviously be an asset to grow up in Sweden's most prominent finance family; you would pick up so much know-how and such a network of contacts for free. But in another way . . . He wondered what it had done to her. Had it slowly chipped away at her self-confidence? Or had it made her more anxious to show what she could do?

"Your boss speaks very highly of you," David said. He wanted her to know that.

"Thanks. It feels a little weird to sit here talking like this. Don't you think so? I know so much about you, in a way—through the media—but I don't *know* you, not actually, not really." She furrowed her brow, and he knew that she was thinking about how they had gotten to know each other the previous night. Of how well they knew each other in that way. But Natalia was right. They didn't know one another, regardless of what they thought they knew. He wondered if she, this super-bright woman, had as many secrets as he did. Suddenly he wanted to get to know her better, wanted to share something about himself.

"What do you want to know?" he said. "Ask whatever you want."

"What's your limit?" she asked quickly. As if the question had been buzzing around in her head for a long time. "What would you never do?"

And David knew she was talking about work. So typical of her to choose to ask about what was dearest to them both. Because they were alike there, too—their work defined them as people.

"I buy and sell companies. I break them up. I make them more efficient. And a lot of people have opinions about that," he said, knowing that was a mild understatement. People—like Natalia's father, for example—didn't have *opinions*; they thought David was blasting venerable companies to bits. "But I would never speculate in schools or health care. That's unethical." He had never wanted to invest in those types of companies, had far too much respect for them. "I don't think a venture capital company should be running businesses like that for profit. That would never be good."

She raised a dark eyebrow. The movement made her look like a curious, proper schoolteacher. Her hair, which she wore up, and her austere blouse contributed to that impression, of course. "A venture capitalist with morals?" Her voice was filled to the brim with skepticism.

"It depends on who you ask," he said sardonically.

"What if I ask you?" She looked at him, and David allowed himself to be transfixed by her clear-eyed gaze.

"I'm no better than anyone else in this world, but I'm no worse either. And Hammar Capital has never profited off weapons, oil, or tobacco," he added, almost ashamed at how badly he wanted her to understand him, so that later on she would remember more about him than just his deceit.

"I understand," she said without blinking, without smiling.

God, how he wanted her when she looked like this. Poised. Composed. Curious. He wanted to peel the layers of cool linen and expensive lingerie off her and kiss and lick and bite her until her skin was on fire. He thought back to what she felt like—warm silk, taut and pulsing, welcoming, demanding and yielding at the same time.

He couldn't remember what they were talking about.

A voice said, "David Hammar?"

David tore himself away from her eyes and looked at the man who had walked over to them, an acquaintance, scarcely even that. David quickly stood up, shook his hand, and exchanged pleasantries. Out of the corner of his eye he saw that Natalia had risen from the bench as well. In quick motions she strode off to throw her wrapper in a trash can quite a distance away.

"You didn't want to be seen with me," he remarked after the man had left and Natalia had returned and they were seated on the bench again.

"I'm sorry, but I don't really know what this is between us," she said forthrightly. He wondered if she'd ever lied in her whole life.

"And I'm in the middle of a deal," she continued. "An enormous deal. One that will affect Investum and my whole future. My father wouldn't be happy if we were seen together."

"I understand."

"It's actually crazy," she continued. "I've tried to warn my father several times, but he won't listen to me."

It took a second before he understood what she'd just said. She wanted to confide in him. Fuck, he couldn't have this conversation with her. "You shouldn't tell me this," he said sharply.

She startled and bit her lip. "I know, but you just told me how moral you are. I feel like I can trust you."

This was so dangerous. He didn't want her to hate him more than was necessary; later it would be an unavoidable consequence, but not yet. So he didn't want to hear her secrets, things that she would later think he'd used against her father and against Investum.

He already knew everything he needed to know.

"It's late," he said instead, navigating away from dangerous territory. They had been talking for a long time. The sun had started to cautiously graze the rooftops. And she'd been awake, with him, the better part of the preceding night. "You must be tired."

"No," she said, raising her chin in a determined gesture. "I'm not tired. Do I think it's inconvenient for us to be seen together? Yes. But I want to be with you." She looked at him, her enormous eyes like molten gold, her skin so light, like carefully polished marble. "Tonight."

This was totally mind-blowing. Her words sank in, and David felt his body coursing with expectation. He raised his hand and placed it on her leg, cautiously stroking it over her thigh before pulling it away. He understood her fear of being seen with him. When this was over—and it had to end, anything else was sheer madness—it would be better for her that no one had seen them together.

But Jesus Christ. Just touching her leg, through the thin fabric of her skirt no less, woke his whole body up. *One more time, what difference would that make?* it whispered through his head. And David couldn't think of a single reason to say no, to deny them what they both apparently were desperately longing for.

"Where do you want to go?" he asked. He would do this really well, he decided, so that she wouldn't regret it.

"I don't have any condoms left at home. No food, nothing. And my housecleaner comes first thing tomorrow. So preferably not my place." She blushed a little, and it was clear that she wasn't used to talking about this kind of thing. But she straightened her back and looked him right in the eye, and David laughed. She was a brave woman.

Hammar Capital had a guest room at the office, a refrigerator stocked with the basics, and a well-tended roof terrace with a view of the water. They could go there. But his office was also covered with plans to take over Natalia's father's company, so . . .

"We could go to my place," he said slowly, surprising himself.

His home was extremely private. He rarely took women there. He actually couldn't remember the last time he'd done it. He didn't like to let people in that far, preferred to be the one who got up and left. He never had parties, didn't socialize in his apartment, and it was closed to the media. Not even Michel had been there. It was just his. But he couldn't take Natalia to a suite at the Grand Hôtel for a number of different reasons, primarily because it felt *wrong*. "We can stop on the way and I'll pick up what we need," he said.

She nodded and stood.

"Well, that settles it," she said. She hugged her purse. He wanted to stretch out his hand, hold her hand, give her a kiss, and say that he planned to take good care of her this evening. Tonight. But instead he raised his hand and hailed a taxi, painfully aware that no matter how well he took care of Natalia, it could never compensate for what he was going to do afterward. He brushed aside these thoughts and held open the door of the cab that stopped. Natalia had been wrong about his character. When it came to taking something he wanted, then he had almost no morals, practically no qualms at all.

18

Natalia had almost believed David would fling himself on top of her in the cab. The air between them was so charged that she had a hard time breathing. Was this really happening?

His hand lay on the seat next to her. Strong and broad, the hairs black against his skin. She could hardly wait until those big, capable hands were on her again. She glanced out the window, tried to steady herself. Her nipples were hard and sensitive against the inside of her bra, her thighs hot and her palms moist. She would have liked to shower before this, but somehow she hadn't imagined that a mere hour after leaving work she would be sitting in a taxi on her way to David's place for the express purpose of having sex.

David told the driver to stop. He hopped out, quickly ducked into a 7-Eleven, and came back out with a paper bag in his hand. She tried her best to appear cool, as if she often traveled by cab and stopped to buy condoms.

"Where do you live, anyway?" she asked, because she hadn't heard the address and they were heading away from Östermalm. It occurred to her that she didn't know anyone who lived anywhere other than Östermalm. Aside from Djursholm and on Lidingö, of course, which were even more affluent. Well, aside from her house-cleaner, actually. She had no idea where Gina lived. The thought almost made her erupt into nervous laughter. Could a person be any more sheltered?

"Here," David answered as the cab pulled to a stop. He got out and came around to hold her door open for her. When she got out she took his hand and squeezed it hard.

She felt him with every single one of her senses. His scent, his overwhelming size. The quiet rustling of the paper bag. The metal tinkling of his keys. He put his hand on the small of her back, guided her through a door. The stairwell with the elevator echoed. It was light and elegant but a little impersonal. No names on any placards.

"I own the whole building," he said briefly. "I know everyone who lives here."

She realized he'd intended to reassure her; he must be able to see how nervous she was, but it felt like an omen. If anything happened, no one would know where she was.

She shook off the morbid thought and stepped out of the elevator when it stopped on the very top floor. David unlocked a heavy door and let her enter first. The door slid shut behind them without a sound. The whole building was like a silent, discreet, efficient machine.

"Go straight in," he said, pointing down the hallway. "I'm just going to go do something."

He disappeared up a steep, spiral stairway, and Natalia walked down the hall into the living room. She stopped on the threshold. She didn't know what she'd been expecting. Stainless steel and black leather maybe. A big flat-screen TV and shelves full of DVDs. Masculine and nouveau riche.

But this . . .

Sturdy bookshelves stuffed with books, puffy sofas, warm colors, and thick rugs. No TV and a completely ordinary, analog sound system. Loads of classical music. A fireplace, burned-down candles. A little untidy, but clean and fresh and terribly cozy.

David appeared behind her.

"It's so homey," she said.

"You sound surprised," he laughed, and when Natalia turned around she saw that his arms were full of white terrycloth.

"Come on," he said. "We're going all the way to the top."

She followed him up the stairs. The floor above was dominated by windows facing every direction. She glimpsed a bedroom. But what made her breath catch was the view.

"Come on, we're going even higher." He went up another flight, and when they emerged onto the rooftop terrace, Natalia couldn't help gaping.

"I don't know what to say."

The view was mind-blowing. The peaks of roofs, the sky, the sunset, and the water. A wooden deck, deck chairs, palm trees in enormous pots. And in the middle—a sunken pool or Jacuzzi, kidney-shaped with turquoise water and recessed spotlights that glittered in the steaming water. "I never dreamed anyone lived like this," she said reverently. It was perfection.

"I brought you a bathrobe and a towel. I'll open the wine while you get in."

She hesitated, but then started to undress. She unbuttoned her blouse, took off her skirt, panties, and bra and was then completely naked. David stood with his head discreetly turned away while she lowered herself into the water. It was heavenly. He turned around, smiled, and came over and leaned down to hand her a glass of wine. As she sipped it, he undressed. She watched him surreptitiously over the rim of her wineglass. She'd never fully appreciated the attractiveness of the male body before, but now she really did.

Naked, he lowered himself into the water across from her.

He drank some of his wine and watched her. His eyes surveyed her face and then moved down her body, which glowed white in the warm water. Natalia straightened a little so her breasts popped up, and she saw the hunger ignite in his eyes. Then he kissed her, hard. He took her glass from her and set it aside, and she wrapped both arms around him. His arm curled around her waist and he lifted her. He sat down on the underwater ledge and then placed her astride his knee. The warmth of the water, the alcohol in the wine, and the completely unsurpassed sensation of sitting out under the open sky and kissing wildly made Natalia's head spin. He put a hand behind her head and she felt her hair come loose and fall down as she writhed in his lap. She rubbed against him. His hands stroked her hips; he held her against him while he leaned forward and took a nipple into his mouth.

She moaned, could have come just from that.

"So unbelievably sexy," he murmured. Natalia moaned again, buried her fingers in his hair, pushed herself against his lips, his body, his erection. She didn't know how long they kept that up, kissing and making out like teenagers, drinking wine and kissing again.

"Let's continue this on land," David said hoarsely.

The evening was warm, almost tropical, and she didn't shiver at all when they left the pool. David was naked, but she wrapped a towel around herself before lying down on one of the deck chairs.

He sat down next to her, unwrapping the towel from her so she lay completely naked. He put a hand over her sex, cupping her mons. "I love that you're not waxed," he murmured.

She gasped as he took one of her legs and moved it up onto the armrest. She squirmed, aroused and embarrassed at the same time.

"Shh," he whispered, caressing the inside of her thigh as he placed her other leg up on the other armrest. "Relax, Natalia," he murmured. "Trust me, I want to do this."

She thought she ought to protest. It was a vulnerable position; she was wide open and didn't feel completely comfortable. But his voice was so convincing, his eyes so intense. Besides, her senses were dulled, so she leaned back, sank into the soft cushion and closed her eyes.

He started tracing circles with his fingers and his mouth on the inside of her thigh, and she trembled. He caressed her and kissed her, but without really touching the spot she wanted him to touch. She started moving on the deck chair, restless and full of longing, but constrained by her position.

He laid his hand on her stomach, spread out his fingers and palm, and pushed her down slightly onto the cushion. He gently kissed the crook of her knee and the inside of her thigh, and she moaned. His mouth traveled slowly and carefully.

"David," she said, frustrated in her arousal. She wondered if he was taunting her. She had never really had good experiences with this kind of thing, to be honest. Men were rarely as committed to it as they wanted to appear, and like most women she had suffered her share of uninspired oral sex.

No sooner had she thought that than David did something with his mouth and finger that definitely was not aimless or uninspired. And when he kept doing it . . . Natalia had no idea just exactly what he was doing, but a level of lust so overpowering it felt almost unreal surged through her. And she thought she would die if he stopped.

"Oh, God," she moaned, so close to coming that she had almost passed the point of no return where the waves just came when he stopped and she wailed, "No!"

She opened her eyes. Saw her spread legs, saw him caressing her thighs very intently without looking into her eyes. He leaned his head down. She felt him spread her open with his fingers before he took her clitoris into his mouth and sucked. Her thighs shook, literally shook, and then he paused. She was breathing so hard that her throat was dry.

He started slowly stroking her with one finger, in and out. "You're so sexy," he said, his voice raspy. "I could come just from licking you."

She heard a sound, a whimpering sound that must have come from her.

"Do you want me to keep going?"

She closed her eyes and nodded. *Yes!*

"Say it."

"Lick me," she said, her voice cracking as his finger entered her again. "Please don't stop, you have to keep going, I can't take any more."

He stood up, quickly retrieved a wineglass, and then positioned himself between her legs again. Slowly he poured the wine over her belly. The cool liquid trickled down over her sex, and he leaned forward.

David caught the wine with his mouth and tongue, drinking and lapping, enjoying how the taste of her and the chilled wine mixed. She was like nothing he'd ever experienced. He spread her open with two fingers. She was beautiful, glistening, and that scent. He let a finger slide into her, listening to the sounds she made.

She was a tightly controlled woman, calm, collected. But like so many other capable, confident women, she was full of passion once finally enticed to relax her control. He felt her surrender herself to him, saw her spread her beautiful thighs and let him play with her.

How he loved this, getting the serene Natalia De la Grip, countess and banking superstar, to quiver as she pleaded for him to go down on her. He was hard, had been since they had first sat down in the taxi, and all he wanted was to bury himself in her strong, quivering body, to take her until she screamed his name.

He could picture it.

His finger was surrounded by her heat. She was tight, and he slid another finger in, stretching her gently, heard her gasping. She was so ready.

He bent his fingers, searching and listening. She murmured something inaudible and he found it. He pushed on that soft spot with his fingers, bent down between her legs, covered her clitoris with his mouth, and sucked. Natalia exploded. He kept going while the orgasm shook her body. And he kept going until she started to come back down a little before slowly pulling back.

She lay there with her eyes closed, her face relaxed, her hair a wild mass. She was arrestingly beautiful this way. He took a condom, ripped open the wrapper, and rolled it on. She was still lying completely still, one arm over her head, her other hand on her belly.

He put his hand on his cock and guided it in. Her hips started moving and she opened her eyes. He was transfixed, looking into her golden eyes, didn't look away for a millisecond, could see from her eyes that she enjoyed how he filled her. She was like warm silk around him, hot and wet, swollen following her orgasm. Actually he wanted to take her hard, selfishly, but he forced himself to be careful, not really knowing what she would accept or enjoy.

Her eyes focused a little and she smiled at him, a smile that lit up her face. She moved slightly, her legs still over the armrests, gloriously open.

"Is this alright?" he asked. "Is it uncomfortable? Should I put your legs down?"

Her smile became bold. She moved a little, rocked her buttocks, unexpectedly curvy, soft, and very feminine. He had to be careful; otherwise he would come way too soon.

She raised her legs from the armrests—she was as lithe as a cat, strong as a dancer—and wrapped them around his back so he was suddenly encircled by them. He started losing ground when her hoarse voice said, "Fuck me, David, hard."

She hadn't talked like that before. It was as if another Natalia had taken her over, a freer, bolder Natalia who released all the raw sensuality and passion he had suspected she kept bridled below that cool, professional exterior.

He thrust into her harder and she gasped. He did it again, the blood rushing to his cock, to her, to them. Again, harder. She blinked, raised her hips toward him, and he continued until he pumped into her so hard that he might have been concerned if he could have thought a single rational thought.

She murmured something, but he didn't hear what. Her nails tore at his back, her hands pulled him closer. David brought a hand between them. He stroked her, angled his hand, increased the pressure, and as she started to contract around him, as her long legs around his back squeezed tighter, he pushed himself deep into her and then exploded in an orgasm, a release that made everything go black. He didn't want this to end. No, he wanted time to stand still, to just let him stay here, surrounded by her legs and her warmth and, yes, her cunt.

And then Natalia's legs started shaking uncontrollably, and David pulled out, afraid he might faint if he didn't manage to sit up first. There was absolutely no blood in his head. He turned around, fell backward, and just breathed. Then he started laughing, a contented, satisfied, happy laugh, right out loud.

Natalia listened to David's laughter. She was completely limp. Not a single muscle would obey her. The sun caressed her body, and she moved lazily. "I'm going to be a nudist," she murmured.

She heard him laugh again, and his joy was contagious.

She had come twice. She had never believed in all that stuff about multiple orgasms and g-spots and men who knew what they were doing, but now she was a real convert.

David's deep laughter, so outrageously sexy, the images of what they'd just done, aroused her again. She studied his body, realizing that just now it was insatiable. Could two people really have chemistry like this? Silly question, clearly they could.

"What are you doing?" she asked.

"I think I'm dead."

"Is there anything to eat in this evil venture capitalist's lair?" she asked.

She was ferociously hungry, famished. It was very draining to be a sex goddess.

They ate well-seasoned little tapas-like things, turnovers and pies and rolls that smelled and tasted exotic.

"My cleaning lady's husband is a Persian chef," David explained.

"They live in the building and look after my apartment for me," he said. "She cleans and does the laundry; he gives me leftovers."

"These are some leftovers," she said.

As the evening cooled down, David led her to his bedroom one floor down, where they made love again. He was tender and rough. And then considerate and then forceful again. She was insatiable and smiled at the thought that she, Natalia De la Grip, was going to be stiff and sore tomorrow, from sex.

Afterward she lay completely still in his bed. All the bedding was clean and smelled nice, ironed and luxurious.

"This is the best bed in the whole world," she murmured.

He lay next to her, stroking her skin. He pulled down the sheet she had just pulled up to her chin. He studied her body as if she were a painting, a work of art. She lifted her hand and ran one finger down his upper arm. He was so muscular, and he made her feel so sublimely feminine.

"Did you always know you wanted to work in corporate finance?" he asked, and started stroking her hair, disentangling as he separated the locks across the pillow.

"I decided in London." She lay still, letting him attend to her. From time to time he kissed her, on the arm, on the shoulder.

"After the School of Economics?"

"Yes." She closed her eyes. After she got her degree, she had worked in New York for a year as a consultant. After that she had gone to Philadelphia and gotten an MBA from Wharton, the school that had educated some of the world's leading financial minds. And then the whole world had been open to her. She knew that David had gone to Harvard. But while her father had paid for her education, David must have paid his own way. She had never wondered what an education like that cost, never really thought about how much she had gotten for free.

"And then?" David's voice was just a low, sensual murmur, and she realized she had drifted off. Her hair was now spread out around her.

She opened her eyes. "The Bank of London headhunted me."

"They only recruit the best."

"Yes."

She had put in a few dog years in London, along with other promising young finance people. They worked around the clock, were owned by the bank, could be sent anywhere in the world at one hour's notice. A lot of them had jumped ship, fed up with the inhuman demands, but she'd loved it, loved finally being able to utilize all her abilities, being encouraged, being challenged, feeling like she was good at what she did. "I'm sure you know that more than ninety percent of the corporate finance world is men, right?" she said.

"No," he said, sliding his finger all the way from her neck down to her stomach. "I thought there was more gender equality than that."

"It starts out very equal, but the women disappear as you go along."

"Some people say that's because women are too smart to want to work that much," he said, lifting her hand and kissing her fingers, one by one.

"And other people say it's because women can't deal with hard work by their very nature," she retorted. "That what they want most of all is someone to take care of them."

She wondered how many times she'd heard her father say those exact words. And her mother always nodded in agreement. And said that gender equality had gone too far when women wanted to be exactly the same as men. And that that was why Jonas had left her, because she worked like a man.

"That's bullshit," David said. "The best women work twice as hard as the best men. It's going to change. I met some smart girls when I was teaching at the School of Economics. And more and more companies are waking up to the idea that women constitute a recruiting base they can't afford to overlook."

David sounded as if everything he was saying was irrefutable, and something happened in Natalia as she realized she had never before talked to a man who actually, truly thought the way she did, who didn't distinguish between female and male. It was a huge turn-on.

"When I was growing up, I used to love to talk about business and the family company," she said. "I used to force my brothers to debate different strategies for Investum. They hated it."

David picked up her hand and smelled her palm. "And why aren't you working at Investum now?" he murmured.

"I want to prove myself first on my own merits," she replied mechanically.

And if I can just show that I'm good enough, then Daddy will have to ask me.

He turned her hand over, kissed the back of it, nibbling a little. "And then you came back to Stockholm." He smiled. "Two years ago."

Natalia nodded; that information was no secret, just required a little Googling.

"J-O was hired on here to lead the Swedish office, and he brought me along." She'd moved from her apartment in London, which she'd shared with people she hardly ever saw because she spent so much of her time working and traveling. She and Jonas had gotten engaged in London; he'd commuted by plane from Sweden.

"My fiancé at the time lived in Stockholm."

"Not now?"

She turned her head to look at him. "Uh, no. I wouldn't be here if there was someone else." That question worried her a little. She had assumed David was single, but now she remembered with discomfort that she'd seen a picture in a gold frame of a beautiful blonde in his living room, a very attractive woman with the arm of a happy-looking David Hammar around her shoulders. It was common knowledge that David didn't have any family. Apparently he'd had a sister, but she'd died young in some accident, and his parents were dead. So who was that blond woman? And who—or what—was Natalia, herself, to him? Was she just David Hammar's little summer vacation fling while his beautiful blonde was off doing—what?

Natalia furrowed her brow. It shouldn't bother her this much. She hadn't done anything wrong and they hadn't agreed on anything more than just this: insanely good sex. If David had a little affair, that certainly wasn't her problem. But it actually did feel like a problem. How dumb could she be? Why hadn't she at least asked?

"What is it?" David asked.

"Nothing."

"No, you went somewhere else there for a second. Tell me." He watched her seriously.

She took a deep breath. Might as well say it. "I don't sleep around," she said. "And I hate infidelity. I don't know what this is between us, maybe it's just sex and maybe we don't need to talk about it. Maybe we don't need to say this, but . . . I'm not sleeping with anyone else."

David rested his head on his hand. He had beautiful eyes. Everything about him was stunning. Like a model. Although he was much more muscular, more like a construction worker. The girls at the boarding school must have been crazy about him.

"Natalia," he said, and then waited until their eyes met. "What the two of us have, I've never had with anyone else. I don't sleep around. Not more than any other guy, probably less. I don't know what this is, but I'm not seeing anyone else right now, okay?"

"Okay."

"And I'm not very fond of infidelity either," he added, gently running his hand over her forehead.

"Okay," she said, feeling ridiculously happy. She blinked and then suddenly yawned. "What time is it actually?" It was almost dark, and suddenly she felt completely drained.

"You must be tired," he said.

"I can't stay. I have to go home, change, pick up some things."

"I understand." He ran his hand over her hair, traced her eyebrow with a finger. God in heaven, that felt so good. She yawned again. She was really worn-out, physically and mentally.

"Stay," he said softly. "Don't go. Sleep for a bit. I can wake you up early if you want."

It was so tempting. And he did something with his voice, made it deeper and soothing, convincing, caring.

"Early," she said. "I can't go in late two days in a row."

"I promise."

Two seconds later she was asleep.

David kept his promise. He woke her so early that the dawn air coming in through the open window still smelled of dew. He was dressed in a T-shirt and light-colored slacks, and was freshly shaved, with his breath smelling of mint. He served her coffee, hot and strong, which she drank in bed. She took a long shower, pulled on her wrinkled clothes, and padded down to the kitchen. He buttered a slice of toast for her, refilled her coffee, and watched her skim the business section. Then he called for a car, handed her her purse, and said good-bye at the door. A firm hug, a quick kiss, and fifteen minutes later she was home in her own entryway.

19

David walked around his apartment after Natalia left. The memory of her laughter and their incredible sex lingered like an echo or a scent.

He hadn't planned on this happening, and it couldn't continue. This was pure insanity. The countdown continued around the clock.

Through dummy corporations and brokers, he and HC now owned enough Investum shares that someone *must* be starting to wonder. So many unknown shareholders, so much activity—it really should be setting off alarms, summer holidays or not. There couldn't be more than a week, ten days max, before someone raised a red flag. It didn't matter. They had known it would show up on the radar sooner or later. But with only twelve days left, less than two weeks, before they went public in the press, what he had just done was insane. Although it didn't *feel* insane.

It felt fucking fantastic.

David stopped in the living room. He looked at the photo in the gold frame. He hadn't thought about that. Had Natalia seen it? Had she wondered?

Probably. He should have realized when she'd started talking about infidelity.

There was so much he couldn't tell her, that she wouldn't understand, and that made him feel dirty, unworthy.

He liked Natalia; she wasn't some interchangeable stranger. She was a good person and an astoundingly, unbelievably sexy woman. Whom he couldn't seem to break up with even though there were so many reasons that he should.

He grazed the happy blonde's face with one finger. He had to call her, call Carolina; she was already mad that he'd pulled away. He had to take back control. This craziness with Natalia had to end.

That was the only right move.

Fuck.

20

Saturday, July 5

"We're not together, but we're sleeping with each other," Natalia said, straightening in her saddle. Her chestnut mare, Lovely, nickered softly. "So I actually have no idea. Is this how things work these days?"

Åsa, who was already seated in her saddle, her back straight, securely holding the reins of her light-gray horse, said, "You weren't born in the fifties, were you? Yes, this is how things work these days. In the twenty-first century. You test your way forward, step by step. Or sleep together and move on."

Natalia adjusted her position on her horse. She found this all terribly confusing. She peered around the countryside. The sheep were in the meadow with their lambs. The water glittered beyond the fields and pastureland. The yellow castle was to their right.

Peter and his wife had offered them an aperitif of sherry on the terrace before the meal, but Åsa and Natalia had been graciously permitted to go for a ride instead.

"When did people start doing things this way?" Natalia asked, urging Lovely on.

"He's still good in bed?" Åsa asked over her shoulder.

"Extremely."

"Can he carry on a conversation?"

"He's unparalleled. I've never met his match."

"Natalia, sweetie, can't you just wait and see where this goes?'

"I guess. I mean, it's not like I have any choice."

Natalia and David hadn't seen each other since she'd gone home Wednesday morning. It was Saturday now. David had sent her one message, but it had been a courteous, downright impersonal text message. Natalia had replied, and then he'd texted that he was going to be traveling for a few days. She hadn't asked where he was going, they hadn't been in touch, the weekend had arrived, and she was more confused than ever. Was it over now?

"Every time we see each other I get the feeling it's the last time. And then he contacts me and is totally amazing, and I have no idea what's going on."

"You're suddenly very dramatic," Åsa said. "You're not PMSing or something, are you?" Åsa was wearing a brand-new riding outfit and thus totally breaking with the age-old aristocratic custom of wearing worn, old clothing. She bought shiny new clothes and didn't give a hoot what people said about it.

"If you ask my family, I have PMS all the time," Natalia said bitterly and glanced up at the yellow façade. Gyllgarn was so beautiful, emotion caught in her chest when she looked at it. It had been in the family for three hundred years. Kings had slept in its rooms. Natalia had spent some of her best times here with the horses and animals and with the children who lived in the area. Peter had taken over running the place last year when he married Louise.

The whole family was here today, aside from Alexander, of course. Peter and Louise, Mom and Dad, and then Åsa, who was a member of the family in so many ways. Åsa's mother and Natalia's mother had been childhood friends, and their daughters—Åsa and Natalia—had become fast friends despite the four-year age difference. When Åsa's family died in a head-on collision, the then teenaged Åsa had moved into the De la Grip household. She had lived in the guest room, cried in Natalia's armchair, and snuck alcohol from the liquor cabinet. And now Åsa worked for Natalia's father. And joined them for dinner a few times a month, either out here at the family seat or at Natalia's parents' place in Djursholm.

"Hey, can I stay with you in Båstad?" Natalia asked. "J-O ordered me to go, but I can't live with my parents. Alex is coming and he always gets the guest room. And Louise is going to be tramping around in the flower beds, as usual, tallying up what she's going to inherit next."

"Louise has to be the most disagreeable person I've ever met," Åsa agreed. "Not even Peter deserves to be married to a battle-ax like that. Weird that she hasn't managed to get pregnant yet." Åsa fell silent and then gave Natalia an apologetic look. "Sorry," she said quickly. "That was insensitive. Just for that you can stay in my guesthouse. That can be your little love nest. Is he going?"

"David? I have no idea."

Because we don't discuss the future. Because this is what people do. And I think it's over. And I hate all this modern stuff.

"Wonder if he's bringing his thick-headed partner with him?"

"Oh my God, you two still haven't seen each other?"

"Why would we see each other? Did you hear something? Did David say something?"

"Why don't you just call him?"

"Bah. He can call me if he's interested," Åsa scoffed. "I've been dating all sorts of men, all week long. I don't have time to be interested in Michel." She adjusted her riding helmet and jutted out her chin. "And he doesn't seem interested either, does he?"

"Of course that might have something to do with your acting like a snobby bitch the last time he saw you," Natalia pointed out.

Åsa sneered. "All this sex you've been having hasn't improved your social skills," she said. "Michel was the one who was unpleasant, in case you didn't notice. He can contact me if he wants anything."

"What happened to living in the twenty-first century?"

"The twenty-first century is highly overrated, if you ask me."

Amen to that, Natalia thought. *Amen.*

There were six people around the dinner table. Appetizer, soup, entrée, and fruit.

"We're keeping it simple," Louise said smugly as the antique china, the polished-silver plate covers, and the local delicacies were served by an elderly woman from the area.

Peter was sitting next to their mother at the table, and Natalia could hear fragments of their conversation as she tasted the soup, which was actually exquisite. Of course, Louise hadn't made the food herself, but she had a good cook. The local population around Gyllgarn Castle contributed, as they had done for centuries, to their noble overlords' ability to live in comfort. It was like a holdover from feudal days, which had really only ended about half a century ago.

"He married some young thing," their mother said. "So now we have to put up with her coming to the party. It's so discourteous to force the rest of us to associate with that type of person."

Peter mumbled supportively. That's what Peter did best, agree. The conversation continued to revolve around who was coming to Båstad and was important enough to see. Relationships, marriages, and degrees of worthiness were debated. Peter's voice was quiet and conciliatory. As the food was served, Natalia heard the conversation take a different turn, from people and parties to the future. She braced herself. It wouldn't be long now before her mother had a go at her with the usual questions about her plans for the future, observations about committed relationships, and reminders that she wasn't getting any younger. If it hadn't been so annoying, Natalia would almost have found it comical how the conversation was the same every time.

"I never understood why Natalia and Jonas had to go their separate ways," Mother said with uncanny timing. She moistened her lips with the wine and set down her glass. Her blond hair shone. "They were such a good match," she said. She wasn't addressing anyone in particular. "All my friends agree. And I was so sorry to see it end."

Sometimes Natalia thought she must have been a disappointment to her mother from beginning to now. In elementary school, where her class had included one of the royal children but she had never succeeded in hanging out in the right circles. At boarding school, where she hadn't acted like the other girls, hadn't networked, hadn't gone to balls any more than absolutely necessary. In her professional life, where she had gotten a real job instead of taking a few fluff courses and pursuing a man with the right pedigree. The only time her mother had been proud of her was when she got engaged to Jonas. Her mother had taken the breakup personally and hadn't spoken to Natalia for several weeks after finding out. Her mother did that whenever anyone or anything displeased her. Froze them out and ignored them. It had always been that way—her mother punished her with silence, by withdrawing her love. There was no way to defend against that tactic, and it left its marks, creating small, hard-to-heal wounds.

"Yes, Natalia, bad on you for not still being together with Jonas," Åsa said loudly with a slight slur over the main course. "For the family's sake."

"That's my opinion," Natalia's mother said coolly. "And I'm entitled to it."

Åsa gave Natalia a look of encouragement. *Tell them*, her eyes urged. *Tell them why he dumped you. It was so beyond low of him.*

Natalia shook her head in warning.

Åsa emptied her glass and refilled it herself. Natalia clenched her silverware. The meal was almost over; then she could go home.

"I heard you had lunch with J-O," Peter said, turning to his father. Natalia perked up her ears.

"We discussed the merger," her father said, without looking at Natalia.

"You had a meeting without me?" Natalia asked. She put her hands in her lap. She watched her father with courteous attention, without giving away how trampled on she felt. By both her father and her boss.

She loved and admired her father, but he had done things like this a few times, and it was just as unpleasant each time. The last time had been two years ago. Natalia had applied for a prestigious management position at Svenska Banken, where her father was the chairman of the board. It was a position with a lot of responsibility that she'd been qualified for, but she hadn't gotten the job. She'd heard through the grapevine later that her father was the one who had prevented her from getting it. When she fished, her informant told her it was because she was a little too young and that they didn't want to play favorites just because of her name, but then the position had gone to a man who was only a few years older than she and a De la Grip cousin, no less. After that she decided to create a portfolio outside of Investum and accepted the job J-O offered her in Stockholm. She knew her father was from a different generation; she got that. She understood that on some level he just felt more comfortable talking to J-O, that it didn't have anything to do with her personally, but it still stung. And in purely professional terms, her father's attitudes hadn't done her career any favors either.

"I wasn't aware that I needed to tell you whom I meet with," her father said.

"Of course not," she replied as calmly as she could. "But this is my deal. I should have been informed. What did you discuss?"

Her father set down his silverware. "Why are you so damned worried about everything? If you can't handle big deals like this, then you shouldn't be working on them."

"I . . . ," Natalia began, but her mother interrupted her.

"That's exactly why I have always believed it's better for the men to deal with these matters," her mother said. She daintily dabbed the corners of her mouth with her linen napkin. "We ladies have our ways."

Louise smiled at her in agreement.

Åsa scoffed and caught Natalia's eye. They both hated this passive-aggressive side of femininity.

"Women are more emotional. That's just how it is," her mother stubbornly maintained. This was her favorite argument. That and the phrase "good sense." She looked at Louise, who nodded in agreement.

"I'm sure that feminists must be deeply unhappy women," her mother said. "Man-haters."

Louise sniggered and reached for her wineglass so that her large engagement and wedding rings sparkled. Natalia was sure her sister-in-law was deliberately showing them off—being married was hands down the highest achievement a woman could attain in Louise's worldview.

"I'm not particularly worried," Natalia began again. "Just careful, Daddy." She struggled to sound professional and levelheaded. "I want it to go smoothly. I hope you know that and will count on it." She smiled.

But her father seemed to be on the warpath. "There's a difference between being careful and being unsure. Sometimes you have to act, not just sit around staring at computer screens. Svenska Banken is strong. The Danes will make money off this merger. There's no reason to dillydally. I had lunch with J-O because I wanted him to assure me that a bunch of female hormones weren't going to get in the way when it really mattered." He curled his lip. "This is serious, Natalia, not some kind of make-believe on the Internet or YouTube." He banged his fist on the table, and she jumped. "These deals are real, the kind that build this country. I'm so tired of all that feminist nonsense. After all, we men have been at the helm for a long time, no matter what you modern ladies think you need to prove. Always the same goddamn nonsense."

Natalia chose to focus on her food for a moment. She knew that this idea of women at the top was a sensitive subject for her father, and she wanted to pick her battles.

A few years ago Svenska Banken's biggest competitor, Nordbank, had appointed a new CEO, Meg Sandberg. Her father had openly criticized the choice. He had made statements to the media about all the reasons she was a bad choice. Privately he'd also mocked and ridiculed her manly appearance, her garish fashion sense—not a lick of which had anything to do with her ability to run a company. Meg Sandberg, however, had proven worthy of her board of directors' faith in her, and the outspoken redheaded CEO with the gaudy fashion sense had shepherded Nordbank to great success. Natalia was sure that was one of the reasons her father was now pushing the merger that she and J-O were working on. Her father wanted Svenska Banken to retake its position as leader.

"I care just as much about Investum and Svenska Banken as anyone else here at the table," Natalia said. "I know what it means to you, Daddy. It's just as much in my blood and genes as yours and Peter's and Alex's." She smiled to take the edge off her words.

Åsa blinked and raised her glass in a silent toast, but Natalia's father wouldn't look at her, and Natalia was dangerously close to losing her composure if he kept ignoring her so blatantly. She should have known it was a bad idea to come here.

"I talked to the Danish chairman of the board," her father said to Peter. "He assured me personally that everything is going well. I'm not worried."

"So you didn't talk to just J-O over my head?" *How the fuck could he undermine her like this?*

Even Peter had the sense to look pained. If she didn't have Gustaf's support, at least outwardly, no one was going to trust her. She squeezed her wineglass.

"The last time I checked, I didn't need to ask your permission about anything," her father said, smirking, as if the conversation were a joke. Natalia was used to his domineering tactics, used to meeting men like him and dealing with them. But when it was her own family, it always brought up a bunch of emotions.

"No," she said. "But it is my deal. I am leading the project, and it's a little strange for you to go over my head." With one of the biggest efforts in her life, she gave him a friendly, albeit stiff smile. "What did you promise him?"

"Stop it. There's nothing more to discuss."

"Darling, can't you talk shop after we gals have left the table?" Mother pleaded. She looked at Natalia. "All of this, really, I think it's gone too far."

"All of this?" Natalia said sharply.

"Women have to be women," her mother said. "Everyone can't be the same, that's all I'm saying. Don't you see how you're blowing this all out of proportion and disrupting our dinner? Women's rights have gone too far."

"Seriously, Mother, how can women's rights have gone *too* far?" Natalia asked. "Too much equality, Mother? For whom?"

"Am I somehow no longer entitled to my own opinion?" Ebba De la Grip asked, looking around. "Everything used to be so lovely. The men dealt with the business world, went hunting, and got to be men. And women were women. I don't understand why things can't continue that way."

Natalia had hated this her whole life, that the men stayed at the table and talked shop while the women retired to the living room to discuss caterers and preschools. It was like living in the 1800s.

"It's a lovely tradition," her mother continued.

Louise leaned forward and patted Ebba's hand.

Natalia didn't say anything else; there was no point. She'd been fighting this battle her whole life. She looked over at Peter, but he avoided making eye contact. He would never defend her against their father. Louise sneered and mumbled something that Ebba nodded to. Ebba and Louise were in complete agreement that women quite simply were not biologically suited for business.

Natalia waited while the table was cleared. Åsa had sunk into introspective silence. Mother and Louise talked in subdued, feminine voices. Father was saying something that Peter was listening to attentively. Natalia glanced at her brother and then at her sister-in-law.

They were seated far apart, as if they didn't really belong together. Natalia thought Louise had blossomed after her marriage to Peter. It was as if Louise had been waiting her whole life to become a lady of the manor, to organize hunting and fishing trips, to supervise the art collection, and tend to the cultural heritage. But Peter looked tired, worn-out. As if he were always trying to keep up, but wasn't quite up to it. He worked in the city with Father, commuted all the way back out to Gyllgarn in the evenings. They had a lot of social obligations, their home often appeared in prestigious lifestyle magazine spreads, and Louise was known for her dinners and parties. Louise was living her dream, but sometimes Natalia wondered if Peter were paying the price for her keeping up appearances.

"David Hammar is in town again," Peter said suddenly, and Natalia paid closer attention. Peter tugged on his tie and said, making a face, "I saw him the other day."

Father furrowed his brow but didn't say anything.

Natalia's heart did an uncomfortable summersault. It wasn't by any means the first time David Hammar had been discussed in the family home, but before he'd always been just one of a crowd of nouveau-riche upstarts who were despised and bad-mouthed. Not a person Natalia had slept with. Not a man she'd been so nakedly intimate with. She glanced over at Åsa, who just shrugged.

"God, he's so vulgar," Louise said.

"A damned parasite," Father said. "He has never known his place."

"Darling, didn't we go to Skogbacka with him?" Louise asked Peter, her face twisted in spite. This was what David had encountered, every day, at the boarding school, Natalia thought. Scorn and innuendo.

"He was there on a scholarship. A charity case," Peter said.

"His mother worked at some bar," Louise said. "And she was sleeping with the headmaster." She sniffed scornfully. "So horribly low class."

Peter shook his head. "He never grasped the rules."

"He's done quite well for himself," Natalia said sharply. She flashed Louise a poisonous look. "And surely he's not responsible for what his mother did or didn't do."

Louise raised an eyebrow but didn't say anything.

"He lines his own pockets on the backs of decent people," Father said. "Even worse. He plunders companies that other people built."

"He operates on the same terms as everyone else," Natalia pointed out. "And he's good at what he does."

"He's unscrupulous and shortsighted. You don't have to be particularly good at anything for that."

"Some people aren't worth wasting your energy on," her mother said. "That beastly man is one of them. Let's not sully this lovely dinner that Louise has arranged any more now."

"But . . . ," began Natalia.

"That will do, Natalia," her father interrupted tersely.

Natalia blinked. But it wouldn't help to get angry—she never won. And it was her against them all. Not even Åsa got involved in these types of debates. *Screw them all.*

"It's sad when people like him are allowed to come in and ruin things, that's all I mean," Louise said in her insipid voice. Feminine and vapid. The way women were supposed to be, if you asked upper-class men. Harmless fools who froze out the people they didn't like and never took a stand for anything important. Natalia couldn't help thinking of how David had talked business and gender equality with her.

"As usual, you don't know what you're talking about, Louise," Åsa said suddenly and loudly. She shook her head, as if she'd had enough. "I don't understand how you can stand to be so dense."

"I'm just saying out loud what we're all thinking," Louise said, red blotches appearing on her neck. Her eyes darted around; she moistened her lips but didn't back down. "Some people have no style, no finesse. And I think that's clear from the beginning. That's just the way it is. It's inborn. There's a difference between proper folk and, well, people like him."

Peter looked down at his plate, his facial expression impossible to interpret. Natalia wondered if he was as weary to the core of these conversations as she was. But she never knew what Peter thought; they hadn't been close to each other for many years.

When she was little, she had hung the moon on her big brother. He was six years older, and she had looked up to him a lot as a child. Alex had been born only a year after Natalia, and in a way she and Alex had become allies as Peter disappeared more and more with each passing year, until it felt like they were more strangers now than siblings.

Father's face was expressionless, as usual. But he didn't need to say anything. No one needed to say anything. Natalia still knew what they were all thinking. Sometimes all this silent communication was so uncomfortable that she just wanted to scream. Her mother sat motionless, just waiting for them to return to the pleasantries. Louise smiled, Peter cleared his throat and praised the food, and then they did what they usually did: carried on as if nothing had happened. Natalia gave up.

After dinner, coffee, and brandy, Åsa decided to spend the night, but Natalia wanted to go home. She said good-bye, hugged Åsa, took one last look up at the beloved yellow façade, and then started her car. It would take her a while to recover from this family dinner.

David was restless. He had spent his entire Saturday with Carolina, taken a valuable day and seen her. She'd been happy, and he felt a little less guilty. Now he was back in the office again, trying to make up for lost time, even though it was Saturday night and, honestly, there wasn't much he could do now. Michel was out with his parents at their suburban villa, and the office was totally empty.

David glanced at the phone but didn't have any messages. Or at least none from Natalia. But he hadn't been expecting one either. He'd been intentionally short with her, and it was probably all over now, he presumed, just as he'd planned. It just felt so incomplete, so damned unsatisfying. He scrolled through his contacts. Dialed her. He decided that if she didn't answer after three rings, he would hang up.

"Damn it, hang on, let me plug in my headset," he heard. And then, "Yes?"

"Natalia?"

Long silence. "Hi, David," she said as if she couldn't decide if she was happy, surprised, or something else. "Sorry, I thought you were my boss."

David glanced at his watch. It was almost eleven. "You did? Does he usually call you this late on a Saturday night?"

"Well, you know J-O," she said sarcastically. "What do you think?"

"You're right. Did I wake you?"

"No. I'm in my car. I was with my folks. Although actually we were at my brother's place."

David pictured the yellow building, remembered his helicopter trip. "The castle?"

"Yeah, although we don't call it a castle. We call it an estate." Short silence, quiet laugh. "Sorry, I can't believe how arrogant that sounded. I mostly go there to ride my horse. My family is just a part of the deal."

Outwardly the De la Grip family was known for their unity, but something in Natalia's voice told David that their relationships were more complicated than that.

"You ride?" he asked, although he knew she was an expert equestrian. There was something about the thought of Natalia in high, shiny boots and spurs that made his blood flow faster.

She laughed, a low laugh that made him remember how she had writhed beneath him, gyrating under his body, so amazingly hot.

"Yes, David. I ride." Her voice was low, and the double entendre wasn't lost on him.

"I don't know if this is the wrong thing to say, but the idea of you in riding boots turns me on. Do you have some of those tight pants, too?"

"Very tight," she said slowly.

He pictured her long, strong legs, her round, full buttocks. "What are you wearing?" he asked in a deep voice.

"Fuck," she muttered.

"What happened?"

"I'm going 85 mph. I can't have phone sex."

He sat up, suddenly thinking very clearly. "That's over the speed limit. Could you slow down a little?"

"It's fine, you just took me by surprise is all."

"Have you been drinking? Do you want me to come pick you up somewhere?" The worry was so automatic that he didn't think, just spoke.

"I wasn't drinking, and I'll be home soon."

"Okay," he said. "Drive safely."

"Oh, David, I do everything safely," she said, her voice like a soft, seductive melody. God, he loved it when she flirted with him.

No more now. Hang up.

"I just wanted . . . ," David began, but couldn't think of anything sensible to say. He shouldn't have called. He knew that. "I was thinking about you," he finally said, quietly and honestly. *Dumb, so dumb*.

It went completely quiet.

"David?" She almost exhaled his name, and David could sense her pressing the phone to her ear.

"What?"

"I'm not so used to this stuff, so I don't know if I should say this, but I'll be home soon. I've had an awful evening. Do you want to come over?" She breathed quietly, and he thought he heard the faint rumble of her car engine. "I want that," she said. "No matter what is or isn't going on between us, I want you to know that. I want to see you. Again."

Oh, fucking hell. Of all the things she could have said, that was the worst. He debated with himself. And lost by a mile. "I'll be over in an hour," he said.

21

Peter lay awake for a long time after Natalia went home. After Åsa and his parents had said good night and withdrawn. Long after Louise had fallen asleep next to him.

He couldn't shake the feeling of unease.

The feeling of impending doom had begun when he saw David Hammar during rush hour the previous Friday.

He stared at the antique stucco ceiling, not knowing if it was his imagination. It scared him, how little he could rely on his feelings, how he mostly didn't feel anything.

Although that wasn't true either, he thought, rolling over. It was a hot, stuffy night, and of course the house didn't have any air-conditioning. He did feel some things. The problem was just that everything was so darned uncomfortable and he did what he could to avoid it. Unfortunately, he couldn't choose which feelings to suppress, so he lost them all.

He remembered when he'd started at Skogbacka. He had thought it would work out, that he would land on his feet, that he would get to start over, leave the misery of elementary and middle school behind him and finally fit in.

But he'd never had an easy time making friends, and that hadn't changed just because he started at Skogbacka. There was hazing from the older students. Even though that was just a part of it, it had been tough. You were on your own in those situations. Everyone had to go through that humiliation on their own. "You have to bite the bullet, Peter," his father had said the one time he'd made the mistake of calling home, crying. "Don't cry like a fucking girl."

After that, Peter just put up with it, did everything that was expected of him. Strangely enough, you could get used to anything.

And then it had been his turn.

New students came, and he wasn't the youngest anymore. David Hammar had been one of the new ones; even back then he'd been tall, with angry eyes, a childhood unlike anyone else's, and those rumors about his mother sleeping around. David didn't stand a chance from the start. The initiation rites had begun, and even today it startled Peter how quickly his cohort, who had been victimized the previous year, became the agressors. Especially him.

But that was all just part of boarding school, he thought, explaining it away in his head, apologizing just as he'd done his entire life. It didn't make you a bad person. Everyone understood that.

Except for David Hammar, of course.

That outsider never had the sense to just bear the humiliation and shut up. David had refused to follow all the social codes that Peter observed to the letter. And Peter remembered how angry and deceived he had felt, almost personally violated. Who did David think he was? A charity case, a working-class boy attending the school on a scholarship—how did he have the balls to think he was better than anyone else? Peter didn't remember how it had happened, but he had decided he was going to break that guy, not least because the girls at the boarding school were crazy about him.

Even Louise.

Peter glanced at his sleeping wife. Even in her sleep Louise was the perfect woman: tranquil, quiet, and fresh.

Louise probably didn't think Peter knew it, but he'd overheard her talking about David at a party. He'd seen her eyes beam with arousal as she spoke about that tall working-class boy.

And Peter had seen how mortified she'd been when her approaches had been rejected.

Strange that he hadn't thought about that before. He'd forgotten the whole thing, but the memory had resurfaced when the subject of David came up at dinner, as he listened to how Louise poured her scorn over David Hammar.

Peter had never been sure he was good enough for Louise, so he had been astonished when she chose him in the end. She had been with some of his buddies before the two of them got together. Everyone had considered Louise a catch, and he'd proposed without reflecting on anything other than the fact that he had been tremendously lucky to land a woman like that: blond, cool, and with exactly the right pedigree. He had always been awkward around women. He didn't really get them, just knew that you needed to earn a lot of money and be successful; otherwise they would look down on you.

He moved a little in the bed, ran his hand over his pajama bottoms. It had been a long time since they'd had sex, but honestly he just hadn't wanted it as much. Could that be age already? He was only thirty-five, and he wasn't particularly happy in his marriage. Maybe he ought to care about that more, but ultimately Peter wasn't really sure he deserved to be happy, not after what he'd done. He pulled his hand back, didn't even feel like jerking off. And if Louise should wake up . . . She would probably vomit.

He sighed. His thoughts returned to David Hammar again.

He'd attacked David with all his strength at Skogbacka, with all his bitterness and envy and frustration, hadn't even known he had that much emotion inside.

The consequences had been disastrous.

Oh, how they'd harassed David, how it had escalated.

And then . . .

No, he wouldn't think about that. He couldn't; it would make it almost impossible to breathe. That's why it was better to try to forget. Actually he wanted to get up, light a cigarette, and smoke, but he wasn't up to explaining that to Louise.

He blinked, trying to urge sleep to come, but there didn't seem to be any chance. Maybe this was just about the merger? As soon as the deal was done, his father would retire, withdraw, and turn everything over to Peter, the eldest, the dutiful son.

Then he would be the CEO. That would be the crowning achievement of his career, proof that he was good enough. Everyone who had ever whispered that he only got his job because of his name would be silenced. Everything would be better then.

Peter turned and stared out the window.

Maybe inner peace was too much to hope for. But he really wanted to be rid of the baggage he carried around all the time, all the memories he could never share with anyone, all the stuff that sometimes made him feel like he was losing it.

It would start to get light out in a few hours. Sweden had so many hours of daylight in the summer. Maybe that was why he couldn't sleep?

Louise mumbled in her sleep, and he studied her. He decided he would talk to her if she woke up. But she didn't, and he knew that he could never undo what had been done. The best he could hope for was to forget. He'd been trying to forget for almost two decades.

He would try even harder.

Eventually it would have to get easier.

22

Natalia was like a drug to him. David couldn't describe it any other way.

He couldn't think clearly.

Or he didn't want to.

Because somewhere inside himself, even as he climbed into the taxi and gave the driver Natalia's address, David knew that if he were thinking clearly he would not continue this relationship. Not with everything that was on the line. Investum stock was changing hands at an exponentially increased rate now. Five of the biggest brokerage firms were ready. They had bought shares for Hammar Capital under various dummy corporations and would sign over ownership to him the moment they received word.

Legally he was operating in murky territory, he thought, as he watched the city go by outside the cab. It wasn't strictly illegal, but it was definitely unethical, and it would make a lot of people in the financial world hit the roof, especially those following their own double standard. All of David's backers had come through with the funds they'd promised, which meant that Hammar Capital now had a staggering hundred billion Swedish kronor at its disposal. Without a doubt this was the biggest takeover ever in Sweden, maybe in all of Europe. It would be on the front page of the *Wall Street Journal*, and their renown would reverberate well beyond the financial sector.

It was actually inconceivable that nothing had leaked yet. Indeed, no one besides David and Michel had the whole picture. And it just wasn't imaginable that anyone would go after Investum, the backbone of the nation. The finance world had its unwritten rules, and

David was poised to break pretty much all of them. He would succeed. David felt that in every fiber and cell of his being. They would force Investum to its knees. The giant would bleed and fall. The history of Swedish business would be divided into before and after this event.

He needed a clear head for this, to be able to focus on the complexity of what they were doing.

So he couldn't have his head full of Natalia this way, couldn't drift off into thoughts about sex and laughter and some strange emotion he wouldn't name.

So *one last time*, he told himself, as the cab stopped on her quiet street and he paid. That was what this was. He would be with her one last time, end this as nicely as he could, and then he would be free. With precision and focus. That was all this was about. Ending it.

There was no alternative.

None.

He called up from the front door and was buzzed in, took the stairs, couldn't bear the thought of standing still in the elevator. His heart hammered and his blood coursed, and when Natalia opened the door he buried himself in her, put his hands on her cheeks, kicked the door shut behind him, and pushed her against the wall with his kiss. She gasped and caught fire in his embrace. He pulled on her tight pencil skirt, tugging it up over her thighs, tore her panties to the side. She was wet when he cupped his hand over her.

"David," she breathed.

He inhaled the scent of her. She pushed herself against his hand. She was so easy to read, and he stroked her until she came, fast and hard, almost furiously against his hand. She clung to his neck with her skirt around her hips and her satiny heat convulsing around his fingers. They panted against each other's skin, and when he wrapped a hand around the back of her head, she was sweaty. He unbuttoned her blouse without a word, pulled her bra down, and laid a hand over one breast.

She took a deep breath and said in a wobbly voice, "Would you like to come in?"

He almost laughed, realizing they were still just inside her front door. "I really would," he said.

She pulled her skirt back down over her hips, took his hand, and led him down the hallway to a door.

It was a bedroom, which smelled clean and like Natalia.

The bed was made, white sheets, so very erotic in all their chastity.

"We've had sex on your sofa," he said. "And in the front hallway and on your balcony, but this is actually the first time I've seen your bedroom."

"I know," she said, undoing her bra and letting it drop to the floor. "I've never experienced anything like this before." She stepped out of her skirt and panties, and stood there, poised, naked, graceful.

She helped him off with his T-shirt, ran her palms over his chest, then over his upper arms. She looked determined, so David let her proceed, knowing he would get to do what he wanted with her soon. She unbuttoned his pants, pulled down the zipper, and stroked him with the same intense seriousness. He saw her breathing speed up, saw the heat sweep over her, coloring her pale skin pink. He closed his eyes as she curled a hand around him. "I've been longing to have you inside me," she said hoarsely.

He raised an eyebrow. "Rough day?"

She nodded. "Do you have protection?"

He pulled out the packet he'd brought.

She lay down on the bed, stretched out. Those long limbs, her arms over her head, one leg over the edge of the bed, the other pulled up, completely unashamed.

Never in his life had he put a condom on so quickly. He lay down on top of her, spread her legs, clasped both of her hands in one of his, and pushed, pressed, plowed into her. Her hips flew up; he placed one of her legs over his shoulder and then took her until he was close. She looked like she was almost there.

He brought a hand between them and stroked her.

"Natalia?"

"Mmm," she mumbled.

"Are you with me?"

"I think so. This is so nice." Her voice was husky. He studied her, so very close to coming.

"Can you look at me?"

She opened her golden eyes and looked at him through a veil of arousal. He thrust into her, pressing with his hand at the same time. Her eyes glazed over.

"Don't disappear," he commanded and did it again. And again. He watched her orgasm begin, felt it in her body, and when she contracted around him, squeezing him with her internal muscles, he came too. He didn't look away, loved watching her come just as he pushed into her one last time, buried himself, and exploded inside her.

He tried to catch his breath. Realized he needed to move, that he was too heavy. And then he shifted off her and collapsed on the spacious bed.

They lay next to each other, gasping for breath. His senses began to come back online, one by one. The scent of the room. The light from the window. The silence of the neighborhood.

"I'm glad you came," she said.

"I'm glad *you* came. Twice."

She laughed, and he stretched out his arm as she rested her head on his chest. It felt good to have her there.

"This is nice," she said, resting her hand on his rib cage.

"Better than nice," he said emphatically and pulled her in closer. She was sweaty, and her long hair twisted around them both.

"I was so glad you called," she said, and he knew he ought to defend himself against the warmth in her voice, felt himself being pulled out to sea.

But instead he candidly said, "I was glad you invited me over. You didn't have a good time at your folks' place?"

She exhaled against his chest. "At my brother's place. He took over the house last year. He and his wife."

"Louise, right? I've met her." David vaguely remembered a chilly blond woman. Girls like that had been a dime a dozen back at Skogbacka. "You said you go there to ride? Do you have your own horse?"

She nodded.

Of course she did.

"Do you ride?" she asked.

He laughed at the absurd question. "No. I don't even like horses. I don't like the countryside, and I don't like horses. And besides, they're a bad investment. I only pursue things that pay off."

"You're lying. You like to read, you gave me tickets to Sarah Harvey, and you bought me a hot dog. I don't think you're as hard-nosed and tough as you want to appear."

If only she knew.

"I love horseback riding," she continued. "It demands all your attention. You can't think about anything else. You know, they say you have to fall off at least a hundred times to be a good rider?"

"Are you good?"

"Yes."

He could picture her, purposeful after a fall, covered in dirt, joints stiff but determined to get up again and keep going. "I suppose that's true of most things," David mused. "You have to be competitive, to hate losing."

"Oh, how I hate to lose," she said so emphatically that he laughed. He felt the same way.

She ran her hand over his chest and stomach, tracing the contours of his abs with her finger. "So, if you don't ride, how do you get your exercise?" she asked. "Or are you just naturally super muscular?" She put a hand on his thigh.

"I run," he mumbled. "And I play tennis, mostly with clients." Her hand moved.

"Do you play tennis?" he asked. He would really like to see her in a short, white skirt. His cock jumped. She studied it and smiled, filling him with anticipation. When was the last time he'd had this much energy?

"I'm an upper-class girl. I play tennis, and enjoy horseback riding and skiing. Although I draw the line at golf."

"I play soccer," he said.

"Soccer?" She stroked his thigh, and he forced himself to focus on the conversation.

"Yes," he said. He actually never talked about this, not with business contacts, not with the press. It was too private. But now he heard himself telling Natalia, "Michel and I coach a youth team northwest of Stockholm." It was far out, in one of the really rough neighborhoods, and it felt good. And very, very private. "I'm actually quite good at soccer." He wanted her to remember that. That he did at least one unselfish thing in this world.

Her hand stopped moving. "You should be careful, David," she murmured. "Soon you'll have me believing you're not an evil venture capitalist at all."

He pulled her briskly to him, under him, and moved over her. He looked deep into her eyes, and as he kissed her, he knew that if his goal in coming over here had been to get over Natalia De la Grip, then he'd really been deluding himself. "I don't know if I can handle letting you go quite yet," he mumbled.

"That's totally fine," she smiled, and they kissed again. Her tongue was so warm and lively. But when her hands slid around his back, he stiffened and tried to pull away.

But she didn't let go; she spread her hands and fingers out, covered his whole back and refused to be brushed aside. "No," she said.

David gave her a look of warning, but Natalia shook her head, stubbornness making her eyes burn. "I want to," she said with determination. One finger traced a rough scar, and David felt a wave of discomfort.

"Lie on your stomach," she said. Her eyes bored into him.

He looked at her for a long time. She was going too far, coming too close.

Natalia looked at the serious expression on David's face and knew he was planning to refuse her. Their eyes locked in a battle of wills. She saw emotions flickering over his face, emotions she chose not to analyze.

She just persisted and decided not to cave.

"Natalia," he said in warning.

"No," she repeated. Hadn't she just told him how strong-willed she was? She wasn't planning on backing down now.

And suddenly he was shaking his head. "Stubborn woman," he muttered, but he obediently rolled over so he was lying on his stomach.

Good Lord.

His back was in a ghastly state. "Who did this?" she asked quietly. There were so many scars, it was impossible to even count them. How long did it take to whip someone like this?

"It wasn't just one person."

She waited.

"It was at school," he sighed and she knew he was talking about Skogbacka. Skogbacka Grammar School, framed in greenery . . . With its notorious bullying, the scandals. And that was only what had reached the press—Natalia knew that was probably just a fraction of it. Suddenly she regretted insisting, wasn't sure she could bear to hear the truth. She realized the scars didn't hurt anymore, but she wanted to caress them, ease the pain that must have been unbearable at one time.

"I had a hard time adjusting to the hierarchy," he said, his head resting on his cheek on the mattress. His voice was calm, sounded totally unaffected. "I refused to allow them to humiliate me—you know, with their baptism by fire and all that shit. It went on a long time. My attitude really bugged them, my being different." He shrugged. "I was sixteen and so fucking arrogant, and of course that made it all worse. One day they tricked me into going down into the basement. I was supposed to be punished for something I'd done that they hadn't liked. There was a soundproof room down there. They whipped me and left me there. For a long time. The wounds didn't heal the way they were supposed to."

"What happened to them?"

"What do you think?"

"Nothing. It was hushed up?"

He nodded.

First David's schoolmates had taught him that he was inferior to them, just because they went to these ridiculous dinners in tuxes and drove sports cars while he was poor, and then they had physically abused him for daring to stand up for himself.

Natalia had never been as ashamed of belonging to her social stratum as she was now, but she decided not to press him any further, suspected she had already gotten significantly more out of him than he usually revealed.

She followed his big body with her eyes. David Hammar was so much more than his scar-covered back. His arms swelled, and his shoulders spread across her bed, and she knew she would really like to have him here more often, much more often. She ran a hand over his back, felt him inhale, slid her palm downward, smiled at how his firm buttocks tensed under her fingers. She cupped her hand, heard him gasp for breath before she continued down over his hips and thighs. He moaned, and that deep sound spoke directly to her body. If David had gone to her school, she—and all the other girls, Natalia just *knew*—would have been crazy for him. And for the moment he was hers.

"Turn over," she ordered.

He turned over. His weight rocked the bed, and a wave of desire coursed through her as he obeyed.

David made himself comfortable on his back. She wound up beside him.

She placed a hand on his thigh. "Spread your legs," she commanded.

His eyes narrowed, but he did as she said without taking his eyes off her for a second. He was hard, and she kneeled between his legs—one hand by his hip and the other encircling his arousal—and took him into her mouth. He gasped.

She feasted on the sensation of hardly being able to fit him in her mouth, sucking and licking without any shame at how much she was enjoying this. She kept going until David seemed to have had enough of the passive role. He sat up and laid her down on the bed. She watched as he rolled on a new condom and entered her. Her legs flew up around his back, and he tugged her to him.

It was crazy hot.

The lovemaking. His body pumping into her, the sounds, the words. And when she came, now with him behind her, in her, with her, with his enormous hands around her waist and his kisses on the nape of her neck and then, later, with his arms around her, close together, with salt and sweat and scents, she knew it was rare, really rare, that you experienced something completely new, and if she hadn't been so happy she would have cried. She just curled up against him, allowed him to pull her into his embrace, surrounded by his body. Their violent passion now replaced by tenderness, she lay completely still and tried, really tried to just be, to live in the present.

But her mind wouldn't let her be.

What were they actually to each other? Were they a couple? Were they in love?

"David?"

"Yes," he murmured in his deep voice.

She wanted to ask, *What kind of a relationship is this? Are you my boyfriend? My lover?* But she didn't dare. Didn't want to hear a lie, couldn't brave asking for the truth. *You're a coward, Natalia, such a pitiful coward.*

She rubbed her cheek against the arm he had wrapped around her. "I'm really glad you came over," was all she said.

His arms hardened around her. "Me too. Can I stay?"

"Yes, stay," she said.

"I have to work tomorrow. Or I guess it's today already."

"It's Sunday."

"I know," he said, pulling the sheet up over her and kissing the back of her neck.

They slept, cuddled together.

She woke up when he emerged from the shower. Still half asleep, she flung her arms around him. He was still wet, and they made love again before he said good-bye with a kiss on the tip of her nose.

"Bye, my sex goddess."

"Bye."

She stayed in bed.

She was falling. She could feel it in every fiber of her body and soul.

Careful, Natalia.

She couldn't go back to sleep, so she padded out to the kitchen. The coffee maker was out, and she smiled when she saw that David had prepped it for her. She pushed the ON button and waited patiently. She heated some milk, poured in some sugar, and took her mug out to the balcony.

She looked down at the empty street and the little park where a neighbor was walking his dog. She sipped her coffee and thought about her night. And then a thought hit her, one she could hardly bear to pursue. Something she wished had never occurred to her, something that David's story had brought to mind.

She drank her coffee and thought about her family: her parents, her brothers.

Peter was her big brother, and she loved him, but despite his appeasing, almost weak style, he wasn't always a nice person. He could be awful, particularly to his siblings and to anyone he had power over. He had spoken of David with scorn. And no matter how reluctant she was to admit it, she knew that Peter was a typical bully, tyrannized by Father, pressured to perform, capable of cruelty. And he had been at Skogbacka at the same time as David.

Had Peter had anything to do with the scars on David's back?

23

Sunday, July 6

Count Carl-Erik Tessin glanced at the invitation. He received so many that he didn't always open them. Piles of letters and invitations to everything from premieres and art exhibits to parties and balls. Summer was the worst.

He just tossed most of them. But he recognized this coat of arms, and it brought back so many memories, so many emotions.

He fingered the heavy, expensive paper, read the black lettering, the more formal sections embossed with gold, that arrogant signature.

Carl-Erik rarely said yes, especially not to this specific party, but this time he hesitated. It had been so long. The years passed. There was so much he regretted, so many things he should have done differently.

He looked at the two happy faces in the antique frame on the mantelpiece. They had no idea. They were satisfied with their lives. Should he leave the past alone? Could he?

He slowly pulled the desk drawer open, selected a fountain pen.

He responded ceremoniously.

Maybe it was best this way after all.

Alexander De la Grip looked around at the little airport, full of people, but no welcome committee, no parents, no cousins, nothing at all.

Thank God for that.

Out of the corner of his eye, Alexander saw a tall, redheaded woman waiting by the baggage claim. She'd been on his flight from New York as well. He smiled to think that here they were now, at the same small Swedish airport.

He'd noticed her because she was almost unbelievably beautiful, tall and stately like an Amazon. She'd turned down the drink he'd wanted to buy her. And she'd dropped a comment about his drinking that wasn't all that flattering, so he assumed she hadn't exactly fallen for him.

She was clutching her purse with short, unpainted nails, and he wondered what she was doing here. They had spoken English on the plane, and it hadn't occurred to him she might be anything other than American. But here she was at a small airport in southern Sweden.

"I didn't realize you were Swedish," he said, sidling up next to her.

She looked confused. "Excuse me?" she said in English.

He switched over to his own flawless English. "We met on the plane. I'm Alexander," he said, holding out his hand.

She looked at his outstretched hand for such a long time that he thought she wasn't going to shake it.

"Isobel," she said finally, grasping his hand quickly before pulling hers back again.

Alexander smiled his most charming smile.

A tattered Samsonite appeared on the luggage belt, and he could tell from her eyes that it was hers. He picked it up and handed it to her.

She took a firm hold of it while he lifted the first of his hand-stitched calf-leather suitcases off the belt.

"Can I offer you a lift somewhere?" he asked.

She wrinkled her straight nose and looked at his luxurious baggage, which continued to tumble onto the luggage belt. She stretched her back, becoming even taller in her flats. She glared at him and said, "I'd prefer it if you went and fucked yourself." She picked up her worn suitcase, turned on her heel, and left him.

24

It was a five-hour drive from Stockholm to Båstad—if you didn't make any unnecessary stops and weren't a stickler about speed limits. It was faster to fly, of course. But in a car Michel and David could talk undisturbed, without having to worry about anyone overhearing. What they lost in terms of time, they gained in privacy. Besides, apparently David had bought himself a new car.

Michel looked at the car, one of Bentley's most expensive sports models, if he wasn't mistaken. "Isn't it a little early for a midlife crisis?" he asked, opening the trunk. He stuffed his bags inside and slammed it shut.

"It was the only one they had that I could get on the spot," David said casually. "I wanted to own a car."

"You never mentioned that before." Actually David had always claimed it didn't make any sense for him to own his own car since he was so rarely home. And unlike Michel, who loved expensive luxury goods, David wasn't ostentatious.

David jingled his keys. "Nah, I decided to do it yesterday. I headed over to the Marble Halls showroom and bought it on my lunch break."

Michel just stared. He was well acquainted with the fashionable and ultra expensive Marble Halls. Located since the 1920's on Grev Turegatan, one of Stockholm's most expensive addresses, the automobile showroom was a well-known address to him. Actually Michel liked to go there every now and then, to check out the sportscars, to soak in the atmosphere. But as far as he knew, David had never shared this interest.

"They handed me the keys on the spot." David grinned. "What do you think?"

Michel wondered if his boss and colleague was starting to feel the strain after all. For as long as Michel had known him, David had *never* done anything impulsive or impetuous. David's brain worked with extreme speed. He was a master at processing information, and it sometimes looked like he was being impulsive, but Michel knew better. David never did anything without thinking it through carefully.

Aside from buying a car worth a million and a half kronor, apparently. In baby blue.

"It's very, uh, blue."

"Hop in, let's go. Did you talk to Malin?"

Michel nodded. Yes, right before he'd left the office. He could hear Malin Theselius yelling all the way to the elevator.

"She's a little miffed that we're leaving her at home," he said, seriously understating the situation. Their communications director had been as angry as a hornet. "Apparently she'd already bought clothes for the party. I didn't quite catch the last bit of what she said, but I think she might be expecting an extra-large Christmas bonus now."

David started the car, and its powerful engine rumbled to life. "I know, she e-mailed me a whole list of reasons why she should come to Båstad, but she's needed here. Everyone else had to stay here too."

The mood in the office had been anything but merry, but David was right, Michel thought. Still, he was glad that he didn't have to be the one who killed democracy at Hammar Capital. "We'll just hope there's no mutiny back at headquarters while we're off enjoying ourselves in Båstad," he said. "There will be journalists there. You know how they hound you; Malin could have helped you screen."

"Malin has to prepare the press release, and she knows that," David said. "I can screen journalists myself. But I canceled our hotel room and rented a house instead."

"Good, it'll be quieter that way," Michel agreed. No risk of running into curious journalists or drunk young finance guys who wanted to chat about what they really thought of venture capitalists, self-made men, and dark-skinned foreigners.

* * *

David drove out of Stockholm, onto Essingeleden highway and then southward. The car trip passed quickly—they had a lot of information to swap and discuss—and David was satisfied with his somewhat impulsive decision to drive instead of fly. And he liked his car.

His mother had never been able to afford a car, and he found himself wondering what Helena Hammar would have thought about this, which was unusually sentimental for him. She had always been fond of fancy, expensive things, he thought with a pang in his heart.

They stopped once along the way to stretch their legs and eat a quick lunch; later that afternoon they reached the outskirts of Båstad.

The blue exit sign finally appeared, and David got off the highway and saw the sea. Natalia was supposed to be here, he thought. Hammar Capital was one of the Bank of London's most important clients, so naturally he and Michel were invited to the party J-O was hosting.

"Is Åsa coming?" he asked.

"Don't know," Michel said.

"You still haven't called her?"

"Sure I have," Michel replied saronically. "I called her once the day before yesterday, but then I changed my mind and hung up. And then I called her again yesterday to explain."

"What did she say?"

Michel's jaws were working as he gazed grimly out the window. "Don't know," he said tersely. "I hung up after a couple of rings."

David stifled a laugh. "You know that caller ID will show her who called, right?"

Michel kept staring out the window. "I know," he said. "I can't think clearly when it comes to her. But I can't see how there could possibly be anything between me and her. My family would go nuts."

"You don't have to tell your family," David pointed out.

"And besides, she works for Investum. You know, the company we're about to take over."

Unlike Natalia, who only owns part of the company.

He couldn't ignore the fact that Natalia was here and they would surely see each other tonight. They hadn't been together since Sunday morning, had only had sporadic contact via text message.

But then David had almost sent Natalia a message that was supposed to have gone to Carolina, and that had shaken him. So much was at stake, he couldn't mess it up now.

"Åsa owns a ton of Investum shares," David said. He knew exactly who all the biggest shareholders were. "Among other things," he added. "Do you know how rich that woman actually is?"

"She inherited everything when her family died, and she's managed it well, so I assume she's one of the richest women in Sweden."

"How old was she?"

"When they died? Eighteen. She inherited the lot. And the line will die out with her. That's quite a one-two punch, losing your family and inheriting all that at the same time. She was wild when we were at school together—studying but smoking, drinking, sleeping around. I think she came unhinged."

"She sure seems to be good at her job now, so I assume she's recovered. And there's definitely something between you two."

"And speaking of not following your own advice," Michel said, "how's it going with Natalia?"

"It was nothing," he said curtly. "It's over now."

Michel scratched his scalp. One of his many chunky rings flashed, twenty-four-karat gold and a three-carat diamond. Gold chain around the neck. Boy from the hood who'd made it. "So, first it was nothing?" Michel said skeptically. "And now it's over?"

"Exactly." Because it *was* over. He was completely sure. He was over her.

"You saw her again," Michel said. He shook his head.

"We saw each other," David said, sounding defensive. "Once at her place, maybe twice. And once at my place. But that was it, and there won't be any more."

"At your place? In your apartment?" Now Michel was staring at him. "Yes."

"The place that no one, not even I, am allowed to visit?"

"You can come over," David said, turning into a parking lot and pulling to a stop. "You can come swim in my Jacuzzi."

"You are not making sense," Michel said.

"Maybe not, but at least I don't keep calling girls and hanging up."

25

"I don't see how you can walk in those," Natalia said, studying Åsa's extremely high-heeled pumps. By comparison, her own sandals looked almost modest despite their four-inch heels.

"These shoes aren't for walking," Åsa explained. She wiggled her foot. "They're for catching men. You won't be on your feet in them for very long." She looked around, nodded to a Swedish *Idol* winner, waved at a movie star. "Michel called me twice and then hung up," she said. "It's payback time."

Natalia surveyed the snakeskin-patterned dress Åsa was wearing. It looked as if she'd been poured into it. Her blond hair, curlers removed, was now bobbing around her face, and her curves, stretching the fabric of her dress—she was so obviously a woman on the warpath that Natalia almost felt bad for Michel Chamoun. In her current mood, Åsa would slaughter him like a lamb.

Natalia took a glass of champagne from a silver tray and waited while Åsa gave a government minister and his latest unofficial girlfriend kisses on the cheek.

Natalia and Åsa had been in Båstad for two days already, sunbathing and swimming and—in Natalia's case—meeting clients.

The little town bustled with activity, but there were actually only two parties that mattered, where people wanted to be seen. One was her parents' party tomorrow. This was the other, the giant Bank of London party. The guest list was chock-full of rich, powerful, famous names, and Natalia knew that people broke down in tears if they didn't receive one of the sought-after invitations. After the Nobel Prize dinner and the princesses' weddings, *this* was the party everyone wanted to be invited to.

J-O waved at them, and Natalia waved back. The garden was already overcrowded with people in fancy dress, and more kept pouring in. Champagne in tall, chilled flutes and oysters on crushed ice were offered as welcome drinks and appetizers. A band played, and celebrity performers took turns singing and entertaining the guests. In the courtyard, the country's foremost master chefs were ready with their grills lit and their enormous pans, cooking away. The food preparation was its own show, and Natalia saw a television crew filming the spectacle. Soon they would have to clear out, though. Television cameras were only admitted for a very few moments at the beginning of the party.

Politicians, journalists, and celebrities mingled. Åsa flirted first with a Monégasque prince who'd flown in for the party, and then with a famous hockey player, while Natalia sipped her champagne. She only knew a fraction of the people, definitely not as many as Åsa, but the mood was jovial, and she was enjoying herself.

And then suddenly she heard, "Hi, Natalia," and she was pulled into an enormous hug.

"Alex! How great to see you." She disentangled herself from the tight hug and beamed at her little brother, Alexander De la Grip, who wasn't so little anymore. He grew bigger and wider every time they saw each other.

"Hey there, sis." He looked her over more closely. "You're a babe." And then his smile got even bigger, a smile that made his already handsome face beam. "And Åsa Bjelke," he said, his voice honey and sunshine. "You look magical, as usual. Can I bring you ladies some more champagne?"

They nodded and watched Alex walk away.

"I always forget how gorgeous he is," Åsa said. "It's as if God woke up one morning in his very best mood and decided to give one man everything."

Alexander came back, and they each took a champagne flute.

"So, are you legal yet?" Åsa asked.

Alexander, who was only a little more than a year younger than Natalia, and who, as far as Natalia knew, went through women at a pace that would make Åsa's escapades look like a chaste Sunday stroll in the park, laughed. He had been thirteen when the eighteen-year-old Åsa had moved in with the De la Grip family. They had always had a special bond, flirty and a little lacking in boundaries. And they had a lot in common, Natalia thought. Smart and attractive, but unhappy. And sexually promiscuous. Alexander leaned forward and whispered something in Åsa's ear that made her howl with laughter.

Natalia pushed against his arm. Alexander was her little brother, and she didn't care what he did or whom he did it with.

"Are Mom and Dad here?" he asked, setting down his glass, which he'd emptied in record time. Not even Åsa drank that fast.

Natalia nodded her head. "Haven't you seen them yet?"

"No, and thank God for that. The longer it takes, the better. So, what's new? Do I dare hope that Peter is divorced from that witch yet?"

Natalia was about to answer, but she squeezed Alexander's arm instead.

"What is it?" he asked.

"Shit," Åsa said, having realized what was going on. "It's Jonas."

Natalia felt as if her legs were going to give way. Jonas was heading straight for them. They hadn't seen each other since the breakup, and she had no idea what he intended, coming over here with that serious look on his face.

She squeezed her brother's arm again. He patted her hand. "Come on, Nat, you're a De la Grip. You can handle this. Or do you want me to beat him up? I have nothing against fighting. To the contrary, actually."

"Thanks, but it's fine," Natalia said. The very last thing she wanted was for her little brother to end up in a fistfight at J-O's megaparty.

And then Jonas was in front of them.

First he shook Alexander's hand, always the men first. Natalia saw that Alex squeezed Jonas's hand so hard he grimaced in pain. She couldn't help but smile. Alexander was one of the most immoral men she knew, but he was loyal to the end to the few people he loved.

Jonas kissed Åsa once on each cheek and then looked straight at Natalia.

"Hi," he said quietly. Nice eyes and a friendly smile made her heart constrict.

"Hi," she said.

"You look wonderful."

"Thanks," she said, already feeling better. This wasn't so bad. The first shock had subsided, and Jonas was himself. He wasn't a bad person, not really. This wasn't anywhere near as hard as she'd feared. She exhaled and gave him a polite smile.

"I hoped you would be here," he said.

"You did?" Her voice was calm and level. And strangely enough, that's how she felt, almost neutral.

"Yes, I've missed you."

"I've missed you too," she mumbled, although she realized it wasn't true. The last two weeks she hadn't thought of Jonas even once.

A press photographer came over and asked if she could take Alexander's picture. He always attracted the press, and they waited while he let her take some pictures. Then a young woman came over and lured Alexander away. Natalia watched her brother go. He was almost *too* attractive for his own good; women flocked around him, and he manically cultivated his playboy image. If only he was happy, she thought. If only he didn't have that hunted look in his eyes. Wasn't drinking so much.

She saw him stop by a stunningly beautiful redheaded woman who was talking to J-O. The woman wore a pale-pink dress that made her red hair glow, and whatever Alex said to her, she didn't like it. Natalia heard Jonas say something to Åsa, but couldn't bring herself to turn back to them.

And then Natalia felt it.

David's presence wound its way through the buzz and the mingling and the guests, and she felt it, like an electric pulse. The hair on her arms stood on end, the quality of the sounds around her changed, her focus shifted. It was so strong that she thought she must be imagining it. She realized that she'd stopped breathing, so she took a deep breath and slowly set down her glass. She systematically activated all her muscles and all the strength years of horseback riding, dance, and sheer will had given her. She slowly turned her head, felt a tingle in her back. Her lips curled. And then their eyes met, his and hers.

Bang.

Åsa slid up close beside her. "Do you see?"

"Yes," Natalia breathed.

"They're both here."

"Yes."

"Damn, but they're hot."

Natalia thrust out her chin. She had new clothes, new shoes, and a new hairdo. She was ready. "But we're hotter."

"Yes," Åsa agreed. "This is our scene, Natalia. Are you in?"

"All in."

26

David saw her. She was standing there amid a crowd of partygoers, almost luminous. People moved around and behind and sometimes in front of her, but she stood out like a radiant star in a dark sky. How could he ever have thought that Natalia was anything other than breathtakingly beautiful? Had there really been a time when he had described her to himself as common and insignificant? There was *nothing* ordinary about her. She had done something to her hair—it fell around her shoulders in big glossy waves that continued down her back. And she was wearing red. A Ferrari red dress, short and made of some material that looked alive, swirling around her body in triumphant serpentine swaths. And those long, sexy legs that quite recently had rested on his shoulders as he brought her to climax.

At first he couldn't identify the word he heard in his head; he was too preoccupied with drinking her in with his eyes.

But then he heard it again, a single word that drowned out all the others, a primal roar.

Mine.

She is *mine*.

Which was beyond stupid, of course. He had no right to her, never would. It didn't matter what they'd done. It was only sex.

Only sex.

He wanted to walk over to her. He wanted to caress those bare shoulders, put his arm around her, pull her to him, kiss her deeply, thoroughly, satisfyingly. Wanted to see her face start to glow, see her eyes widen. It was almost impossible to resist. Impossible to remember why he should resist that impulse that was so primal in its force. He did what he apparently always did when it came to Natalia—he started bargaining with himself.

One last time, what did it matter? Because *this* would really be the last time, truly. This was the last night they would see each other before—well, *before*.

She cocked her head to the side and watched him, alluring and tempting him like a modern-day siren, and David just threw it all overboard. He dumped his good intentions and reason as if they were ballast, holding him down, and made up his mind.

Mine.

He was about to start walking toward her, had already taken the first step, when he suddenly saw a tall man slip up behind her, as if he'd been standing there the whole time and was now staking his rightful claim. With a slow wink Natalia looked away from David. She turned to face the man. He whispered something in her ear, she nodded in response, and David saw the couple move a little and then they were swallowed by the crowd of party guests.

The moment was past.

He swallowed. He should be grateful it had happened. Now he had the chance to move on.

But he didn't move on.

He just stood there.

And he wondered: who the hell was that man?

Michel had tried not to stare at Åsa. But it was like starving to death and trying not to stare at a buffet. And every time his eyes were drawn to her, Åsa looked back at him, through ever more narrowed eyes. She was wearing something tight-fitting, like a second skin. As Natalia De la Grip moved away with an unknown man, Åsa remained.

Michel pushed his way over to her.

"Åsa," he said as he reached her, his heart pounding so hard he thought it must show.

She raised a blond eyebrow and gave him one of her truly aristocratic looks.

"Yes?" she said.

Åsa had always been good at putting him off-kilter. A word, a look, and he started waffling like an idiot.

They were the same age, had both been twenty when they first met. Michel still remembered it. The first day of the semester at university, studying pre-law. He had sat there, exhilarated, eager, the pride of his family, extremely early in the very front row.

Åsa had sailed in, late, swishing past him without a second glance, surveying the whole lecture hall. He hadn't heard a single word of the lecture, had just sat there, sneaking peeks at her as she sat with her pen in her mouth, swinging her foot back and forth. After the lecture the other students had swarmed around her, girls and boys. She hadn't even looked at him once. And Michel, who didn't drink alcohol, had started going to student pubs. He had hung around, his beer untouched, watching her, seeing her go home with different men each time.

One night they'd started chatting. She was flirty but also smart, and strangely enough, they had a lot in common. They started studying together, eating lunch together, but no more. Åsa kept going home with different men, and he kept fantasizing about her. And then one night . . . Michel couldn't really think about it without feeling the familiar anxiety: one night it had all changed and they weren't friends anymore. After school they'd disappeared from each other's lives, and scarcely a day had gone by in the last ten years when he hadn't thought of her.

If anyone asked him, love at first sight was damned overrated.

"I called you," he said. All the complicated old emotions made him sound terser than he'd intended.

She cocked her head slightly, a lock of blond hair grazed her cheek, and he wanted to run his hand over it, twist it around his finger, smell it. She was more beautiful now at thirty-something than she had been at twenty.

"But you didn't say anything, just called and hung up. No message. I'm not a mind reader, Michel," she said, and his name sounded like fire and sex in her mouth.

"I know," he said. "I apologize."

"What do you want?" she asked nonchalantly, as if she were asking him his favorite color or something else equally insignificant.

What do I want?

Michel wasn't sure there were words in any of the languages he spoke that described what he wanted.

"I want us to be friends," he said. Their friendship had been genuine. He hadn't realized how much he missed it.

"Åsa!" a loud voice behind them cried out. "Oh my God, it's been ages!" There were people everywhere, and Michel heard the loud voice and the hollered words from behind him. He saw Åsa automatically look to see who had spoken, mentally starting to pull away from him, and something just snapped.

That's what she did, pulled away, turned off, shut people out. He wasn't sure he could survive it again. He moved, stepping in to block the path between Åsa and whoever was trying to get her attention.

Åsa's eyes widened. "What do you think you're doing? You have no right to . . ."

But Michel shook his head and took a step closer to her, moving into her personal space. He was taking the right. He grabbed Åsa's wrist. Oh, the scent of her, always this vanilla scent that made him think of Åsa, no matter where he was.

"You and I need to talk," he said. He pulled her to him and their eyes met.

It was like looking right into her soul.

"Talk about what?" He saw a sliver of fear before she shut him out and sneered instead.

"About us," he said.

Her eyes narrowed. "There is no *us*."

But he was running on new fuel now. The insecure student was gone, and he'd seen something in her eyes, something soft and vulnerable, something that revealed that she wasn't anywhere near as chilly as she seemed, and that gave him hope. He just said, "There most certainly is. Come on."

He hoped the gamble would pay off, that if he were pushy enough, she would be sufficiently flummoxed to just go along with it. He really hoped so, because he didn't have a plan B and he didn't have all that much courage in reserve.

He held out his hand.

Åsa looked at it for a while, as if she were trying to figure out what it was, but then she laid her hand in his, and he squeezed it hard, and she didn't try to pull away as he turned around and started walking.

She was completely silent behind him as he pushed his way through all the people. She didn't say a word as he pulled her up some stairs, searching aimlessly for a quiet corner where they could be alone.

Finally he opened the door to a room and saw with relief that it was empty. A sofa, an armchair, a coffee table, and a small TV—some sort of family room. He shut the door behind them.

He looked at Åsa; she was breathing hard.

"Michel," she whispered. "What are you doing?"

He didn't know. He had just acted, without thinking. But they had never talked about what had happened. Maybe it was too late, maybe it was crazy to try to pick things up where they'd ended ten years ago. Maybe he needed to understand.

"I want to talk," he said.

"I hate talking," she said sharply.

He smiled a little. "I know."

She turned her turquoise eyes on him and said, "I'll give you ten minutes."

Natalia smiled at Jonas, another one of those reflexively polite smiles she'd bestowed on everyone for the last fifteen minutes. Jonas chatted with a man she didn't know about something she couldn't really concentrate on. They were surrounded by people she certainly knew but had never had anything in common with, well-heeled women her age, dressed in low-key pastels, so similar to each other they were practically interchangeable. The men talked in this world. The women stood next to them and smiled.

A couple that Natalia and Jonas used to socialize with stopped and said hello. The woman kissed the air next to her cheek and complimented Natalia's appearance. The man shook hands and laughed loudly and heartily. The man joined in the conversation about golf or sailing; the woman admired someone's shawl.

Natalia tried to look like she was listening, but her mood was tanking. She tried as best she could to cling to the festive, expectant feeling she'd had. But Åsa had disappeared with Michel, who had looked like he had seriously important intentions. And David had also disappeared without a trace.

Their eyes had met, and every single one of her hairs and limbs had been electrified. She'd thought he felt the same way. She couldn't deny it any longer, at least not to herself. She'd fallen for him.

But then Jonas had come back, and she'd lost sight of David, and now he was gone, swallowed by the five hundred guests, at least a quarter of whom were ridiculously attractive women. Maybe it was just as well. No one needed to convince her that it was a genuinely bad idea to fall for David Hammar. For a host of reasons. Not least of which was the tiny detail that he didn't appear to have fallen for her; rather, he seemed to be keeping his distance. Besides, she was a sensible person, Natalia convinced herself, a person who would never stoop to being with a man who wasn't into her.

And yet, all the same: She wanted to be with David. She wanted whatever she could get, whatever he would give. He'd made her greedy. It was as if she had become aware of what she was entitled to expect from life. She nodded automatically to a question, said something vapid, and just wanted to get out of there.

Jonas touched her now and then just as he used to. It was actually a little creepy. She pulled her arm away. She was worried about Alexander. He hadn't looked happy. And she scanned the crowd for J-O, hoping he was satisfied with the party and with her. She was tense about running into her father, and on top of all that there was the draining uncertainty about how things *actually* stood between her and David.

Suddenly Natalia saw the whole thing as if in an abundantly clear light.

Men. Everything had to do with different men and how she related to them. It felt like an important insight, like something she wanted to pull back and dissect in peace. Why should everything she knew and thought be defined in relation to a man?

She emptied her glass and took a new one, swirled it with her brow furrowed. She felt that she was onto something important. She finished the champagne, which was ice-cold. It was hot out—hundreds of guests, a late-summer evening, and all those hot barbecue grills were gradually making it even hotter. She took another glass from a tray and took a few quick gulps.

"Shouldn't you drink a little water?" Jonas whispered.

"What?" she asked sharply. She looked into his eyes and saw consideration but also a little worry, and something clicked inside her. Slowly, without taking her eyes off Jonas, she drained her glass, set it down, and then took another.

"Natalia," he began.

"You . . . ," she started, pointing at him with her glass so that the champagne sloshed. "You are not my fiancé." She made a show of drinking another gulp. "You," she said. Everyone else around them looked at her in curiosity. She had raised her voice. A woman never raised her voice, never drew attention to herself, not in these circles. It was *vulgar*. "*You're* the one who broke up with *me*," she continued, her voice finally breaking a little at the end. "So, Jonas Jägerhed, you no longer have any right to an opinion on anything I do. None. Zippo."

Jonas looked as if he were thinking of saying something, but Natalia held up her hand. "No," she said, handing him the empty glass. "I'm going to go find my brother now. And my boss. And maybe someone else." She covered her mouth and burped as discreetly as she could. "Coming through," she said, pushing her way past the startled onlookers and allowing herself to be swallowed up by the sea of people. Let them talk. She continued on aimlessly before she gratefully spotted her little brother's broad back.

"Alex," she called, pushing her way through and tapping him on the back. He turned around with a broad smile. "Natalia, I thought I heard you chewing someone out back there. Fascinating. And exactly what that pompous Jonas needs."

"I thought you liked Jonas?"

A hard glint flickered in Alexander's eyes. He was blond as a Viking but had long, dark eyelashes and cheekbones a woman would kill for. "That was before," he said. And then he smiled and his standard cheerful expression slid into place. "My dear sister, may I present you to—pardon me, I've forgotten your name?" Alexander turned and Natalia saw whom he'd been talking to.

Aha.

"I know him," Natalia said. "His name's David. He's a venture capitalist." She wobbled a bit in her sky-high heels. "You know, the kind of person our family hates."

Alexander grinned. "My dear big sister, are you by any chance a little tipsy?"

She sniffed dismissively. "Aren't you?" she asked.

"Always," Alexander said. He turned to David again. "Sorry, what did you say your name was?"

Natalia saw David's eyes twinkle, and she thought he had no right to look so darned good.

"I'm David Hammar," he said. "And if it's okay with you, I'd really like to speak to your sister for a moment."

Alexander was about to say something, but Natalia interrupted him. "What do you mean, if it's okay with him?" she asked, irritated. "Don't I have free will?"

David looked at her, for a long time. The look in those gray-blue eyes was impossible to read, but if anything he seemed amused, and she felt so drawn to him. Her body was starting to lean toward him; her fingers wanted to slide over his biceps, into his hair.

The silence dragged on, and then with a dry laugh in his voice, Alexander said, "Well, I suppose I'll be moving along." He gave Natalia a quick kiss on the cheek and said, "My offer to kick Jonas's ass is still good. I'll be here somewhere if you need me." His eyes fixed on a young woman with large breasts and long hair, and he smiled broadly. "For a little while anyway. Ciao." He sauntered off.

David was still looking into Natalia's eyes. "How are you?" he asked once Alexander had left.

"Just dandy," she said with feigned nonchalance. "And you, how are you?"

"Good. I've been working a lot this week."

His voice was quiet, and she leaned toward him until she smelled the scent of his aftershave. She wanted to close her eyes and just breathe in his scent. Pull off his clothes, rub against him. Damn, she had it bad.

"You look really amazing," he murmured, looking as if he were caressing her with his eyes, skimming down her neck, stopping at her breasts. Her breathing sped up; she became aware of everything: the fabric of her dress, the sensitivity of her skin, his scent, the heat in the air.

"Thanks," she said and cleared her throat. She wished she had a glass in her hand. "You look great too," she said honestly. Because he was dressed all in black—formfitting black slacks, shiny leather belt, black shirt—and was ethereally good-looking. God, how she wanted to taste him, bit by bit.

David smiled, and Natalia had the awful feeling that she'd said that last bit out loud.

"When did you arrive?" she asked, retreating to safe, polite topics. She could be polite in five languages.

"Michel and I drove. We got here today."

"Where are you staying?"

"I rented a house. Down by the water. And you?"

Natalia thought about her sex nest. "Åsa loaned me her guest cottage," she said casually. "I'm staying there."

The noise of the party got louder with each minute. They'd started serving the food, and the band was playing. It was almost impossible to carry on a normal conversation.

"Do you want to get out of here for a little while?" he asked.

She hesitated. This was J-O's party. He was the host, and she was his closest colleague. But people were partying and drinking. No one was going to miss her. Not if they were only gone for a little while. "Yes," she said. "Just give me a sec."

David watched Natalia walk away, her long legs, her short red dress swinging. If his intention was to put an end to whatever was going on between them, then he had failed catastrophically. Everything, every last thing about her, drew him to her.

She returned with red lips and a huge smile.

And something inside him fell apart.

What he was planning . . .

It wasn't going to sadden or disappoint Natalia. It was going to *crush* her.

This was his very last chance not to hurt her any further. He ought to say something meaningless about this being bad timing, about having to prioritize his work, and leave her. He knew that. That would be humane and decent. If she already thought he was an asshole, then the later blow wouldn't be so hard.

He *knew* that.

And then she swept past, gave him an expectant smile, and all he could think was that she was the most beautiful, the sexiest, most fun woman he'd ever met, and that this was their last night together, and that he was unscrupulous enough to want to enjoy as much of her as he could.

They strolled down to the water. There were people everywhere—on the beach, on the docks, at the cafés—and David didn't want to attract any unnecessary attention, so he didn't touch her. Didn't want her to have to explain her relationship to him.

Fuck, the press would slaughter her if they found out.

At least he could do that, protect her from prying eyes. David looked out at the waters of the Kattegatt, which connected the Baltic Sea to the North Sea.

"That was Jonas Jägerhed you were talking to earlier," he said when he put two and two together, remembering where he'd seen the man before.

She laughed. "Sometimes it feels like you have some kind of dossier on me that you've memorized. Yes, that was Jonas. That was the first time we'd seen each other in a year."

He helped her down a steep step. "Those shoes weren't made for walking," he pointed out. Narrow high heels, even narrower straps around her strong ankles.

"No, Åsa says they're shoes to capture men with."

He laughed. "Are they working?"

She blinked at him. She didn't seem drunk anymore; she just looked happy and a little naughty. "Well, you're here, aren't you?"

She looked out at the water, and David positioned himself behind her, shielding her from onlookers from behind. In front of them was just the sea.

"It was weird to see Jonas again," she continued. "But it wasn't as awful as I thought it would be. Emotions are such a strange thing. Time makes everything better eventually. It's a little sad, how change-able everything is."

"A little comforting, too," he said, putting his hand on her arm. She leaned lightly against him, moving her shoulder blades slightly against his chest. He ran his hand over her skin.

She trembled, drew in her breath. "I suppose so," she said quietly.

"Why did it end?" He asked the most personal of questions, the one he actually had no right to ask. But he just found it inconceiv-able. How could anyone be with Natalia De la Grip and not slay drag-ons for her?

If everything was different, if she was his girlfriend . . .

Natalia was silent for a long time, looking out at the quiet sea. The sound of the waves on the pier and the occasional splash was all they could hear.

"My period started yesterday," she said, and David thought she was changing the subject. "It's never worked right, but this wasn't anything unusual. This morning it was already over." She smiled, and he knew that they had to have sex tonight; he couldn't leave her without sharing that incredible experience one last time.

"I never thought there might be anything wrong. I've always wanted to have a family, and Jonas is very fond of kids." She rubbed her palms on her upper arms to warm herself up, still looking out at the water. Her voice was quiet and steady, almost distanced. "But Jonas is the oldest son; he has a title and a large estate. Only a biological child can inherit a noble title. In some circles that's incredibly important."

She turned around and looked at David. The sun was still up, but the light was turning golden, and as her eyes caught its rays they began to sparkle like pure gold.

"This might sound like a first-world problem, but for many years my period was my biggest enemy. God, how I hated when it came."

She shook her head and looked out at the water again, up at the sky, anywhere far away.

David waited. When her voice began again, it was so empty, so sad that he shivered.

"Jonas left me the same day he found out in black and white that I can't have children."

27

Åsa peered at Michel, who was standing in the middle of the room scratching his forehead. Man, was he sexy with his shaved head. She'd never gone for the gangster look before. Most criminal types were insufferable narcissists, and the way she saw it, there was only room for one egotist in her relationships. His shiny suits, garish shirts, and flashy rings were in a league of their own, of course. She crossed her legs in front of her. But they turned her on, no doubt about it. He wasn't one of those slick finance boys, nor some tough thug. He was Michel, the nicest and most respectable man she'd ever met. The fact that Michel had turned her down once didn't make him a bad guy. She realized that today, ten years too late. But that didn't mean it hadn't hurt like hell.

"You must have noticed," he said, snapping Åsa out of her revery. She'd been so lost in her own thoughts she hadn't even heard what he said. She furrowed her brow. She had been serious about what she'd said when she allowed him to drag her in here. She didn't want to talk. No good ever came from talking, regardless of what Natalia and Åsa's irritating psychotherapist thought.

Talking *hurt*. People said rotten things and you never came out of it feeling good. So she really didn't want to talk.

She ran her eyes over his legs and hips and stomach, her gaze drifting to his crotch.

What she wanted was to get laid.

Natalia was always saying Åsa used sex to deaden her feelings, but Åsa didn't agree. She used alcohol to deaden her feelings; she just really enjoyed sex. She was good at sex. And Michel wanted her, even a blind person could see that.

"Are you listening to what I'm saying?" he asked indignantly.

"Sorry," Åsa said, making a show of looking at her watch. Three minutes had gone by.

She got up from the armchair where she'd been sitting. Michel almost jumped back. She traced one finger along her décolletage, looking deep into his eyes. Two seconds and then he would be hers.

Michel shook his head. "You're not listening," he said. "I wanted to apologize for how badly I behaved when we ran into each other at the bar. I was surprised and I said things I regret. I'm sorry." He backed away farther.

"It doesn't matter," she said impatiently, with a dismissive wave of her hand. She took a high-heeled step toward him. He watched her warily. She smiled a little. "I let all of that go," she continued, which was maybe not entirely truthful, because he had hurt her, at one time anyway, and it was still there, like an encapsulated spike in her heart. But that was then, and this was now, and nothing ever came of thinking about old issues, she reminded herself firmly.

She cocked her head and lowered her voice to a hoarse purr. "You have a few minutes left." She smiled, blinked slowly, and approached him.

He shook his head. "No, Åsa," he said seriously. "We need to talk. I mean it. *Just* talk."

And there it was.

The panic.

Åsa stiffened, lowered her arms. If Michel didn't want to have sex with her, if he really just wanted to *talk it out*—there was no expression in the world she hated more than that—then there was no point in their even seeing each other. She had imagined that they would argue a little, he would pursue her, she would tease and taunt and then regain the power that he'd stolen from her that one vulnerable evening. Then they would end up in bed and have an explosive night. Michel would see what he'd missed out on, and then it would be over. She would have won. But this? No. The panic made her break into a cold sweat and opened floodgates that were supposed to stay closed.

When she'd met Michel she had still been in shock. Apparently you could be in shock for years.

Her family had been obliterated, so maybe it wasn't so strange. An accident, a phone call from the police, and her whole world suddenly collapsed.

She'd moved in with Natalia's family. There had been papers to sign, lawyers to listen to, decisions to make. When she occasionally thought back on that time now, it was like it had all happened to someone else.

School and then Michel had been her bedrock in the chaos. At school she'd just been one student in the crowd, which had been so wonderful. And Michel had always been there, waiting, never in the spotlight, but always dependably waiting in the wings. And they'd become friends. She'd teased him, flirted with other guys to test him. Nothing had happened. He'd just watched her with those black eyes of his, impossible to decipher. Sometimes she'd thought she'd seen hunger. Sometimes compassion. Always friendship. Somewhere along the way she'd fallen in love, of course. She'd had to drink until she was really drunk in order to muster the courage to approach him, which was so horribly childish and embarrassing. He'd rejected her. Just like that. Hadn't wanted what she'd offered.

She'd gone home with someone else that night, obviously.

But that was lifetimes ago, she reminded herself, forcing air into her lungs. She was a grown-up. She could command herself not to think about that.

"Michel, do we have to talk about that now? Couldn't we maybe . . ." But her voice lacked conviction. She'd gambled everything on that one card; she'd bet it all on sex and had lost. Again. He was turning her down, again. This was starting to become a very unpleasant habit. She sank back down into the armchair.

Michel squatted down in front of her and put his hands on her legs, and Åsa nearly flew out of her skin. In all these years, he'd never touched her, not really, not like a man. His hands were big and rough, just like the rest of him. His arms and legs bulged inside the fabric of his suit.

She looked into his eyes, black and nice. Or was that pity she saw? She couldn't think anymore, couldn't breathe. She stretched her back. She was Åsa Bjelke. She could walk right back out to the party and in record time have a dozen men fawning over her. She didn't *need* this.

She pushed his hands away, stood up, and smoothed out her dress. "Your ten minutes are up," she said coolly. "You really can't have anything more to say to me. You're not interested, that's fine." She shook out her hair, gathered her strength where she always gathered it— from anger, from indifference. "Thanks for this little chat. I'm sure we both agree that we don't need to repeat it."

"Åsa . . . ," he said.

She shook her head. She'd had enough. "Good-bye, Michel," she said.

28

The guest cottage Natalia had borrowed was well down below the main house, quite private, and all the way out by the water.

"This is incredible," David said as they stood in front of the enormous windows admiring the view.

"I know," she said. The windows ran from floor to ceiling, and outside only the sea was visible. No beach, no people, nothing other than water until the horizon met the sky. The July night was still light, but the sun had set, and a full moon hung over the warm water.

The cottage consisted of just one room, a kitchenette, and a bathroom. Everything was white. The wood floor had been painted white, white textiles, white walls. The sea played the starring roll. The sea and the bed, made with white linens and white pillows.

David looked at the bed for a long time and then at her. Natalia shivered. There was pure hunger in that look. She stepped right into his embrace, hard and urgent. She felt brave and bold, and she kissed him until they were both panting. He moved his hands to her neck, to her cheeks, and looked at her, studying her carefully.

He was like that, attentive, a quick study. She had never felt so important, as if what she wanted, what she liked, was important to David, maybe most important of all. It was as if he studied her, tested his way forward, rejected what she didn't like, gave her more of what she wanted. It was potently erotic. And in the midst of all the sensual darkness: safe.

He stroked her throat, down to her collarbone, following his own movements with intense focus. Natalia lost track of anything besides his eyes and fingers. He pulled her dress off, she undid his belt, and they undressed each other with almost familiar motions.

He smiled at her extravagant lingerie. She hadn't realized it before, but the sheer lingerie, expensive and French, was representative of what she was with him, what she became with him. A sexy, hungry woman, a woman who expected and demanded, without shame, the best the world had to offer her, a woman who wanted this man and dared to claim him.

Their previous lovemaking had been either fiery or playfully passionate. Today it was so intense that Natalia could hardly breathe.

She lay down on the bed, and he lay down beside her. He spread her legs apart and carefully caressed her while showering her with airy kisses.

He bit her on the shoulder and murmured, "Let me make this good for you. I need to make this good for you, better than before."

The raw emotion in his voice tied her insides in knots. "Yes," she whispered, and then she was swept away by his tongue, his hands, and his body, coming in a quick orgasm.

Afterward she lay on her back, sweaty and relaxed. David kissed her with feather-light kisses, stroked her hair. He brought water and watched while she drank. He took the glass, took a few gulps, and then set it on the floor. She reached for him, wanted him in her, but he pulled away.

"Not yet," he said quietly. He kissed her on the ribs, gently on the breasts, so incredibly tenderly. She sank down into the bedclothes, closed her eyes, letting him caress her, pulling her into yet another wave of sensations. Unbelievably enough he brought her to another orgasm, and she almost curled up into a ball afterward, as if her body couldn't handle any more. He ran his hand down her back, helping her unfurl again, carefully laying her on her stomach, rubbing her back, down over her buttocks—so amazingly sensitive. Hot blood and warmth and lust surged, emptying her of all thought and leaving only emotions, sensations, and her body. Her thighs: the inside, the backs, so many sensations in that thin, tender skin, so much desire. And although it was impossible, even though she was spent, Natalia's body responded again.

It was as if she was somewhere else, far inside herself. He rolled her onto her back. She was limp like a doll. He laid her legs over his own legs, his hairs scratchy beneath her thighs. He stuffed a pillow under her head, held a heavy arm over her legs. When she was comfortable, he spread her legs, stroking her, bent down and kissed her.

"David, I can't. No more," she murmured. The touch was too intense.

"Shh," he said. And his finger found its way in, gentle but secure. So skillful. "You're going to come again, Natalia," he said. "You know you can, and I want it. I want you to come for me." And then another finger, and he found all the most sensitive spots with his slow methodical movements. The stroking and her passive position made her breathing heavier and heavier. And finally, when she was writhing, he pulled on a condom and entered her.

Natalia could hardly move as he filled her. It was as if every part of her had been made to receive him, buried in the bedclothes, surrounded by pillows and fresh air. He brushed the hair out of her face; she was sweaty and hot and floating around in the soft bed, the mild night, and the sounds of their lovemaking. He kissed her. He tasted so good, warm and familiar, big and safe. She opened her eyes, and he was so close, so close, and it was *too* intense and something in her couldn't handle all the intimacy, so she closed her eyes again.

"Natalia," he whispered in her ear. He nibbled her earlobe. "Look at me," he said, and she obediently opened her eyes again.

They were so close, no space between them. He was looking right into her as he moved inside, deep, determined movements that pushed and pressed until the impossible happened and she came again. As her emotions overflowed, her tears were near.

"Natalia," he whispered again, just her name, over and over again.

She put her hands on the sides of his face, holding him close, so close. She draped one leg around his waist, never wanted them to be separated. He put one hand on her face, and she let herself sink into him, with her body and soul and heart.

He thrust into her, slowly but rhythmically. Again. And again. He murmured her name, softly. And slowly as a summer breeze, lazy as a placid sea, completely effortlessly, their eyes locked on each other, she started to come again. His beautiful eyes, gray and blue, became so veiled and glassy, and she watched him come, silently, intensely, without taking his eyes off her, and something broke inside her, the tears welled up and she had never been so close to another person, another soul, hadn't thought it was possible.

"David," she whispered.

He started to say something but stopped, as if his voice wouldn't hold, and she had to close her eyes again. It was too raw, too tender. She was forced to shut him out for a little bit, otherwise she would come apart.

David kissed her eyelids and she sobbed.

He stayed put and it was perfect.

"Natalia," was all he said.

She flung her arms around him, buried her face against his throat, ran her fingers over his scars. There were no words, she thought, because that had been an experience you would really need to invent new words to describe. She stuck out her tongue and licked his skin. She bit gently, heard him moan, and then he covered her mouth with his. Of everything they did, she still loved his kisses the most. Without interrupting the kiss, he scooped her up—God, he was so strong— pulled her into his lap, and she sat that way, in his naked lap with the sea and the moon outside, and they were kissing. Skin to skin, heart to heart.

Later, when the night had actually gotten a little dark, they pulled the bed all the way over to the open windows and lay in it watching the sea. She lay on her stomach, with her hands under her chin, and felt how he climbed onto her, with his hands on either side of her body. He entered her slowly, filled her until she gasped from the bed-clothes. He made love to her in silence, slowly while the sea breeze and the salt air wafted in the open windows.

She woke up hours later, still with her head down by the edge of the bed but with a sheet over her body and a pillow under her cheek. She just remembered him whispering her name, and then she must have fallen asleep. She wondered how long she'd been out. When she looked up, David was out on the dock that ran along the outside of the cottage like a simple balcony. He was standing in the moon-light. The moon was full, and the light was a late-summer gold. He was barefoot, wearing pants but with his torso bare, and he leaned with his hands on the railing and seemed completely lost in thought.

"David," she called softly.

He turned around and came inside to her, sat down on the edge of the bed and brushed a lock of hair out of her face.

"Can't you sleep?" she asked. She was sleepy and limp, as if everything in her was relaxed.

"I have to go," he said.

And Natalia understood. He didn't want them to be seen together, and he was leaving for her sake.

She was the one who had insisted the whole time that they should be discreet. But she didn't want to be discreet anymore. Her heart swelled. This was more than just a passing liaison, and she knew he must feel the same way. She had seen it in his eyes, had felt it in the heat and intensity of their lovemaking, in the intimacy they shared.

But they would have time to talk, so she nodded and he got up. He pulled on a shirt, put on his shoes, and then looked at her for a long time. He seemed as if he was on the verge of saying something, but then he just shook his head.

"Good-bye, Natalia," he said solemnly.

"Bye," she said with a smile.

He nodded, and she saw something come over his face. She wanted to ask if everything was alright, but then he was gone.

She sat there for a while before she crawled under the sheet, breathed in the smell of him, and fell back asleep, certain that she loved him. And that he felt the same way.

29

Åsa stretched out, floating in the clear blue water. The sea was cold the way only a Swedish summer sea could be, but she needed to cool down, so she took another few tooth-chattering swim strokes before she gave up and started treading water.

Natalia bobbed a little ways away, on her back in a striped bathing suit, with her eyes closed against the sun. She was humming, splashing and smiling, and it took a while for Åsa to put her finger on what was different about Natalia today.

Then it hit her: Natalia was happy.

Åsa, on the other hand, was irritated. Not even her new bikini, which flattered her body so very well, put her in a good mood. Because what good was being super attractive if it didn't *lead* to anything?

"I still can't believe you got laid and I didn't," Åsa called petulantly.

It wasn't just that Michel hadn't wanted to have sex yesterday. It was also the humiliating fact that for a moment Åsa had been so close to getting down on her knees and begging for it. She shivered in the cold water. No one could ever find out about this. She would die if they did.

"But you can have anyone you want," said Natalia. "Why didn't you just go out and find someone else?" She gave Åsa a look, a contented, lazy look that made Åsa cloud over even more.

It wasn't that she begrudged Natalia anything, but did the woman have to look so *satisfied*? The kind of contentment that only a whole night of really good sex could give a woman? Åsa wanted to howl with envy.

"You've done it before," Natalia continued, sounding both concerned and focused on finding a solution at the same time, as if she hadn't realized that this business with Michel was something completely different from the normal meaningless sex Åsa filled her life with. "This place is teeming with men. You just need to close your eyes and point and you'll get what you want," Natalia concluded.

"That's just it," Åsa complained. "I don't want anyone else." Was she coming down with something? This didn't make sense. "All we did was talk."

"Sometimes talking is good."

Åsa didn't agree. "Can we swim back in now?" she asked. "I'm freezing my vagina off."

They swam back to shore. After they put their clothes on, brushed their hair, and put on some lotion, they walked up to the beach promenade. Åsa hid behind her sunglasses and a broad-brimmed sunhat. Natalia had wrapped a silk scarf around her hair and looked audaciously elegant. Åsa nodded to a couple of acquaintances but didn't stop for anyone. She wasn't done with the subject of Michel.

"I'm going to meet him for coffee," she said, wondering why she'd agreed to subject herself to that specific humiliation. He'd texted, and somehow she'd said yes instead of no. "Before they head back to Stockholm. I guess we're going to talk more. Have I mentioned that I hate talking?"

Natalia shielded her eyes with her hand. "They're going to Stockholm? When?"

"Today, I think. Didn't David mention it?"

Natalia shrugged. "He's not under any obligation to tell me anything. Besides, we were busy doing other things." Natalia grinned wantonly, and Åsa groaned. She *hated* their roles being reversed.

A tall man waved at them, and Natalia said, "Oh, my boss. I wonder what he thinks about my ducking out yesterday?"

"I think I'll take this opportunity to skedaddle," said Åsa, who had no desire to see J-O. She'd spotted a group of men she knew. Dumb, cocky young finance guys, exactly what her battered self-esteem needed. She pointed to them. "I'm going to go over and shake things up a little. I'll see you at the barbecue?"

Natalia nodded, and Åsa scurried off, passing J-O with a nod and receiving an appreciative smile in response before setting her course for the men.

Natalia saw how the young, well-groomed men welcomed Åsa with cheek kisses and a general uptick in rooster-like behavior. Natalia waited apprehensively for J-O to reach her. They met in the middle of the shoreline promenade. The sun was high in the sky, and despite her chilly swim, Natalia was sweating.

"There you are," J-O greeted her. "You disappeared yesterday."

"Yes," she said, but without further comment. J-O was her boss, but he certainly didn't *own* her time.

"Was it anything I need to be concerned about?" he asked as they began strolling along side by side. "Because several people asked about you."

"No," she said. "I talked to the Danes. They seem calm." She wondered if she should bring up J-O having had lunch with her father without including her, but she decided no good would come of that.

"Good." J-O nodded toward one of the many press tents that were set up. "Walk with me."

Natalia walked over to the press tent with him. J-O greeted a journalist and introduced her to Natalia, who greeted her politely.

Natalia noted J-O's approving looks. He was satisfied with her. And she thought she conducted herself well. She shook hands with a member of parliament, met a potential investor, and thought that this, this was what she did best: talk finance, network, build relationships.

David saw Natalia standing there mingling with some people over at one of the press tents along the waterfront promenade. He had just concluded a panel debate with an economics professor and a business owner. He was only half listening to the follow-up discussion now as he tried to steal an extra glimpse of Natalia. She was coolly dressed in linen, with J-O as a safe harbor at her side, and seemed to be in her element. With a beach bag over her shoulder and sunglasses on top of her head, she looked confident and efficient, energetic, competent, and actually completely radiant.

It was as if something constricted over his chest, and he swallowed at the sensation.

"Could I ask a few questions?" wondered a journalist, a woman he'd spoken to often over the years.

David tore his eyes off Natalia, smiled reflexively, and nodded in response. This journalist was always well informed and professional, and he usually tried to be accommodating for her. But he took one last look at Natalia, couldn't help himself. Her hair looked wet. Had she been swimming? She was probably an excellent swimmer. Oh, how he wished he could walk over to her, wished he could stop time, wished he could . . .

"David?"

He was lost in his own thoughts, and now he'd missed the journalist's question. He smiled apologetically. "Sorry," he said.

"No problem," the journalist said, but he saw her glance over at Natalia and J-O with curiosity, as if she were trying to work out what had distracted David.

She began her interview again, asked her questions, and then let her photographer do his job.

As soon as the journalist thanked David, he noticed J-O and Natalia coming his way. His heart thumped, ridiculous but true. Natalia's face was tranquil, almost without expression, but David could see her mind racing. She was worried, he realized, and he wanted to calm her down. He would never embarrass her in front of J-O. He knew what her job meant to her, how important her integrity was. How reluctant she was to be tied to him. Strangely enough, that hurt a little, even though he was the one who was about to betray her.

And then David spotted someone behind Natalia and J-O.

Ah.

This could get complicated.

When they got to him, David shook J-O's hand first. Then he looked Natalia in the eye, and it felt like oceans of time passed.

"You know Natalia De la Grip, don't you?" J-O said, and David was sure he was implying something.

David held out his hand to her. "Yes," he said calmly. "We've met."

Natalia hesitated for a fraction of a second, but then shook his hand, mumbling a polite greeting. She swallowed, and her slender throat tensed.

His eyes grazed the tender skin along the neckline of her blouse. A few hours ago he'd kissed that very spot. The scent of her still surrounded him, like the memory of an unusually vivid dream.

"And this is Eugene Tolstoy," Natalia said, introducing a gray-haired man. She smiled warmly. "My uncle."

David made his face go completely expressionless.

Just what the two of us need, even more complications.

"My mother's brother," Natalia added. Of course. Eugene's sister was Natalia's mother, Ebba De la Grip.

David shook hands with the Russian. They'd already met, which naturally he couldn't reveal, especially not to this group. He smiled politely at Eugene, the eccentric and extremely rich Russian who happened to own quite a bit of Investum stock. Eugene blinked at David. David bit his tongue. The man probably couldn't even spell the word *discretion*.

"What a small world this is," Natalia commented without seeming to have noticed anything unusual. She smiled at her Uncle Eugene and J-O. "How everyone knows everyone else, I mean."

And, David thought, it was even smaller than she realized.

Natalia looked at her uncle for a long time and then at David. She furrowed her brow slightly and then asked the question that David would really rather not have had to hear: "You two already know each other?" Her eyes were calm and slightly intrigued, but David knew she was dangerously smart. The smallest clue and she would start putting the puzzle together faster than any computer.

He wished he'd insisted that he and Michel leave town this morning the way he'd wanted. He had wanted to focus on all their commitments and just go, but Michel had been uncharacteristically stubborn, and they had stayed, and now Natalia was standing here questioning one of the men David really didn't want to start talking. He didn't know the Russian well enough, didn't know how reliable he was.

And then: saved by yet another relative.

"Alexander!" Natalia cried, looking away from her uncle. She beamed at her brother, who joined them. More handshakes and cheek kisses. David found himself shaking Alexander De la Grip's firm hand. The younger man's piercing blue eyes, completely unlike Natalia's, looked into his own. Alexander De la Grip was like a younger, more vital-looking version of his Russian uncle. And he squeezed David's hand quite hard. "It's David, right?"

David wrinkled his brow. So Alexander De la Grip, the direct descendant of at least one Russian grand duke and notorious for his immoral lifestyle and his general lack of interest in anything other than his own pleasure, had decided to dislike him.

But David couldn't have cared less what a spoiled rich kid thought or didn't think of him. He pulled his hand back, looked at his watch, and saw that it would soon be time to leave Båstad. He made sure to excuse himself during the minor commotion that followed in the wake of Alexander's arrival.

He saw Natalia notice his departure and gave her a subtle wave. She looked so happy here, surrounded by her friends and relatives. He wanted to remember her this way, competent, together with her ilk, sun-kissed and laughing. She trained her twinkly gold eyes on his, and they shared a look, held it for a long time before David forced himself to look away. He nodded to her and then did what he should have done a long time ago: walked away.

She watched him go.

He felt her gaze on his back, on the back of his neck, but he didn't turn around.

Good-bye, Natalia.

Alexander noticed Natalia watching David Hammar stroll away, irritatingly self-confident, as if he owned half the world and would soon own the other half as well. There was no mistaking the look on Natalia's face—nor the look she and David had exchanged—and he wondered what was going on between his clever big sister and the force of nature that was David Hammar.

Natalia had never looked at Jonas like that, not that that had ever bothered Alexander. The rest of the family had been disappointed when Natalia and the ever-boring Jonas broke up, as if he were the best Natalia could get. But Alexander had always thought Jonas was too weak a person for his sister. Natalia was diplomatic and low-key, calm and levelheaded, but she was also strong as all hell, maybe the strongest person in the whole family. She needed an equal, not a nature buff like Jonas. But that said . . .

The ice-cold David Hammar was hardly a better choice. David was gone from view, but Natalia—his big-hearted sister who was capable of so many fine sentiments that Alexander knew he could never be capable of—was still watching where he'd been with an abandoned expression.

"Well, that's a little strange," he said casually. Natalia raised an eyebrow.

"I would have thought David Hammar would hate us all," he explained.

"What do you mean?"

"Well, I started at Skogbacka a few years after Peter and David graduated," Alexander began. "But the rumors lived on." He shook his head. They were so macabre they had to be true.

"What rumors?" she asked sharply. So sharply that Alexander realized she already knew something.

"Something happened to Hammar at Skogbacka, something bad."

"Harassment?"

"More like hazing," Alexander said tersely. He'd hated his boarding school years.

"David has scars on his back," she said quietly. "From a whip."

Alexander avoided thinking about exactly how his sister came to know what David Hammar's back looked like.

"Be careful," he said.

"*You're* giving me relationship advice?" she said with a smile. "Really?"

"He's not a nice person," Alexander said.

"There are those who would say the same of you," she pointed out.

Alexander shook his head, knowing she was right. "What happened at Skogbacka was serious. It was hushed up, but I know a girl was involved. According to the rumors, she died."

It did actually happen that people died at those schools. Accidents happen.

Yeah, right.

"There was some kind of settlement," Alexander continued as his memories began to crystalize. The school had been abuzz with rumors. "And I'm pretty sure it was about a girl."

It always was, he thought. Sex or money. So depressing.

"But why would he hate *us* for that?"

Alexander looked her in the eye, her gaze wide and uneasy. Shit, she was in this deep. Alexander shook his head. This wasn't good— she should steer well clear of David Hammar.

"Because they said Peter was the one who whipped him," he said quietly. "Peter abused him."

She blanched but didn't say anything, just looked at him for a long time. Alexander wanted to say something astute and comforting, but he'd never been very good at playing the role of the considerate brother.

Someone drew Natalia's attention, and she turned away. Someone else asked Alexander to pose for a picture, so he rubbed his eyes and then faked a smile. Damn, he was tired. He looked at the glass in his hand. And clearly he was already drinking. He didn't remember how the glass had gotten into his hand, and now it seemed to be empty. He looked at Natalia.

This was problematic, this business with Natalia and David. That notorious venture capitalist had a lot of secrets. And many of them seemed to have something to do with the De la Grip family.

Alexander excused himself and walked over to one of the bars serving drinks along the shore promenade. It was lunchtime, he rationalized, avoiding reflecting on what self-delusions like this actually meant.

He twirled his glass and let his mind wander.

Yesterday at J-O's massive party, he had wound up behind a heavy curtain. A thick velvet drape, long enough to hide a couple who needed hiding when someone unexpectedly walked into the room where they'd been having sex over the back of an armchair.

He'd hastily flung himself behind the curtain, along with the far-too-young second wife of one of those men who considered themselves pillars of the nation. She was a bored, thrill-seeking woman with exhibitionist tendencies. But she was also a woman who would really prefer to stay married. So when the door opened, she had quickly pulled Alexander behind the curtain.

With her eyes wide from suppressed laughter, she continued to satisfy him with her hand. She had talented hands, and Alexander had never been one to object. So he'd stood there behind that heavy curtain, in a window on the second floor of J-O's extravagant house, and let himself be jerked off by a pampered housewife seeking affirmation while he listened to the man who'd entered the room have a quiet conversation on his cell phone.

Alexander hadn't seen the man who was talking, but he had still known who it was. And the conversation had clearly been with a woman. The man's voice had been warm and loving. The whole time the conversation (and the hand job) had been underway, Alexander's eyes had been on the yard below. The estate had been filled with partying guests. He'd seen many people, including his big sister. Dressed in red, Natalia had been drinking champagne, chatting with J-O and laughing in the middle of the garden.

Natalia had *not* had a phone in her hand.

Therefore Alexander was entirely sure that the person David Hammar had been talking to on his cell phone, the person Alexander was convinced must be a woman, and to whom David in a gentle, loving voice had said, "I love you," could by no means have been Natalia.

This could only end one way.

Badly.

30

If J-O's Thursday party was the most festive and extravagant of Bås-tad week, then the De la Grip family's customary Friday barbecue was the most traditional. The average age of the guests was somewhat higher and the snoot factor, based purely on the number of royal and titled attendees, a notch greater. Natalia's father socialized with a group of men who knew the king, and Natalia's mother cultivated those connections carefully. No detail could be off; no one was permitted to deviate from the code of conduct when the royal couple was expected.

The party was held at her parents' villa. Somber music filled the air. The black-and-white-clad wait staff worked efficiently. The wine being served came from the De la Grip family's vineyard in France. Linen tablecloths and the silver table service were family heirlooms, and everything that could be polished gleamed. The refrigerators were filled with midnight snacks. The aroma of the food wafted over the grounds—the same menu every year, tables heaping with meat and game. Classic, Swedish dishes.

Natalia scanned the room where the guests were quietly mingling. French doors opened out to the garden; door attendants made sure the right people got in and that everyone else was kept outside. Natalia saw Louise chatting with her mother by the antique credenza. They wore nearly identical dresses and similar jewelry and gesticulated in the same feminine way. Louise was actually more like the daughter Natalia suspected her mother had always wanted, blond, interested in interior design, art, and genealogy. And just like her

mother, Louise mostly communicated through subtle digs and pregnant sighs. With her arrogant ways and her blond French twist, Louise
actually resembled the rest of the De la Grip family more than Natalia
ever had. She turned away. Uncle Eugene, with two cut-crystal vodka
glasses in his hands, was heading her way.

"Natalia, darling," he said effusively, handing her one of the glasses.
He took a swig of his own drink and then looked over at his sister Ebba
with a slightly curled lip. He shook his head and then said to Natalia,
"Things haven't been easy for you, *milochka*."

Natalia tasted the vodka. She'd always wondered why Eugene
looked down on his own sister so much, but she'd never dared ask.

"It's always the same people who come to all the parties," she said
instead. All these cookie-cutter people, she thought gloomily, men in
identical suits, women with their discreet little dresses and even
more discreet plastic surgeries. Somehow it felt more stifling than
usual. "Don't you think it's depressing?" she asked, taking another
sip. Maybe she should just get a bottle of vodka and sit down by herself in a corner somewhere?

Eugene studied her closely. "Are you missing someone in particular?" he asked casually.

Natalia looked away and took another little sip of the cold liquor.
"Who is that Alexander's talking to?" she asked, skirting her uncle's
far too insightful question. Apparently she hadn't been as careful
with David as she'd thought.

David.

Just thinking his name quietly to herself set her heart aflutter.
Damn it, she really, *really* had it bad.

She nodded at Alexander, and Uncle Eugene looked that way.
Alexander stood with one hand nonchalantly in his pocket, smiling at
the redheaded woman she'd noticed at J-O's party. She did not return his smile at all. It was so unusual that a woman wouldn't be
completely spellbound in Alexander's presence that Natalia was actually startled. When Alex directed his charm at someone, they usually
had no chance.

"No idea," Uncle Eugene said without any interest. "Some doctor,
I think." He studied the two more closely. "Alex can just give up on
that one right now," he confirmed.

Natalia smiled. "He's not very used to encountering resistance."

"No," Uncle Eugene agreed and then greeted a man who joined them. "Have you met Count Carl-Erik Tessin?" he asked.

The man, who was Natalia's father's age, was gray-haired, sun-tanned, and distinguished in his conservative suit. A man who spent a lot of time outdoors, Natalia thought. She smiled automatically and held out her hand. He shook it, but he was looking at her so intently that she thought maybe they already knew each other. "Have we met before?" she asked in an apologetic tone. She didn't recognize him at all.

But Count Tessin shook his head. "No, but I know who you are. You're Gustaf's daughter. I went to Skogbacka with him." He smiled a smile that did not really reach his eyes. Count Tessin generally seemed to be bearing some underlying sorrow. "Ages ago," he added.

He seemed pleasant, and Natalia tried to call to mind more exactly who he might be. Her mother and Louise would have known, of course. Those two had the who's who of Swedish nobility memorized. They would have known whom he was married to, the name of his estate, and how many children he had.

"Carl-Erik and I live near each other," Uncle Eugene explained. "We're almost neighbors."

Uncle Eugene had been living at Alexander's mansion south of Båstad for a couple of years as some sort of house sitter. The von Essen siblings, Ebba and Eugene, had grown up in Sweden, but while Ebba had carefully tended her Swedish noble heritage, Eugene had taken their mother's maiden name and never called himself anything other than Eugene Tolstoy. He had spent many years in Russia, but Natalia had never really had the guts to ask him what he did there. Despite his Russian teddy-bear-like charisma, her uncle had some sharp edges and dangerous contours. But in recent years Eugene, who was openly gay, had settled permanently in Sweden. In the mansion that Alexander owned but rarely visited. Natalia was glad her uncle had friends, because despite his booming laugh, he often seemed lonely.

"We drink brandy and talk about better days," Carl-Erik laughed and looked as if he were about to say something else, but they were interrupted by the appearance of Natalia's father.

The mood in the group changed instantly.

As usual, Gustaf De la Grip dominated the space with his presence. He was like a king, used to obedience and attention, secure in his position, convinced of his own superiority. But that created friction, and the mood became more strained.

Eugene greeted Gustaf with a handshake. Gustaf looked at Count Tessin. The two men sized each other up. They were the same height, the same age, and actually equal in all regards. But something in their postures revealed the balance of power. "It's been a while," Gustaf said. "I didn't think I'd see you again."

"And yet here I am," Carl-Erik responded quietly. "Thanks for the invitation."

It wasn't actually a strange conversation. Their tone was polite, their phrases courteous, and their faces calm. But there was a hostile undercurrent between them that Natalia couldn't put her finger on, a barely evident aggression that seeped through, making their gestures jerky and their tone staccato. Gustaf turned to Uncle Eugene and said something about hunting and his hunting club. Carl-Erik moved back, pulled away. He apologized to Natalia and surprised her by taking her hand and kissing it in the old-fashioned way before leaving them. Natalia watched him go, still unsure what she'd just witnessed. But something had just gone on below the surface, she was sure of that. Unspoken words and scarcely concealed looks had been exchanged. She had a frustrating sense that she should have been able to interpret them and thereby solve some mystery.

"Dad," Peter said, joining them.

So typically Peter. He was probably scared to death that Gustaf would say something important. Peter was always protecting his interests, always uneasy. First he nodded to Gustaf with his usual fawning respect. Then he shook hands with Uncle Eugene but made sure to avoid the Russian kiss on the cheek. Peter had never liked physical contact. Maybe that's why he and Louise were such a good fit, Natalia thought unfairly, and then greeted him with a nod but nothing more. She had the lowest rank and they never hugged. Although, it occurred to her, no one in the family aside from her and Alex hugged. How was it that she'd never reflected on that? Her mother hugged Louise. And her mother had hugged Jonas. But never her own children. Wasn't that strange? Why hadn't that struck her before?

"Have you heard anything else about the stock price?" Peter asked, and Natalia paid attention.

"What are you talking about?" she said.

Peter gave their father a questioning look, as if asking for permission to tell her. As if they had secrets that they needed to decide whether they could share with Natalia. "Tell me," she said sharply.

Gustaf nodded his brief consent.

"Investum shares are being traded," Peter began. He spoke slowly and sparingly, his eyes on his father the whole time, as if he were prepared to cut himself short if he happened to say too much. "We've been following it all week. No one knows what's going on," he continued. "But some unknown names have started turning up in the shareholder list. No one knows who they are. We're going to have to look into it next week."

"Can't we look into it right now?" Natalia asked. This could affect the deal she and J-O were working on. Shares changing hands and winding up with unknown parties was never good. "How many shares are we talking about?"

Peter turned abruptly to her. "*You* haven't said anything about the deal to anyone, have you?"

She stared at him and then at her father. What the hell did they think of her? "No," she said brusquely. Damn it, she was angry. She swallowed, feeling a little jumpy, because she had been so close to saying something to David. If he hadn't stopped her, maybe she would have told. "No," she repeated.

It wasn't as if David had anything to do with the movement in the stock price, right?

Or did he?

David was driving his blue Bentley. Michel had finished his coffee with Åsa Bjelke, and they were finally on their way out of Båstad. David hesitated and then made a hasty left turn. The road to Stockholm disappeared off to their right.

"Which way are you taking?" Michel asked, perplexed.

"This is just a little detour," David said.

As they approached the big villa, they saw the crowd of people outside and inside the garden. The guards at the gate let invited guests in through the wrought-iron fence. Outside, people stood and gaped at all the extravagance. The music could be heard out on the street.

David slowed down. It felt as if he still had a choice.

"Uh, what are we doing here?" Michel asked. "Isn't this the De la Grip mansion?"

David nodded. He looked, knowing that ultimately there still wasn't any choice. He'd been planning this for half his life. And he had to think about Carolina, not about a woman he'd known for . . . what, two weeks?

He looked out at the laughing guests in their party clothes, the elite. Some of them were actually people he cared about, people whose lives he was going to impact.

"David?"

He shook his head in response to Michel's question. He took his foot off the brake, took one look in the rearview mirror, and pulled out.

They drove home in total silence.

David dropped Michel off and then drove home.

He parked the car, took his bag, and went in the door. They had agreed to meet at the office at seven the next morning.

It was time.

31

"Thirty–love."

Natalia hit the tennis ball over the net with all her strength.

"What the hell," Åsa complained with no more than a very half-hearted attempt to reach it. "I can't take any more now. Can't we go get a drink instead?"

"It's eight o'clock in the morning," Natalia pointed out, fetching a new ball. "Ready?"

Åsa nodded gloomily. Natalia served the ball, and Åsa returned it.

Natalia had had an early tennis reservation at the Royal Tennis Hall, and in an unusual momentary lapse of judgment, she'd forced Åsa to join her.

"Why did you agree to come if this is so awful for you?" she asked when Åsa swore again.

Åsa twirled her racket and then swung it menacingly. "Because otherwise I'm going to kill someone. I have to burn off some hormones."

Natalia more or less felt the same way. She served another ball. She hadn't heard a peep from David since Friday in Båstad. Now it was Monday morning, and she refused, absolutely refused to sit home and be depressed about a man, dissecting everything he'd said or hadn't said, compulsively checking her e-mail and text messages every five minutes.

She had texted him on Saturday. He hadn't responded. And now here she stood angrily smashing balls at a grumpy Åsa.

"You want to play another game?" she asked, wiping the sweat off her forehead.

It was hot and stuffy, and she felt tired, really worn down. Båstad had been unexpectedly exhausting. She'd left her parents' party early, had lain in bed and watched the sea, inhaling David's scent on the sheets. On Saturday she'd swum and slept, and on Sunday she and Åsa had come back home together. Natalia needed to work in Stockholm for at least another week, and Åsa had suddenly decided not to stay in Båstad after all. They were pathetic.

"Are you going to see Michel again?" Natalia asked over the net.

"Maybe," Åsa said. "I don't know. Maybe. I can't handle any more right now."

They showered and sat in the club café, each with a smoothie. Åsa sipped her drink, muttering something about wasting good cocktail mixer material.

Natalia absentmindedly picked at her open-faced cheese sandwich. "When you said they had some kind of job they needed you to come home for," she began, "did you get any sense what it was?"

"Why are you asking?"

Something wasn't right.

Natalia felt it so strongly it was almost palpable. For some reason she found herself wondering about Investum's stock price, which was behaving so oddly. And she wondered why the price had been slowly, very slowly going up the last six months.

"Have you ever heard Peter say anything about Skogbacka?" she asked, feeling her pulse start to pick up. "He and David were there at the same time. Apparently Peter did something to him." She thought about the scars on David's back.

"Like bullying?"

"Yeah, but worse." *Peter whipped him.*

Her head was spinning.

Everything is personal.

There was a woman involved.

The blonde in the picture frame.

J-O thought Hammar Capital was working on something big.

"I haven't heard anything," Åsa said. "I could ask around a little if you want. Are you feeling alright? You look really pale."

Natalia dropped her sandwich. She couldn't eat. Waves of nausea washed over her.

"Do you think Hammar Capital is working on something involving Investum?" she asked slowly, hoping that Åsa would laugh out loud at her silly question.

"Do *you*?" Åsa asked seriously.

Natalia had never really understood why David had asked her out to that first lunch.

All the Investum shares with unknown owners.

David's hasty departure from Båstad.

The hatred between her family and David.

Skogbacka.

Shares with unknown owners.

Never satisfied.

She blinked. Could it be true? She turned to Åsa, but her eyes were almost glazed over.

She had to get to work. ASAP.

Because now she had identified the look David had given her when he left.

She'd thought the look had been about the beginning of something great and new.

But it hadn't been about a beginning at all.

It had been about an ending.

32

David was in the office early on Monday morning, freshly showered, clean-shaven, and focused.

He got himself a cup of coffee, sat down at his computer, and waited for Michel.

It was just a question of moving forward now, nothing more. He forced his thoughts into different mental cubbyholes, closing the doors on all the ones that didn't have to do with this deal.

When he had rashly plunged into this relationship with Natalia, he had thought he could handle it because it wouldn't involve any feelings.

But he had developed feelings for her, feelings that were far too strong. And now, when he needed all his focus, his concentration was disrupted by an impossible distraction. Because it *was* impossible, doomed.

He scanned his e-mails and started sorting through the stacks of paper on his desk. He stretched his neck, which was stiff, but otherwise he was fine, *had to be* fine.

Michel came in, serious but apparently energized.

David hesitated, but he had to say it. He couldn't think clearly anymore, and he needed his friend's reassurance.

"I have something to tell you before we begin," he said, gesturing to the chair next to his desk.

Michel sat down. "Does this maybe have anything to do with Natalia De la Grip?"

"In a way."

Michel eyed him skeptically. "Do I want to hear it?"

"Probably not, but I need your opinion. I'm at a loss. I need to hear that I'm doing the right thing, that what we're going to do makes financial sense."

Michel swore a long string of curse words in French and then shook his head. "I need some coffee," he said, standing up. "Then we'll talk about this behind closed doors."

David waited. Michel came back with coffee. He shut the door. It was early, but people were already starting to come in.

"I slept with Natalia," David began.

Michel raised an eyebrow. "Again?"

"Yes."

"That wasn't smart."

"No," David agreed.

"I mean given that you're about to destroy her family."

"I know what you meant," David snapped.

Michel studied him. "What kind of feelings do you have for her?"

"I don't feel anything for her."

Michel sipped his coffee. He made a face. "I'm in love with Åsa."

No shit, Sherlock. "Have you guys talked?"

Michel nodded.

"Michel, there's more I have to tell you."

"More?"

"We've gone over this so many times," David began. "Decided this was a sound business plan, right? Everyone says so. There's a real financial reason to do this. And we have a good chance of making a lot of money."

"Yes," Michel said slowly.

"And you know we've always said business can't be personal. That's what we've been best at, keeping a cool head, being professional, not caring about prestige and all that."

"I'm really not going to want to hear this, am I?" Michel said with a heavy sigh.

"When I was a student at Skogbacka something happened, between me and Peter De la Grip."

"Something?"

"It was really bad," David said, remembering how he'd sat in that soundproof room in the basement with blood pouring from his back. "Life-and-death bad. His father, Gustaf, was involved. And my family too. It's a long story. It was after that incident I decided."

"Decided what?"

"That I was going to become rich enough to crush them, wipe them out." David shrugged. "Get revenge."

Michel blinked.

David waited for what he'd said to sink in.

"Fuck. You should have told me," Michel finally said.

David exhaled. It was an incredible relief to have that said, to give all that information to Michel. Almost all of it. "Yes, I should have," he agreed.

"We've always been upfront with each other, open, no lies—those are your words, your values."

"Yes," David said.

"But you hid this from me. I have a right to be mad."

"Absolutely," David said. "How mad are you?"

Michel shrugged. "I'm hurt that you kept this to yourself. But from a purely business perspective, it doesn't change anything."

"No, I didn't think so."

"Do you want to back out? There's still time to turn around, I assume," Michel thought out loud. "But if we do, we're going to bleed. And it would weaken Hammar Capital." He looked seriously at David. "Is that what you want to do? For her sake?"

David shook his head. "No, we're still on."

"But she's going to *hate* you."

"Yes." Natalia was going to hate him. Maybe that was just as well. She deserved a good man, better than him, better than he could ever be.

"Hey, you," Michel said hesitantly.

"What?"

"While we're confessing things to each other . . . ," he began.

David pinched the bridge of his nose. Oh lord, they'd never had a conversation like this before. He wondered which of them was more uncomfortable. "What?" he asked curtly.

"When we had coffee, Åsa asked if I knew anything about someone vacuuming up Investum shares off the market."

He'd known the whole time that they couldn't underestimate her. "What did *you* say?" he asked.

Michel made a face. "I broke down and told her everything. What do you think? I flatly denied it, of course. But now she's going to hate me."

"Join the club. I think Natalia suspects something too. If we had been dealing with those two instead of the men, we would never have made it this far." Investum's board was one hundred percent male. Seven white middle-aged men. That's what happened when you recruited buddies from your good old boy network. You lost out on talent.

There was a knock on the door. "Everything's ready," Malin Theselius said, sticking her head in the doorway.

David looked at the clock. There were still twenty minutes left until the stock market opened. He nodded to her. "We're on our way."

The Stockholm Stock Exchange had been computerized years ago. No trading actually took place in the beautiful old 1770s building in Old Town Stockholm anymore. Everything happened at Nasdaq OMX down in the Frihamnen waterfront neighborhood and was then immediately displayed on monitors around the country, in banks, brokerage firms, the offices of fund managers. The market opened at nine o'clock.

They'd already made a massive buy early this morning, before the market opened. With that buy, in one fell swoop, Hammar Capital now owned ten percent of Investum. Deals of that size were traditionally occasionally permitted after hours, in order to minimize halts in trading.

"Did you flag it?" Michel asked.

David nodded. As soon as anyone owned more than five percent of a company, you had to flag it by reporting it to Sweden's Financial Supervisory Authority. For Hammar Capital to suddenly own not just five, but ten percent would have explosive results on the market. "I just e-mailed them," David said.

"They're going to audit us."

What David had done ran along an extremely fine line between unethical and illegal. "They won't be able to prove shit," he said.

David and Michel stood up. They buttoned their jackets and looked at each other. They walked out to the lobby in silence. The Reuters screens, monitors that reported stock prices without a time delay, hung in the conference room, and they headed there. Malin came in too. A couple of the analysts came and sat down at the table.

Nine o'clock arrived.

The market opened.

The prices blinked, ticking by row by row. The Investum share price started climbing. And climbing.

"I'm going to send the press release now," Malin said ceremonially.

David nodded.

She hit SEND.

The price kept going up.

Soon they would find out what would happen when the market realized what was going on. You never knew for sure. The stock market had a mind of its own. It was erratic. But they had their hunches.

David looked at Michel. "Are you ready?"

"Yes."

"Let's do it."

Michel nodded. Malin nodded.

The war had begun.

33

Natalia and Åsa had gone their separate ways after tennis. Åsa had taken a taxi to Investum, while Natalia had put on her sneakers and walked from the Royal Tennis Hall to her office at Stureplan.

She was tired and hadn't slept well, so she thought a little more exercise might do her some good. The city was quiet and mellow, and the urge to rush had dissipated. She needed to think. She bought a bottle of water on the way, and tried to focus her mind.

When she reached the bank's half-full offices, she got to work, convinced that this was the best way she knew to handle her anxiety, powerlessness, and fatigue.

There didn't seem to be any sign. The office was calm. Everything was under control. She persuaded herself that she was wrong, that she'd overreacted.

All hell broke loose at five minutes past nine.

Every phone started ringing, almost simultaneously. Texts and e-mails chimed in, every electronic device started blinking and making noise. After a look at one of the e-mails, she knew it was bad, really bad.

"Oh my God," she whispered.

It was as if she were at the top of a building that had started to collapse beneath her.

She acted without thinking. She grabbed her purse, threw her cell phone into it, and rushed out.

"I have to go to Investum," she called to the receptionist.

The whole way there, she tried calling: her father, Peter, J-O, but every line was busy. She was forced to stop and catch her breath at a street corner. Her hand on her side, she was on the verge of vomiting.

She couldn't believe it was true. Despite all her suspicions, despite her musings that morning, the shock was still numbing.

She was breathing so hard she saw spots. Her hands were shaking, her legs were numb. She forced herself to keep going.

Ten minutes later she pulled open the front door, ran up the stairs, and opened the door to Investum's headquarters. The lobby was in chaos. No one even looked up when she came in, standing there breathing so hard she could taste blood in her mouth. Phones were ringing, people were talking loudly, their faces red, their eyes glazed. Women and men ran around with papers in their hands. The big TV on the wall was showing live financial news, and someone had turned up the volume. The monitors for the various stock prices blinked cataclysmically.

Natalia knocked on the door to Åsa's office and stepped in without waiting for a response. Åsa had her feet up on her desk, the red soles of her pumps bright and shiny. She waved Natalia in while she kept talking into her BlackBerry in a steady voice.

"Gustaf is on his way home from Båstad," Åsa said by way of a greeting after she hung up. Her phone rang again, but after a glance at the caller ID, she sent the call to voice mail. "Peter and the others are coming too," she added.

"Alexander?" Natalia asked. It felt like a time when the family ought to be together.

Åsa shook her head. "Haven't talked to him. He's already on a plane to New York, apparently he was just here for the weekend."

"What did Dad say?"

Åsa shrugged. "You know how he is. He stays calm. On the surface."

Natalia knew. Her father never lost his cool, although he must be furious now. Peter, on the other hand, would be frazzled. And even now Peter was surely trying to find a scapegoat for this catastrophe. A shiver ran through Natalia. She had an incredibly bad feeling about this.

"What do we know?" Natalia asked.

Åsa's phone rang again, and this time she took the call, but she waved to Natalia to stay, so Natalia sat there in the visitor's chair, slumped, sapped of energy, mute from shock.

Åsa finished her conversation. "There's going to be a press conference at ten o'clock," she said. "They're doing the broadcast from Hammar Capital's headquarters. Come on."

They walked out to the lobby. Every time a phone rang, every time an e-mail or a text message came in, there was yet another catastrophe to add to the previous ones. This—whatever was going on—would hurt the business in unforeseeable ways. Natalia looked around. It was like a battlefield. Someone was crying. Someone was screaming.

"It's starting!" someone called, and they gathered in front of the TV.

A blond woman, communications director Malin Theselius, began the press conference at the exact specified time and stated in a steady voice that Hammar Capital, based on the quantity of shares they now owned, would be calling a special general meeting. The journalists shouted their questions, trying to drown each other out. Natalia had never seen such a heated press conference. It was like a bad movie. Malin answered as best she could. She gave a calm, composed impression, polite and accommodating. David had recruited someone who really knew what she was doing.

Yes, the major owners and backers are with Hammar Capital.

Yes, David Hammar wants a seat on the board.

Yes, things will be done totally by the books.

The questions never ended.

And the phones were still ringing in the office. Natalia watched Investum's own communications director, a fifty-year-old man in a suit, answer his cell phone, and then she saw his face go totally ashen. Whatever he'd been told was really bad.

Natalia looked down, cold and nauseated. This was only just beginning. She heard the communications director raise his voice and thought that it was never good when the man whose job it was to be the outward face of the company was screaming like an angry drunk. She looked at the TV, where the blond Malin Theselius was courteously answering the journalists' questions. The contrast was striking, but maybe she was being unfair. As far as she knew, this was the first time in the company's history that anything like this had happened. It wasn't really so strange that they didn't have any strategies for handling it.

David was on-screen, off to the side behind Malin. Michel stood on her other side. Both men looked refreshed and exhilarated, and David totally oozed power and confidence. It came through loud and clear. Natalia wondered if he would say anything and if so, what. And she wondered if there was some manual for how she was supposed to feel in a situation like this. The first shock hadn't subsided yet. Maybe some shocks never did.

She was completely closed off from her feelings. As if she was watching herself and the situation from the outside. As if there was some other Natalia standing a little ways away, watching what was happening, a Natalia who was trying to analyze the situation but who didn't feel a thing. She noted simply that she had been tricked, betrayed, and deceived.

She started to feel dizzy. She couldn't take this in, couldn't.

Her phone rang, and through completely foggy eyes, she saw from the caller ID that it was J-O.

"Where are you?" she answered without saying hello.

"On my way in," J-O replied. She heard airport sounds in the background and tried to remember where he might be. "Where are you?" he asked.

"I'll be in the office in ten minutes," she replied. "I'll see you there."

"The Danes are going to pull out."

"I know."

This was going to have completely unforeseeable consequences. And on so many different levels. Heads would roll, people would lose their jobs. And Investum, the unsinkable company, the pride of the nation . . . Natalia couldn't even imagine what would happen to Investum. She took a deep breath and stood up. She didn't have time to fall apart. Because when this caught up with her, she didn't know if she would be able to get through it.

"I have to go back to work," she told Åsa, who hardly looked up.

Inside the Bank of London's offices at Stureplan things were significantly calmer; people were watching live broadcasts and muttering comments, but working as usual.

Natalia sat glued to a TV screen in the lunchroom, following the developments with one hand over her mouth. She tried her father and Peter on their cell phones, over and over again, but no one answered. She called David. When it went to voice mail for the second time, she left a message and then sat staring at her phone, trying to will him to answer. Nothing happened.

When the staff came in to eat lunch, she shut herself into her office. She just sat there as if someone had poured lead into her joints. Her blood was pounding, but she was so tired. And she was cold and a little sick to her stomach. I'm in shock, she persuaded herself. It's the body's way of protecting itself against mortal danger.

J-O came in after lunch. By now the websites of all the major papers had the news on their home pages—*Hammar Capital Goes After Investum. David Hammar vs. Goliath.*

Later, she went out and bought all the papers. The news was everywhere.

Here's how it affects you.

The power struggle.

Playboy billionaire's brazen power grab.

At three o'clock a grim J-O confirmed that the Danes had pulled out. The banking deal Natalia had been working on for so long had fallen through.

At three-thirty, her father and Peter landed in Stockholm. Peter texted her from the taxi.

Dad wants you to come over to their place. At six.

Her fingers cold and trembling, she replied that she'd be there.

This nightmare had only begun.

When she left the office at five-thirty, David still hadn't responded to a single one of her texts or voice mails.

34

Feeling as if she were still wrapped in a thick fog of shock, Natalia took a taxi out to her parents' villa in Djursholm. Her mother, father, Peter, Louise, and Åsa were already there. Her father's face was like a stiff mask, and he hardly greeted her. Peter looked like he'd aged several years in just a few days. Her mother and Louise each sat, straight-backed in antique chairs, wringing their hands, like pale women from the 1800s. All that was missing were the smelling salts and fans.

Her mother's housecleaner, Gina, the same young woman who cleaned for Natalia, served them tea. She slid through the room silently, moving among them. Peter waved her away in irritation, but Natalia gratefully accepted a cup. "Thank you so much," she murmured. Åsa was standing by the window talking on her phone. She took a cup of tea without looking at Gina.

Natalia turned to her father and brother. "What's the news?" she asked.

"There will be an extraordinary general meeting in two weeks," Peter said bitterly. "He wants to re-vote on the board."

"Do we know who he's suggesting?"

"Yes. And there's not a single name from the old board, not even anyone from the family, and we own the company. It's so fucking arrogant."

Swapping out the whole board—that was so unusual that Natalia wasn't sure she'd ever heard of it being done. Replacing every single one, not utilizing the expertise and knowledge that was there; it was a motion of censure that was so arrogant she never would have believed it from anyone else. But she could believe it from David.

"He wants to take over completely, wipe us out; there's no doubt about it. That son of a bitch."

"Has anyone called Eugene?" Natalia asked.

"Why should we call him?" Peter's voice was snappy as he cast an unobtrusive glance at his father. Åsa finished her phone call and looked at Natalia.

Mother and Louise didn't say anything. It was like a chamber play, claustrophobic and stuffy with a frighteningly predictable plot. Her father's icy fury, Peter's overwrought breakdown, Åsa's gloomy face. And an ending that would change everything.

Natalia set down her cup. She hadn't eaten all day and was starting to feel dizzy. It was so quiet. Every time someone said something, it sounded louder than usual. All of Djursholm was quiet. No one was home at this time of year. It was like a ghost town of million-kronor mansions where only the gardeners and cleaning-service employees moved about discreetly, like shadows. "I suppose we're going to have to talk to everyone who holds A-shares," she said, realizing her voice sounded calm. Her whole body felt as if it was about to fall apart. Her heart was racing, her lungs heaving; sometimes she thought she went numb for a moment, but then she forced herself to focus on the practical matters, refused to let herself feel. Every now and then, an emotion managed to force its way in, a streak of profound despair, but so far she'd managed to hold it at bay.

She wondered how much longer she would be able to do so. She glanced at Peter, who had his hands in his pockets. He must have a bunch of keys in his pocket that he was squeezing over and over again. The jingling sound was driving her crazy. "Do *you* know anything about why he's doing this?" she asked.

"Because he's insane," Peter hissed back.

Åsa stared at Natalia. At that moment, Natalia wished she'd never confided in her about what she'd done with David. What was happening was so egregious. The shame, the sadness, the rage—all of these painful emotions would be easier to bear if she didn't also have to deal with Åsa's reaction. She looked Åsa in the eye and then turned back to Peter again. "This could have to do with something else, couldn't it?" she asked persistently.

"What do you mean by that?" he snapped.

But despite his denial, Natalia knew she was on the right track, because Peter suddenly looked pale. She continued, "I know some-thing happened between you at Skogbacka. Could what's happening now have something to do with that?"

"What are you talking about?" her mother asked indignantly. "Na-talia, that man is crazy, a nouveau-riche upstart who's trying to make a name for himself at our expense."

"But . . . ," Natalia began. She wasn't trying to defend David, but she wanted to understand what was at the root of this. What were they hiding?

"He's done this before," her father said curtly. It was the first time he'd said anything since Natalia had arrived. "To other companies. I really never thought he would dare take on Investum. But he's done this exact same thing before. On a smaller scale."

"Tell me," Natalia said.

"The moment David Hammar gets it into his head that someone has wronged him, he takes his revenge in every way he can," Gustaf said, and Natalia knew that what he was saying was the truth. She knew it because she knew David. She looked around for a place to sit. She found a chair.

"David Hammar already crushed one man who went to Skogbacka with him, a classmate who hadn't done a thing to him, but I suppose David imagined something. He took over the man's company and completely butchered it."

Mother sniffled softly.

"And then David seduced the man's wife," Gustaf continued. "Just to humiliate him completely. That poor man never recovered." Her father looked at her. "Hammar is a psychopath, Natalia, he has no conscience."

Peter nodded. "He's crazy," he said. "You could already tell at school. He couldn't accept the rules that everyone else followed. He never understood how things worked. And now he does this."

"But that's terrible," her mother said. "Can't he be reported?"

Natalia was feeling sicker and sicker. Was Peter right? Were these the acts of a crazy man? How many people had David gone after?

He'd seduced his enemy's wife to humiliate him.

Her head started spinning. Everyone else's agitated voices floated around her.

David had tricked her. Suddenly she saw that very clearly. David had used her to get at her family. *That's* what their original lunch had been about. He had been looking for weaknesses. He wasn't just out to take over Investum. He wanted to crush her entire family. Using her. Terrible things had happened between David and Peter—hazing, abuse, whipping—and now David was exacting his revenge.

Åsa was trying to catch her eye again, but Natalia looked away. She didn't want to believe that this was true, but there were heaps of evidence, and it was getting harder and harder to ignore.

She had continued to text David, over and over again. Countless times, almost compulsively. He hadn't responded a single time. Of course he hadn't. Because she meant nothing. She was just a means to achieving a goal, a pawn in a dirty game. She was so stupid, so unbelievably stupid. She wanted to double over and wail. The shame was almost unbearable. Shame at what she was, at what she had believed she'd meant to him. And guilt at what she'd done . . . She closed her eyes. Oh my God, what had she done?

35

"Let's go sit on the terrace," David said, getting a beer from the fridge in their office kitchenette. It was a warm evening, and there were plenty of nice chairs up there.

Malin and Michel—the only ones from the management group who were still at the office—each grabbed a bottle and nodded. The head of personnel and the CFO had gone home fifteen minutes earlier. The last of the rest of the staff had also left for the day. Only the three of them remained after what had definitely been the most eventful day in Hammar Capital's history.

"Good job," David said, and they clinked their bottles in silent cheers before they each sat down on the terrace. The sun had sunk down toward the horizon, and the water—the terrace had a terrific view of it—sparkled blue with some fire-colored hues.

"What a day," said Malin, kicking off her shoes and putting her feet up on a stool.

"Mmm," said Michel, and he took a big swig from his chilled bottle.

The press releases had continued to flow out of Hammar Capital all day long. The office had been practically besieged. Malin and her assistants had worked tirelessly and effectively, and David was proud of them. They were a good team. And Malin had appeared on every TV channel today, both on regular TV and online, sounding calm, collected, and professional.

"Good job, yourself," she said, but he could tell she appreciated the praise.

David had also been on pretty much every TV station. He'd done a number of interviews from the conference room in front of the Hammar Capital logo. He'd answered the same questions that Malin had fielded, over and over again for what felt like hours. Every single financial journalist he'd ever talked to had sought him out, and he had made time for most of them. He was sure he'd never talked so much in his life.

"It's going to be a long day tomorrow, too," Michel said.

"The next several *weeks* are going to be long," Malin predicted.

"And while you two put on a good show on live TV, our staff did a wonderful job back here at the office," Michel said. His eyes were bloodshot, his clothes were wrinkled, and for once he wasn't wearing his suit jacket. He was right. Their team had manned their positions. Everyone had worked hard and intently. David, who had handpicked every single one of his coworkers, was proud of them.

"If we sold everything today, we would make a real killing," Michel mused. Investum's stock price had shot through the roof. The papers were already calling this the Hammar effect.

"I'm going home," Malin said, yawning behind her hand. "My husband is starting to forget what I look like."

"And your children?"

"They're so content to have their father at home," Malin said, making a face. "I'm pretty sure my chances of winning a gold medal for motherhood have passed me by." She set down her beer bottle and put her shoes back on. "See you tomorrow."

David and Michel said good-bye to Malin and continued sitting there next to each other. Michel drank his beer with his eyes closed. It was totally quiet now that all the phones were turned off. Listening to all the ringing had been too much, and they'd decided to shut everything off an hour ago. They wouldn't be contactable for a few hours. David only had his private phone on, but the volume was off. He looked at it where it sat silently. The texts from Natalia had stopped coming a while ago.

"It's going to be brutal tomorrow," Michel said.

"Oh yes," said David.

The papers had already started digging into their backgrounds. It wouldn't be long before someone started wondering about the Skogbacka connection. The most bizarre rumors were already circulating, and they were still just a faint breeze compared to what was to come.

Tomorrow Malin would start leaking the information she had on Gustaf and Peter. Things that would not be at all favorable to them. Things that would discredit their positions at Investum, things involving secret agreements and favorable deals. Of course it would affect the entire De la Grip family, he thought. Even Natalia.

"Have you talked to her?" Michel asked slowly.

David shook his head. It was difficult for him not to feel like a complete asshole. "And you?" he asked, shoving aside the almost overwhelming feelings of guilt. "Have you heard anything from Åsa?"

Michel raised one eyebrow sarcastically. "Yes, I have," he said. "Åsa left a very detailed voice message on my cell." He scratched the stubble on his scalp. "That woman could win Olympic gold in insults. But after that, nothing. It's almost worse that she doesn't say anything."

"They want to see us—the family, I mean."

Michel brought his beer bottle to his lips and drank. He set the bottle down. "What did you say?"

"We're going to see them tomorrow. Malin is going to arrange a neutral location, probably the Grand Hôtel. We don't really want them here. And it's not like we're going to be welcome at their place." David laughed joylessly. "They'll be armed to the teeth with lawyers." He gave Michel a warning glance. "And you can count on Åsa being there. She's their best." He hoped Natalia wouldn't be there. There was no reason for her to attend, but you never knew.

"Well, that is going to be one delightful meeting," Michel muttered.

"Exactly." But David was glad he'd told Michel about Skogbacka. Even though he hadn't told him everything, of course. Not the part about Carolina.

"Maybe we ought to go home and get a little sleep," Michel said, stretching so that his joints popped. "Are you going too?"

"Soon."

Michel said good-bye and left, but David sat there, looking at the sky.

He had fantasized for so long about how this moment would feel, how it would be to finally get his revenge. In a way he'd thought it would fulfill him, fundamentally change him, that the act of breaking up and destroying Investum would feel good.

He sat for a long time as the midnight sun disappeared and the sky grew dark. The strange thing was that he didn't feel anything. He was just empty.

36

The next day Åsa arrived at the Grand Hôtel with Gustaf and Peter in Investum's company car, complete with chauffeur. The mood in the car was tense. Even more Investum lawyers followed in the car behind them, like some kind of suit-wearing private army.

The cars stopped, and everyone got out and walked into the hotel in a line.

David and Michel were already waiting in one of the conference rooms, serious and unwavering.

As Gustaf and Peter sat down at one end of the table, the lawyers fanned out in an almost comical fight to get the best, most strategic, most prestigious seats. Åsa nodded briefly to a junior attorney that he should move, and then she sat down next to Gustaf. She crossed her legs, heard her thin pantyhose rustling, and forced herself to look unaffected, almost bored, before she looked Michel in the eye for the first time. They hadn't seen or spoken to each other since they'd had coffee in Båstad. But that wasn't so strange, she thought morosely, given that he must have been extremely busy planning his hostile takeover of her boss's company.

Michel's long eyelashes trembled when their eyes met. His chest heaved inside his garish shirt—she didn't think she'd ever seen a man wearing such a pink garment. She nodded cursorily, as if they were strangers, as if he didn't concern her in the least.

Somehow he had managed to penetrate her defenses, but she would never let him see that. Her only goal today was to get through this meeting without losing her cool. Otherwise she had no expectations that this would be anything other than a massacre.

She had consistently advised Gustaf not to attend this meeting. But did Sweden's leading patriarch listen to her? No. So he, Peter, and all the young legal bucks had only themselves to blame. She would wash her hands of it. As the only woman here, she would observe what happened. And then, she thought, she would go home and get hammered on everything in her bar cabinet. Not her most Nobel-Prize-worthy plan, but still. She brusquely ordered one of her subordinates to keep the minutes. She absolutely refused to be a damn secretary.

The meeting degenerated rather quickly. Investum's lawyers started talking in loud, superior voices. They blurted out a continuous stream of legal complaints and objections, read aloud from memos, and waved their gold-signet-ring-laden fingers. It was downright tiresome, and Åsa had to pinch her thigh to keep herself from yawning. She glowered at Michel while her subordinates kept rattling off nonsense phrases they must have been practicing all night in front of the mirror.

Gustaf sat by in haughty silence. He alternated between shooting David icy glares and ignoring him completely.

Peter did not succeed in looking equally unfazed. He was obviously shocked and aggrieved. His face was red, and he radiated a corona of rage. Peter ought to be careful that he didn't have a heart attack or something.

Åsa looked at the two men from Hammar Capital, watching them as she pretended to write on her notepad.

David Hammar really was unbelievably attractive, like a fucking supermodel. And he looked so controlled sitting there in his tailor-made suit, as if he weren't physically capable of being nervous.

Åsa would never, *ever* admit it, but David scared her a little.

She moved on to the man next to him, steeling herself against the feelings she was so reluctant to accept. Michel was also calm, of course, even though she could tell from his black eyes that he had emotions. He wasn't able to look quite as cold as David. Michel had always had pathos and passion and couldn't quite hide that now. His insanely long eyelashes fluttered. Damn, he was hot.

They weren't getting anywhere at all.

Åsa's head was starting to throb. She gave Gustaf a meaningful look. *End this.*

Gustaf nodded, as if he'd heard her. Despite his poorly hidden disdain for women, he usually listened to her advice—it had something to do with her having an even more refined pedigree than he did, combined with the fact that she never got into a conflict with him—and after yet more meaningless phrases and poorly veiled threats, they marched out. The owners, her, and a whole mob of lawyers.

No one shook hands with anyone.

"What do we do now?" asked Peter when they sat back down in the car.

He was looking at Åsa, but she was staring out the window.

No fucking idea. They're going to tear us to shreds.

"We'll have to wait and see," she said, thinking it didn't matter what Michel did to her or her boss, remembering how he'd tricked her with his fancy words about wanting to talk and get to know her, all the while planning this goddamned takeover.

Åsa left the car when they got back to Investum, quickly went into her office, and shut the door behind her.

No matter what he did, she still wanted that damn Lebanese.

The next day, after working considerably more than she was actually comfortable with, something struck Åsa. She stood up from her desk chair, walked out into the hallway, and knocked on Peter's office door. He looked at her blearily. Åsa hadn't noticed before, but Peter had started going gray at the temples. He was only a couple years older than she and already going gray. And he looked like shit, haggard and drawn. She wondered if he'd been drinking. Not because she judged people for drinking, but despite his Russian lineage, Peter couldn't hold his liquor very well.

"What?" he snapped at her. He looked like he was losing it. If he didn't watch out, he was going to make Louise a widow.

"When was the last time you and Natalia talked?" Åsa asked. She didn't have the energy to feel empathy for Peter and the sad choices he'd made. If people wanted to screw up their lives, that was their business. She was busy with not learning shit from her own mistakes.

Peter just shook his head in irritation. His phone rang, and he waved her away.

Åsa returned to her desk. She put her legs up and stared at the ceiling. Should she worry? She wasn't very good at worrying. People thought she was a good lawyer because she seemed levelheaded and cool, when really she just didn't care very much.

She studied her hands and her nails. She wanted a manicure, a massage, and sex, not crisis, chaos, and emotions. She hated emotions. She closed her eyes, but opened them again when her secretary knocked. Åsa raised her eyebrows at her.

"You have a phone call. She called the main number, a woman named Gina."

"Gina?" Åsa asked. The name didn't ring any bells. It sounded vaguely foreign, and Åsa didn't know any foreigners. Aside from Michel, of course. She gave her secretary an irritated look. The whole point of having a secretary was not having to take unimportant calls all the time, right?

"I think you'd better take this call," her secretary said calmly.

Åsa sighed. "Put it through then." Her phone rang and she answered. "Yes?"

"Is this Åsa Bjelke?"

"Who is this?"

"My name's Gina. I'm Natalia De la Grip's housecleaner."

The worry was so immediate that it felt as if someone had punched Åsa in the chest. She'd received a phone call like this before, an unexpected call that came out of nowhere, a polite call that degenerated into chaos.

I regret to inform you, everyone is dead.

Is there anyone you can call?

The periphery of her field of vision started to go black, and she wanted to collapse to the floor. *If anything's happened to Nat, I'm going to kill myself.* She felt no hysteria. That was simply a statement of fact. Because there was only so much loss one person could take, and Åsa had never had the illusion about herself that she was particularly strong. If Nat died, she would die too. That's just how it was. She squeezed the phone so hard her hand hurt.

"Hello? Are you still there?"

The calm voice on the phone snapped Åsa out of it. She pushed aside her morbid thoughts. The woman sounded much too calm.

"I'm sorry," said Åsa, her voice trembling. "I don't know who you are, but what is this about Natalia?"

A short silence followed. "I'm worried," Gina said on the other end of the line. "Natalia won't let me in. She paid me to clean, but I can't get in."

Finally Åsa understood. "You're her cleaning lady?" A fuzzy memory of an earnest-looking foreign woman came to mind.

A short silence followed before the woman calmly repeated, "Her housecleaner, yes."

Åsa had already picked up her purse and started for the door. "I'm on my way over." She stopped. And then, not entirely comfortable with gratitude, awkwardly said, "Thank you for calling me."

But by then the maid—the housecleaner—had already hung up.

Åsa took a taxi and got out in front of Natalia's building just a few minutes later. She called up from the front door. When there was no answer, she started systematically pressing each of the buttons until someone let her in.

The elevator creaked slowly upward, and that gave Åsa time to continue blaming herself. In the middle of all the chaos, she hadn't had a chance to think about how Natalia was doing. Fuck, she knew how into David Natalia had been. But her egotism and preoccupation with Michel had made her forget that this whole mess was even more personal for her best friend.

For Natalia to be let down again by a man wasn't good. Jonas's betrayal, the way he'd dumped Natalia right when she was grieving the news that she wouldn't be able to have children—that had been terrible to see. And Åsa—she knew she was a dreadful person because of this—hadn't known how to handle Natalia when she broke down after Jonas left her.

Poor Natalia, who had always fought for a place in the family, who had struggled against the feeling of never being good enough, who wasn't really confident in herself as a woman. Nat had loved Jonas, Åsa was sure of that. Her love had been loyal, and Natalia had wanted to have a family. Being unceremoniously dumped, in that way and for that reason, had really hurt her self-confidence as a woman. And then David Hammar had shown up, and Natalia had fallen hard for him.

Not good at all.

Åsa listened to the rattling chains and the creaking of the aging iron elevator. Natalia was strong, but there was also a frailty to her that she probably didn't think Åsa was really aware of. But Åsa knew that Natalia always held that darned frailty in check with work and rest and the occasional burst of exercise. The question was, what had happened now?

She rang the doorbell. When no one answered, she didn't stop, just kept ringing and ringing. When there was still no answer, she started knocking on the door. And then she yelled, "Open this fucking door!"

A neighbor peeked out, her security chain still on.

Åsa ignored the neighbor. "Natalia!"

The neighbor's eyes widened.

And then Åsa heard the lock click.

The door slid open, and Natalia's face appeared. "What do you want?"

Åsa's relief gave way to anger. "What the hell, Nat, you scared the shit out of me. Let me in before some idiot calls the police."

Natalia nodded at her neighbor. "It's okay," she said in a hoarse voice. "We know each other." And then to Åsa, "Come in." She held the door open, and Åsa stepped inside.

It was dark and smelled stuffy. Mail and newspapers lay untouched beneath the mail slot. Natalia shuffled along ahead of her. She had a blanket around her shoulders; her hair hung loose and unbrushed, and she was wearing a pair of shabby slippers. Even though the sun was out, the apartment was shrouded in darkness, and Åsa noted that the shades and curtains were all drawn. This couldn't be good. And Natalia's appearance. She looked like she was having a breakdown.

Åsa fought the wave of panic she felt, fought her desire to flee and the anguish that surrounded Natalia like a formless cloud, oh so contagious. She hadn't known that before therapy: anguish is contagious.

"Have you talked to J-O?" Åsa asked. Her voice sounded far too loud in the silence.

"I called his assistant and said I was sick. I'm just not up to talking to him."

They went to the living room, and Åsa sat down on one of the sofas. Natalia sat down in an armchair. With her feet pulled up under her, she looked like a pale teenager. She was hollow-eyed, her skin practically transparent. Åsa tried not to show how shocked she was.

"Have you eaten anything?" she asked.

Natalia put her chin on her knees. She had gray circles under her eyes. "I Googled everything David has ever done," she said, her voice hollow. She pointed to the printouts that lay in drifts around them. David's face was visible in the photos. The headlines varied. "All the people he's ruined over the years," she continued. "Women he's slept with, families he's destroyed. Did you know he bought a mansion once just to tear it down? A historic building? Here." She held out a newspaper article. When Åsa didn't take it, she dropped it and picked up another. "And here. This man was his enemy, so David had sex with his wife. He was behind their divorce."

"It doesn't say that, does it?" Åsa said, shocked.

Natalia shrugged. "I checked that social media website, Flashback. David Hammar has quite a reputation there. He's clearly a dick," she said in a conversational tone. "They use other words there, too, but they're all variants on the same theme." She twisted a lock of hair around her finger over and over again.

"Natalia . . ."

"I see it now," Natalia interrupted. Her voice was suddenly animated and combative. Her eyes seemed to burn in the closed-in darkness. Åsa felt a cold force creep under her skin.

"I should have realized it before," Natalia continued. "He was just sleeping with me to punish my family, to get revenge. Don't you see?" Her voice broke. Åsa saw that her friend's lips were totally dry. "He's out for revenge. Who knows who's on his side?" Her voice rose and she blinked hard, over and over again, her eyes dry. Åsa remembered that exact feeling, remembered the shock when the inconceivable happened, the inability to take in what couldn't be true, the free-falling sensation, like a nightmare that didn't end.

She swallowed. She didn't want to be here, not in the middle of this anguish. Her whole adult life had been about escaping anguish. She had no strategies for this.

"When was the last time you ate something?" she repeated. "Do you have any food here?"

Natalia coughed. And then again. Her body sort of crumpled up in a coughing fit. She wiped her mouth.

"Do you want me to get you some water?"

"It hurts so much," Natalia whispered.

"I know." *God, do I know.*

"It hurts everywhere. I can't do anything."

Åsa nodded. She knew how it was, when all systems just shut down.

She got up and went to the kitchen. The fridge was completely empty. And there weren't any dishes in the sink. Natalia hadn't eaten. No glasses, no bottles, so clearly she hadn't been drinking either, but she had never drunk very much alcohol. Åsa filled a glass with water and brought it back to Natalia.

"Shouldn't you be with the family?" she said helplessly. "Should I call your mom?"

Natalia accepted the water glass and gave her a sarcastic look. It was a glimpse of the old Natalia, the one who hadn't had her heart crushed, the capable, intelligent Natalia. "No one has contacted me, and I'm grateful for that," she said. "I'm not up to talking to them."

She drank a little water and made a face, as if it hurt. "I'm really sick," she complained hoarsely, curling up in the armchair. "Some kind of flu, I think. I'm nauseated, my stomach hurts, I have a sore throat." She sniffled and put her hand on her chest. "It hurts here, in my heart."

Natalia really looked sick. Unless . . . Something had occurred to Åsa, and then, without thinking, she said, "You're not pregnant, are you?"

The hatred that flared up in Natalia's eyes for a second made Åsa freeze. In all the years they'd known each other, Åsa had never seen her friend so furious. Red splotches flared up on her chalk-white throat.

"We used condoms," she said hoarsely. "I had my period." She took a deep breath. "And in case you'd forgotten, *I can't get pregnant!*" she screamed, and Åsa had to force herself not to back away.

Natalia was staring at her. The tendons in her neck were working, and she wasn't blinking, just watching Åsa with her eyes wide. "And I don't have the strength to pretend I don't care about it anymore. If you're my friend, stop being mean. Otherwise you can leave. Just go."

Natalia's voice trembled. And then the fury was gone just as quickly as it had come. Replaced by completely excruciating pain. The abrupt mood swings frightened Åsa more than anything else. Because if Natalia lost her composure, then nothing in the world would be stable anymore.

Åsa swallowed. "I'm your friend," she said quietly. "I know that this is unbearable and that he did this to you . . ." She shook her head and felt something very akin to hatred for David Hammar. "I can't even imagine how you're feeling." She didn't really dare touch Natalia. They had never been particularly physical with each other, and everything about Natalia signaled that she wanted space. "But I'm your friend, Nat. And you're my friend, my only real friend. I didn't mean to say anything hurtful. I'm here, and I'm not going to leave you."

Natalia's eyes were dry but shining. She looked feverish. More red splotches appeared on her neck. Maybe she really had the flu? And then she started shaking in the armchair. Her shoulders shook uncontrollably under the blanket. How could a person waste away so much in only two days?

"He won't take my calls," she said. "And that hurts so much." She sniffled and gave Åsa a look that was so full of desperation that Åsa wanted to cry. She would never forgive David Hammar for this.

"It hurts so much I think I've had a breakdown," Natalia whispered.

"I know."

"I'm not up to being strong."

"No, I'll be strong now. I'm here. I'm at your side, just yours."

"Promise me," Natalia said, her voice small, like a child's.

Åsa reached out her hand and placed it unaccustomedly on Natalia's shoulder. "I promise," she said.

"Thank you," Natalia said.

And then she started to cry.

Finally.

37

"**D**avid?"

David looked up from his computer. He'd been deep in concentration, and it took him a moment to adjust his eyes. Malin Theselius was in the doorway, looking concerned. "Yes?" he said.

"You have a visitor. The receptionist didn't know what to do."

David furrowed his brow. His assistant, Jesper, was supposed to deal with any visitors, make sure that no one unauthorized made it in. They'd been besieged by journalists and reporters since Monday, but so far no one had managed to get in unannounced. "Where's Jesper?" he asked.

Malin gave him an admonishing look. "It's Friday night," she said. "Jesper has been working almost around the clock since Monday."

"So?"

"He fell asleep standing up in the kitchen a while ago."

"You can fall asleep standing up?" David asked, deeply skeptical.

Malin stretched one shoulder. "At any rate, I sent him home."

David looked at the time. It was after eight, so he decided he'd be lenient. But he wondered which journalist it was this time. It felt like he'd already talked to all of them. "Who is it?"

But Malin shook her head worriedly. "It's not a journalist," she said. "It's Natalia De la Grip."

He froze.

Natalia.

She'd stopped texting late Monday evening, and after that he hadn't heard a peep from her. How many times had he thought of her since then? A hundred?

"Should I ask her to leave?"

"No," he said quickly. They couldn't show her the door. They were going to have to see each other sooner or later. He ignored the strange sensation, convinced himself that he didn't feel anything.

"Where is she?"

"She's waiting in the small conference room."

He shut down his computer. "Thanks. And, Malin, you can go home."

"I can stay if you want."

But David shook his head. Malin looked completely worn out. "Go home. And don't come back before Monday morning. That's an order."

She smiled tiredly, with big circles under her eyes. "Call if there's a crisis," she said and left.

David stood up and went to the small conference room.

She was standing by the window, and something swept through him—a feeling, a sensation. She stood poised like a ballerina, her hair up in a tight bun. Apart from the glimmering pearls around her neck, she was dressed all in gray, and he happened to think of the term they used for the best of the corporate finance folks: the gray eminences. "Hi," he said quietly to her back.

She turned around.

Those enormous eyes almost burned in her pale face. She looked serious, bordering on resolute. No smile, no warmth, and no out-stretched hand. David hadn't expected any of these, but still—damn, did it hurt to see her like this.

She stretched. "Hi, David," she said coolly.

It was like standing in front of a stranger. He noticed that her fingers, which were clutching her purse, were white, but otherwise she looked composed. Impossible to interpret.

"I won't take up much of your time," she began, and her voice woke something in him. He watched her earnestly, searching her face for something. "But I need to know: was I part of the plan?"

He blinked. "What?" he asked, even though he had a sense where this was heading. *Fuck, fuck, fuck.*

"I've come to realize that you have your own reasons for wanting to take over Investum. No one in my family will tell me anything, but both you and I know that this isn't just about business."

"No," he said. "It's not just business."

"But sleeping with me?" Her voice was calm, almost easy; just a little quaver at the end revealed any emotion. "Did I mean anything at all to you? Or was that also part of getting at my family?" She crossed her arms. "Everything was a lie, wasn't it? A game to cause as much damage as possible."

David stuffed his hands into his trouser pockets so that she wouldn't see how they were shaking. He didn't know what to say, felt completely empty. The last several days must have been awful for Natalia. Every newspaper had scrutinized the De la Grip family in great detail: her parents, her brothers, their business dealings, and Natalia as well. He looked at her, standing there pale and dressed in gray, almost transparent. This private woman with her integrity—everything had been made public, in printer's ink, on blogs, and in the tabloids to varying degrees of awfulness. Some had blabbed about her infertility. Jonas Jägerhed had been profiled as well. Another one of Natalia's earlier boyfriends had been interviewed, had made a statement. Everything had been dragged out in the open. And that was partially his, Malin's, and Hammar Capital's fault. He felt sick when he thought of the information he had leaked about Peter and Gustaf, information about bonuses, benefits, and secret backroom deals that had reached the mass media through their efforts and damaged the men. It was a game—just a game really, but it had also unavoidably tarnished the rest of the family, hurt Natalia.

"Natalia, I . . . ," he began, but she interrupted him.

"Did you know that Investum was in the middle of a bank deal that made them vulnerable? That was my deal, mine. We were at a sensitive point. A *confidential* point." She took a step forward, and he saw red roses on her cheeks. Her eyes glistened, as if she had a fever. "Did you know that, David?" she asked, and her voice was hard and cold as arctic ice. "Was that why you sought me out with your fucking flattery and flirting?"

David slowly shook his head. The pain in Natalia's face was almost more than he could bear. She deserved so incredibly much better than this.

And yet . . .

If he could turn back time, would he have done anything differently? Would he not have done all the things he had done? The truth was that he didn't know, because he couldn't imagine a scenario in which he and Natalia hadn't gotten to know each other, hadn't become lovers.

"I suspected something was going on," he said. "You know as well as I do how rumors get around. My job is to sift out the facts from the rumors, and yes, I had my suspicions that a merger was underway."

Her face went gray, and he knew what she was thinking, that she was remembering how close she'd been to confiding in him, before he'd stopped her.

"And I said . . . ," she began. Her voice cracked, and she had to clear her throat before she began again. "I told you . . ."

"You didn't reveal anything," he said curtly. "Nothing that I didn't already know." That was true. But he realized that Natalia would still blame herself.

He clenched his fists in his pockets. He had figured he would hate himself. And he had figured that Natalia would hate and despise him. He had convinced himself that it would be hard but bearable.

But what he hadn't counted on was that Natalia would blame herself and that that would feel as if someone had punched him over and over in the chest until he almost couldn't breathe. If unbearable pain existed, then that's what this felt like.

Natalia looked at David's expressionless face. He hadn't said very much, mostly listened, his eyes cool and his jaw clenched. She didn't really know what she'd hoped to get out of seeing him, but seeing him had felt necessary, seeing the man who'd tricked her in almost every conceivable way.

Åsa's visit the day before yesterday had been a turning point. After she'd cried herself hoarse, she slept, with the help of Åsa's pills. When she woke up the next morning she'd been able to breathe again in some sense. Åsa had called Gina, and when the housecleaner had laid out food on the table, Natalia had obediently eaten. She had slept for a few more hours and cried a little more. But then she'd realized she *had* to see David. She needed some kind of resolution. Whatever that might mean.

Showering and getting dressed had taken every bit of her energy, and she had forced herself to focus on the practical. The flu had made her weak, and she'd had to rest frequently as she got herself put together. Even so, she almost hadn't had the strength to make it to Hammar Capital's offices. She'd had to stand down in front of the building and wait until she gathered the strength to go up. Her courage almost failed her many times. And it wasn't until she'd reached the almost empty reception area that she noticed what time it was. It was as if she'd been living outside time and space the last few days.

She'd been on the verge of turning around in the doorway, but the friendly blond communications director had shown her in. Natalia glanced around the room. It was eye-poppingly lavish, smelling of money and capital and success. Every item and painting looked priceless. The furniture and décor had obviously been chosen to impress. This was what David was, superficial and obsessed with money.

And when Natalia looked at David's stiff, obstinate face, she knew it was good that she'd come. That everything David had been accused of was true. That what had existed between them was an illusion.

A lonely, easily duped woman's desperate fantasy.

Yes, he'd used her. But she had also allowed herself to be used, even though she should have known better. Well, fine. Strangely enough, this meeting with David restored some kind of energy to her. Now that she saw the cold look in his eyes and realized that she had never meant anything to him, she finally reached bottom. And from the bottom there was only one way to go—up.

Natalia focused her attention inwardly, searching for something, and finally finding it, the emotion that would keep her going from this point forward, which would give her strength and everything else she needed: rage.

Fine, because now she could take all the grief and shame and guilt she felt and put them to work for her.

"Good-bye, David," she said. She turned on her heel and left, her back straight, her gait steady.

She would take all her rage and do the only thing she could do. She would fight.

38

"Natalia De la Grip?"

Natalia closed the magazine she'd been browsing. Luckily it was an old edition—in other words, no gossip about the hostile takeover. There had been some pictures of Alexander, though, from some society event in New York.

"Yes," she said loudly, setting down the magazine, getting up and shaking hands with the doctor who had come to get her in the waiting room.

"Hi," the doctor said. "I'm Isobel Sørensen. Welcome."

Isobel's handshake was firm, almost hard, and she was implausibly beautiful with her red hair and freckles. "You already gave us a blood test, right?" she asked with one eyebrow raised.

Natalia nodded. "Several vials," she replied.

"That's good. We'll take excellent care of you."

Natalia studied the doctor more closely. "Have we met before?" she asked, because there was something familiar about this redheaded Amazon.

"In Båstad," Isobel replied with a nod. "We were at the same party."

Natalia remembered the redhead she'd seen with Alexander. "Are you a friend of my brother's?" she asked.

A sarcastic smile, which Isobel either didn't have a chance or didn't bother to hide, fluttered across her lips and then vanished again just as fast. "No," she said simply and showed Natalia into her examining room. "This way."

Natalia sat down on the visitor's chair.

Isobel sat at her desk, looked at her chart, and then looked straight at Natalia. Her demeanor was objective and professional. "It says here that you'd like a checkup," she began. "That's why we started with the blood tests. How are you feeling?" Intelligent gray eyes studied Natalia attentively.

"I'm feeling pretty good. I had some kind of flu last week, but that's not why I'm here. I've been working hard, and, well, there's been a lot going on lately . . ." Natalia paused, unsure how much Isobel already knew about her. She felt totally transparent, despised all this exposure. But she wanted to do this. The meeting with David on Friday had snapped her out of her shock. Now that the weekend was over, she was ready to look to the future.

"I understand," Isobel said calmly, and somehow it felt as if she really did understand.

Natalia shifted her position in the chair. Her normal doctor, an older man, had retired, and now she had this woman instead, and she wasn't feeling completely comfortable with a doctor who was almost the same age as she. "I just want to make sure everything's the way it should be," she said by way of explanation. "Taking care of myself. Coming here felt like the right thing to do."

She paused and looked around at the room. The walls were mostly covered with colorful posters and pictures. An anatomical chart showing muscles and tendons hung next to the window. There were two photographs from some foreign country pinned on the bulletin board, two serious little squares in the midst of all the other light, impersonal stuff. One showed Isobel in the middle of a group of laughing black children. The other showed Isobel weighing an underweight infant in a simple scale. Natalia recognized the emblem of the aid organization in one of the pictures.

"Do you work for them?" she asked.

Isobel nodded. "When I'm not working here. It's a nice change."

Natalia bit her lower lip, ashamed of her first-world concerns. What did a little fatigue or vitamin deficiency matter? She was healthy and vaccinated, had a roof over her head, and ate her fill every day.

"It's good you came in," Isobel said somberly, as if she had a sense of what Natalia was thinking. "While we wait for the blood test results, I'll do a proper physical exam. Does that sound alright?"

* * *

Afterward, once Isobel had examined Natalia with succinct, efficient movements, once they'd done an EKG and Natalia felt thoroughly poked and prodded from top to bottom, including her lymph glands and breasts—yes, Isobel had even examined her breasts—Isobel concluded with, "For women your age, with the symptoms you've described, I like to do a pregnancy test as well."

Natalia straightened her clothes. "There's no need. I just had my period, and I can't get pregnant."

Isobel nodded, entered something into the computer, and then looked at Natalia. "You're not on birth control pills?"

Natalia looked down at her clasped hands. She hated these kinds of routine questions. "No, like I said. I can't get pregnant."

Isobel nodded encouragingly. "How do you know this?"

Natalia bit her lip. "My former fiancé and I were tested. That's what the tests showed."

"I see. Have you had any unprotected sex recently?"

Embarrassingly enough, Natalia blushed. "No," she replied. "I mean, yes, I've had sex recently, but not unprotected. We used condoms. To protect against STDs." She thought about laughing a little, but the laughter stuck in her throat. Oh my God, she hadn't caught an STD, had she?

"Smart," said Isobel. She handed Natalia a small container. "It's just routine," she said in a tone that did not exactly encourage further dialogue.

Irritated, Natalia took the container, went to the bathroom, and did what she'd been asked. She handed the urine sample calmly back to Isobel, who took it, excused herself, and left the room.

Natalia picked at the tape and the gauze in the crook of her elbow. She decided she didn't like this bossy new doctor.

Isobel came back in with some papers in her hand. "Your blood test results are back," she said.

"So fast?"

"We have a top-notch lab right here in the building." Isobel looked over the results and then looked up at Natalia. "Your blood work looks good," she said. "No causes for concern. Liver, iron, glucose, everything looks fine."

Well, then. She would buy some vitamins and supplements, and then she'd be her old self again. Natalia got ready to gather her things and go.

There was a knock on the door. A nurse came in wearing noiseless white rubber-soled shoes and handed Isobel another sheet of paper. Isobel thanked her and quickly perused it. A little wrinkle appeared on her forehead. She looked at Natalia. "You said you had the flu last week?"

"Or a cold."

Isobel looked at Natalia for so long that Natalia started blinking her eyelids nervously. Something was wrong. She sensed it.

"What is it?" she asked.

Isobel gave her a friendly smile. "The pregnancy test came back positive."

Natalia laughed, a short, joyless laugh. "I just told you," she pointed out. "That's impossible."

Isobel looked at the piece of paper again. "Not according to your urine sample. It's very early, but you're definitely pregnant."

"But I *can't* be pregnant," Natalia repeated, now angry. How dare this woman sit there and mock her? "You must be looking at the wrong results," she said. She came from an almost unbroken line of Swedish noblewomen and Russian grand duchesses. She was born a countess, even if she never used the title, and when she really wanted to, she could sound quite stuck up, and she did now, furiously. She stood. "And besides, I don't *feel* pregnant. I don't feel anything." Isobel must have misread the results. Or maybe she wasn't even a real doctor, just an intern or maybe a model, mocking her.

"Are you tired?" Isobel asked, completely unflappable.

"Yes, but . . ."

"Are you nauseated?"

"Maybe."

"How do your breasts feel?"

Natalia's forehead crinkled. Isobel's exam had been gentle, but she'd really felt it. "Tender?"

Isobel shrugged, as if that settled matters. "You're pregnant," she said.

Natalia blinked. But then she came to her senses. This was utterly absurd. She gave Isobel one of her chilliest stares. Enough was enough. "I have papers that show I can't get pregnant," she snarled. "And as I just informed you, the last time I slept with someone we used protection." Relief coursed through her when she also remembered, "And I had my period the other day, which I also mentioned to you." She pointed to the notes on Isobel's desk. "Just a couple minutes ago." It was outrageous to treat her like this.

She was going to demand to switch doctors.

"I see that this wasn't planned," Isobel said. She still seemed completely unruffled despite Natalia's outburst.

"Planned?" scoffed Natalia. "This must be some kind of sick joke. Are we done yet? Can I go?" Suddenly she hated this redheaded Amazon of a woman. What did someone like Isobel even know about what Natalia had been through? Isobel Sørensen looked like some sexy fertility goddess. She probably had four kids at home that she'd popped out in between prestigious doctor gigs. Natalia was leaving and never coming back. She was going to report Isobel, call some boss and complain, maybe the Ministry of Health. You just couldn't do this kind of thing to people.

Isobel leaned back in her chair and put her fingertips together so that her hands formed an airy triangle. Her red hair screamed like a stop sign against her white lab coat. "The period you had. Was there very much blood?" she asked.

Natalia tried to remember. It had been in Båstad. She shook her head. "No, but it's always varied quite a bit."

Isobel cocked her head to the side. "That's called spotting. It happens when the egg implants in the uterus. And in terms of infertility, it does happen that women who thought they were sterile get pregnant." She shrugged her shoulders apologetically. "Nature isn't an exact science."

"But we used a condom," Natalia said weakly. Now her head was spinning again. This just *couldn't* be true.

"No form of birth control is one hundred percent effective," Isobel said. "You can put them on wrong. They can break or be old. Condoms aren't meant to be stored for a long time."

This wasn't happening.

This just couldn't be happening.

Because Isobel was right. The condoms she'd had in her dresser drawer weren't exactly spring chickens. Suddenly Natalia felt like she was falling. She sank down onto the chair.

Isobel stood up, filled a disposable cup with water, and handed it to Natalia.

Natalia took the water. All the anger had streamed out of her. She swallowed and swallowed. "Have you ever heard of something like this before?" she asked quietly.

The beautiful doctor's eyes filled with something that Natalia couldn't put her finger on, boundless sadness maybe.

"I've worked as a doctor in war zones and refugee camps. The things I've seen . . ." She smiled a little and nodded at Natalia's stomach. "This still falls within the bounds of normal."

Normal.

It didn't feel normal.

"Are you in a steady relationship?" Isobel asked.

"I'm sorry?"

"Do you know who the father is?"

Natalia nodded weakly. "But it's impossible," she said even more weakly, because she couldn't take this in. For so many years she had longed for exactly this. So many months when a pregnancy would have been the only thing she wanted from life, that enormous, all-encompassing desire for a baby, which she'd been forced to give up.

"I can see that this is a lot to absorb," Isobel said. "It's still early. A pregnancy is counted from the first day of the last period. You become pregnant during the third week. If we assume that that was spotting you had, then that happens in week four, which means that you are in about week six now, which matches what the test said—they're incredibly sensitive nowadays. As I said, it's very early. It's not even a fetus yet, just an embryo, a little cluster of cells. If you wanted to terminate the . . ." Isobel stopped. She was being completely professional toward Natalia. There was no judgment, no opinion, just enormous calm.

I'm pregnant.

Natalia tried to get her head around the word. She put a hand on her stomach, which was almost ridiculously flat. She was six weeks pregnant. With David's child. It had probably happened that very first night, the very first time. What was the word she was looking for?

Surreal.

That's what this was—completely surreal.

"Are you quite sure?" she asked.

Isobel nodded. "If you decide to keep it, you will have to think about telling the father."

"Do I have to?"

"This is the twenty-first century. Most men usually want to participate in their children's lives. And children need their fathers."

Natalia stood up, her legs wobbly. She walked over to the sink, placed her hands on the cool porcelain. She leaned over and threw up.

She was breathing heavily. She wiped her mouth and looked at Isobel, who sat in her chair watching her.

"Are you sure-sure?"

"Yup."

Natalia swallowed, closed her eyes, and took a few breaths.

She opened her eyes, looked down into the sink, and vomited again.

It was that kind of a day.

39

Michel dragged the thin, Lebanese bread across his plate to wipe up the last of the oil and yogurt and stuffed it into his mouth.

"I should eat Lebanese food more often," David said with his mouth full of hummus and eggplant. Michel's mother had sent Michel home with meze, and he and David were enjoying the food immensely.

Michel reached for his mineral water, drank out of the bottle, and then stretched out his legs on the office terrace. There was a nice breeze off the water up here, and the views of Stockholm were amazing. They had hung their suit jackets over the backs of their chairs and eaten the late lunch in relative solitude.

"My mom's mad at me. And you."

"Why? I thought your mom loved me," David said.

"She thinks we're picking fights with people. I'm supposed to stop picking fights and get married and give her grandchildren."

David shook his head.

Jesper Lidmark, David's assistant, moved among the planters on the terrace. He watered a plant here, plucked off a dry leaf there. He looked over at them and asked, "Should I bring coffee?"

David nodded. "Could you ask Malin to come up, too?"

Jesper nodded eagerly and disappeared.

Michel furrowed his brow and watched Jesper leave. "Is he still . . . ?"

David shrugged. "Maybe a little." It was impossible to interpret the look in his eyes behind his sunglasses, but he was smiling.

Jesper, who had worked at Hammar Capital for two years, had gotten completely drunk at the last office Christmas party. He had weepily admitted both that he was gay and head over heels in love with David.

In a world as homophobic as the financial sector, it was darn near social suicide to be anything other than one hundred percent, no questions about it, straight. That's why everyone had cute female assistants and participated in manly sports and slapped each other vigorously on the back all the time. Michel had always suspected that David had chosen a young male intern from the School of Economics just to stick it to all the middle-aged white guys. Then when the kid turned out to be gay . . .

Jesper had kept drinking at that notorious Christmas party until he passed out.

The next day he hadn't come to work. No one knew what to do. The office had been abuzz. David called Jesper personally, and ever since that phone call (though it was unclear how word had gotten out) the story had been told and retold as an urban legend at Hammar Capital.

David had informed Jesper that he didn't personally have any problems with anything except people not coming to work when they were supposed to. "I'm straight," he added. "And I'm your boss, so it's out of the question that there could be anything between us. Plus I'm much too old for you. Now get in here."

Jesper had been at Hammar Capital one hour later, trembling and hungover, and since then he hadn't missed a single day of work.

When Jesper turned up with bruises after Christmas vacation, not looking anyone in the eye, David had summoned him to his office. David managed to get it out of Jesper that Jesper's own father, a well-known Swedish director, had beaten up his son when he had come out to him.

David had had one of his rare blowups. In a cold rage, he stormed right down to the restaurant where the director was enjoying a three-course business lunch. In front of the man's guests and employees, David had told him exactly what would happen to him if he so much as lifted a pinky against Jesper—one of Hammar Capital's most cherished employees—ever again.

David had returned to the office, still fuming, and said that he was buying a building on Kungsholmen and that if Jesper wanted, there was an apartment there that he could rent effective immediately.

Since then, Jesper had been seeing a prominent reality TV star and moved in with him, but Michel suspected that if Jesper ever had the chance, he would give up his life for David.

"This is a messed-up industry," David said.

Michel didn't object. "Talking about messed-up people, what about that Russian uncle? Where are we with him?"

"Eugene Tolstoy? He'll come up for the meeting and vote," David said.

"Is he reliable?"

David shook his head. "Hope so. But he's like a steel ball in one of those labyrinth maze games. Almost impossible to control or interpret."

"Rumor has it that he's got ties to the Russian mafia," Michel said.

"Wouldn't surprise me in the least."

"Why is he going against the family anyway? Gustaf is his brother-in-law, Ebba his own sister. Wonder why he's doing it."

"Don't know. But I get the sense that he has his reasons."

"Does that mean we have the votes we need? What do you think?"

There was no way to be certain. A lot could happen in the week that was left before the meeting. Michel kept a running tally, but there were so many variables that he couldn't say anything for sure anymore. This far into a deal, it was as much psychology as money that mattered. And everyone knew that the only thing that was definitely certain in this industry was that no deal was done until it was done.

"It wouldn't hurt to have more," David said, reaching for an olive.

"Have you talked to Alexander De la Grip?" Michel asked as Jesper came out with the coffee. "Thanks, Jesper," he said, taking the espresso.

David looked pensive. "Alexander seems to have an agenda all his own. He hates me, I think. It feels almost personal, which is weird, because we haven't had much to do with each other."

"And you're so popular."

"How do you think Åsa's going to vote?" David asked.

Michel snorted. "She's totally loyal to Investum. Besides, I'm quite sure Åsa Bjelke's only desire in this life is to cause me and you, but mostly me, as much pain, humiliation, and defeat as she possibly can."

"Well, you can't blame her too much," David said. "She looked like she wanted to torture us to death."

Michel was moderately amused.

The meeting at the Grand Hôtel had put a definite end to his and Åsa's potential new start, that much was clear. "She's going out with other men," he said even though it hurt just to think about it. "All the time. Different men, every evening. And she's doing it—partly anyway—to bother me."

"How do you know that?" David asked. "You're not spying on her, are you?" He didn't look like he was kidding.

"No," Michel said, pulling out his cell phone. "I haven't sunk quite that low yet. She sends me pictures." He showed David picture after picture of Åsa laughing with different men by her side. A laughing, kissing Åsa. "A new man every evening since Tuesday, when we saw each other last. Seven so far."

"Harsh," David said. "Impressive, but harsh."

"She's really pissed. I shouldn't have started talking to her." He'd told himself that during the last week, that he should have stayed away. But he wasn't even convincing to himself. He was condemned to this, to pine for a woman who hated him, looked down on him, and was super pissed at him. He'd known it would be like this, that the takeover he and David had orchestrated would render a relationship with Åsa impossible.

"Of course she's mad," David said, unconcerned. As if Åsa Bjelke wasn't the only woman Michel could imagine being with for the rest of his life. It was like one of those movies where you rooted for a happy ending, but in the end someone died in a bicycle accident.

He sighed. His family wouldn't have been happy if he'd brought Åsa home. He had six sisters, he was the only son, and his family's wishes were clear. Åsa Bjelke wasn't really the daughter-in-law his mother and father envisioned.

Michel shook his head, as that wasn't exactly a looming problem, given that Åsa hated him. Those looks she'd given him at the Grand Hôtel, that meeting. He shuddered.

If he ever somehow succeeded in getting close to her again, managed to break through her rage, then he'd better be prepared for all-out war. It would be a battle, and she would fight hard to make sure he didn't win.

"We really ought to have someone from the old guard on the board," he said to keep himself from revealing to his boss, his colleague, and his best friend his inability to let go of the idea of Åsa Bjelke. "Someone who knows the company."

"I know, I've been thinking that too," David said contemplatively.

There were seven seats on the board of directors. Naturally Michel would take one of them while David took over as chairman of the board. And they had several candidates for the important positions. Then the board's first and most important task would be to kick out the old managing director and appoint a new one. They already had one in mind, but Investum was an enormous company to get acquainted with. Having someone on the board who already knew the company would make it easier.

"Natalia would have been perfect," Michel pointed out wryly. "If you hadn't gone and duped and double-crossed her, of course."

"She would have been good," David agreed, without smiling. Michel knew his joke had been in poor taste, but he wasn't sure about David's feelings for Natalia. In all the years he'd known David, he'd seen him with many different women—smart, attractive, funny women. But he'd never seen his friend fall for anyone. From where he was sitting, it looked like David had fallen for Natalia.

"How's she doing?" Michel asked.

David shrugged. "We talked last Friday," he said. "But I don't actually know."

"What did she say?" Michel pushed.

David didn't answer; he just shut down, and Michel felt a chill creep up his spine. David looked really devastated. "Um, hey . . . ," Michel began, but David interrupted him: "Investum is preparing some kind of countermove," he said, and his icy stare made it clear that he didn't want to talk about Natalia anymore. "I think they've got me under surveillance. Have you noticed anything?"

"No," Michel responded. But they both knew that they had to step up their day-by-day vigilance. There was no room for careless-ness.

David looked at his watch. "I have to go," he said. He stood up and took his jacket from the back of his chair.

Michel watched him go, noticing that David hadn't said where he was going. He shook his head. This deal . . .

David took the stairs down. He walked out to his car, then turned around. He didn't see anyone watching him, but he would talk to Tom Lexington, he decided, and review their security procedures. He looked at his watch again. Carolina was coming in; he should go pick her up at the airport. Soon he'd be forced to tell Michel about her. Yet another secret that he'd kept to himself for way too long, yet another crucial piece of the puzzle that would affect Michel.

He sat down in the car and started the motor.

But then he closed his eyes behind his sunglasses for a brief moment.

For a man who'd been planning something half his life, he really had an awful lot of loose ends to tie up.

40

Two days after her doctor's visit, Natalia went out to Djursholm to talk to her parents. She had called in sick to the office after seeing the doctor, not up to working when her whole life had just been turned upside down.

Again.

There'd been a lot of that going on lately.

She had actually managed to make it in to the office for a bit yesterday. She'd worked for a few hours, but then she'd felt so sick she'd had to go home again. Better that than throw up all over her coworkers. This morning she'd given up and called in sick again. And then fallen asleep on the sofa. That was so not her that it was like being in someone else's body.

J-O hadn't called once, and Natalia wasn't sure if that was a good or a bad sign. Maybe he wanted to give her a break.

But now she'd at least made a decision: she would tell her parents. The pregnancy would affect them too, and she was hoping for their support. And no matter how you looked at it, whatever their relationship was like, she was still a young woman pregnant for the first time. She so wanted to share this with the people she loved.

Natalia took the E18 north, trying to imagine her mother and father's reactions. Would they be angry? Disappointed? And yet, it was a child, their first grandchild. Did she dare to hope for a little joy once the worst of the shock had subsided?

She bit her lower lip, because she really had no idea what to expect. Yes, she'd made a mistake, gotten involved with a man who'd tricked her, but she was only human, and once the shock wore off, surely they would understand? She hardly dared consider the possibility that they really wouldn't understand, that they wouldn't support her. They were all she had. They *had* to understand.

"I have something to tell you," Natalia said once they were seated in the living room. The house was totally silent and the air almost stagnant.

Her mother sat stiffly with a delicate wrinkle between her eyebrows. Her father had his arms crossed.

Natalia nervously moistened her lips, wished that she had something to drink. "It's about David Hammar," she began.

Her mother blinked and put her hand to her chest. "I really hope you're not having anything to do with him," she said.

Her father's eyes narrowed, but he didn't say anything, just watched.

Natalia swallowed. "David and I . . . ," she began, but the words failed her. She really needed something to drink. She was enormously thirsty.

"Natalia," her mother said. "What did you do?"

"Let her speak," her father snapped.

Natalia got ready. After all, it wasn't like she'd murdered someone. She stretched her back and said, "A few weeks ago, I had a short relationship with David Hammar, and I . . ."

Her mother leapt out of her chair and bawled, "Are you insane?"

"Quiet," her father said. He was looking straight at Natalia. "And?" he asked coldly.

Natalia looked down at her lap, saw her fingers twisting around each other, and forced them to lie still. "It's over between us," she said quietly. "But I'm pregnant."

Her mother's hand shot up to cover her mouth. "That can't be true!"

"I found out two days ago," Natalia said. "David doesn't know. I came to you first." She watched them pleadingly. "You're my parents."

Her mother started to cry behind her hand. *That must be the shock,* Natalia thought. Her mother could be cold and selfish, but she was still her *mother*. Certainly she must . . .

But a terrible feeling began to spread through her gut. She hadn't really imagined that they would react like this. She tried to make eye contact with her father. Her father was hard, but he loved her, in his way. Surely he understood how this felt to her, surely he understood that the family must stand as one. She only had them, after all. "Papa, I . . ."

"He did this to get to us," he interrupted her. His voice was steady, almost devoid of emotion.

"No, Dad, it wasn't like that," she said, trying to sound certain even though she was convinced of the same thing.

Her father sneered at her mockingly. "Maybe you think that Hammar fellow wants you? And your baby?"

"You don't understand what you've done," her mother said, sounding stifled.

"I knew it," her father said. He looked out the window, as if he couldn't even bear to look at her anymore. "Bad genes always show through. I've been waiting for this."

Her mother shook her head. "Gustaf, don't say that." But her voice lacked conviction.

Her father turned back to Natalia. The look in his eyes was harsh, without even a flicker of warmth or understanding. "I knew the whole time. Any daughter of *mine* would never act like some cheap, low-class hussy."

"I understand that you're upset," Natalia said as calmly as she could. "It was a shock for me as well."

"Gustaf," her mother pleaded. "Not now."

Gustaf flashed Ebba a quick glance, and she looked away, retiring back into her position as a submissive aristocrat's housewife.

Her father stood up. "If you think I'm going to tolerate some tramp's brat in my family, then you're wrong," he said.

"Surely we can discuss this," Natalia said, more shocked by his coldness and choice of words than she wanted to show. "It's a baby that we're talking about here, your grandchild." *And we're living in the twenty-first century. And I need you,* she thought.

"You really see how the vulgar heredity comes out now."

"Papa!"

"You really don't understand," he hissed. "Listen carefully now. You are not my daughter. You never were. I don't give a fuck about you or your bastard. I am going to stamp out David Hammar like the rat he is." He pointed to the door. "Get out of my house."

"But . . ."

"You explain it so she understands," he ordered his wife. "I don't want to see her again." He slammed his fist on the coffee table so hard that a vase jumped. "Never again, you hear?"

Then he left, without even deigning to look at Natalia.

Natalia stared after him. "I don't understand," she said. "What does he mean? I am loyal to the family, surely you see that? Mother? He can't be serious. It's not like I've *done* anything."

"I didn't want you to find out like this," her mother said, sniffling into a tissue she pulled from a box on the coffee table. "Actually, I didn't want you to find out at all."

"Find out what?"

"Are you really pregnant?"

Natalia nodded. "Six weeks."

"And it's his?" She made a face. "That man's?"

"Yes."

"You have to get rid of it."

"That is not your decision."

Her mother clenched the tissue tightly in her fist. "How could you do this to us?"

"I didn't *do* anything to anyone." She couldn't even express how hurt she was, how betrayed she felt, how lonely and scared she was right now. She'd come here for comfort, because she thought she'd hit bottom and because she had been counting on her mother and father's support. On this point, she had truly misjudged the situation.

"For all these years, I've tried to get you to think about your behavior," her mother said, her tone reproachful. "To think about what you say. Tried to make you understand how important it is. To be careful." She shook her head. "You have so much to be grateful for. And then you do this." She looked at Natalia with dry eyes. She wasn't crying anymore, and Natalia saw no compassion, just that her mother had decided something.

"I can't do anything about this," her mother said, crumpling the tissue. "It's out of my hands now."

"I don't understand any of this," Natalia said genuinely.

Her mother smoothed her skirt, straightening the fabric until it was flat, and then calmly said, "Gustaf isn't your biological father."

And then everything changed.

Everything she had believed.

Everything she had known.

Everything.

She wasn't a De la Grip.

An enormous wave of exhaustion overtook Natalia. She was so tired she hardly had the strength to blink. Maybe she was actually at home in bed sleeping and soon she would wake up and realize that this summer had never happened, that she had never met David, that . . .

"This is hard for me too," her mother continued, and her voice was already stronger, as if it were all over now as far as she was concerned. As if she'd already chosen a side and had no intention of changing her mind. "I've always tried to protect you. But you've gone too far this time. I have to be loyal to your father—to Gustaf. He needs me. And I need him; you know that."

Natalia blinked. Her heart raced in her chest. Was this really happening? Was her own mother rejecting her?

"I made a mistake," her mother said. "Peter was so little. I was alone, and I felt so unappreciated. I did something foolish. But your father and I agreed to stay together, to go on as a family. He gave you his name and forgave me for what happened."

For what happened? I'm *what happened.*

"Then Alexander came along. You children had everything," her mother continued, as if she were defending the choices she'd once made. "We have lived well, traveled a lot, had nice things."

"He's always treated me differently," Natalia said, because suddenly so much made sense. How she'd been kept out of Investum's inner circle. How the mansion and the family jewels had been systematically transferred to the sons. The whole time she'd thought it was because they were boys. But really it was because of their genes. She wasn't Gustaf's biological child, and therefore she had to be kept out. She, who had always detested infidelity, was the result of an illicit affair. The irony was epic.

"Gustaf is a stern man, but you've always meant a lot to him," her mother said. "He never made any distinction between you children."

But her mother was lying, and they both knew that. There had been a distinction. And no amount of skill or accomplishment had been able to make up for it.

"Does Peter know? And Alex?"

"No one knows."

But Natalia had seen the flicker of uncertainty. Her mother was lying. Again. All these lies.

"Uncle Eugene knows, doesn't he?" Natalia said once the final pieces slid into place.

"Yes, Eugene knows. He's never forgiven me. He always thought you should know. This has actually been really hard for me. And for your father."

I have to get out of here, Natalia thought, panic-stricken. *I have to get out of here, get away.* She stood up while her mother was in the middle of saying something. Natalia walked out of the living room without saying good-bye. Out of the house, her eyes vacant, an icy lump in her chest.

She sat down in her car.

Her hands were shaking so hard she could hardly take her phone out of her purse. She called and closed her eyes as the call went through.

Åsa was on her way out the door when Natalia called.

"Can I come over?"

She could tell right away that something had happened. She just said, "Come." She had a dinner date with a young fund manager and had already planned the picture she was going to send to Michel later. Tight red jersey dress, décolletage to die for, and long red finger-nails. A little on the vulgar side, certainly, but she knew what men liked. Who would have thought that driving Michel crazy would be so much fun?

Ten minutes later Natalia was standing in her apartment shaking, and Åsa only needed to take one look at her friend to see that this was going to take all night. "Come in," Åsa said. "I just have to call and back out of a date."

Åsa called and canceled. Then she told Natalia, "You look like shit. I'm going to order a pizza," she decided because she was starving. "Do you want some?"

Natalia shook her head, but Åsa ordered a large one anyway so they could share. Natalia looked like she needed some energy, and Åsa had been suppressing all her unfulfilled sexual desires with food lately. "Extra cheese," she said into the phone while Natalia collapsed flat on the sofa.

Natalia kicked off her shoes, put one arm over her forehead, and said, "More drama. You want to hear about it?"

Åsa sat down on the other sofa. "Spill it."

After Natalia filled her in, Åsa was quiet. Considering that Natalia had been the one who led the more boring, undramatic life, she was really catching up.

"Did you know?" Natalia asked. "That Gustaf isn't my father?"

Åsa slowly shook her head. "Embarrassingly enough, I never even suspected anything. I'm way too self-absorbed. How are you doing?"

"Oh, I'm doing great," Natalia said sarcastically.

"Well, who is your biological father then?"

"Can you believe I didn't even ask? I have no idea. And I can't bring myself to call my mom and ask right now. It could be anyone. The pool guy, maybe."

The doorbell rang, and Åsa went to get the pizza. She returned with the box, set it on the coffee table, and then went to the kitchen to get utensils, plates, and glasses.

"It smells heavenly," Natalia said when Åsa came back. The box was open, and the aroma of garlic and basil filled the living room.

Åsa served them each a slice, dripping with cheese. "I have a nice red wine in the kitchen. Do you want a glass?"

Natalia had just taken a big bite of pizza. She set down her slice and wiped her mouth. "Oh my God, I'm so sorry. I forgot to tell you my other news." Her eyes danced with glee. "Not only am I a bastard, it turns out I'm pregnant, too."

Her hand flew up to cover her mouth, and her shoulders shook from hysterical laughter.

Åsa set down her utensils. For all these years Natalia had just sailed calmly through life. Apparently those days were over now. "I think I'm going to skip the wine, then," Åsa said. "I need a real drink, and then you're going to tell me everything."

* * *

When they finished the pizza and Åsa was comfortably drunk after a couple of vodka tonics, Natalia leaned back on the sofa. She had her legs pulled up Indian-style and looked surprisingly with it considering she'd just been duped, dumped, accidentally knocked up, and then informed that she was a bastard, all in a little over a week.

Åsa downed the last of her drink. "What are you going to do now?" she asked, fishing out an ice cube and crushing it between her teeth.

"I don't know. Everything is such a mess, to put it mildly. But I don't even have the strength to fall apart. Is this hard for you, by the way? Talking about all this? I mean, you're close to my mom and, uh, Gustaf."

"I'm fine. And I meant what I said before. I'm on your side, Nat."

"Thanks," Natalia said. Her phone rang. She picked it up and looked at the caller ID. "I have to take this," she said with a crooked smile. "It's not like things can get any worse—at least there's that!"

She put her phone to her ear and listened. Åsa went out to the kitchen to mix herself another drink. When she came back Natalia was already done with the call.

"That was fast," Åsa said. "Who was it?"

"That was J-O." Natalia was staring straight ahead, as if she were thinking hard.

Åsa looked at the time. "What did he want?"

"J-O?"

Åsa nodded, sipping at her drink.

"Oh, he was just calling to tell me I was fired."

41

The next morning, which was actually a totally normal Thursday morning, Natalia strolled downtown. It was nice to get out and walk, and something had loosened after yesterday's bizarre turn of events.

Yes, she was pregnant by a man whom she suspected was an unscrupulous psychopath.

Yes, she was unemployed.

And yes, she'd just learned she was an illegitimate child, the result of her mother's infidelity. And she had probably been disowned by her family.

But—and this was an important but—she was healthy, had food to eat and a roof over her head. It could actually be much worse.

She blinked behind her sunglasses and turned her face to the sun for a little while before she steered her steps toward the glass kiosk on the wharf below Berzelii Park. There were only tourists in line, and she waited patiently until it was her turn. She bought a waffle cone with strawberry ice cream and then sat down on the same bench she and David had sat on to eat hot dogs more than three weeks earlier.

She had known David Hammar for less than one month. It hadn't even been two weeks since they'd made love in Båstad. It shouldn't be possible for a person you'd known for such a short time to be so significant, to take up so much room. A man who had so coldly exploited her, used her like a game piece . . . Natalia pushed aside her pointless thoughts, which threatened her delicate and extremely fleeting sense of well-being.

Her mood changed on a dime these days. Total despair, profound grief, and choking rage were only seconds apart, and it was exhausting. On some level she understood that she was in crisis, but she didn't have *time* for a crisis. She didn't want to give up. She had to focus on what gave her strength and made her feel like she was in control, which was why she'd spent the last week—between bouts of morning sickness, attacks of vomiting, and bits of bad news—calling around to every person she'd met in her professional life from whom she could call in a favor. She'd talked to old clients, major brokers, and managers, and she had argued with every single one of them, listing the reasons why they should listen to her.

Because she was going to do everything in her power to make sure David didn't win at the general meeting. Everything would be decided there, and she would do her utmost down to the very last minute to foil his plan. The problem was that this was a well-planned hostile takeover, and he had such a big head start.

She ate her ice cream pensively, lost in her thoughts. She had never been unemployed before and had actually barely had any leisure time in her whole life. She hardly knew what to do with herself if she didn't have a job to go to. She looked up, studying the passersby. They were mostly tourists, but some seemed to be hurrying to or from work or meetings. She hadn't thought about it before, the difference in pace. A boat tooted its horn and took off from the wharf. She saw a child wave and was on the verge of waving back.

If everything went well and if she kept the baby, then she would be a mother next summer. That was completely unreal. And what would she do about the fact that she hated the child's father? Was the doctor right? Did she have to inform David? Or could she be selfish enough not to say anything? He didn't want to have kids; he'd said that himself.

Her thoughts were interrupted by a shadow and a quiet, "Hi."

She'd been off in her own world.

She looked up automatically.

It was as if her thoughts had summoned him, made him materialize right in front of her. Because it was David, serious and just as handsome as ever, standing in front of her. And despite the fact that she'd just been thinking about him—or maybe that was *why*—the shock was paralyzing.

"Hi," she said, not actually even wanting to say that, but the imprinted habits of politeness trumped all her other feelings, although she couldn't think of a single other word to say.

"Early lunch?" he said, with a questioning look at her ice cream. He was still standing, and Natalia had to tilt her head back to be able to see him properly. His sudden appearance shook her more than she'd thought was possible, and she didn't want to give him the satisfaction of seeing her off balance. She had been so content with her exit last Friday, but that was almost a week ago, and her reserves of strength were severely stretched.

She squinted at him, contemplating as objectively as she could the man who had hurt her more than any person had ever hurt her. Did she see something in his eyes, or was that her imagination? What was he feeling, standing there looking at her with that expression in his eyes? Pity?

"Do you want me to throw that away for you?" he asked while Natalia remained silent.

Natalia looked at what was left of her melting ice cream cone, which she'd forgotten she was still holding in her hand. She wanted to tell David Hammar that she could throw her own ice cream away and he could go to hell, but she didn't want to seem weak or vulnerable. She wanted to be strong and levelheaded, so she handed him the ice cream without a word and then watched him walk over and toss it in a trash can before he came back and sat down on the bench next to her.

Without touching her, he looked out at the water. She sat with her back upright, stiff and with her heart pounding, and just stared straight ahead without seeing anything. Why had he come here? Of all the thousands of benches in Stockholm, why did he have to sit right here?

As unobtrusively as she could, she snuck a peek sideways, at him. He had turned toward her at exactly the same time, and it was like being exposed, revealed. That penetrating look and then all the energy that was him.

She was the first to look away. The tension between them was so strong that she could hardly breathe. Or maybe she was the only one who felt it.

Maybe he didn't feel shit. Maybe he slept with people, crushed their self-esteem, and then casually sat down next to them without caring. Maybe he'd been with scores of other women while he'd been with her. Maybe she was just one among many, maybe . . . Furious tears started to well up inside her. She bit the bullet. She wasn't going to sit here and fall apart. She wanted to be cool, casual. She should go, anywhere.

"Natalia," he began.

"What, David?" she interrupted him. Her voice was angry and sputtering, but better angry than sad was all she could think. Anything was better than sobbing. "*What* can you have to say to me?"

"I understand that you're mad," he said, soothingly, as if she were a hysterical child, and she almost suffocated as her rage completely exploded. So, he *understood*—well, how goddamned fucking understanding of him! Natalia clenched her fists and then stretched her fingers out again, inhaled, gathered the strength she had always been able to rely on, which had carried her through her childhood and her adult life, summoned up every last bit of reserve she possessed. Her heart was pounding so hard it hurt. And then she did something she'd never done before. Something she used to be proud that she'd never stooped to: she laid into him. She struck and wounded him where it would hurt the most, on purpose.

"No, I'm not that mad," she began, hearing through the roaring in her ears that she sounded downright calm even though she wasn't calm, even though she wanted to wound him and injure him. "Why should I be? You know where I come from. People like me might slum around with the dregs for a while, but I can honestly say that it didn't mean any more to me than it did to you."

She brushed a crumb off her arm and gave him a chilly, patrician look directly copied from every single aristocrat she'd ever met. "Sleeping with you was a nice change, I agree. But honestly, David, after a bit it got to be a little, well, how can I put this, a little wearing for me. I couldn't have put up with all that for much longer anyway."

Even before the last words had left her mouth, she knew she'd gone too far. The lie was so big, the implications so ugly. As if he was dirty, as if she'd felt revulsion.

David's face hardened. "Well, if that's how you . . . ," he began. She saw that the words stuck in his throat. She'd never seen him angry before, not like this.

"David, I . . . ," she began, because she already regretted it. It was beneath her to lie and belittle him. "I shouldn't have . . . ," she said, but David seemed to have stopped listening. His whole face had actually changed. He furrowed his brow. Turmoil and attention made those harsh features even harder, and he was focusing on something that didn't have anything to do with her, but with something behind her. Reflexively, Natalia turned around. David got up off the bench, and she felt the turmoil that enveloped him now. And then without any doubt at all, Natalia saw what, or rather *who*, had made him react so powerfully.

It was her.

The beautiful blond woman from the picture that David kept in a lavish frame in his living room, a picture that Natalia had never been meant to see. The woman had longer hair and was more tanned than she'd been in the picture, but it was definitely she. She radiated joy and health as she hurried toward David on her long, attractive legs in her expensive pumps.

The woman flung her arms around David and burrowed into his embrace. The gesture was intimate, and David's arm around her was protective and loving. Natalia stared at them, forced herself to endure the pain, because it hurt. It didn't matter that she hated David. This was awful to see, and yet she couldn't look away.

"I know you asked me to stay at the café," the woman said. She tossed her head in the direction of a café a little ways away and smiled apologetically. Her voice was gentle, and she had an accent that Natalia couldn't quite place. Her Swedish was perfect, but something in the rhythm and pronunciation suggested some other country.

The woman looked at Natalia, hesitant but not worried, as if she were secure in her role in his life. And Natalia saw what she wanted to see least of all: the love between these two people. It would have been obvious even to people who weren't looking particularly carefully, and Natalia was looking oh so very carefully. She saw a warmth in David that she hadn't seen before, a softness in his face and movements, that was like a fist in the gut.

The blond woman put her hand on David's cheek. She had long fingers with rings that sparkled the way only real stones do, and she said softly, "I missed you." Her voice was gently reproachful when she added, "You were gone so long."

She turned to Natalia, still with David's arm around her shoulders. She leaned a little against his chest, as if to show whom he belonged to, whom *she* belonged to. Her mouth formed a smile, but her eyes sent an unmistakable message to Natalia about ownership and obvious belonging.

"This is Natalia," David said. His voice was stiff and uncomfortable. "And this is Carolina."

"Hi," Carolina said, but she didn't hold out her hand, and Natalia wasn't going to do it either, just mumbled something as she got up off the bench.

The sun burned on her back. It was hot, *too* hot. A bead of sweat ran down her back, and she felt that she would die if she didn't get something to drink now, at once. She clutched her purse tightly and looked at them one last time before walking away. Blindly. Without looking at David. She didn't say good-bye, couldn't think of anything she could have said to the couple, who excluded her as if she were no one. She hoped that she was out of earshot when the first sobs began.

David followed Natalia with his eyes. He watched her for far too long, couldn't stop. Her back was straight, and she looked composed, but he'd seen how shocked she'd been when Carolina showed up.

He inhaled, tried to calm himself down. She'd said she was slumming it with him, that she was tired of it, and it had felt as if the ground began to sway. And then Carolina had unexpectedly turned up. That was unlike Caro. He'd asked her to stay at the café, and she usually did what he wanted without question, but he really couldn't be angry that she'd turned up. It was just so damned complicated, all of it.

Carolina touched his forearm. "Is everything alright?" she asked.

David nodded.

"Is that her?" she asked quietly.

David stiffened. Sometimes Carolina could be very perceptive. "What do you mean?"

But he hadn't succeeded in sounding blasé. And Carolina both knew him and didn't know him. She knew everything and nothing. He pulled her into a hug again.

Carolina burrowed her nose into his chest. "I'm not used to so many people," she murmured. "Can we go home?"

He nodded, relieved that she seemed to have dropped the subject. "Of course."

"And David?" She glanced up. Her face was serious, and he knew right away that she wasn't going to drop this. "We need to talk," she said.

42

Peter had practically been living at Investum for the last few days. His father was also at the office from early in the morning until late at night. As if it mattered whether they were here, Peter thought, burying his face in his hands.

He had a hard time seeing how this coup-like heist was going to end in anything other than complete disaster. But his father was firmly determined to fight, which of course meant that Peter was there too. It was easier to go with the flow than to stir up a counter-current. And besides, the truth was that if they lost Investum, then Peter's future would be seriously jeopardized. His buddies, his col-leagues—everyone he knew, including Louise—would see him as the worst kind of loser.

He rubbed his eyes and looked up from his desk as his father walked in, looking gloomy.

"You have to look at these," Gustaf said, holding up a brown folder. He opened the folder and started spreading large photographs out on the table.

"Are those from the private investigator?" Peter had hired the PI firm that was tailing David Hammar and reporting back. Nothing odd about that, they did it all the time, kept tabs on competitors or other threats. Mostly it was a waste of money, but sometimes . . .

Peter studied the pictures.

He didn't really get it. Why was David talking to Natalia? He looked more closely. That looked like Berzelii Park. Based on the date in the lower corner, the pictures were from today.

"Do they know each other?" he asked, still not able to make sense of how close his sister and David seemed to be standing to each other. "Outside of work, I mean?"

"They know each other," Gustaf said tersely. Something about his father's voice made Peter feel as if something was being kept from him, but then he saw something that made him completely forget David and Natalia, a face from the past, and it took his breath away, literally.

It couldn't be true.

Peter stared. It was her, for real. *Her.*

Carolina.

She was older in the pictures, not a young girl anymore, but a sophisticated grown woman. And Peter would have recognized her anywhere. He could still picture her features at night, when he woke from a sweaty dream or stared into space when he was daydreaming. He stared at the photos spread out on the table. They looked like they were from a detective movie, grainy enlargements, close-ups.

Carolina.

Oh my God.

"She's alive," he whispered. His voice wanted to break. He looked at his father in a panic. "You said she died, but she's alive."

43

David looked tiredly at his computer screen. He'd been doing that for half an hour now. Numbers and tables glowed fixedly back. He kept thinking back to the meeting in the park yesterday.

Going up to Natalia had been stupid. He realized that fully, especially now, after the fact. But somehow he was unable to make smart decisions when it came to her.

He closed his computer and stood up.

That look in Natalia's eyes when she greeted Caro . . .

He hadn't wanted Natalia to meet Carolina that way. Hadn't wanted them to meet at all, of course. And he knew it would be lunacy to contact Natalia now. But he needed for her to understand. Didn't want her to hate him more than necessary. If you could even differentiate hate that way, into necessary and less necessary strata.

He walked over to the window, stuffed his hands in his pockets, and returned to dwelling on the thoughts that wouldn't leave him. He didn't want her to hate him. And the thing was that he *could* explain, about Carolina anyway.

All that other stuff had been irretrievably set in motion. But Natalia deserved an explanation. From him.

David picked up his phone, found her number, and called, before his thinking brain had a chance to point out that what he was doing was rationalizing, nothing more.

It kept ringing. Was she busy? Did she see it was him and didn't want to answer? When he got her voice mail, he hung up.

He looked out the window again, saw heat waves in the air. He should take this as a sign to let go of her for good.

Screw signs. He called again, waited impatiently.

She answered on the third ring.

"Hello?"

She sounded dismissive, but David was relieved that she was talking at all.

"Hi, thanks for taking my call," he said.

Long silence. "David," she said and then the same silence again. Finally, "What can I help you with?"

"I'd like to see you," he said. "To explain."

"You don't need to explain anything," she said.

"I get that you don't trust me."

"No."

He looked at the time. It was four o'clock. "Are you still at work?" he asked. She didn't say anything, and David picked up something, he wasn't sure what, a hesitation of some sort that he didn't understand.

Then she said, "No."

"Can we see each other?" He couldn't talk about this on the phone. At least that's what he told himself. The truth was that he wanted to see her.

"I'm at the National Museum," she said finally. She was still being very terse. But she hadn't said no.

And he knew right away what she was doing there.

"At the icon exhibit?" he said, and he could picture her among all those exquisite Russian icons.

"Yes."

David thought. He was quite sure he was under some kind of surveillance. He'd seen a car and a camera, and he didn't want them to be seen together. But a Friday afternoon in the middle of the summer? The likelihood that someone they knew would see them at a small Russian exhibit was minimal.

"Can you wait for fifteen minutes? I'm on my way," he said.

"Okay," she said and hung up before he had a chance to say any more.

David opened the door and yelled, "Jesper, can you come in here?"

The boy came in, smiling, with a notepad in his hand.

"Listen carefully now. No, don't take any notes. I need your help. Take my car," David began, trying not to feel like he was in a spy movie. But the more careful he was, the better for Natalia. "Take my car and drive away." He pulled out his car keys and tossed them to Jesper, who eagerly caught the key ring.

"The Bentley?" Jesper asked.

"Do you have a suit you can wear?" David asked, looking at the boy's linen pants and black T-shirt.

Jesper nodded. "You want someone to think I'm you, huh?" He gave a big smile, as if it wasn't the least bit strange to pretend to be his boss to trick anyone who might be tailing him. And then he lit up even more. "I could take that," Jesper said, pointing to the suit David had had made at Savile Row that spring. "Then you can take my T-shirt. And I'll take your Ray-Bans, of course."

David shook his head. "You can take the suit, but I draw the line at my glasses." He looked at Jesper's lanky body and thought it probably wouldn't work. "Give me your shirt," he said, resigned. There must be a pair of pants around here somewhere.

Natalia stood in front of the glass protecting an ancient icon, staring at it blankly.

She knew very well that of all the stupid things she could do, agreeing to meet David took the cake. But nothing in her life was going the way it should, so she'd answered when he called a second time, and then she'd said yes to meeting even though her brain had screamed no.

Now her heart was ticking like a time bomb as she tried to concentrate on the Russian masterpieces. She wandered between display cases—some were made of bulletproof glass and contained priceless relics—and reminded herself that this wasn't a date. David belonged to another woman, and he'd lied to her, in more ways than one. *Danish*, it occurred to her suddenly. The woman had a Danish accent.

She put on some lip gloss, stuffed it back down in her purse and closed it. She moved along, knowing that she looked cool and elegant and feeling satisfied with that.

As long as she didn't puke, everything would probably go fine.

She heard a quiet sound, looked up, and saw David.

Broad-shouldered and dressed in black, he was standing in the doorway, almost filled it. Natalia held her breath and felt the hair on her arms stand up. The museum was air-conditioned, and there were high ceilings, but it felt as if all the air had suddenly gone out of the room.

David came over to her with long, silent strides and stopped without touching her.

"Thanks for waiting," he said quietly.

"I love icons," she said, grateful that her voice sounded normal despite the roaring in her head. "I could stay here forever."

She began to walk slowly to the next display case, unable to bear the tension in the air between them.

Her whole life she'd been drilled on manners and politeness: sit still, stand up straight, say "thank you very much," but it was as if that were all gone in a flash. Her brain was empty, devoid of small talk and conversational graces. She hadn't counted on it hurting so much to see him again. Her pulse sped up, and even though they weren't touching each other, hardly even looking at each other, it was as if he completely flooded her senses, filled everything, took all the room and air there was.

She stopped in front of a display case. He stopped too. His arm, bare in the short-sleeved T-shirt, brushed against hers. Natalia almost jumped. It was inconceivable that she could have such conflicting emotions. She should detest him, and she did, but at the same time: the memories of what they'd done together, how they'd laughed and made love until they were sweaty, how intimate their conversations had been, how close they'd come to each other. David had *seen* her like no one else. Or had that just been a ruse? Could a person be so totally mistaken? Several weeks ago, David Hammar had been an unimportant extra on the periphery of her existence. Now he felt like the person her entire being revolved around.

It was practically unbearable.

David nodded at the icon lying on velvet in the display case. "That's beautiful," he said softly.

It was one of the smaller icons in the exhibit, and it was the one Natalia liked best in the whole room.

This was her second visit to the exhibit. She'd come here today for a little serenity. The Russian artwork held a strange power over her, a reminder of her heredity, one that no one else in the family was particularly interested in.

She hadn't heard from either her mother or her father—Gustaf, since she'd fled their mansion in Djursholm. She'd called Gustaf, but he hadn't answered. The same thing with her mother. The phone rang forever and eventually went to an impersonal voice-mail system. Peter certainly took her calls, but he sounded frayed and irritated and hardly listened to her suggestions about how they should mobilize against the hostile takeover. Alexander hadn't answered either. Maybe the whole family was pushing her out of their collective conscience?

Tears threatened to obscure her view. She didn't even know if her brothers knew. No one said anything.

"It's on loan from the Hermitage," she said quickly, looking at the golden icon. She'd compartmentalized everything. Unemployment into one box. Illegitimate birth into another. Pregnancy . . . She pushed that totally aside, forced herself to pay attention to the moment. She would just have to deal with one cataclysmic, life-altering catastrophe at a time. The Madonna's face was mild. Her halo was made of gemstones and glowed in rich jewel tones. For all its petiteness, the icon made an unbelievably strong impression, as if all the power in the room was centered there upon the velvet inside this bulletproof glass display case. According to the card next to it, its value was estimated as "priceless."

"She looks like you," David said, studying the serious Madonna. "Strong, unwavering."

"Thanks," Natalia said. "I think."

She wasn't sure "unwavering" was exactly her favorite compliment. But she really wanted to be seen as strong, especially now when she was so very, very frail.

"Hey, you," he said and his voice was raw with emotion. He sounded completely honest. That was highly dangerous. "About what happened yesterday."

Panic welled up in Natalia.

"You don't need to say anything," she said quickly. She swallowed and swallowed. *Don't start crying, don't ask a bunch of questions, just get through this,* she instructed herself.

But her jealousy was vicious. She would never again look down on people who were jealous. From now on, she would understand the despair and hopelessness that feeling caused. She clung to the last shards of her dignity. *Don't beg, don't plead. Be unwavering now, Natalia.*

"Carolina is my sister," he said, looking her right in the eye. The light in the museum was muted, but he looked like he was being honest. He didn't blink.

This was so bewildering that at first Natalia didn't really understand. She was forced to look away, staring blankly into space. She couldn't think when David looked at her that way. As if he were baring his soul to her.

"You said you don't have any family," Natalia pointed out, forcing herself to look at his face again, to steel herself and dissect what he said, not allow herself to be tricked by her own unreliable emotions. Emotions weren't truth. Emotions lied, often. "You said your sister was dead." Her suspicion grew, because David must be lying.

"I lied before, but I'm not lying now," he said in that tone that always made it feel as if he was reading her mind. "Carolina is my little sister."

Natalia put a hand on the glass display case even though there was a sign that said you shouldn't touch anything. She hoped she hadn't just set off some alarm. "Are you messing with me?"

"No one knows. I've never told anyone, not even Michel. You're the first person to know. I wanted to tell you yesterday, but it's not just my secret. We've kept it hidden since we were teenagers." He shook his head. "I can hardly believe I'm telling you now."

"Does she know? That you're telling me?"

And why is it a secret? People don't have secret sisters, do they?

Apparently the whole world had secrets. But why not? She was illegitimate. And was going to have a secret baby. Why shouldn't David Hammar have a mysterious, secret sister? This was like a soap opera. She was struck by a sudden desire to burst into inappropriate, hysterical laughter.

"Yes," David said. "We had a long talk yesterday. She knows I'm telling you. We're very close. But she hasn't been doing well, and I've been very protective." He smiled. "*Too* protective, if you ask her."

"Is she sick?" Natalia searched his face.

He had a sister.

A sister, not another woman.

"She's fragile." David seemed to hesitate. "But there's more than that, Natalia. And it's not going to be pleasant for you to hear."

Of course there was more. And of course it was something awful.

She tried to remember exactly when her life had turned into this— a melodrama full of chaos and secrets.

"Tell me," she said.

David looked around, but they were still alone in the room. "Let's sit down," he said and pointed to a bench.

"The reason Carolina has been 'dead,'" he began once they were seated, making quotes in the air around *dead*, "is that there was a threat against her. The decision was made a long time ago, for her own safety."

Natalia remembered how a scarcely discernable vulnerability had seemed to surround the blond Carolina, as if she were a little too frail for this world. She gave David a questioning look.

"When I was at Skogbacka, our whole family moved to the small town where Skogbacka is situated. My mom took a job working in a pub there. The nights were long, and she was away a lot."

A shadow fell over his face. A distant look settled in his eyes.

"One night Carolina was attacked," he continued. "She was so badly abused that she ended up in the hospital. That was the culmination of all the harassment that had been directed against my family, which had been going on for a long time. It continued even after the attack. People gossiped, and our whole family was targeted. It was a small community, and we weren't from there, and . . ." He shook his head, then cleared his throat and continued. "Finally it got so bad that my mother decided to move Caro to Denmark."

"To Denmark? Why?"

"Caro was always special, sort of frail. After . . . the attack . . . she withdrew into her own world. The doctors said she was traumatized, but no one knew what to do with her. My mom heard about a therapist in Denmark who specialized in these types of patients. She was desperate; otherwise she would never have allowed herself to be separated from Caro." David looked down at the floor. Had he never discussed this with anyone? "Caro moved there. She was only fifteen, but it was good for her. She lived out in the countryside by the sea. It helped her heal." David fell silent, and Natalia tried to visualize what he was telling her. A small Swedish town, the locals who turned on a family of outsiders.

"My mom never recovered," David continued softly, and it was as if Natalia was seeing the young man he'd been then, still a teenager but with one foot in the adult world, an outsider, worried about his mother and sister. "We grew apart, the three of us, in different ways. Caro stayed in Denmark. I moved to Stockholm to study. My mom died while I was at the School of Economics."

"But your mom stayed there? In spite of everything that had happened?"

"Yes, she refused to leave. My mother could be very stubborn."

Natalia smiled a little at how David had very clearly inherited that stubbornness.

"If you can die of a broken heart, my mom did," David continued. "And I was no help. We grew apart, and then, one day, she was just gone. I didn't even know she was sick. Pneumonia that she didn't get treatment for in time, so pointless. At the funeral I told everyone that Caro was dead and no one questioned it. Maybe that was wrong, but she was doing so well in Denmark, and it felt safest. It wasn't until the last few years that she started to go out, see people." He smiled a sad smile. "To be more like other people. There are no signs of her breakdown anymore. But we don't talk about what happened. I can't and she . . . I don't know, actually."

Natalia's heart was pounding. Somehow she suspected he hadn't told her everything.

"But what was it that happened?" Her question sounded like a whisper in the quiet exhibit room.

"Carolina was raped." David said it calmly, but she saw the effort it cost him. Natalia felt an icy chill race through her body.

"It was a gruesome rape," he said, pulling his hand over his face. He leaned forward, resting his forearms on his knees. The back of his neck was bare and looked vulnerable. Natalia wove her fingers together in her lap. "Of course all rapes are terrible," he continued. "But this . . . I thought Caro was going to die. It was awful. And I blamed myself."

"No, why?"

"Caro had always been a little different, even before." He looked up. "I should have been home with her. Mom was working, and Caro didn't like to be alone. But I was young and restless, didn't want to sit around home and babysit my sister. So I slipped out. And they came in and . . ." He stopped.

Natalia tried to picture it. A frail fifteen-year-old at home alone. Men who broke in, took her trust, hurt her forever.

"But who were they?"

"Four boys from the school. Caro knew them, and they tricked her to get in. She thought they were well-meaning—Caro always thought the best of everyone. She was incredibly sweet as a teenager, and she was like any fifteen-year-old girl. But they were there to get back at me."

"At you?"

"I'd gotten into a fight with some of the older students at the school. These four wanted to teach me a lesson."

That sounded completely insane, like what would happen in a war. Men taking revenge on women and children.

"Natalia, it's hard for me to say this," David continued. "But Peter was one of the attackers."

"Peter?" She blinked, still busy digesting what she'd heard. "Peter who?"

David didn't answer. She looked at him. Slowly shook her head when the significance of what he'd said sank in. And she was forced to comprehend the impossible.

Of course. That would explain so much.

But that was sick. David *couldn't* mean . . .

"No," she whispered.

David watched her steadily. "There's more," he said.

"More?" How could there be *more*? Whatever she'd been preparing herself for when they'd started talking, this wasn't it.

"Of course a crime like that would be reported. I was completely beside myself; my mom called the police, the school. But it was hushed up. Do you understand? Your father—one of the school's biggest donors—and the headmaster hushed it up, said it was Caro's fault for inviting them in. You know how it goes."

Natalia nodded, devastated. It happened every day. Girls were raped first and then blamed for it, a double attack. First physical abuse, then shaming.

"Our family received threats, our name was dragged through the mud. You can't believe what people said about us, about Caro. It was awful. And when I tried to report the crime anyway, well . . . you've seen my back. Peter and his buddies did that. Finally my mother begged me to stop." David shook his head. "I did. For her sake. And I started studying instead, thought that's how I would get back at them, become so powerful that no one could do anything like that to my family ever again."

Natalia couldn't breathe. Her chest was on fire.

David was destroying her family. Because of something her brother and father had done. It was a vendetta, a feud, real blood vengeance, the kind you only read about.

Nausea washed through her.

"Natalia?"

David's voice was distorted and distant. She couldn't breathe, couldn't sit still. She stood up, clutching her purse until she couldn't feel her fingers.

"I need a minute," she said weakly.

David had stood up too. "I'm sorry, truly. But I wanted you to know who Caro is. I could tell you thought something else."

Natalia didn't know what to say. David had spent his youth protecting his mother and sister against violence and threats—from *her* family. He'd devoted his adult life to plotting revenge against her father and brother. Peter had . . . No, that was too much.

"My biggest motivator since then has been securing Caro's future," he said.

"By getting revenge against everyone who was involved," she noted, because suddenly everything made sense. David's missile-like trajectory throughout his professional life. How many of the people he'd ruthlessly ruined had been involved in the events at Skogbacka? In the rape and the cover-up? All those articles she'd read about him, all the rumors—they were true. They were part of his plan for revenge.

"The headmaster and the others. You destroyed them financially, one by one, didn't you? You took their companies, tore down their houses, seduced their wives. They're not lies, that's the truth. Those were the men who raped your sister, right?"

"That was about business," he said.

"That was *revenge*."

"Does it matter?"

Yes, Natalia thought, it mattered, to her anyway. Maybe not in his world. But for her there was a difference between business and personal acts of vengeance.

"That's going to destroy you as a person," she said, at the same time wondering if maybe it hadn't already. "Can't you see that?" she pleaded. "They wronged you, and now you're getting your revenge. I can understand the emotions, but David, no good can come from revenge. Do you really think this is what your mother would have wanted for you? For the two of you?"

"You can't know what my mother would have wanted," he said, leaning his shoulder against the wall and crossing his arms over his chest. "The very idea that you think you know is so arrogant. Natalia, don't you realize how sheltered you are in your blue-blooded bubble? You don't know what life looks like for most people."

Strangely enough, those words really stung.

She had thought that he *saw* her, saw past all the external stuff, saw how she'd fought her own battle. But she was just some upper-class bimbo to him, narrow-minded and ignorant.

Apparently there were no limits to how dumb and humiliated a person could be.

"We come from totally different backgrounds," he continued, cocking his head to the side and studying her. "Can you honestly say that you didn't sleep with me because that idea was exciting?" He smiled. "How did you put it yesterday? That you were slumming it a little?"

"I'm sorry about that," she said quietly. "I shouldn't have said that; it wasn't true. I'm sorry."

"You haven't said anything about it being your own family who's behind everything," he said, straightening up. "I get that you're mad at me, but aren't you mad at them? For what they did?"

She bit her lip. "I . . ."

"You don't believe me," he stated. "A part of you thinks I'm lying."

Natalia looked down. "I don't know what to believe," she said sincerely.

He had sounded credible, but the story was so dreadful. Could something like that happen? Could her own brother do something so brutal? Could a whole community turn on a defenseless family like that?

But yes, she believed him, she realized. "If it's true, then I was a part of your revenge as well," she said, and the ground swayed beneath her. Peter had raped Carolina. So David had taken revenge by sleeping with Peter's sister.

"Retaliation for what Peter did," she added flatly.

It felt so sordid.

David's eyes narrowed, and Natalia shivered.

"Peter and his friends violently raped Carolina," he said. "They injured her in ways you don't even want to know. You wanted to have sex with me. That is an important difference, wouldn't you say? That you were more than happy to sleep with me."

She nodded, pulled her fingers through the scarf she was unwrapping from around her neck. "Yes, there's a difference," she said. "But do you know what I think?" she asked.

He shook his head.

"You're doing this for your own sake. You like taking revenge, you enjoy the power it gives you." She looked him straight in the eye. "You're using what happened to your sister as an excuse to make money and gain power. I think it gives you satisfaction to manipulate people."

"I didn't manipulate you into anything," he said. "And you know that."

"You shouldn't have contacted me," she said and swallowed. "Or arranged the tickets, or flirted. You should have left me alone."

"But I didn't want to leave you alone," he said, moving closer to her.

She backed away.

"You can convince yourself that I tricked you, if that makes you feel better. But what happened between us, Natalia," he said in a husky voice, coming a little bit closer still, "you wanted that, just as much as I did."

He was so close now that he towered over her.

Natalia took another step backward and felt the wall against her back.

"But there can never be anything between us," she said, her voice starting to break. She cleared her throat. "You knew that from the very beginning. That is a crucial difference, at least to me."

"Just because there's no future doesn't mean it can't be good now," he murmured.

She felt sweat breaking out on her scalp. What was he doing?

David raised his hand and caressed her, so incredibly gently, running his thumb over her cheek.

She couldn't breathe.

"What are you doing?" she whispered, sounding strangled to her own ears. The loving touch was so unexpected; she was completely unprepared for the answering flood wave of feelings. Her heart pounded against her ribs. She couldn't take her eyes off his face. Of all the things they'd done, she'd fallen hardest of all for his kisses. Nothing was as intimate as kissing, and he was so very good at it.

He put one hand on the wall behind her, slowly leaned forward, as if to give her a chance to pull away.

Natalia didn't pull away.

And he kissed her. Softly, tenderly, caressing her lips with his mouth. She was breathing, hard. She foggily thought she ought to push him away, that this could only end with even more hurt feelings. But she wouldn't have been able to push David away if her life depended on it. She needed this, more than she needed air or food. She closed her eyes, leaned into him with her whole body. They kissed until she gasped.

A muffled clank made her pull away. A guard had walked in; he glanced at them briefly, looked around, and then left again. David hadn't taken his eyes off her. His gaze was dark and intense, and his chest heaved as he pulled away from her. She could have kept going until they were lying in a heap on the floor.

He smiled slowly. "Are you going to keep lying to yourself, Natalia?" He reached out with his hand and ran a finger along the neckline of her blouse until she trembled. He smiled at the effect he'd had, watching her, staring deep into her eyes. "I never needed to seduce you, if that's what you've persuaded yourself. You fell like a ripe plum. I just had to reach out my hand and pick you." His finger continued moving down, until he touched her breast, and unwelcome tears welled up in her eyes. "You still want it," he murmured. "Despite everything you know about who I am and what I've done."

He leaned toward her again.

And Natalia, who had never done anything violent to anyone in her whole life, who had always argued with her family in favor of nonviolence and peaceful solutions, raised her hand and slapped David right on the cheek with all her might. The slap was so powerful it made his handsome face snap to the side.

"Fuck you," she said.

She stared at him and their eyes met.

"I'm going to fight," she said. "Don't you think I'm going to make this easy for you, not in any way."

And suddenly she knew what it felt like to want revenge, to retaliate for unforgivable wrongs. He had pulled her into this. He had made this personal, for *her*. It no longer had anything to do with Investum, not to her. She was planning to fight for herself, for her unborn child. "It isn't over until it's over," she said and if it sounded like a line from a bad movie, so be it.

She took a deep breath, gathered the remnants of what had been her self-esteem. David hadn't even gotten mad about the slap; it was as if he hadn't felt it. He was undoubtedly used to worse. Surely she wasn't the first hysterical woman to slap him.

He handed her her scarf, which had fallen on the floor, and she snatched it out of his hand. He watched her, and for the life of her she couldn't interpret the look on his face.

"You know what?" she said angrily. "The rape, the assault, and what your family was subjected to—no one should have to go through that. Justice should have been served; they should have been punished, all of them. But this, what you're doing now, isn't this just as bad? This is *now*. You can't change the past, but what you're doing is going to destroy your life *now*."

"That's a naïve argument," he said.

"Maybe," she continued. "But isn't it better to be naïve than to be dead inside? You're completely stuck in the past. I don't know how I would be able to move on after something like what you went through. But I know that people *have* to move on. Otherwise it's like the perpetrators won."

"No," he said. "I'm going to win this, and don't you believe otherwise."

"You're going to destroy my family."

"Yes."

And it was at that moment that Natalia realized she was never going to tell David about the pregnancy. There was no future for them. Before she had thought that the board meeting would be the end of it. But she'd been wrong, she realized as she tied her scarf, hands trembling, and straightened her clothes. Because this was just the beginning. From here on out things were only going to get worse.

All those years ago, David's family had been broken up. Now it was her family's turn.

Chaos and hatred would follow. Maybe it would even continue into the next generation.

She struggled for breath. She'd made up her mind. This was enough.

"Good-bye, David," she said.

44

It was Friday afternoon, and David had vanished from the office, without a word, wearing black like a burglar or something. Michel got up from his desk and took out his gym bag. He had no idea what David was up to. Instead, he opened the bag and checked to see that he had everything he needed, zipped it shut again, and then headed to the refrigerator in the kitchenette to get a bottle of water.

"I'm going to the gym for a while," he told Malin, who was standing in the lobby leaning over a stack of paperwork.

"Things are starting to calm down," she said. "Everything's ready for Monday."

"I'm coming back," he explained. "I just have to clear my head."

Malin nodded.

"Where's Jesper?" Michel asked.

"He left," Malin said with a shrug.

Michel shook his head. Something was going on. David, who was the most reliable, levelheaded, and disciplined man Michel had ever met, was acting increasingly irrational. Acting on his feelings, afflicted with doubt, like a goddamned rookie.

As Michel drank his water, took the stairs down, and started strolling toward his gym, he thought in all seriousness that they should maybe think about getting out of all this. David had been going at an almost inhuman pace ever since the School of Economics. Maybe it was too much for him in the end? They could cut their losses and pull out if they wanted. After all, this wasn't nuclear physics. They would hemorrhage money, of course, but it was hardly life or death they were talking about.

Michel emptied his bottle, tossed it into a recycling bin, and opened the door to one of Stockholm's most exclusive gyms. He greeted the receptionist and put his thoughts aside. He changed, and ten minutes later sweat was pouring out of him.

Åsa couldn't remember the last time she'd still been at work past four o'clock on a Friday, but today was the last weekday before that stupid goddamn general meeting, so she was still at Investum like some common drone.

She had been at work early on Thursday (hungover after her shocking evening with Natalia) and even earlier this morning (actually hungover today as well, but she was going to stop drinking soon, any day now).

She was doing her best to deal with this mess. Natalia talked about fighting, but the problem was that the takeover was devilishly well planned. Natalia was rightfully pissed at David Hammar, that fucking traitor, but Åsa didn't actually have it in her to be quite as pissed at Michel any longer.

The financial sector was brutal. People were sharks, and as soon as someone started to bleed, they attacked. And a little part of her felt that Gustaf only had himself to blame. This was what happened when your board consisted of mediocre middle-aged yes-men. The level of expertise sank like a Baltic share price on a Black Monday. David Hammar might be a ruthless and arrogant businessman, but he knew what he was doing. He was well organized, whereas Gustaf always thought he knew better than anyone else and therefore never took any advice or listened to anyone else. Now Peter, Gustaf, and all the other Investum employees, high and low alike, were running around alternately panicked, furious, or utterly exhausted.

Åsa yawned widely and closed her eyes for a moment. Peter was out in the corridor bawling about something she couldn't have cared less about. He really wasn't handling this crisis well. If she'd had a shred of sympathy for him, she would have been worried. She wondered how he would react to this business about Natalia not being Gustaf's child. Jeez, what a shocking evening *that* had been. Åsa had no doubt that Gustaf really meant it when he said he wanted nothing more to do with Natalia. Natalia was still hoping they would reconcile, but Åsa doubted that would happen.

Since her own parents had died, Gustaf had functioned as a sort of stand-in father for her. It was always uncomfortable because Åsa felt that Gustaf liked her better than Natalia. She hadn't discussed it with anyone; she'd just known it, which had been really hard. Her solution had been to keep her distance emotionally and to act out. If you acted out, the inevitable always happened and people left you. It was easier than math or Intro to Common Law. And drinking a little too much was a solution to most other problems, in her expert opinion. Acting out and being drunk a lot—those were the two pillars her existence rested on.

Åsa put her feet up on her desk and closed her eyes again. She knew that Gustaf and Ebba had really wanted her and Peter to get together so that she, the girl with Sweden's finest pedigree, would marry and produce little De la Grips with crown prince Peter. That was how it was done, after all. You married the inner circle, swapping fiancés and girlfriends with each other in an almost incestuous way. But she would rather stick a barbecue fork in her eye than have any more to do with Peter.

She scratched her forehead and sighed loudly. It was hot and she wanted to go home. If she didn't tell anyone, then she could take a night off and spend it at home with her TV and a couple of sleeping pills for company. She didn't have the energy to date, to get dressed up, flirt, and send more pictures to Michel. He didn't want her; she gave up. It would never have worked anyway.

A while later, Åsa was walking home from work, swinging her briefcase and watching people. Purely on impulse she decided to take a detour on the way to her apartment. Instead of her usual Östermalm route, she would walk along the water.

There were a lot of people down by the pier, and her high heels kept getting stuck between the cobblestones. As she leaned down to pry a heel free again, her phone rang.

She answered without looking to see who it was. "Hello?"

"Åsa?" said a familiar voice.

Fuck. There she stood, bent over, with her briefcase under her arm, holding her phone under her chin, unable to think of the smart things she'd planned to say if he ever called.

"Hi, Michel," was all she said, tugging on her heel, which finally came free.

"Hi," he said; it sounded like he was smiling, and her mind went blank. She started walking again. The sun was hot, the pier full of people, and she had to push her way along. She tried to force herself to think of something witty to say, hated that she wanted him so much. Couldn't stand this need to see him, to hear his voice. It *hurt*.

"What are you doing?" he asked.

She looked around. People everywhere, sticky children and tourists pointing at stuff. "I'm just meeting a friend for a drink," she said. Thank heavens he couldn't see her like this.

The heel on her shoe was loose, so she was limping a little. Her white suit—she loved white—hadn't held up well to the chaos of her day at work, so it was both dirty and wrinkled.

"Where are you?" he asked.

She brushed the hair out of her face. She was also sweating, and she hated that. The day menopause started giving her hot flashes, she was going to kill herself. Her bra slipped, and she held onto her phone and briefcase in one hand and tried to push her breast back into the cup.

"In the city." A boat leaving the pier tooted its horn, and she heard an echo over the line. She furrowed her brow. "Michel?"

"Yes?"

"Where are *you*? I thought I heard a boat horn."

"Here," he said and then he was standing in front of her, smelling good, with a bag over his shoulder and wearing aviator glasses.

Her heel got stuck again. *Goddamnfuckingshit.*

Michel had spotted Åsa as he left the gym and hadn't been able to resist the impulse to follow her for a bit. With her white suit and blond hair, she looked like an angel—if angels had four-inch heels and curves that would make a twisty, turny Italian mountain road seem straight and uneventful.

She didn't look happy to see him, but then Åsa had never liked surprises. She blew a blond lock out of her eyes and glared.

"Where are you *really* going?" he asked, holding out his hand to her. She seemed stuck, the heel of her shoe wedged between two cobblestones.

With a wary look on her face, she put two fingers on his arm, used him for support, and pulled her heel loose. "I hate cobblestones," she said, letting go of his arm. She smoothed her skirt, and he snuck a glance at her hand as she ran it over her hip. The white fabric was taut over her buttocks and thighs, and Michel almost had to resort to violence against himself to keep from staring. He dragged his eyes back up to her face, lingering at her mouth, and then looked into her eyes.

"What the hell are you doing here?" she asked.

"I'm just coming from the gym," he said. "I saw you."

"And then you decided to stalk me?"

He shrugged. "Where are you headed?"

"Home."

He raised an eyebrow. "This way?" He knew exactly where she lived, at one of the quietest and most exclusive addresses in Östermalm. He'd stood outside her building more times than he would ever care to admit.

"I decided to take a stroll along the water. Rotten idea. I'll never do it again."

He laughed. "No, you've never been a fan of strolls," he agreed. He'd always loved her for that, her decadent attitude toward physical activity.

She studied him. "You're looking awfully good. Are you going on a date?"

"I just worked out," he said. When she looked at him like that, running her eyes over his muscles and openly studying his body, he had to force himself not to start flexing and clenching like some idiot. She affected him, and he had to hold on tight to maintain control. Åsa could nose out weakness, and if she had any idea of the effect she had on him, she would crush him under one of those heels of hers.

"What do you want, Michel? What are you doing?"

"I'm just having a conversation," he said.

"You know what I mean. I don't want to talk anymore."

"No," he said. "I know." But he refused to be one of those men she slept with and then got rid of. He thought for a moment. "I think I'm courting you."

"Courting?" She made a snorting sound. "Does that word even exist anymore? Are you drunk?"

"No," he said.

"You can't decide what our relationship will look like," she said. "You can't come into my life and just point at things and think I'll care."

"I can point however much I want. You just need to choose whether you're going to follow or not."

She glared at him. Her pale skin had some color now; light-pink patches flared up on her cheeks. "You're an asshole," she said. There was fear lingering in her eyes, curled up there like a scared child.

He leaned over and kissed her quickly on the lips and then released her again just as quickly. "In seventy-two hours all of this will be over," he said. "Then I'm coming to see you. Then we'll be done talking." He glanced at his watch. "But now I have to get back to the office before the market closes," he said. "I'll see you."

"Just go," she said. "I'm doing fine without you. I hope that's clear to you."

"Åsa?"

"Yes?"

"Stay away from cobblestones."

He turned around again and walked away, whistling.

"I hate you," she called after him.

He laughed. *And I love you.* But he didn't say that out loud. In spite of everything, he was no fool.

45

David strolled the short distance from the National Museum back to his office, deeply lost in thought. His meeting with Natalia had been bewildering, to say the least. He'd deserved that slap in the face. He hadn't been particularly nice. He rubbed his cheek. She was strong.

David opened the front door to the office and greeted Malin, who was standing in the reception area.

"Are people still with us?" he asked. It was five-thirty. As soon as the market closed, everything would be totally calm.

She nodded. "Nothing's going to happen now. Everyone's waiting for the meeting."

Malin was right. He nodded as he glanced through a report she handed him. Nothing would happen from now until after the weekend was over.

"I'm leaving in half an hour," she said as Michel appeared in the doorway. Malin walked off to make a phone call.

"Where have you been?" David asked.

"The gym," Michel responded, setting his bag on the floor. He pulled off his sunglasses and wiped his forehead with the back of his hand. "Where have *you* been? And where's your car?"

David had completely forgotten about Jesper and the car. "Can you come into my office for a minute?" he asked. "There's something I need to tell you."

David waited in his office while Michel put away his bag. Michel came in carrying two bottles of water and shut the door behind him with his elbow. He handed one of the bottles to David. They sat down on either side of the desk.

"Jesper took my car," David explained. "Have you noticed that we're under surveillance? I didn't want to be followed."

"Mmm, I see. It's not like this is the first time." It wasn't the first time they'd been tailed; the financial world sometimes stooped to out-and-out espionage. After all, it was an industry where information was the hardest currency of all.

"I'm sorry I ran off without saying anything," David said. "I had to take care of something."

"It's alright."

"I saw Natalia," he said.

"Was that really a good idea?" Michel asked, fingering his water bottle.

"No," David agreed. "But I had to clear something up. And now I want to tell you."

"I'm all ears," Michel said with a sigh.

So David told him the whole story.

About the meeting between Carolina and Natalia in the park yesterday, about the assault at Skogbacka and Peter's role in it, everything. He told Michel absolutely everything. And it felt great. Just as it had to tell Natalia. For a little while there, inside the museum's icon exhibit, David had felt at peace. For a little while, before they wound up bogged down in conflict yet again, he had felt calm and harmonious. He'd finally told someone about Caro. Natalia had listened, and it had been like confessing. He hadn't realized what a burden the secret was.

Natalia had been shocked, of course, and he wondered if there was anybody he'd deceived as many times as he'd deceived Natalia. If he'd read her right, she was never going to forgive him, never going to trust him, and that hurt more than he could bear to think about. But he was glad he'd told her about Caro. At least she'd heard it from him and hadn't read it in some tabloid exposé. Most of the media attention had blown over by now. Journalists still asked about Skogbacka and hazing, but not that often. Neither the rape nor the whipping had been reported to the police, after all, so the worst of the details remained hidden. And none of the people involved had any interest in the story being made public.

He glanced at Michel, who sat silent with a shocked look on his face.

"This is absolutely incredible," he said, stunned.

"Yes."

"You have a secret sister. That's insane."

"Yes."

"And you never told anyone about her."

"No."

"And Peter De la Grip did . . . that to her." He stopped.

"Yes."

"This whole deal has been so weird," Michel said. "With you and Natalia and all the various personal vendettas. And now you have a sister I've never heard of, that *no one* has ever heard of."

"I'm sorry," David said. "But it was all for her own safety."

"I understand that," Michel said, waving his hand dismissively. He seemed to be thinking. "You said there was a threat against her?"

"That was a long time ago, but you can't be too careful."

"So why is she here? In Stockholm?"

"My sister owns Investum shares," David said with a smile. He'd bought them for her over the years. By now she owned quite a bit.

"Is she going to vote?"

"Yes. I tried to get her to send a proxy instead, but she wanted to come in person. She can be really stubborn."

Michel raised an eyebrow. He set down his bottle of water. "I have to digest this for a bit."

"I understand."

"But that's all? You don't have any more secrets? No more hidden relatives I need to be aware of, I mean?"

There was a knock on the door.

David shook his head and said, "No more," before he called, "Come in!"

Malin stuck her head in. "David?"

"Yes?"

"There's a man here to see you."

"At this time of day? Who?"

Malin gave him an embarrassed look. She glanced at Michel and then back at David again. Her eyes flitted back and forth, as if she were watching a tennis match. She cleared her throat. "I don't know how to say this."

"Say what?" David asked.

Michel gave Malin a puzzled look as well.

She looked from one to the other a few more times. Then she said, with a heavy sigh and in an apologetic tone, "He says he's your father."

46

The silence that filled David's office was palpable. Michel slapped both hands onto the desktop so that his heavy rings clunked. One gem sparkled, menacingly. Slowly he stood up, leaned forward, and gave David a dark look. "You go right ahead. This is all yours," he said, his voice sounding so choked it was almost cracking. "Mister venture capitalist, founder, and superhero." His jaw was clenching and unclenching, and then he continued, emphasizing each syllable separately, "But then you and I are going to talk. For real. About the future, your and my future." He gave David one last furious look, took his hands off the desk, grabbed his empty water bottle, and crumpled it up. He nodded at Malin on the way out.

"Send him in," David said once Michel was gone.

He stood up. *This won't take long.*

Malin mumbled something, and then he saw the man.

"You can go on in," Malin said, and David's normally confident communications director looked uncertain as she showed the visitor in.

David crossed his arms over his chest and studied the man who walked in. "Carl-Erik Tessin," Malin said. "*Count* Tessin," she, the woman who was never nervous, added nervously.

"Thanks, Malin," David said. "You can go home. This won't take long." He was deliberately impolite, allowing some of the rage he felt to be heard in his voice. How *dare* this man even think about coming here?

Malin quietly closed the door on them, and they were alone.

"Hi, David," Carl-Erik said. He spoke in that quiet, articulate voice that David more than anything else associated with the upper class and abuses of power.

"What the hell are you doing here? And what the *fuck* do you want?"

Carl-Erik's face quivered. "I've tried to reach you."

"So?"

Still no anger from the man, but then Carl-Erik had always been a cowardly, evasive person.

"I wrote to you," he said quietly. "And called. You don't answer."

"No," David said tersely, didn't say anything more than that, didn't want to prolong this conversation, didn't want to *have* this conversation. There was nothing Carl-Erik could say that David wanted to hear. He hated this man, his count of a father. Just that word—father, *dad*—the most meaningless and noncommittal word there was, turned his stomach. This count with his genteel southern Swedish dialect and his rarified pedigree was the man who had had two children—not one, but two—with a young, beautiful Helena Hammar. The man who had met the uneducated waitress out on the town in Stockholm in the late seventies and started a relationship. Got her pregnant and never thought about separating from his wife, a woman with the right background for a count. There were no words to describe the disdain David felt for Count Tessin. He stared blankly at him, made himself cold, and radiated unavailability. If anyone knew what it felt like when an outstretched hand was met with indifference, it was he.

"I saw you in Båstad," Carl-Erik continued.

David had also seen him, but in the same way that Carl-Erik once had refused to recognize his illegitimate children, David refused to acknowledge Carl-Erik's existence.

"And I read about you in the papers. I read everything."

There had been a time when this whole business of having a father had been important in David's life. There had been times as a child when he'd wondered what he'd done wrong, since his own father hadn't wanted him. One time he'd taken the bus, without telling his mother, all the way down to Skåne, a bus ride of many, many hours, and stood outside the fence of the mansion where his father lived with his wife and his *legitimate* children. Tired and sad, he'd returned home and then shut the door on his past for good.

Years had gone by, and Carl-Erik might as well have been dead now. To David he *was* dead. Aside from the fact that David hated him, and a rational part of him realized that you couldn't hate someone who was dead. But he hated this man standing before him with a mixture of remorse and hope in his eyes every bit as much as he hated Gustaf and Peter. This man who always backed away, who exploited and left, who disappointed and was weak. David wanted to believe that there wasn't a single cell in him that was like Carl-Erik Tessin.

"Like I said, what do you want?" David inhaled, tried to contain his anger, didn't want to show that he cared. "I'm giving you two seconds, then I would like to see you get out of here. For good." He loathed that he was so angry. He wanted to be indifferent.

His mother had loved this man. If Carl-Erik had been there for her, everything would have been different. Carolina wouldn't have been hurt, his mother wouldn't have had to work so hard. Maybe they would have lived happily ever fucking after.

"I would really like to get to know you, to have a relationship."

David didn't say anything.

"I wasn't there for you when you were little, and I have to live with the guilt of that. But now . . ."

"Now?" David interrupted. "There is no *now*."

"If you only knew how much I wish I'd done things differently, that I'd been there for you more, for your mother, for Helena. But she wouldn't let me into her life."

David remembered the tears and the bitterness. "Maybe that has something to do with the fact that you were married to another woman," he said icily. He had no memory of anything good when it came to this man who had the balls to claim to be his father.

"I couldn't get divorced, but I wanted to help her. She refused to take almost everything I offered her, I could only . . ."

"Is that all?" David asked coldly.

"I came to ask for your forgiveness. And your sister's . . ."

"Caro?" David blurted out, despite having decided to remain silent no matter what the old man said. "What does she have to do with any of this?"

Carl-Erik's face softened. "Carolina and I see each other sometimes. I've visited her at her home in Denmark. And we had coffee together in town yesterday."

David tried not to show how shocked he was. They were in touch with each other? Carolina had never told him that. He'd always thought Carolina told him *everything*. He tried not to feel betrayed.

"Carolina is a grown woman, David," Carl-Erik said with a friendly smile, a smile that made David want to punch his aristocratic face. Of course he knew Carolina was an adult; he just hadn't quite understood that she had her own life. Maybe sometimes he thought her life revolved just around him, but he certainly knew she was an adult. It was just a shock to find out about her independence this way. Coffee in the city, no less.

"Carolina wants me in her life, and I'm extremely grateful for that."

David clenched his teeth so hard he heard them grind together. His patience was at its limit now.

"She's worried about your hostile takeover. She's worried about you."

The fury was like an explosion in his body. Carl-Erik had no right to discuss Carolina with him, no right at all. The rage sat in his chest like a seething black mass.

"Go," David said in a quiet voice. It was either that or scream. He had trouble thinking and choked out the word: "Go!" The anger came in waves now, as if it was breaking against a rocky shore, as if he might lose control at any moment. "Get out of here," he said. "Out. Now."

"David . . . ," Carl-Erik pleaded, holding up his hands beseechingly.

Something broke inside of David.

The tension, the rage, all the old feelings he'd been convinced he was done with were given new fuel, and he lost control. He stepped forward, grabbed Carl-Erik's clothes, an extremely firm grasp that made the elderly man blanch. With the count in one hand, David opened the door with his other and threw—literally *threw*—him out of the room. Then he slammed the door shut with so much force that the whole wall shook.

He had to lean against the door frame and bend over to get the blood to his head. He never lost his temper, hated people who berated and yelled to demonstrate their power, but he'd come close to murdering an old man.

He took another deep breath and felt something akin to reason returning. It was evening and the office was empty. He couldn't keep throwing people out haphazardly. The old man might have had a heart attack and died out there.

David ran both hands through his hair. He adjusted his clothes and put his hand on the doorknob. He made a face, furious with himself and this whole farce. He opened the door and looked out, but the corridor was empty.

Carl-Erik Tessin had left.

47

Saturday, July 26

Alexander had scarcely had a chance to leave Sweden behind before he was summoned back again. He'd stood in this same passport-control line at Arlanda airport less than two weeks earlier. He'd just started to get over his jet lag back home in New York, but now here he was again, tired and hungover. Ordered home by his father. He didn't usually obey when he could avoid it, but Alex was curious about what was going on. The family business was in danger? Was that even possible? The thought was strangely exciting. Almost liberating.

Alexander picked up his bags from the baggage-claim carousel and sauntered through customs out into the arrivals hall, heading for the line of taxis outside. The tabloids screamed their headlines. He hopped into a cab, but then realized he had no idea where he was going to stay. He couldn't bear to stay with his parents. Hmm. Maybe he ought to buy a place here after all? Say what you will, but Stockholm was beautiful in the summertime. "Take me to Hotel Diplomat," he finally told the driver.

He fingered his phone. He ought to call Natalia; this must be really hard for her. David Hammar, whom she'd seemed so fond of, was picking a fight with Investum. He glanced out the window. The question was, what the hell was going on? And whether he could be bothered to care about it.

48

David studied the sculpture towering in front of him. He wasn't particularly interested in art, and he didn't really understand sculpture as a medium at all. But Carolina was walking around it looking enraptured, so he kept his thoughts to himself and nodded as enthusiastically as he could each time she looked his way.

Carolina had always been interested in art, culture, and other creative expressions, and he knew that those interests were probably what had saved her from losing her mind, so every time they saw each other, he made sure to take her to a museum or an exhibit. It was fun for him, too, although baffling.

There were a lot of people at the exhibit, and he noticed Carolina happen to bump into a man. He stiffened, ready to leap to her rescue. But Carolina just apologized with a smile, without looking afraid, without blanching. David exhaled and relaxed a little.

For so many years, going out in public had downright terrified Caro. He wondered if he would ever get used to her not being as fragile as before.

She came over to him with a smile. The exhibit was outdoors, and the breeze ruffled her hair. She smiled, and there were laugh lines at the corners of her eyes. She lived by the sea and loved the outdoors, the sun and the wind. "You don't look as agonized as usual," she said, putting a hand on his arm. "Do I dare hope you're actually enjoying this exhibit?"

"There's nothing I love as much as staring at naked statues," he said. Then he added, "You look happy."

Carolina squeezed his arm. "I feel good," she said. "I know you worry, but it's true. Someday you're going to have to start believing me."

Caro was right, David realized, dismayed. She actually looked robust. For so many years, he'd worried about her, been so preoccupied with trying to do right by her that he hadn't taken the time to stop and see what was increasingly obvious: Caro was thirty-two and doing great. She was practically radiant.

"Now don't be mad at me," she said, "but I'm thinking about finding some cozy hotel to stay at for the rest of my time in Stockholm." She bit her lower lip and watched him carefully, as if to see what his reaction would be.

"But why?" he asked. Obviously she was free to do as she liked, but this came out of nowhere. "I thought you were happy at my place," he said, feeling a little guilty.

"Really?" Caro said with a smile. "And what are you basing that on? Given that you're never home, I mean." She was still smiling, as if to take the edge off her criticism, but she was right. He'd been neglecting her.

"Your apartment is great, but I'm way too old to stay with my brother. No, my mind's made up. Actually, I already called and booked a room," she said, looking satisfied.

"Okay," David said, still caught a little off guard by this turn of events. Carolina had never been particularly impulsive, nor independent either. She'd always relied on him, let him make the decisions. He supposed he'd just instinctively viewed her as fragile, but here she stood, radiating self-confidence and authoritativeness, *deciding* things without consulting him. Like any grown woman.

"But if you're going to stay at a hotel, you're going to need some form of bodyguard or security," he said, because Caro wasn't just any woman, and he had to consider what was most important: her safety. "I'll talk to our security firm about that."

"You don't think that's a little extreme?" she asked, her head cocked to the side, her long earrings dangling against her cheek.

"If anything were to happen to you, Caro . . ."

She squeezed his arm. "David, you can't protect me from life."

"You know what I mean," he said, and his guilty conscience for feeling relief at having his apartment to himself made his voice a little sharp. "I don't like this. I'm sorry you've been feeling neglected," he added.

But apart from feeling ashamed that he hadn't really made time for her, Carolina was right. They were adults with their own habits.

And after Natalia had spent the night at his place . . .

The fact was that David had a hard time having anyone else there.

Carolina squinted up at a narrow sculpture. "And since we're talking about this anyway, I've actually been thinking about buying myself a place here."

He stopped and looked at her. This was news to him. "In Sweden?" he asked.

"Yes," she nodded. "In Stockholm. I love Stockholm. I remember how we used to go into the city when we were little. Stockholm still feels like home."

David wasn't sure he liked that idea. The risk of her running into Peter or Gustaf was much too great. She might seem happy and healthy now, but what would happen if she ran into Peter, the man who'd injured her so badly?

"I thought you were happy in Denmark," he said. "You've always said you love living by the sea."

As a fifteen-year-old she'd lived in a residential treatment center, of course, but then the years had passed and she'd stayed, and the foreign country and the ocean had done her good. Now she lived in a house David had bought her, with a view of the sea and an enormous studio. It was in the middle of nowhere and windy, but she'd always loved it.

"I do. But I can have two homes, can't I?" She stopped in front of a sculpture of a bird with outstretched wings. "I like this one," she said, studying its slender lines for a long time. "I met my accountant last week. We looked over my assets together. I've got plenty of money, so I should be able to afford this." She gave him a broad smile.

He'd managed her finances for many years, bought stocks, invested, transferred over as much as he could, always worrying about her well-being. He'd grown up constantly on guard lest something should happen to him or her; all his plans had been about making their investments as safe as possible. And that had paid off. Caro was financially independent.

"I have to say, it's handy to have a brother who's a financial genius," she said gently. "Both my accountant and I were very impressed."

She walked on, her long skirt swishing around her feet.

A Carolina who met accountants, booked hotel rooms, and made financial decisions on her own. David was at a loss. When had this happened?

"I can contact a real estate agent I know," he said when he'd caught up to her. But he was fighting his distaste for the idea. How could he protect her if she was in Stockholm?

"You're a real mother hen," she said. She ran her hand over a pedestal, read the inscription, and then looked at David. She was smiling. "You know Mom would have been proud of you, right?"

I doubt that.

Caro had always thought highly of him, David knew that. But Helena hadn't. Mostly his mother had been hugely disappointed in him. She had thought David let the family down, over and over again, that he was selfish and irresponsible. And she had been right, of course. If he'd taken better care of his family, a lot of things would have been different.

"You're my sister," was all he said. "I want you to be happy."

And safe.

Carolina moved on to the next sculpture. He followed.

"I heard that you saw Dad," she said after a bit.

"Yes," he said uncomfortably. Thinking about the unexpected—unwanted—visit still left a bad taste in his mouth. "Carl-Erik come to the office, completely uninvited."

Carolina shook her head. "David, it's okay to reconcile with him, you know. He's still your father."

"I didn't know you two were in touch with each other." David's voice was chillier than he would have liked, but he couldn't help it.

Carolina gave him a mildly reproachful look. "He came to see me in Denmark a few times. I'm sorry I didn't tell you, but I knew you wouldn't be happy." She watched him with her big, blue-gray eyes, so like his own. And with a shock, David realized that both of them had inherited Carl-Erik's eyes. It had never occurred to him before.

"You know he's the one who paid for me to run away to Denmark, right? He paid for the treatment center. Mom let him do that."

"I didn't know that," David replied resolutely. But he had wondered how there had been money for Caro's treatment. His mother had never talked about where she'd gotten the money. Had he suspected, on some subconscious level, that their father had chipped in? Maybe. But did that mean he had to respect the count for that? Hardly.

"It's going to take me some time," he mumbled, well aware that that was a lie. He would *never* reconcile with the count, no matter how much coffee the man drank with Carolina. No matter how much money he provided.

"If Mom were alive, she would be so incredibly mad that we'd seen him," Carolina continued. "You always had to choose sides with her." She brushed her blond hair out of her face and tipped her head. "Did you know that he tried to contact us, but that Mom stopped him? He wrote to us every week, but Mom sent the letters back. He still has them. Mom could be very black or white."

David looked at his sister in astonishment. They almost never discussed the past and rarely their mother. He'd just assumed that they felt the same way about their parents.

"I never thought about Mom like that," he said, realizing that he'd never had a single negative thought about his mother. In his world she had never been anything other than good, which was strange, actually. No one was ever completely good.

"No, you and Mom had a totally different relationship," Carolina said. "With a ton of guilt and blame. I went to therapy, you know. You learn a lot about yourself. That first year was really tough." She let one of her colorful necklaces slide through her fingers and took on a vacant look for a moment. "But then things turned around. They were wonderful down there. They left me alone when I wanted it, talked when I needed it. And they taught me so much. The therapy saved me." She smiled, a little apologetically. "It must have been expensive. I didn't realize it at all, but, David, Dad said you took over all the bills after Mom died, that you took over all the responsibility. You must have really struggled to be able to afford everything you did for me, everything you gave me." Her eyes got misty.

David shook his head. Of course he'd prioritized her well-being. He loved her. But he knew that some of his behavior toward Carolina would always be driven by feelings of guilt. If he'd stayed home that night, if he hadn't provoked Peter De la Grip and the other boys. If he'd been a better person, a less selfish person, then nothing would have happened to Carolina.

"David?"

"It's fine," he said dismissively. They were so close to each other; they only had one another, and yet they knew so little about each other's innermost thoughts and feelings. Carolina was a grown woman. Of course he'd known that, but in some way he'd always regarded her as the frail, traumatized teenager who'd been hurriedly sent abroad. But the woman standing in front of him today was mature and self-confident, and laughed often. No matter how he looked, he didn't see any traces of the things he'd always associated with her.

"I'm just so glad you're doing better," he said genuinely. Maybe it was time to start seeing Carolina as an individual, not as a victim. Weird that he'd never had that thought before.

"And of course you can hang out with Carl-Erik if you want to," he added, almost meaning it. "And in a few days, all this other stuff will be over, and then there won't be an Investum anymore, and they'll have received their punishment."

"Punishment?" Carolina said with a sharp crease in her brow. "What are you talking about? For whom?"

He could hardly bring himself to say their names to her. "Peter and Gustaf De la Grip," he said as concisely as he could.

She gave him a serious look. Her earrings and necklace sparkled in the sun. She'd always loved colorful things. "Is *that* what all this is about?" she asked, and he'd never heard her sound like that, accusatory.

"Of course, what did you think?"

"I didn't think anything, David," she said, her voice sharp. "Since you didn't tell me anything. And when you talked about Investum and my shares, when it came up in the newspapers, I thought it was all about good business, some deal that made good sense here and now. Not some kind of plan for revenge. Is that what you're up to? Vengeance?"

He couldn't believe Caro was criticizing him. "I had to. What they did to you . . ."

"But that stuff happened a really long time ago," she said. "It *was* awful," she said, but her voice didn't tremble at all. "I've spent my whole life putting it behind me, working through it. I'm over it," she said. "People can do that. I'm over it, and I hardly ever think about it. You can't start mucking around with that; you can't let the past decide. David? Is that what you're up to?" Carolina furrowed her brow. "Why?"

"Why?" he burst out. "*Why*? You can't be serious."

"Of course I'm serious." She put her hand on his arm and looked him right in the eye, seriously and in a very, very grown-up way. "You've made so many sacrifices already, tell me this isn't all about revenge."

"Not entirely," he said. Carolina had never ever questioned him, and the whole situation felt goddamned uncomfortable.

Carolina crossed her arms in front of her. "What about Natalia De la Grip then?"

"What about her?" Caro was his sister, but there were lines not even she had the right to cross. His relationship with Natalia was none of her business. He gave her a warning look.

"Don't you look at me like that," she said.

"Like what?" he snarled.

"Like you're some kind of emperor and everyone else is beneath you. You *like* her."

He'd told Caro select bits, not everything of course, but Caro was smart and she was intuitive—she'd always had that skill. Of course, she'd pieced together far more than he'd chosen to tell her. But he couldn't grasp how this had happened. He'd invited his little sister out to see some art on a Sunday morning and now they were practically yelling at each other. People were starting to look at them oddly.

"It's clear that she's important to you," Carolina continued. She'd lowered her voice. "It's obvious from the way you look at her."

"I care about *you*," he said.

She waved her hand, as if that went without saying. "I've never doubted that, not ever. No one could wish for a better brother."

"Don't say I'm a good brother. If you hadn't been alone that night . . ."

"Did you actively do something that caused me to be raped? Well?"

"Of course I didn't," he said, shocked. "But . . ."

"There's no *but*. It wasn't your fault. If anything, it's thanks to you that I recovered as well as I did. That's what my therapist said: that you were always there for me unconditionally; that's the kind of thing that makes it possible to recover and move on. You can't change what happened back then, it's in the past."

"But I can change how it looks now, and protect you."

"Enough. I can take care of myself. You have to think about you. And I want you to be happy. You've sacrificed so much for me, but David, you're not happy. You need to move on too."

"I can hardly move on with Natalia De la Grip."

"No, not if you're going to destroy her whole family."

"But what they did to you . . . ," he repeated.

"That was a long time ago."

"Some things a person doesn't forget," he countered, and couldn't believe he even needed to tell her that. Although of course they'd never discussed this, he realized, not ever. He'd just assumed that Caro felt the same way he did, that she had been ruined, that it was a wound that could never heal.

"But that's exactly what I'm saying." A note of frustration had snuck into her voice, and she waved her hand dismissively. "It's *over* for me. I don't want to live in the past."

"You don't understand," David said. "They hate me. Us. And you don't realize what they're capable of."

"But I think they've already been punished in a way," she said. "And I've left it at that." It was clear that the subject was closed as far as she was concerned. She gave him a little smile. "And I've met a man."

What?

She moved on to the next pedestal and statue. David hurried after her, took her by the arm, and made her stop. "What do you mean you've met a man?" he asked.

"What do you think?" she said, giving him a sharp look, so belligerent it was like looking into his mother's face. Their mother had always had a fiery temperament. David just hadn't realized that Caro had inherited it.

"Is that so implausible?" she said. "Yes, it was awful that I was raped, it was disgusting." She pulled her hand back. Her voice didn't tremble at all when she quietly said, "But I want to live my life. And I want *you* to live *your* life, not live mine for me. Don't you understand how much pressure you're putting on me if you're out for revenge in my name?"

He and Carolina had *never* argued like this before. He felt shaken down to the core, as if everything he'd believed to be real had turned out to be collapsible theatrical props.

"I didn't know," he began and broke down. He didn't know where to begin. Was he living Carolina's life for her? Was that how she saw it? And all this stuff about letting go of the past, could that even be done? Just like that? He wasn't at all convinced. "I don't know what to say," he finally said. "What do you want me to do?"

"I can't make a decision for you," she said gently. "And I trust you. I trust that you'll do whatever's most sensible. I'd really like to go to the general meeting tomorrow," she added.

That was an extremely bad idea. Carolina might have a bunch of ideas about how she was doing better, but this general meeting was probably going to be unpleasant. And who knew what Peter or Gustaf might do if they saw her. Good Lord, they thought she was dead.

"You shouldn't come," he said. "You can send a proxy, someone to vote for you."

Carolina's eyes narrowed. "I can do my own voting, thank you very much."

"I know, but if you're there, then I'll worry the whole time," he said, aware that he was shamelessly manipulating her by trying to make her feel guilty.

She shook her head. "We'll see," she said, and for the first time ever David actually felt that he didn't have control over what she decided. It was a dizzying feeling. Not completely comfortable, but also not expressly uncomfortable.

"This man you're seeing, do you want to tell me anything about him?"

"Not yet. It's too new."

"But do I know him?" David asked.

"No. But I don't want you to start investigating his background or doing anything else super controlling."

"I would never do a thing like that," he lied.

Carolina smiled. She put her hand on his cheek. "You most certainly would," she said.

49

Michel was back at the gym again. His body was tired, but there was nowhere else for him to be if he didn't want to go insane. No matter where he looked, he saw Åsa. From the moment he woke up he saw her voluptuous curves and blond hair. All day long her mocking smile and pink lips hounded him.

He closed his eyes, sitting in the weights machine, then pushed until the sweat was pouring out of him. He forced himself to count his lifts, forced himself to ignore the protests from his muscles. And he didn't stop until he couldn't lift his arms anymore. Then he moved on to the next machine and started again.

He would take a long vacation when this was over, maybe go to one of those retreats where you're not allowed to talk, just work out and sleep. He had to get out of this mess of revenge and things that kept popping up from the past, away from Åsa.

He groaned and pulled on the back machine until his muscles trembled. The gym was barely half full since most normal people were outside hanging out, sunbathing, or swimming. They weren't at the gym, well into the second hour of their workout, trying to exercise away anything having to do with erections or sex or fantasies or platinum-blond women.

He could still picture her as he moved to the next machine. Saw her in that white suit, in that tight dress she wore in Båstad, or in a pair of simple jeans like she wore one time back in law school. Åsa was not a jeans person, but that time she had worn jeans and a white T-shirt. He'd glimpsed those extraordinary breasts, and her blond hair—longer back then—had hung in a simple ponytail.

She was a hundred percent woman and a hundred percent sex, and he would probably have to stay for another four machines because now he was hard as a rock. He punished himself and his aroused body by loading up the leg press more than he'd ever done, but when he got off it, heading toward the free weights on trembling legs, the only thing he was thinking about was the soft curve of her neck and the only thing he wanted to do was lick her entire body. He picked up two free weights and counted lifts intently as he stared into the mirror. His testosterone was coursing, his skin glistening, and he kept going until his arms refused.

Afterward he showered for a long time, then lathered himself up, standing with his back to the door. He was totally alone in the changing room, and it took him less than ten seconds to come.

He rinsed himself off grimly, watching the bubbles and sweat and semen run down the drain, and thought that he must have reached some sort of all-time low. Masturbating in a public shower—classy, real classy.

He pulled on his T-shirt and pants. His body was totally pumped, and he was still sweating, so he bought a bottle of water, pulled down his sunglasses, and walked out into the broiling sunshine.

His phone was in his bag, and it took a while before he realized it was ringing. He'd promised his mother he'd come out to the house for Sunday dinner, so he assumed it was her. Maybe he could head out there a little earlier, he thought as he dug around. He liked hanging out with his family. His sisters would be there, his father of course, and some of his uncles. They would drink lemonade and play with some of the kids who were always running around, and maybe he would be able to stop thinking about Åsa for a couple of hours. He managed to dig out his phone and stared at the caller ID.

So much for not thinking about Åsa.

"I thought you weren't going to answer." He heard her deep, throaty voice as he clicked to answer the call.

Michel closed his eyes, letting himself be pulled along by the impossible feelings he had for this woman. He allowed himself to lower his guard for a short, short time, since she couldn't see him, before he straightened up and said, sounding steady and self-confident: "Hi, Åsa."

He heard her breathing on the other end. Oh God, just the sound of her breath turned him on.

"I didn't know who to call," she whispered.

"What happened?"

"Can you come over here? Do you know where I live?" she asked, and her voice was a little strained. "Do you know the address, I mean?"

Did he know the address?

"Did something happen?" Was she hurt, had something happened to her? "Åsa?" he asked worriedly.

"Can you come?"

"I'll be there in ten minutes."

"I'll text you the code for the front door," she said. "Hurry."

"But Åsa," he began, but she'd already hung up the phone.

Michel stared at the silent phone. It buzzed in his hand as her front door code arrived in a text. Michel ran his thumb over the glossy display, wondering what kind of game she was playing. Because he really shouldn't let her control him. If he let her take charge, she would swallow him whole. But she'd sounded upset, for real.

He dialed a number as he started walking.

"Mom? It's me. Unfortunately I can't come. No, I'm busy. Yes, all evening. Say hi to Dad."

He hung up and then veered off, jogging toward upper Östermalm.

Less than ten minutes later, Michel typed in her door code. The door was large, more like the door of a palace, and the whole building exuded the same discreet opulence as the rest of the neighborhood. He ran up the stairs and rang her doorbell. He heard the quiet swish of a well-oiled lock sliding open, and then Åsa was before him in the doorway.

Michel swallowed.

She was wearing something thin and billowy. Every breath made her soft curves push against the almost transparent veils of fabric. Pink toenails on bare feet peeked out from beneath the hem. He stared. He'd forgotten her feet. Perfect little toes, and then that innocent, erotic color on her nails, like the inside of her lips. There and then Michel realized something: he would never make it out of this meeting intact. Honestly, he didn't even know if he cared anymore.

Åsa watched him in silence. She checked out his freshly worked-out arms and Michel flexed his biceps, reflexively and unspeakably embarassing.

She raised an eyebrow. "Come in," she said, stepping aside.

He stepped in, passed her scented body, and was surrounded by lavish but impersonal luxury. He dropped his bag on the stone floor.

"Come on," she said and turned around, walking away.

Michel followed her. How could she look so calm? How could her voice be so cool when he had to force himself not to jump her, pin her to a wall, kiss her breathless? Everything about her was sensual and soft. There wasn't an angular inch anywhere.

She turned around again—were they there already?—and said, "What?"

"Nothing," he said tersely.

Åsa tried to seem cool and unaffected on her way to the kitchen, but having Michel Chamoun here, in her home, made her weak. And in that tight shirt and with that gleaming chain around his neck, he looked so hard. Like a tough guy from some rough neighborhood she'd never even passed through. Even if she hadn't known him, Michel would have been the kind of man she would have turned around to watch on the street, the kind of man she fantasized about.

She couldn't stop looking at him over her shoulder.

"What?" he asked.

She shook her head. "Nothing."

Honestly she didn't know what had come over her when she'd decided to call him. It had been an impulse, born from an almost overwhelming tidal wave of emotions, and she already regretted it.

She pushed the door to the kitchen open. She had no plan, but she was hot and needed something to drink. She opened the stainless-steel refrigerator, took out a bottle of French mineral water and two glasses. "Would you like some?" she asked.

Michel nodded.

When he took the glass, she noticed his arm again. She was a big woman and had always liked big men, but even by her exacting standards, Michel was enormous. He took a drink, and she hungrily studied his strong throat, watched him swallow, following his dark skin down to the neckline of his T-shirt.

She wanted to lean over, lick the drop of sweat she saw at the base of his neck, follow it down over him with her tongue, take all of him into her mouth.

She was good at sex, and that wasn't bragging, it was a fact. She could picture herself taking him into her mouth, sucking him until he buried his hands in her hair, groaned, and completely lost it.

She took a quick drink, studied him through her eyelashes as he stood there, his hip leaning against her kitchen island. She leaned back against the sink, letting him get a good look at her. She made a move and obediently the slit in her thin dress—it was just a hair's breadth away from actually being a negligee—fell open, revealing her legs.

"Åsa? Why am I here?" Michel asked calmly, setting his empty glass down on the matte-finished granite countertop. It used to be walnut, but she liked the granite better. An interior designer came once a year to change little things around and then sent her an astronomical invoice. "It sounded serious. What happened?"

She sighed. She should have suspected that he wouldn't let her escape.

"Nothing happened. But I was at the cemetery today," she began, sipping the water and steeling herself against the wave of pain that usually arrived when she thought about this. But it never came.

"I haven't been there in a long time, haven't been to see them for several years," she said, pausing and waiting again. Still nothing.

They were all in the same grave, all three of them.

Her mother, father, and little brother. Different birth dates, but all with the same death date. *Eternally remembered*, it said on the gravestone. She didn't remember who'd ordered it, didn't remember the funeral, didn't remember anything. Just that one day she'd had a family and the next day she was alone. So alone.

She looked at Michel standing there, steady as a mountain range.

"How was it?" he asked somberly.

"I guess it was okay," she said, looking down.

It *had* been okay, strangely enough. But now she felt very weak, more fragile than tissue paper or newly formed ice crystals.

Michel crossed his arms. "What happened to your family was so awful," he said softly. "No one should have to go through what you went through."

"Some people have it worse," she said automatically.

"That's always true," he agreed. "But you're entitled to your feelings. And being the only one left, that's certainly everyone's nightmare."

"I had Natalia's family," she said. But Michel was right, she had wound up in a never-ending phase, in which waking up in the morning and being forced to realize that she was still all on her own was the worst thing.

"I didn't understand how I could go on living when I was so sad," she said. Something ran down her cheek, and when she wiped her hand over it, she realized to her surprise that it was a tear. She hadn't even noticed she was crying. She never cried. "Sorry," she said.

He came over to her, took her glass, set it down. He carefully wiped away a tear. "It's okay," he said softly.

She sobbed. "No, I'm sorry about the other thing," she said.

He wiped away another tear, and she wanted to lean on his shoulder, give herself over to self-pity and grief. "At law school, when I stopped being your friend. I'm sorry about that."

"It doesn't matter," he mumbled. "That was a long time ago."

"I was so embarrassed when you refused me. I couldn't handle being your friend after that, and I pulled away."

"Because you were embarrassed?"

She shook her head, thinking it was now or never. "Because I was in love with you," she said, not actually daring to look at him. "You can't be friends with someone you're in love with."

"No, that's very hard," he agreed. "You always want more."

"No one has turned me down as many times as you have."

"I'm sorry," he said.

"You know how people usually say it's better to have loved and lost than not to have loved at all?"

"Yes."

"That's bullshit. *Nothing* is worse than losing the people you love. When my family died, I decided never to be close to anyone again." She bit her lip. "It's such a terrible cliché."

But it had worked.

She'd slid through life, not happy, but then again, who was? Happiness wasn't a human right.

He stroked her shoulder with his hand. It was a comforting caress that almost burned a hole in her. She had a hard time breathing. It hurt to feel so strongly about him. She slipped away and took a few steps. She wanted to leave him behind, erase him from her life, replace him with some other man she *didn't* feel so strongly about.

If they slept with each other, then she'd be able to move on. She leaned her hip against the counter and trained her eyes on him. She'd done this before, been obsessed with having one specific man. It always passed. She was going to put an end to this. She'd waxed herself yesterday, not too much because she loved her blond, curly locks, but she was smooth and fresh, and she just wanted this so much. She wiped away the last of the tears and took a step toward him. "Michel," she said in a low voice, making herself sound tempting and promising.

"No, don't do this," he said. "Not when you're sad."

"I've regretted it for all these years," she said, because this time she wasn't going to accept a rejection. "I've wanted you. Wondered what it would be like. Haven't you?"

"Of course I have," he said, sounding choked.

She put a hand on his chest. She could do this in her sleep, seduce a man. His skin was scorching hot through the fabric, as if he had a fever.

Michel put his hand over hers and a tingle surged through her. This was the best part. Foreplay. She swallowed against the hollow feeling that spread through her chest, pushed it away, and let her hand slide down his chest, rubbing his nipple lightly. She was an expert on the male nipple. He moaned.

Michel raised his hand and tugged on a bouncy strand of her hair. "I really want to," he murmured, letting his finger trace along her thin shoulder strap. "But I don't just want sex. I want *you*."

To her horror, tears welled up in Åsa's eyes again.

Was it really so much to ask?

A quick hook-up, then he could leave her and go. That's all she wanted, she convinced herself. Aside from the fact that if Michel disappeared from her life again, he would take such a big piece of her with him that she wasn't sure there would be anything left.

She stroked his biceps, felt a primitive ache inside. He was so damn sexy.

"I have a clean bill of health," she said. "I've been tested. I'm on the pill. I really want to have sex with you." She smiled. "But I am not a woman who ever wants to have children. I don't want to be tied down."

Michel's parents were definitely expecting grandchildren from their only son, so she was giving him a chance now to agree that this was just about sex, that neither of them was planning something long-term, that she didn't expect him to stay. She didn't know a single man who wouldn't jump at what she'd just offered.

"I'm also clean," he said. "And I want you. Just you. I don't give a damn if you want kids or not. I don't even understand why we're talking about that."

He put a hand on her waist and pulled her to him. Her breasts pushed against his chest through the fabric. And then he finally kissed her, infinitely softly.

Her hands slid up over his arms as she responded to the kiss, and Michel pushed her back against the counter. She made a sound, clung tightly to him, planning to never stop kissing. He pulled apart the thin, silky layers of fabric, and then she had his palms against her bare skin. He grazed her hard nipples, and the arousal ripped through her.

"But Åsa," he said, holding her gently around the shoulders and looking at her seriously. "If we make love, then you're mine. Understand? If this isn't important to you, you need to say so now."

She nodded, slightly overwhelmed. "Okay," she said, but she still wanted to add that this was *just for right now*, that she never made long-term plans and that this would end just like everything else. That she didn't *make love* to men, she had sex with them.

"Say it, Åsa," he urged.

"What?"

"Say that this isn't just sex." His eyes were like black fire. "I've loved you since the first time we saw each other," he continued, and she couldn't decide if Michel thought this eternal love was a good thing or not. But his words gave Åsa something she hadn't ever felt before as an adult: hope.

"But how can you love me?" she said, her voice shaking.

This had to be the most pathetic seduction she'd ever orchestrated.

"I just do," he said.

"This isn't just sex," she whispered.

He exhaled, wrapped his hands around her hair, and kissed her furiously. Åsa clung to his biceps, not just because her legs turned to jelly but also because she wanted to cling to what Michel was for just as long as she could. A warm hand caressed its way in between her thighs; he pulled her cobweb-thin panties aside, and she leaned forward and bit him on the shoulder. She moaned against his skin as his fingers found their way in. Another man would have ripped off those expensive panties, but Michel was careful despite his intensity, and Åsa thought that a man like this was actually what every woman deserved. But he was hers, just hers.

"Where's your bedroom?" he asked hoarsely.

"Is there something wrong with the kitchen?" she murmured.

"No," he said, kissing her again. Oh, he was such a superb kisser. Eager, hungry, just rough enough, as if kissing her made him crazy with desire. It was incredibly flattering. She rode the waves of arousal and then let them take her over. With her head tilted back, she let Michel hold her neck and kiss her throat, nibbling a fiery trail. His hands were everywhere, and she pushed herself into them, into his musky muscles and tender, golden skin.

"Take off your shirt," she said, laughing at how quickly he ripped it off, before he started kissing a burning path down her body, over the dip at the base of her neck and her breastbone, over her thin skin and rosy nipples before continuing down over her soft belly. Åsa loved her body, how it responded and how it felt pleasure. She refused to see her ampleness and her softness as anything other than perfection. And Michel seemed more than satisfied to finally—after fifteen years of foreplay—get to go down on his knees in front of her.

She lazily separated her legs a tiny bit, but he moved them farther apart, determinedly and with force, and burrowed his strong fingers into the softest skin on the inside of her thigh. Åsa emitted a muffled groan. She loved the sound of sex almost as much as she loved the actual act of sex, at any rate when it was good, and this, this was epically good. She made another sound as she saw Michel's head down between her thighs. She closed her eyes. His tongue was zealous and hot, and she squirmed so much under his licks that he finally put his hands around her bottom to get her to stand still, squeezing her butt cheeks and pulling her toward him so that she almost lost her balance.

This was going to get wild—she already felt that.

She'd had sex with a lot of men; she loved sex, and she loved the game. But something told her that Michel was nowhere near as experienced as she was. There was something about the cautious arousal that he approached her with that made her feel worshipped, truly, and she loved it. What did she know, maybe he'd been saving himself for her? She smiled at the thought, opened her eyes again, held on with one hand around his shoulder and the other on the edge of the counter. She looked down, heard the sounds, and felt—God, how she felt—his hardworking tongue and then she came, right in his face.

She gasped and supported herself heavily against the edge of the counter.

Michel stood up and just attacked her with his mouth and his lips and his tongue. He pulled down her slinky dress, let it fall in a heap on the stone floor, and then buried his face in her breasts. He kissed and caressed them, over and over again. *Oh God*, this was so good.

"You are unbelievably beautiful," he said huskily, and if Åsa had been able to speak she would have said that *he* was beautiful, more beautiful than any man she'd ever met.

Each motion intense, Michel turned her around so that she was standing with her face toward the tiled wall and faucets. She barely had time to think how lucky she was that her sink was so attractive—expensive Italian faucets, stainless surfaces, decorative herb plants, and a bowl of limes (she honestly had no idea where they'd come from)—before Michel pulled the thin fabric of her panties down her legs, undid his jeans, and entered her. She felt dizzy because he was definitely not a small man; he was all cock and muscles and hard hands, and when he took her like that she actually lost her breath for a moment. Not that she had anything against that, quite the contrary. She closed her eyes with a muffled moan and let herself be taken against the counter in hard thrusts. He had the stamina of a teenager, she thought as Michel pulled out after a while, still hard. With a hand on the arch of her back, he tore off his jeans and underwear, then took her into his arms and maneuvered her over to the kitchen island, showering her with kisses along the way. Clearly they were going to be inaugurating the whole kitchen today. The island was also topped with granite, cold and black. He took hold of her waist and lifted her up without even batting an eye, as if she didn't weigh a thing, and then set her down on the granite, which was ice-cold for a second before her bottom warmed it up.

"Spread your legs," he said huskily.

She spread her thighs and let him look. The island turned out to be the perfect height, and he stared at her before his enormous cock buried itself in her again. She wrapped her legs around him, and Michel came—with her legs wrapped around his back, his hands on her ass—with a wild, pumping groan. Åsa continued to cling to him and just followed suit. It seemed he could hold her up forever, she noted as he panted into her hair in the aftershocks of his climax.

They kissed again while Michel slowly deflated within her. Sincere, almost insatiable kisses, which neither of them could get enough of. Stupidly, she had tears in her eyes again.

He kissed her one last time, significantly more gently now that he seemed to have recovered a little, before setting her down on the island again. He fetched a new glass of water and handed it to her. She drank and then handed it back. He drank without taking his eyes off her, and she thought there was something tremendously intimate about sharing this glass of water. She admired his body as he set the glass down, studying his muscles and tendons and powerful lines openly and with ownership. Her eyes lingered on his cock. She raised her eyebrows and said, "Already?" because it wasn't that deflated anymore.

"I've been dreaming about having sex with you for half my life," he said, and his eyes were more than intense, they were *passionate*. He slid in again. "Maybe someday I'll have had enough, but not yet, far from it."

Finally they more or less collapsed, entangled with each other, on the floor. Åsa with her head on his chest, he with his arms around her, hard, as if he was planning on never letting her go. They lay like that, took a break, panting and sweaty.

"Do you want any more water?" Michel asked.

Åsa shook her head. She draped one leg over his hips and slid over him as he lay on her freshly waxed marble floor.

"Look at me," she commanded as she put her hands on his chest, straddling him.

Michel's eyes obediently locked onto hers; they were foggy with arousal.

She leaned forward and kissed him. He eagerly kissed her back.

"Are you up for any more?" she asked.

"Are you kidding?" he asked huskily. His eyes were burning hot as he grasped her hips.

So Åsa rode him. Slowly, to begin with, but faster and faster as they found a common pace. She rode him like he was an animal, a slave, a cherished lover.

"Touch yourself," he ordered and she did, until they both came, loud and sweaty and at the same time.

Åsa collapsed onto his chest. Her muscles would be sore. She couldn't remember the last time she'd had such acrobatic sex.

He placed a hand on her hair, still breathing hard, and it occurred to her—a bit too late—that it probably wasn't all that ethical for Investum's chief attorney to be having sex on her kitchen floor with one of the men who was in the middle of a hostile takeover of the board of her boss's company.

Some people would probably call that a moral gray area.

She listened to Michel's pounding heart and knew that right now he cared as much about Investum as she did—which was to say not at all.

What had happened between them had nothing to do with Investum. Tomorrow Michel would continue doing what he could to take over her boss's company. And she would fight him, of course. It was what it was, and it meant less than nothing.

Michel moved beneath her, mumbled something. He was starting to go limp again, but she didn't want to get up yet. She tightened her internal muscles and smiled at his moan.

He'd said he loved her a little while ago. Maybe that was true—probably it was; Michel was a romantic, after all. But there was a lot of other stuff that felt up in the air, that was for sure. Her and him. The future, all of fucking life.

Åsa wriggled a smidge and made a slight face from pain when she lifted a tender knee.

There were a lot of things in this world that were damned uncertain. One thing was certain, though, she thought as she studied her bruised knee, and it was that if she and Michel continued on in this way, she was going to have to talk to her interior decorator as soon as possible.

Because Swedish marble might be nice to look at.

But it was hard as hell to have sex on.

50

Monday, July 28

When the ill-fated Monday morning finally dawned, gray and chilly, Natalia was still lying in bed with sleep in her eyes, her heart ticking away as she tried to go back to sleep. After listening to the blackbirds and something that sounded like geese for a few hours, she gave up and went out to the kitchen. She made green tea, padded out to the balcony, curled up under a blanket, and just let time go by.

When her phone dinged, she jumped, unsure how long she'd actually been sitting out there staring into space. She fetched her phone. A text from Alexander.

In Stockholm. Staying at the Diplomat. Busy?

She texted him back quickly.

I'm home. Come over?

Fifteen minutes later, her doorbell rang.

"Hello there," her little brother said, strolling in and kissing her on the cheek. "I thought we could go together." He handed her a brown paper bag. "I brought you breakfast."

She took the bag, opened it, smiled, taking out the sandwiches. Sourdough bread with brie and vegetables. "Thanks," she said. She'd been awake for several hours and realized she was starving. They saw each other so rarely, and yet Alex had remembered what she liked. He'd always had a great head for details.

"No problem; you are my favorite sister, after all," he said, walking out to the kitchen. It was an old joke, but suddenly it stung. She was only his half sister. Did that change anything? And *when* would she dare mention it?

Natalia made more tea, which Alexander declined. He moved around the kitchen restlessly, and when they sat down at the table he couldn't stay still, but fiddled with everything, stretched out his legs, and drummed his fingers on the table.

"How are things?" she asked.

"Good." He got up, running his hand through his hair. "But I'm not sleeping that well. I hate jet lag."

Natalia ate her sandwich and tried not to let his constant moving about bother her. When they were little he'd always been in motion; apparently he hadn't grown out of it yet.

Her phone, which was on the counter, started ringing.

"It's Peter," Alexander said, looking at the caller ID. He made a face and handed her the phone. "He's called me like five times today."

"What does he want?"

Alexander shrugged. "No idea. I didn't answer." That didn't surprise her. Her brothers' relationship was touch-and-go and filled with conflict.

Natalia answered. "Hi, Peter."

Alexander rolled his eyes, sat down at the table, and stole a slice of cucumber from her sandwich.

"What are you doing?" Peter asked her curtly.

"Eating breakfast," she replied, looking at Alexander. He made a gesture like he was slitting his throat. "I'm home. Alex is here," she added, disregarding his gestures. "We're going to the meeting together."

"Then I'll come over too," said Peter, and he hung up before Natalia had a chance to reply.

"What did he say?" Alexander leaned back in the kitchen chair. He was wearing a suit, something he rarely did, but of course it looked great on him. Long, black eyelashes and dark eyebrows were a dramatic contrast to his blond hair. He looked like some divine creature who'd just been expelled from paradise for morality-related reasons.

Alexander had once graced the cover of *Vanity Fair*, photographed shirtless with two naked female models at his feet. Art, they'd called it. Sexist, Natalia had thought. Rumor had it that Alexander was actually supposed to have been photographed with two other jet-set guys but that they hadn't been able to get a picture where Alexander's beauty didn't completely overshadow the other two men. The solution had been to let him pose with women instead, and the cover had been legendary.

"Peter's coming over," she said and pushed the rest of the sandwiches toward Alexander, eyebrows raised. She was having a hard time getting used to these fluctuations. First she was starving, then stuffed. Nothing in her life had ever been this changeable before; everything had been predictable. Now there was a big storm everywhere. Especially in her body. And all because of a fetus that was the size of a thumb.

She was starting her seventh week today—it was totally dizzying. Every morning she woke up and thought she must have imagined it. But she was still pregnant.

She was on the verge of putting her hand on her abdomen, but stopped herself and set it on her teacup instead. Alexander would have noticed that right away. He was lethal if you underestimated him. She realized that she was going to have to tell her brothers at some point—that she was expecting a child, that she wasn't their sister, that their father had disowned her, that she was unemployed.

"Are you feeling alright?" Alexander asked, studying her. "You look pale."

"I have something that I . . . ," she began, but she was interrupted by the doorbell ringing again.

"I'll get it," Alexander said, getting up and walking out to open the door.

Natalia listened to the voices in the hallway and then to the footsteps approaching. The voices got louder, and even before Alexander and Peter entered the kitchen, they were arguing about something.

Natalia studied her brothers, so similar and yet so different. Peter's face was red with rage, whereas Alexander was looking very aristocratic, with that mixture of derision and disdain that he somehow reserved solely for his big brother.

It was always the same, Natalia thought gloomily, as if they had some constant, ongoing argument. She tried to remember if it had ever been different or if they had always felt this antipathy toward each other. Peter was seven years older than Alexander, she was the middle child—the illegitimate one, she reminded herself—but she had vague memories of her brothers when they actually *weren't* arguing, when a little Alexander had toddled after a laughing Peter, but maybe she was deceiving herself. These days she wasn't really sure about anything.

These days, Alex took every opportunity to openly mock Peter's choices in life and the way he groveled before their father. For his part, Peter picked on everything Alexander did and *didn't* do. At the heart of it, Natalia suspected, Peter had always felt inadequate; he'd never had Alexander's natural charm. But then *no one* had Alexander's natural charm. Being jealous of him was like being jealous of a sunset or a painting.

Peter greeted her with a brief nod, said no thanks to a cup of tea, and leaned against the counter with his arms crossed.

Alexander sat back down in the kitchen chair, with his lips curled into a stiff smile.

Natalia drank her tea, which was now cold. Actually it was sad: three siblings with so little in common.

She snuck a look at Peter, trying to imagine him raping Carolina, raping *anyone*. Was he that brutal? If he had, how could he live with himself? And what did it say about her that she wasn't confronting him?

Alexander drummed his fingers on the table, and it struck her that Alex might know about the rape. He'd gone to the same school, after all. He'd told her about the hazing David had gone through. He must have known *something*.

It was as if everything that was stable in her life had started to disintegrate. No matter what happened, it would never be like before. This insight wasn't new, but it was painful.

Her mother still hadn't answered a single one of her phone calls.

It was slowly starting to sink in how deep this went. Things that had happened, things that had been done or not done, came to the surface and changed life forever. She was going to have to deal with it, whatever *it* was.

Peter snorted at something Alex said. He shouldn't have come if he was just going to argue. But that was Peter in a nutshell. He couldn't tolerate his siblings doing anything without him. He had to be there, keeping an eye on things.

The doorbell rang again.

"I'll get it," Natalia said, leaving the kitchen with some relief to go open the door. She rarely had so much traffic at home, and she wondered who it could be.

Natalia opened the door.

"Hi," Gina said. The housecleaner looked surprised, standing with her keys out. "I didn't know you were home," she added apologetically.

"Sorry, I'd totally forgotten that you usually come at this time," Natalia said. She'd forgotten that it was a normal weekday. Of course, Gina had no idea she was unemployed now and spending a lot of time at home. She'd never realized how complicated it was to have so many secrets.

"Come in. We're nearly on our way out," she said, stepping aside.

Ever since Natalia's breakdown, the atmosphere between her and Gina had been uncomfortable. As if the balance between them had shifted in some invisible way. Natalia led the way to the kitchen with Gina following, like a silent shadow.

Alexander stood up as they entered and greeted Gina with his normal, easygoing charm. Peter totally ignored her, although they must have met several times. He gave her a blank look and furrowed his brow, as if it were beneath him to greet her.

"I'll start in the living room," Gina said, getting her supplies out of the broom closet and lowering her head as she left the room.

"Thanks," Natalia said uncomfortably. She wanted to say something more, apologize for Peter's rudeness, say that it was wrong to divide people by social class, but the moment was lost, and words would hardly have improved the situation.

"You could at least say hello," Natalia hissed.

"What?" Peter asked, looking genuinely surprised. "To her? But she's just here to clean, right? Why should I say hello to her? I didn't even know she spoke Swedish."

"Shh," Natalia said, embarrassed.

"You're such a dick," Alexander said.

Peter shrugged. "I don't give a damn what you think," he said to Alexander. "You don't do anything sensible, you drink and take drugs and sleep around. I hardly need a sermon on morality from you." He raised an eyebrow. "Are you even sober?"

Alexander's eyes flashed, but then he went through that transformation that always scared the life out of Natalia. He adopted a cool, bored expression and sort of disappeared, as if behind a mask. As if there were nothing in the whole world worth caring about. No one could tune out emotionally like Alexander.

"Oh yeah, I'm sober," he said. "At the moment anyway. Try not to fall apart out of moral indignation."

Natalia looked at her brothers. They were actually more alike than either would want to admit. Both were tall and strong, and they were both blond and blue-eyed. Unlike her. How could she have missed that when it was so obvious? She was so unlike them, not just because she was female but also genetically. She let her eyes linger on Peter. Should she tell him that she knew about the rape? She should talk to him, but not when Alexander was listening.

She rubbed her forehead.

Soon she was going to have to sit down and decide what order to do all of this in.

The list of Things I Need to Talk to People About was starting to get quite long. Maybe she should make an Excel spreadsheet or a flowchart.

They heard the sound of a vacuum cleaner turning on in the hallway. Peter looked at the time and got up from the counter with a quick motion. He straightened his clothes and said, "I have to go. I'll see you there."

"Where are you going?" Natalia asked, astonished. Now that they were all here, she had assumed that they would go to the meeting together.

Peter looked over his shoulder. "There's something I need to take care of first."

"Do you know where he's going?" Natalia asked after Peter had left.

"No idea," Alexander replied, unconcerned.

"I was hoping we could talk a little bit, all three of us, come together, you know, show a united front."

"United front?" Alex asked sarcastically. "Really? I know you want to fight for the family business. I know that you've been slaving away like an animal, and I admire you, because you *are* admirable. But, Nat dear, not even you can save this."

"I can try," she said, irritated by his lack of desire to fight. "I talked to Uncle Eugene, by the way. He's coming too." She'd talked to so many people in the last two weeks that her jaws hurt.

"What did he say?"

"Not much. I think Hammar Capital got to him first."

"Natalia, how . . . ," Alexander began in a worried tone. He paused and then started over. "This thing between you and David Hammar, how are you doing?"

"I can't talk about it," she said in a warning tone. "Not now." He really was frighteningly sharp, she thought, freaked out.

Alexander stretched his shoulders as if he'd already stopped caring and quickly said, "Fine. Get yourself together then, and let's get going to our lynching."

"Do you think it's going to be that bad?"

Alexander watched her with his brilliant blue eyes.

"No," he said. "I think it's going to be much worse."

51

Peter walked away from Natalia's building, anxious to get away from there. Seeing his siblings had annoyed him. He didn't even know why he'd gone. Seeing Alex and Natalia and their uncomplicated relationship, being excluded, it all just made him feel irritated. In a way it had always been like that: Natalia and Alex, in perfect partnership, gifted, clever, confident.

Inconceivable that he still cared, even though they were all grown up and living their separate lives. Even though on paper he'd succeeded far better than either of them.

The walk took him just fifteen minutes. His heart was pounding uncontrollably. How many times in recent days had he thought that if he had a heart attack, then it would all be over? He didn't want to die, not really. But sometimes it would be such a relief to escape. All of these demands sat on him like a weight, as if he had to constantly fight not to be pushed into the ground.

He glanced up at the façade of the hotel, glad that they'd decided to continue the surveillance on Carolina Hammar. Now he knew she was staying here, at the Grand Hôtel. She'd checked in over the weekend.

And Peter knew what he had to do.

The only logical thing now that he knew she was alive.

He slowed his pace. He'd been so sure, but suddenly he hesitated.

There was still time for a change of heart. If he did this, it would have totally unforeseeable consequences. It could never be undone.

No one knew he was here.

If he blew it off, no one would find out.

He wished he were better at making important decisions.

He had made so many decisions that had irreparably, almost fatefully, pushed him in just this direction. All these choices and tipping points. The alienation in elementary school. The hard-core hazing at Skogbacka. David Hammar, who refused to submit and whom Peter had taken his frustrations out on. Carolina.

Where had it all gone wrong? What would have happened if he'd never met Carolina?

He knew exactly how it had ended.

But where had it started? *She provoked us. She actually wanted it.* How many times had he told himself those words? An impulsive act, violent peer pressure, a series of circumstances, and suddenly you were a rapist. Although he *wasn't*. No charges had been filed. And Caro had vanished, and everything had been erased, as if it hadn't happened.

Now she was back.

The one person who was witness to what he'd dedicated his entire life to suppressing.

How had it happened? He didn't know.

As if in a fog, he walked through the door being propped open by a smiling doorman.

His father had always said that the choices he made defined him as a person, as a man.

Peter looked at the slip of paper with Carolina's room number. Would this choice define him now? Would he finally be free?

52

David and Malin arrived at the conference center early on Monday. They stood on a glassed-in balcony overlooking the enormous lobby. Lake Mälaren and the Stockholm inlet glittered outside the floor-to-ceiling windows. Below them security personnel from two different companies, wait staff, and conference hosts were all scurrying around.

It was a big facility, the biggest in Stockholm apart from the sports venues. David had known there would be a lot of interest in this shareholders' meeting, but this . . . the RSVPs had poured in.

"What if there's still not enough room?" Malin said, echoing his own thoughts. "People will go nuts if they can't get in."

Tom Lexington, whose company was in charge of Hammar Capital's security, came over to them. He gave David one of his firm handshakes and then did the same to Malin, who managed not to make a face at his tight grip.

"How's it going?" David asked.

"I think they're getting backed up again out there. Is it usually like this?"

"No," David said with a shake of his head. "Most shareholders' meetings are quiet, sleepy affairs."

"This doesn't look like it's going to be one of those," Tom noted.

"No, this one is going to be more like a gladiator match," David agreed. "Can they set up any more seating?"

Malin nodded, her cell phone plastered to her cheek. "I just talked to Investum's communications director"—she made a face to show what she thought of *him*—"and he says they can accommodate seven hundred people in there."

David gave Tom a questioning look, and Tom nodded and said, "That ought to be enough."

Malin excused herself and walked off.

David caught Tom's eye and asked, "Is everything quiet at the hotel?"

He'd succeeded in convincing Carolina not to come to the shareholders' meeting after all. She'd been pale and resolute, but had agreed to send her lawyer as proxy. Maybe she'd realized it would be too much for her, but she'd seemed distracted, and he was worried.

"I have a man over there," Tom said. "Just as a precautionary measure," he added. "We don't foresee any threat against her." He smiled joylessly. "Unlike you. There've got to be at least a hundred people here today who'd really like to see you have a stroke or a heart attack on stage. This is like a reunion for everyone who's ever wanted to see David Hammar's head on a stake."

David laughed. "This is the finance world. Most of them are civilized."

"Yeah, right," Tom said sarcastically, scanning the lobby, where the first of the attendees were starting to be let in. They were meticulously checked off. Then they funneled in and were served appetizers. So far the chaos was quite organized.

Michel, wearing unusually subdued colors, came up to them and said, "This place is besieged outside. The police are setting up crowd-control fences. It's starting to get a little crazy."

"The media is the worst," Tom said, his eyes narrowing. He had started growing a beard since they'd last seen each other, and he looked downright intimidating.

"Try not to enrage the fourth estate too much," David said, knowing that in Tom's world the mass media came just a hair above white supremacists and rabies-infected rats. Tom muttered something inaudible. He was wearing an earpiece and now nodding at something only he could hear. "I have to do a circuit," he said. Then he gave David a look and said, "You don't go anywhere without my knowing, got it?"

Michel watched Tom go. "Am I being silly if I say that guy scares me?"

"Nah, Tom is scary when he's in this mood, maybe in all moods. But he knows what he's doing."

The volume of the din below the balcony was constantly rising. The Investum personnel bore the overall responsibility for the event since they were the hosts, but David had demanded to have his own personnel there. Malin and her staff were focusing on everything that had to do with Hammar Capital—press and information—and Tom and his people were responsible for their security.

Malin came rushing back. "Do you think you could give a few quick interviews?" she asked with a stressed glanced at her watch.

"Just tell me where you want me," David said.

"Great," Malin said. "I'll be back in five minutes."

Meanwhile, Michel's eyes were locked on a point outside the window where Åsa Bjelke had just stepped out of a taxi. It was overcast; the weather had changed overnight, and in the gray daylight, Åsa practically glowed, dressed all in white. Her platinum-blond hair bounced around her shoulders as she balanced confidently on sky-high white shoes.

"She looks like a movie star," David commented.

"She looks like trouble," Michel muttered.

Yeah, that too.

"Here they are," Michel said.

A black Mercedes had stopped. A chauffeur got out and opened the rear passenger door, and Gustaf De la Grip stepped out. Gustaf straightened his conservative jacket and even more conservative tie as he waited for his wife to get out.

No one else got out of the car. Was Natalia coming, or would she send a proxy? And did it really matter?

A couple of journalists spotted the familiar car and came running. Even from this distance they could tell that Gustaf was making a show of ignoring them, walking into the conference center with Ebba at his side.

Malin came to get David for the interviews. She had set up an enormous Hammar Capital logo and showed him where to stand in front of it. David gave her an amused look.

Malin smiled and whispered, "Is it too much?"

"Maybe a little," he said. But he obediently stood in front of the black logo, took the microphone, and started answering the questions that rattled at him like hail, interspersed with flashbulbs going off. From the corner of his eye, he spotted Tom, who had joined them and was standing so that he had an overview of the room and was able to glare at the journalists.

Someone yelled, "There's a rumor that this has to do with some kind of private vendetta between you and the De la Grip family. Would you confirm that?"

David smiled and ambiguously responded, "Of course not."

"What do you want with Investum?"

"The company isn't reaching its full potential."

"Why do you want all the De la Grips off the board of directors?"

"Investum needs a board that can meet the challenge of doing business in a volatile, global marketplace," he responded, managing to imply that the current board consisted entirely of outdated old farts without actually saying as much.

"Hammar Capital has been investigated by the Swedish Financial Supervisory Authority."

He nodded. They had been really irritating. "But they haven't actually found us guilty of any wrongdoing," he said. Although they'd tried really hard.

He went on answering questions while Tom Lexington kept a watchful eye from the side. The noise level in the space grew louder by the minute. And then a ripple began at the edge of the bank of journalists. It spread like a wave through the entire crowd. David saw Gustaf De la Grip approaching him, followed closely by a couple of assistants and what looked like actual bodyguards.

Tom had also spotted them, and he took a step forward, giving David a questioning look, a look that said, "Give me a clear sign, and I'll make mincemeat out of these wimps."

David shook his head. He wanted to see what was going to happen. Normally Gustaf carefully avoided public confrontations, particularly in front of the press. His leadership style was usually more passive-aggressive, based on ignoring and belittling people. He spewed abuse in private boardrooms and behind closed doors but displayed a polished exterior in public. The question now: was he under enough pressure to deviate from these strategies?

Gustaf's bodyguards kept pushing people aside, as if the sea of journalists wasn't letting him through fast enough.

David's face adopted a neutral expression as he felt his pulse increase. He stood completely still, one hand nonchalantly in his trouser pocket as silence settled over the press corps. No one wanted to miss any of what was to come. It was the working-class boy versus the king of Swedish industry and commerce.

New money versus old.

And then Gustaf was there. He looked out at the journalists before glaring at David as if he were something disgusting stuck on the sole of his shoe. And after all these years, after all his success, David still remembered that look. He remembered how Gustaf had come to the boarding school after the rape. How he had taken charge and called the shots, as if Skogbacka and its staff were just an extension of his turf. How he'd denigrated David and his mother to anyone who would listen, told them exactly what sort of lowlife family the Hammars were. And even today David remembered how powerless he'd been, forced to remain silent. The shame he'd felt at having given up in the face of that superior power. They had bullied and beaten him, attacked Carolina, whipped him bloody, gradually broken his mother, and believed that right was on their side the whole time. A certainty that Gustaf and his ilk had taken as their birthright for centuries.

And at this moment in front of the crowd of reporters and next to an outraged Gustaf De la Grip, David knew it had been worth it.

All his sacrifices had paid off.

He would do this without showing any mercy.

Because they had all—Natalia, Michel, and Carolina—been wrong.

Revenge could be good.

He was finally going to do what he'd been fantasizing about ever since he'd cowered before Skogbacka's headmaster, his back whipped into an irreparable network of scars, and been informed that if he did not immediately stop harassing the De la Grip family, they would call in their attorneys, who would make sure that low-class lowlifes like David and his retarded sister and whore of a mother were crushed like the vermin they were. The headmaster had bellowed that last part. The same headmaster who hadn't had any qualms about having an affair with Helena Hammar a few months before all the hell broke loose. The same headmaster whom David had financially destroyed a few years ago. A few years before that he had dealt with the other two men who had raped Caro, and had left their finances in ruins. The things Natalia had read about him had been exaggerated in places, but were basically true. Those men had been made to pay for what they'd done. He'd dealt with them, learned from his mistakes, and moved on.

Only Investum was left now.

Gustaf and Peter De la Grip.

Something inside David let go. He looked straight at Gustaf, saw all the flashbulbs going off, and smiled.

He was really going to enjoy this.

"Gustaf!" a TV reporter cried.

Gustaf gave him a cool look, but the reporter wasn't deterred. The mood in the room was heated, and they smelled blood. "How does this feel? What's going to happen to Investum?"

Gustaf didn't manage to hide his grimace. "It's nice of Mr. Hammar to take such great interest in our company," he said, his voice dripping with sarcasm. "Of course absolutely anyone is free to buy and sell shares on the stock market."

"But what would it mean if David Hammar were to get a seat on the board?" another reporter called out. "What do you think about David Hammar? Honestly?"

Gustaf made a face, as if he really shouldn't have to answer such questions. David looked on with amusement. The pompous Gustaf obviously hadn't planned on answering questions from a bunch of everyday, sensationalist business reporters.

"Ultimately it's the shareholders who will decide," Gustaf half choked.

"We talked to a representative of one of the national pension funds. He didn't seem all that opposed to David Hammar being on the board. How do you feel about that? They're usually loyal to you. Do you think they're going to vote for David?"

"That would be a disaster," Gustaf scoffed.

"What do you think about David Hammar proposing a board without a single representative of the owning family on it?"

"It's completely irresponsible," Gustaf hissed. "An upstart like him doesn't know anything about the real world, about how the financial sector really works."

"What do you say about the high percentage of women on David Hammar's proposed board? How was he able to find so many competent women while you haven't been able to find a single one to date?"

"That's an obvious attempt to sway public opinion," Gustaf responded. "We take our responsibility seriously and make our choices based a little more on expertise."

That wasn't a particularly smart response, David thought. On the whole, this interview was actually proving to be a disaster for Gustaf from start to finish. Gustaf wasn't used to this kind of lack of respect from the press and had allowed himself to be lured into saying what he *actually* thought, not what he ought to say.

The reporters kept calling out questions, and an increasingly stressed Gustaf snarled his answers. David would actually have loved to let him keep putting his foot in his mouth, but he nodded subtly to Malin.

"Thank you, everyone," Malin said loudly, thus concluding the improvised question-and-answer session. "We'll be starting at the designated time, so please head in and find your seats. Make sure your name tags are visible; otherwise you won't get in."

Gustaf pushed his way through the throng of reporters.

"What a delightful guy," Tom said dryly and pushed his finger against his earpiece. The motion caused his jacket to flap open, and David saw something that looked like a holster by his armpit. He really hoped Tom had a license for that.

"We've secured the premises," Tom said after he finished listening to his earpiece. "But if you're attacked, I'll try to extract you."

"You're kidding, right?"

Tom looked him straight in the eye and asked, "What do you think?" Then he pulled out a sleek cell phone that was vibrating noiselessly and looked down at it, furrowing his brow. "I have to take this," he said, moving away just as Michel walked over.

"What?" Michel asked.

"Tom," David replied laconically.

"Oh, yeah, he's hilarious. The way a tax audit is hilarious."

"Yes?" Tom said into his phone as soon as he'd stepped away from David and Michel.

"She had a visitor," said the man on the other end, the man Tom had assigned to keep an eye on Carolina Hammar.

"Who?"

"A man."

Shit, David wasn't going to be happy about this. "Do you have a picture of him?" Tom asked.

"I'm sending it now."

"Where is he right now? Can you see him?"

"In her room."

Fuck. Tom was just about to give the order for his guy to knock on Carolina's door—screw it if he was overreacting—when the man said, "He's coming back out."

"Can you see the woman?" Tom asked just as a text message chimed in. He plugged in his headset and studied the image that arrived as he was wondering whether he should tell his guy to knock on her door to make sure she was alright. The slightest little anomaly and he would order him to storm her room to secure her, and the Grand Hôtel could send him the bill. He wasn't about to let anything happen to David Hammar's little sister. Tom had had to work with the Russian mafia and the most radical of radical al-Qaida factions in North Africa. He would far rather do that again than take the retribution that David Hammar would unleash if anything were to happen to his sister.

Tom studied the image more closely and identified the man who'd visited Carolina Hammar as Peter De la Grip. He had no idea what that could mean. He thought about it, and then he heard a shout and a scream. He looked up, distracted. A journalist was trying to force his way in. Tom shoved his phone into his pocket and went to settle the disturbance.

He approached the journalist. They were all scum, if you asked him.

And a desk jockey and daddy's boy like Peter De la Grip could hardly constitute a serious threat to Carolina Hammar, Tom thought as he yelled at the journalist.

He decided to hold off.

53

Peter walked out through the lobby of the Grand Hôtel.

He caught a glimpse of his reflection in the window, but he looked the same as always. So weird that what he'd done didn't show from his outward appearance.

He didn't know what he felt. Guilt, relief, or maybe regret? No, not regret, strangely enough.

Maybe it would just take a little while for what he'd done to sink in?

It was so monumental.

Now he was late for the board meeting.

He hopped into a cab.

He would just make it.

54

David stood off to the side below the stage, hidden in the shadows. He listened to the low murmur in the hall, scanning the rows of seats, which would soon be completely full. Men dressed in suits shook hands with each other, laughed loudly, and discussed the current hunting season and their sailing vacations. A few female voices broke in now and then, but the front few rows were overwhelmingly male. No journalists were permitted in here, but a few people were taking flash photos with their cell phones.

Up on the stage there was a podium with a lectern and a microphone. Next to the podium there was a table with chairs, microphones, and mineral water.

The seats in the front row, just below the stage, were reserved for members of the owning family, labeled in black letters by name and title. Peter De la Grip's chair was still empty, as was Natalia's, while Eugene and Alexander sat next to each other conversing in low voices. Ebba De la Grip sat, looking reserved and somber. Åsa was next to her, chatting with a young man in a suit. Gordon Wyndt, who'd arrived on the morning plane from London, sat down behind Eugene.

When there were just a few minutes remaining, Gustaf De la Grip and the six men on his current board walked in the door. The two bodyguards positioned themselves on either side of the doorway. People in the front rows stood up to greet Gustaf. Several shook hands. Some even bowed or curtsied. David remained standing while Gustaf took his seat, apparently unaffected by his deplorable performance during the press conference moments earlier.

He should probably go sit down too, David thought, but he was so amped up that he broke with the rules of etiquette and remained standing. Michel sat at the very end of the second row, silent and tense. David couldn't see Tom anywhere, but he sensed his presence. The digital clock on the wall turned to 12:59. Soon the doors would be closed and locked. No one would be admitted after the designated start time. David sensed movement, and Peter De la Grip hurried in. Natalia followed just behind Peter, wearing an elegant suit and a prim hairstyle, and David lost his composure for a microsecond.

Then the doors were closed. Spotlights were aimed at the stage and the lights went down in the rest of the room. The red digital numbers turned to 1:00. David clenched his fists in his pants pockets, preparing mentally and physically.

The next few hours would determine his entire future.

Gustaf stood and climbed onto the stage.

Spontaneous applause and a few cheers broke out. Gustaf nodded seriously, almost graciously. The applause and murmuring died down as Gustaf gazed at the audience. Small shareholders with as few as five votes to big shareholders with over a million peered back.

"Ladies and gentlemen," Gustaf began, "my dear shareholders, I hereby welcome you to this extraordinary general meeting." Calmly and gravely, his eyes swept over the audience of seven hundred. "The first item of business is to select a chairman for the shareholders' meeting."

David listened to the various formalities. The chairman of the shareholders' meeting, an attorney from one of Stockholm's most prestigious law firms, took a seat at the table along with his secretary. Gustaf stepped down off the stage, and a motion was passed to adopt the agenda. Since electing a board was the only thing on the agenda, it didn't take long.

"We note that there are two proposals for the composition of the board," the lawyer said in such a dry voice it practically crackled. "One proposal is to reelect the current board. The other proposal, which was presented by Hammar Capital, calls for a board consisting of the following people . . ." He listed David, Michel, and the remaining people that Hammar Capital had nominated. "First, I'll open the floor to Count Gustaf De la Grip, Investum's chairman of the board, to share with us his vision of where the board should go with the company."

Gustaf came back up onto the stage and made a half-hour-long statement. David and Michel exchanged glances.

"Now I give the floor to David Hammar," the lawyer finally said.

It was time.

The room went silent.

The lawyer stared at the rows of seats.

And then everything went black.

David walked up onto the stage. The room was pitch-black, yet another of Malin's dramatic ideas, which had seemed better when she'd first described it than it did now since David could hardly see his own hands in front of him. But he made it up onto the stage without any mishaps and hoped he was standing at the podium and not too close to the edge of the stage.

And then a single spotlight came on.

It shone straight on David, and at first the light blinded him—he couldn't see anything. The audience whispered. He waited as his eyes adjusted to the light and he started to be able to make out shapes in the audience. He spotted Alexander De la Grip, Eugene Tolstoy, and Natalia's mother.

Natalia sat straight-backed beside her mother. David felt a wave of emotions that he really couldn't explore right now. He blinked and gazed out at the enormous room, full of shareholders, taking them all in and letting them look at him.

A projector came on, and a Twitter stream was projected onto a screen behind him. The tweets, hashtagged #HC and #Investum, rolled by faster and faster, and David had to admit that the effect was impressive. But then Malin had always had a flair for the dramatic.

A sound technician said into his earpiece, "Go ahead and begin."

David took a step forward.

The lighting technician swept the spotlight over the audience in quick bands of light.

David spotted Malin, who was standing and watching him nervously from the side. She gave him a brief, encouraging—or maybe it was a warning—nod.

He nodded to the chairman of the shareholders' meeting.
He pushed aside all thoughts of Natalia.
He took a deep breath.
So.
It was time.

55

Natalia had arrived late on purpose because she hadn't wanted to mingle or chat with anyone, especially not her mother, who had greeted her with just a quick nod and then went back to staring straight ahead, which was what she was doing now in the chair next to her.

Natalia pushed aside the hurt with determination. Actually she shouldn't have been all that surprised. Her mother normally used silence and emotional distancing to deal with conflict. And there were other crises to cope with at the moment. For example, David, who was standing on stage, his charm almost electric. He was wearing a black suit, a slim dark-gray shirt with no tie, dark cufflinks, and a dark belt that looked expensive under the spotlight. He was so handsome—no, so *magnetic*—that it hurt the eye. For a brief moment it had felt as if he was looking right at her, but it had happened so quickly that she might have been imagining it. She realized she was holding her breath. And then he began to speak.

He introduced himself in a loud voice, and little shivers ran over her skin. She knew David from informal settings. Their meetings had been relaxed and private, and that was the David she'd gotten to know. She had never seen him in his role as a self-confident business leader, never suspected how different it would be. Because, oh my God, what an impression he made.

Natalia literally had goose bumps all over her body. His voice mesmerized the entire auditorium. No one whispered, no one tinkered with their cell phone, no one even fidgeted impatiently in their chair. Everyone sat upright, wide-eyed, and listened as David Hammar told them what he would do if they voted for him and his board. Step by step David went through the shortcomings he and Hammar Capital's analysts had identified. Unhealthy perks. Incompetent leadership. Bad investments and poor decisions. Undervalued assets. Outrageous compensation packages. Point by point he hacked away at pretty much everything Investum had done in recent years.

Natalia was almost having difficulty breathing. She hadn't been involved in any of the abuses he described, and she'd never suspected there were so many irregularities. She didn't dare look at anyone in the family as she listened to how he thought the subsidiaries should be broken up, how various offices and ineffective divisions should be shut down and the work outsourced.

And that wasn't even the worst of it.

After David had spoken uninterrupted for almost an hour and gone through PowerPoint presentations about how to reorganize—or obliterate—Investum, he moved on to hidden assets that should be realized. There was land to be sold, assets to be auctioned off, things that had been in the family for eons but which were technically owned by the company. Their worth should be realized and their value passed on to the shareholders. She could see the business side of his plan, was able to see how it made sense. But then sense fled.

"And naturally the family estate, Gyllgarn Castle, northwest of Stockholm, will be sold," David said from the stage. "It would not be fiscally responsible not to sell it."

Gyllgarn, oh my God. Because although the estate had belonged to the De la Grip family for centuries, apparently it was owned now, from a purely technical tax and bookkeeping perspective, by the Investum company. She'd had no idea. Peter and her father must have worked that out together when Peter took over the property. She could picture them—conspiring over the deal. Had her mother known? Had Alexander? Or had they been excluded too? It didn't matter, because now it would be lost. So stupid.

She wondered who could even afford to buy it. But David might have it parceled off and sell the woods and the acreage and the furnishings individually. She looked down at her hands on her knee, didn't want to cry. It was all just stuff. But it hurt her so much, it was like a physical ache.

David kept going. There was a seemingly endless list of actions that would increase the stock price—if he had his way.

She kept listening, in a shocked fog, to David outlining in broad brushstrokes what Investum's future would look like under his leadership. The board would be filled with skilled people. All the improper perks and bonuses would be gotten rid of immediately. Compensation and severance packages would be reviewed and torn up. And so on.

Natalia was so thirsty she could hardly swallow. Around her the shocked silence slowly started to become an agitated murmur. On the white screen behind David, Twitter screamed about hostile takeovers and megalomania. The level of excitement in the room was tremendous.

But if Natalia were to be completely honest with herself, this was a sound plan. The business and finance part of her saw that. At the same time, however, David's plan meant totally destroying a traditional empire. If he won this vote, he would take apart a power hierarchy and disrupt a world order that had lasted for generations. It was almost unbearable. Natalia straightened in her seat. She simply refused to fall apart. This wasn't over yet. She had a few aces of her own up her sleeve. She was no debutante.

She had said she would fight.

And that was exactly what she meant to do.

56

While David waited for Michel to join him on the stage, he peered out at the room and tried to determine how his talk had been received. He didn't need to look straight at Natalia. He saw her anyway; she was like a ball of energy in the front row.

People shouted questions and he answered them rapid fire. When Gustaf had been on stage, their tone had been humble. The shareholders had such unbelievable respect for Gustaf, and no one dared oppose him, here or in any other context. That was the type of treatment Gustaf was used to.

For David it was different.

Questions rattled in from the audience pretty much nonstop, some hostile, some curious, but they seemed never-ending. After a while, he started wondering if each of the seven hundred onlookers was planning to grill him.

"We'll take two more questions for Mr. Hammar. Then the voting will begin," the lawyer finally said into the microphone. "Return to your seats."

The voting would be done using a simplified procedure, which meant that the major stakeholders, those who had the most votes, would be asked first, and they would be asked according to the number of shares they controlled.

Gustaf De la Grip had the most votes. After that came the major funds, and then, in descending order, Åsa, Ebba, Eugene, Alex, Natalia, and finally, last of all, Peter. After that all the small stakeholders present in the room would vote, but by then it would already be decided.

It went as expected to begin with. Gustaf naturally voted for his own board. The fund managers whom David had spoken to and whom he'd won over into his fold voted for him. The ones he had figured would remain loyal to Investum voted against him. Most of them voted the way he'd predicted, with only a few exceptions, but it was close now. He tallied it up in his head. People were still voting, for and against. When it was Åsa Bjelke's turn to vote, she actually appeared to hesitate for a moment. David held his breath. Had they won her over to their side? But in the end she voted against him. Ebba voted for Investum as well. So far it had gone pretty much as planned.

But then their scheme backfired.

When the Russian's turn came, Natalia's uncle Eugene, the man David had spent his summer buttering up, the man David had been convinced was in his pocket, voted *against*. David tried to hide his shock. He glanced at Michel and saw the same reaction in his friend's face. *The Russian has changed sides.*

David couldn't help it; he flashed Natalia a look. A faint, cool grin graced her lips. So this was her doing; she'd managed to turn her uncle against Hammar Capital.

He was going to have a long conversation with the Russian about this.

Then it was time for the rest of the owning family. Alexander voted against and Natalia did the same.

It was neck and neck, much closer than he'd anticipated. Had he made a mistake? Had he counted wrong? Their estimates had never— never—predicted that they might fail, not even on a theoretical level. He cast a quick glance at Michel, who looked calm, but David could tell he was worried too.

And Peter De la Grip hadn't even voted yet.

It was surreal.

David wasn't looking at anything; he could hardly see at all. He clenched his fists tight in his trouser pockets. They were in the lead, but not by much of a margin. And Peter owned A-shares, which were weighted ten times as much as the B-shares that most shareholders owned. It was the traditional Swedish system, often criticized, expressly designed to give the owning family more power. That was why it would have made all the difference to win over one or more members of the owning family. Now it looked like Hammar Capital was going to stumble at the finishing line.

All these years and everything he'd put into this.

For nothing.

He'd sacrificed everything, even the woman he was starting to suspect he was in love with—for failure, a fiasco.

David imagined Michel standing there making the same computations he was making and reaching the same conclusions.

"It's close," Michel said quietly, hardly audibly. "It's so close."

"Do we know how many shares he actually owns?" David asked. It was down to a percentage point or two now. "I mean exactly?"

"It's in our paperwork somewhere," Michel said. He leaned toward David, speaking in a whisper. "Plus he could have bought a ton of B-shares on his own. He is rich, after all. And it's possible that he got hold of more A-shares, even though we did our best to vacuum them up. I don't know the exact percentage of A-shares." Michel scratched the back of his scalp. "What happened with the Russian? I thought we had him."

What happened? Natalia happened.

"I thought so too," David replied neutrally. Would the small stakeholders be able to save them?

Peter voted.

The count flickered up.

They watched tensely. The room waited with bated breath.

What the hell?

David didn't dare breathe.

"What happened?" Michel blurted out. "There must be some kind of mistake."

A murmur spread through the room.

David could hardly believe his eyes, because that must be a mistake, couldn't possibly be right.

The murmur increased. Someone yelled.

And then the room erupted.

So many flashbulbs went off that David was temporarily blinded. Next to him Michel swore loudly and emotionally in Arabic.

Peter De la Grip had definitely decided the vote.

But in favor of Hammar Capital.

Peter De la Grip, their archenemy and opponent, had voted *for*

Hammar Capital's plan and against Investum. He had voted against his father, his board.

It was over.

Hammar Capital had won, and the old Investum didn't exist anymore. The board would be forced to resign effective immediately.

Michel looked him in the eye. They couldn't quite fathom what had just happened.

"I can confirm that Hammar Capital's seven incoming board members already have enough votes. No one else can beat them," the lawyer said loudly. "The shareholders' meeting thereby declares that the majority of the votes was received by the following people," he continued, listing off David, Michel, and the five other people the two of them had selected together, three women and two men.

"These individuals have thus been elected as the new board of directors. I thank the shareholders."

The last bit could hardly be heard. The level of noise in the room rose, and then a few people started clapping their hands, and the applause spread quickly, increasing to a thunderous volume.

"We won!" Michel yelled over the applause and shouting. The shock in his face started to give way and was replaced by a broad grin instead. "We *won!*"

David nodded, and an enormous wave of relief rushed through him, the emotion almost unreal. He vigorously shook the hand Michel held out, up and down. The normally staid Malin flung her arms around David's neck with a squawk of joy, and he hugged her so hard she gasped for breath, laughing all the while. People flocked to the podium to take pictures, offer congratulations, and participate in the chaos. And David did everything he was expected to do while he tried to shake off the surreal feeling.

Hammar Capital had taken over and destroyed Investum.

They had made financial history, redrawn the financial map. This would be written into textbooks and articles forever after. Economics historians would study this event, and write theses and dissertations about it. It was extraordinary.

David looked around, listening to the cheers and thinking that if this had been a TV show, confetti would be fluttering down from the ceiling. The cheers came and went. People were still laughing, and he thought he ought to feel happy too.

But he didn't feel happy. The relief had vanished, leaving nothing in its place, and he felt totally shut down.

He kept shaking hands with the men and women who surged forward from every direction, letting himself be thumped on the back and congratulated. And he tried to persuade himself that this weird feeling would pass soon.

57

Natalia watched David smiling and shaking hands up on the stage. He was overwhelming, like a king or emperor.

And it was over.

Everything was over. Everything had changed.

Her thoughts were racing.

Peter . . . What had actually happened? Had something in his brain snapped? It was inconceivable—literally impossible to comprehend. She looked around for her brother, but didn't see him.

Gustaf was standing with some of the board members—well, former board members—gesticulating with short, tense hand motions.

Her mother sat with her hands clasped in her lap, and Natalia thought she ought to go over to her, offer some comfort, but she didn't dare. Louise rocked back and forth in her seat, blowing her nose over and over again. Alexander sat leaning back, with his legs stretched out as far as he could and his arms along the chair backs. He wasn't looking at anyone or talking to anyone. He mostly looked bored, as if the chaos around him didn't have the least thing to do with him. Uncle Eugene sat next to her mother, patting her clumsily on the shoulder.

Natalia looked at the wreckage of her family.

How *dare* Peter do this to them, to Mother and to his own wife? Why had he done it? Did this have something to do with Carolina? Natalia didn't know what to think, just knew that he'd destroyed his own future. Gustaf would never forgive him. Their mother wouldn't either. And Louise? Natalia looked at her sister-in-law's red, tear-stained face. Louise had married Investum's crown prince, a man who owned a grand estate and was welcomed into the most exclusive circles. Somehow Natalia doubted that Louise would stand by Peter's side now.

And then it *finally* thundered in. Like a late train at full speed in rush hour traffic: the rage against David as he stood up there on the stage like God's gift to humanity, the man who had betrayed her and destroyed her family like some dictator.

This takeover didn't have anything to do with *justice*, she thought furiously. It wasn't about anything other than revenge and power. David hadn't acquired a company; he'd massacred it. People would lose their jobs because of this. The value that had been built up over generations would be sold off.

She rubbed her forehead, already feeling her anger waning, feeling how quickly her strength was running out. She was so done. The last few weeks had drained all her energy, what with everything that had happened, everything that had been written . . . And now she'd lost everything. At least that's how it felt. Outside, the world was probably moving along totally as usual, and she felt an enormous need to get out of here, to get out into the fresh air, to not have to see David and his admirers, how all the women were looking at him with lust in their eyes. Yes, she saw it all, the way they openly stared at him, the leader of the pack, the alpha male, the victor.

She had to get out, away from this room where all her mistakes were gathered in one place, like some exposé of everything she'd done wrong.

Åsa waved to her, but Natalia couldn't do any more than nod weakly back and look away. More than anything else she wanted to go home, but the chaos and the commotion in the room were so overpowering that she just sat there. It would take ages to squeeze her way out, and she wasn't up to it.

She collapsed in her chair.

"Natalia, come!" She jumped and looked up. Her father had barked the order, short and firm. "We're going to meet with them," he said. "We have to save what can be saved now."

"But I . . . ," Natalia began uncertainly. She'd never been involved in the business before, why now?

"Hammar wants you there," Gustaf said in a tone that conveyed extremely well what he thought about that. "Come, now."

Technically no one could force her to go. She didn't answer to anyone. In the end, however, it was less trouble to obey. Natalia got up. Would this ever be over?

58

Peter squirmed. The conference room he and David Hammar were in had big windows, and the water was practically below their feet. David was standing by the window, his back to Lake Mälaren behind him, watching Peter with his arms crossed and a frosty stare.

It felt surreal to be in here, just the two of them. Peter was unbelievably uncomfortable, despite having been the one to request the meeting. He and David hadn't spoken one-to-one since they were teenagers. And even then they hadn't actually ever really talked. They had fought and argued from the first day David started at Skogbacka.

"I know there isn't actually anything I can say to make up for what I did," Peter began. He was forced to speak loudly because the room was long and David didn't approach him, but remained by the window. Peter cleared his throat and steeled himself, but he still couldn't look David in the eye. It took all his courage just to dare to be here, to dare to speak. He couldn't actually look at the man he'd injured so badly.

Peter wondered if he could explain what had happened even to himself: the frustration he'd felt long before he'd ever begun at Skogbacka, the incessant feeling of not being good enough, the jealousy that was so all-encompassing, and, the most shameful of all, the attraction he'd felt for Carolina Hammar. He'd thought she was so pretty, the blond fifteen-year-old with the cheerfully colored clothes and the friendly smile, the working-class girl. She'd been nice to him, and they'd talked to each other a few times, completely harmlessly. It had been like a respite, an oasis. And then people had found out that Peter De la Grip was interested in David Hammar's weird sister.

They'd teased him, and he'd felt ridiculed, so he'd done the worst thing you could do to another person. He and three buddies had gone by her house, had seen her in the window, had rung the bell. It wasn't planned, it just happened, and it was revolting. Not a day had gone by since then that he hadn't been ashamed, hadn't known, to his very core, that he was the lowest of the low.

"But I needed to say that I'm sorry, and I'm grateful that you were willing to meet with me," he said in a half-choked voice. When he'd been told that Carolina had died . . . Her "death," oh God, it had almost *destroyed* him. And now: she was alive. It was like getting a second chance. He felt such gratitude.

"I'm so tremendously sorry for what I did to you and to Carolina," he said a little more loudly. "That's why I voted for you and Hammar Capital in there." He stopped. The words were completely insufficient. "I understand that there's nothing I can say that would make up for what happened. And I don't know what I would have done if I were in your shoes."

David was still standing at the window. He turned away, looking out at the water. His arms were still crossed. The late-afternoon sunlight streamed in, making dust motes visible in the air. Silence swelled between them.

Peter ran his hand over his forehead. He was so tired, so drained after this day—first, the meeting with his siblings at Natalia's place, and then the tension on the way to the Grand Hôtel, and then the meeting with Carolina. It had been like turning back time. She'd been so like herself, and yet different. Colorful and blond, but grown-up and serious. The conversation in the hotel suite was something he would carry with him for the rest of his life. It still felt like a glowing dream. And then the meeting, of course, where for the first time ever—and very publicly, no less—he had opposed his father and thereby also buried his own future in the world of Swedish business.

He looked at David's back. He didn't know what he'd hoped to get out of this meeting. Forgiveness? He didn't deserve forgiveness, but Caro had forgiven him anyway, and that had been like getting a new life. He'd confessed and his sins were forgiven.

"I talked to Carolina," he said to David's back.

David abruptly turned around. "You *saw* her?" he asked incredulously.

Peter nodded.

"When?" David took a step toward him, and it was like facing a menacing tiger or an attacking lion.

Peter was having a hard time breathing. "We've had you both under surveillance," he replied and forced himself not to back away even though it was like forcing himself to stand face-to-face with a dangerous predator who was preparing to attack. "I knew where she was staying, so I went there."

"What did you say to her?" David asked, taking another step closer to Peter. Peter tried to keep his fear at bay, but it was hard. David Hammar was not a teenage underdog anymore. He was a powerful, full-grown man. There was nothing, literally nothing preventing him from beating the crap out of Peter right here. Peter glanced around at the walls and ceiling of the conference room and noted that they even looked soundproof.

"If you did anything to her . . . ," David began. He didn't need to say any more. Peter realized that David was hardly one to make empty threats. There was nothing civilized about this man, just a thin patina of decorum, beneath which he was completely ruthless except to those he cared about. And Peter had never had any doubt that David really cared about his sister.

He was the big brother Peter himself had never been able to be to his siblings.

Peter held up his hand. "I went there to apologize to Carolina. I'd called her beforehand and she let me come. We just talked."

"What did she say?"

"She said that she'd forgiven me a long time ago, which obviously I had no right at all to expect. I hadn't even hoped for that." Peter's voice broke, and he struggled not to let his feelings show on his face. If he started crying in front of David Hammar, he would die of shame. "There's nothing I can say to make up for what I did," he continued. "Nothing, I know that. But I still wanted to see her and apologize."

David didn't say anything, but the worst of the tension in his face began to abate.

"Carolina is okay," Peter said.

"I know," David said. "I talked to her by phone just a little while ago. But she didn't say a word about your meeting."

Peter shrugged. In his eyes, Carolina was a grown woman, not accountable to David, but he wasn't so foolish as to mention that.

David eyed him for a long time. It felt as if he were entering Peter's head and rooting around in there, and it was the most uncomfortable thing Peter had experienced in his whole life.

"You raped my little sister," he said finally.

Peter gasped for breath, but he replied, "Yes."

"You and your buddies whipped me like an animal."

"Yes."

David looked away. Peter waited.

There was a knock on the door. "The others are coming in now," David said. "Are you going to stick around?"

Peter shook his head. "I'm leaving. There'll be enough drama without my father trying to murder me." He hesitated. For a second it had felt as if David had seen him, really seen the man he was trying to be, but he wasn't totally sure. He held out his hand. "Good luck," he said.

David glanced at the outstretched hand for so long that Peter was convinced he was going to refuse to take it. There was another knock. David sighed and finally held out his own hand. Gratitude suffused Peter as they shook hands—not all that warmly, but still.

David quickly pulled his hand back, nodded briefly, and said, "Thanks for your vote earlier." Peter could hear that David wasn't completely comfortable saying the words.

"Thanks yourself," Peter said. And he meant it. He was profoundly grateful that he'd had a chance to acknowledge and take responsibility for his crimes, even if the statute of limitations had run out from a legal perspective, grateful that he'd been given a chance to move on, wherever he was headed now after this. He put his hand on the doorknob and opened it. Michel Chamoun was standing outside. Michel looked at Peter without saying a word and then looked at David with an eyebrow raised. The terrifying man who was in charge of Hammar Capital's security stood outside like a colossus.

"Should I stall them?" Michel asked.

"No, we're done here," David said as Gustaf De la Grip's voice cut through the air.

Peter steeled himself before meeting his father. He'd managed to avoid him directly after the vote, and he assumed his father's mood hadn't improved since then.

Gustaf spotted him and glared at him furiously. "So this is where you've been hiding," he roared. "What the hell did you do? Are you an idiot?"

Peter cowered in the face of his father's rage, felt the familiar fear, and was ready to be beaten. In some way he regressed, becoming small and vulnerable again in front of all these influential men. Fucking shit.

But then the head of security, dressed all in black, took a step forward. He positioned himself between Peter and Gustaf, slowly shook his head, and addressed Gustaf. "Back off," he said coldly.

Gustaf, who apparently had rarely if ever been told to back off before, looked as if he couldn't believe his ears. He opened his mouth, surely to tell the man off, and it occurred to Peter that this was the man who'd allowed him to believe that Carolina was dead. His father had robbed him of the opportunity to stand up and atone for what he'd done. But it was over now, and maybe he could start to be free. The past didn't need to control his life anymore. Peter tipped his head and, taking advantage of the tumult Gustaf's reaction had caused, walked away.

The last thing he heard was the head of security saying, "If you care at all about that finger, I'd stop waving it in my face."

Peter smiled to himself and left.

59

Wondering if he would be forced to intervene between Gustaf and Tom, David watched Peter retreat. It had been a life-changing meeting, and he hadn't managed to fully grasp everything Peter's apology carried with it. He would need some more time to digest it, but first he had a few other things to deal with.

"Tom, you can let them in now," he said.

Tom gave the furious Gustaf a chilly stare before stepping aside.

The patriarch swept into the conference room, flanked by people David identified as Investum lawyers and accountants. Alexander and Åsa were behind them, and last of all came Natalia.

She walked in the doorway past him, and he all but closed his eyes and inhaled her scent. She didn't say anything, just went to a chair and sat down.

Then Michel came into the room, and now Rima Campbell was with him, the woman they were going to appoint as managing director of Investum. Rima shook hands with David. She was a serious woman, one of the best directors David had met, and she'd been his first choice from the very beginning. She'd apparently butted heads with Gustaf a month ago. She eyed him neutrally now. She was brave, David thought, smiling at her. He liked brave people.

Rima sat down, set her phone and iPad on the table, tinkered with her electronics, and then calmly looked around.

Tom was still standing in the doorway. He caught David's attention. "Should I stick around?" he asked.

"Wait outside," David ordered.

Tom nodded and cast one last menacing glance at the Investum people, a look that clearly communicated that they shouldn't even think of getting up to anything, because they would regret it for a long time to come, before pulling the door shut behind him.

Gustaf started right in. "This isn't over, if that's what you think," he began before David had even had a chance to sit down. "You must have rigged the vote."

Michel stood halfway up, but David made a gesture to stop him.

"Of course you're entitled to your opinion," he told Gustaf smoothly. "But I would watch the accusations if I were you." He glanced at Åsa, who nodded in confirmation.

"He's right, Gustaf," Åsa said tersely. "Try to avoid libel, please."

David continued. "The sooner you accept that you've lost, the sooner we can move on."

"I haven't lost anything," Gustaf said.

Åsa shook her head, as if to say she gave up.

Gustaf smiled scornfully, distorting his aristocratic features. "No one is going to touch you with a barge pole after this. You have no power in this country." He leaned back in his chair and crossed his arms. "You are no one and nothing."

The silence that spread through the room was uncomfortable, to say the least.

David watched Gustaf.

For all the years they had known each other, the older man had always been cold and haughty, like a patriarchal relic, born to privileges that he took as his God-given birthright. Gustaf was used to never being contradicted, used to servile submission, and he acted accordingly—as if everything he said and did was unquestionable.

But it was easy to be haughty when you had never experienced any serious defeat.

"I'm afraid you're wrong, Gustaf," David said calmly, permitting himself to sound a little patronizing. "The shareholders have had their say, and as of today I am the chairman of Investum's board." He made a point of looking at his watch. "For at least half an hour now, actually. And that is *something* actually, I would say." He adjusted the cuff of his sleeve and smiled coolly.

Someone suppressed a nervous laugh.

"You goddamned Eurotrash punk," Gustaf said, his voice no

longer as controlled. "You're nothing," he repeated. "You don't know anything. You're trash, the son of your mother, and everyone knew she was a whore. You ought to know your place."

The Investum people started squirming in their chairs. Åsa looked down at her hands and shook her head again. Only Alexander appeared unaffected, as if he'd ended up in this room by mistake and couldn't care less what anyone said.

David glanced at Natalia. She sat motionless, her face pale but composed. He didn't want her to have to hear this. He had agreed— he didn't even know why—to speak to Gustaf on the condition that Natalia was present, but he should have known better, should have realized that it would be nasty.

"And your sister," Gustaf continued, cutting David's thoughts short. "Don't you think I know she's alive? Huh? You're like vermin, worming your way in like roaches."

David still didn't say anything. A strange calm had come over him. The madder Gustaf became, the more insulting he got, the more confident David felt. He would give the man ten more seconds. He listened to the profanities and reflected on how all the sputtering and cursing had the opposite effect from what Gustaf intended. If anyone in this room was acting like trash just now, it certainly wasn't David. And everyone in the room knew it—except perhaps for Gustaf himself, who slapped his palm on the table. All these years the old man had been so cold and controlled whenever they met. Now he'd lost his self-control for the first time. This should feel good, but David didn't give a damn. At last, he'd conquered the monsters of his past.

"Are you done?" he asked neutrally. He didn't even need to force himself to act unperturbed, because it didn't matter anymore. It was over.

"I'm going to drag you through dirt you can't imagine," Gustaf ranted. "I'll make sure you're slaughtered in the press. I have powerful friends. I can go however high up I want. I'm connected."

Gustaf glared at Rima and Michel. "And if you think some gang of gypsies can run my company . . . If you, you piece of shit, think that my life's work can be managed by jungle bunnies like *them*, you're wrong."

Rima made a stifled sound, and if David hadn't known better, he would have thought his new managing director was trying to keep herself from laughing.

Michel shook his head, as if he couldn't believe his ears.

The others squirmed.

Gustaf opened his mouth, but David raised his hand. He'd had enough of this charade; it was time to talk business. "The new board elected me chairman of the board," he said. "Our first resolution was to dismiss the previous managing director." He nodded to Rima Campbell. "Meet Investum's new managing director," he said.

"You can't be serious," Gustaf said, looking as if he were having a heart attack. "You can't choose *her*. You have to at least pick someone who knows the company."

David raised an eyebrow. Until now Investum's leadership team had consisted of men whose foremost merits were that they were Gustaf's friends. They weren't exactly the sharpest knives in the drawer.

"And you have to have someone from the family," Gustaf said, as if he actually had any right to decide. "At least as a consultant. Anything else is inconceivable."

David watched him without saying anything.

"There are rules and principles in this industry," Gustaf continued. "Perhaps it's hard for someone like you to grasp, but I know this world. Everyone listens to me. You need a De la Grip."

David wondered if the man were really so arrogant that he thought his words had any value at all anymore.

"I might offer Natalia a consulting position," he said slowly.

Michel's eyebrows moved up his forehead, which wasn't so strange given that this suggestion had been purely impulsive on David's part, not something he'd mentioned to anyone. But, he argued to himself, Natalia was good, Michel had acknowledged that. The company would benefit from her expertise and knowledge. Surely they could be professional and work together.

Somewhere, deep down, David knew he was fooling himself and coming up with justifications that weren't rational at all.

Natalia just stared at him, her face chalk-white.

"She's not going to have a position in the company," Gustaf roared so that the windows shook.

"There's no other De la Grip I would consider," David said coolly. "You have no authority whatsoever. It's pure courtesy on my part."

"Courtesy?" Gustaf howled. "Over my dead body. And besides, she's not even a De la Grip," he added. "Plus you can't have a leadership team that consists of old women and immigrants. You're going to be ridiculed."

"Gustaf, what the hell," Åsa said tiredly.

David looked at Natalia. He wouldn't have thought it possible, but she looked even paler now. Her eyes were shiny, and the tense features of her face were trembling. He'd never seen her cry, but she seemed on the verge of tears now.

"Out," he said quietly.

"You can't . . . ," Gustaf began indignantly.

"Not another fucking word from you," David roared. He looked around the room. "All of you, out."

The lawyers and accountants were already getting up. Apparently relieved, they gathered their papers and briefcases. Rima Campbell picked up her phone and her iPad.

Alexander got up. "Come on, Dad," he said calmly but determinedly. "You've said enough."

Michel had also risen and was starting to usher people out. Under Tom Lexington's harsh scrutiny, everyone hurried off. One by one they all left. Åsa passed Michel, close, close. They stared at each other for a charged moment before Åsa slipped out.

Natalia stood up as well.

She avoided David's eyes as she fumbled with her purse. She pushed out her chair, prepared to go.

"Not you, Natalia," David said calmly.

She gave him a questioning look.

He shook his head. "You're staying," he said.

60

It's been a long day, thought Natalia. Actually it felt like the longest in her life. And it wasn't over yet.

She watched David empty the room efficiently and dictatorially.

As the last few people exited, she tried to compose herself, and she was almost completely calm by the time the door closed. David turned around to face her, fixed his eyes on her, and asked, "What was that all about?"

"Ha ha ha. Seriously?" she said coolly, fighting the feeling of irritation that flared up in her. She very grudgingly admitted that he had handled Gustaf most impressively, but he had no right to question her. She raised one eyebrow. "You actually think I have to *tell* you stuff?"

He opened his mouth, but then closed it again. He took a seat at the table a little distance from her as if to give her a good view of his whole body: big, self-confident, dominant. Today had already taught her that that was how David worked—he dominated people.

He put a hand on the table and watched her, as if he were searching for a strategy to deal with her.

Good luck with that.

She wasn't planning on making anything easy for him.

He leaned in over the table, and Natalia almost jumped at the movement. She was more tense than she wanted to admit. But David just grabbed a bottle of mineral water, opened it, poured some water into a glass, rose halfway from his chair, and handed it to her. "Drink," he said.

She raised her eyebrow again. Was he *trying* to annoy her?

"You're pale," he said by way of explanation. "It's been a tough day. Have a little water."

It made her feel like a stubborn child, but she refused to take the glass.

He shook his head, set it down in front of her, and sat down again. "I'm not your enemy," he said. "Your greatest wish in life was to work at Investum," he continued in a low, compelling voice. It inspired such confidence, that voice of his. She was on the verge of leaning toward him.

"Why are you saying *no* now?" He looked really bewildered, as if he couldn't fathom why she wasn't jumping at the chance to work with him, *for* him. "Is it because of me?"

"Um, yeah," she replied stiffly.

"I'm sure we can both behave professionally," he said.

Natalia just shook her head. He seemed sincere, and she couldn't decide whether he was just being unbelievably naïve or unbelievably stupid. Regardless of which, she could never in her life imagine working with David.

She wondered exactly how much she'd misjudged him. Maybe he did this all the time? Slept with strategically important women and offered them jobs afterward, maybe as consolation?

It was uncomfortable to realize how differently they'd invested emotionally in the relationship. Uncomfortable and horribly embarrassing. Obviously she would never work with him. It was hard enough to sit in the same room and have him looking at her so intently.

She forced herself to sit completely still and not move a muscle.

"What did your father mean when he said you're not a De la Grip?" he asked. "I don't understand."

Oh, she might as well explain it. What did it matter? It would be public knowledge soon enough. "Gustaf isn't my biological father. I didn't know that before. Now . . . now there have been *repercussions*."

David looked at her for so long that Natalia had to keep herself from fidgeting in her chair. Now she regretted having refused the glass of water. She was insanely thirsty. Nonchalantly she picked up the glass and drank.

"I'm sorry," David said quietly. "I had no idea."

"Don't be silly," she said, her voice sounding artificially chipper. The glass had left a wet ring on the glossy conference table, and she strove to put it back in exactly the same spot. She brought her voice back to the cool tone she so desperately wanted to maintain. When she got home she would treat herself to a breakdown, but not here, not now. "It's not your fault."

"What's going to happen now? With, well, you know, with . . . ?" David made a vague gesture.

Natalia smiled wryly. "With everything? I honestly don't know. Everything is still spinning. But even if you hadn't taken over Investum, I wouldn't have had a future there. Gustaf made that completely clear to me, and now to everyone else as well, as you heard." She wondered if her father was busy informing Alex right now. She trembled, but forced her body to stillness. They had to be almost done here.

"I'm so sorry," he repeated.

"Thanks," she said, even though she was sure that David was truly uninterested in her family situation. She would probably have to change her last name, and she would obviously be stricken from the official list of Swedish nobles. This would surely cost her some of her friends.

But otherwise . . .

Life would actually go on.

She shrugged. "It's not like there's some emergency," she said. "I can always find another job."

He gave her a questioning look. Of course. He had no idea.

"I quit at the bank. Well, technically I was fired because my deal tanked."

And because I blew off work after you broke my heart.

"I had no idea," he said. "So why don't you want to work with Investum now that you have a serious offer?"

She sighed. "David, I honestly can't picture a future in which I'm working for you in one of your companies." How was it even possible that they could have such different views on this?

"You're right," he said quietly.

They sat in silence. She wanted to say something more, but couldn't come up with any words. Strangely enough, she wasn't mad anymore, just empty. She took another drink of the mineral water.

"David?"

"Yes?"

"Since we're talking about fathers anyway, can I ask you something?"

He smiled a little, and she caught a glimpse of the David she'd fallen for, in the laugh lines around his eyes and the twinkle in them. "Absolutely," he said.

"Is Carl-Erik Tessin your father?"

He studied her for a long time. She could tell she'd surprised him, which pleased her. He was so unerring and solid, it felt good to shake him up a little, not to always be the one brought up short. Besides, she was genuinely curious.

"How did you come up with that?" he asked finally.

"You two are very similar," she said. She had liked the low-key count from Skåne. And according to Wikipedia, David had two middle names, Carl and Erik. It hadn't been hard to figure out when she started thinking along those lines. "Is he Carolina's father, too?"

David nodded. "Yes, he was both Carolina's and my biological father."

She raised an eyebrow. "He's not dead either." She couldn't help saying it.

"Apparently not," he responded.

"Do you get along?"

Actually it was almost comical how reversed their roles were now. David's father was a count, while hers pretty surely wasn't. She glanced at his grim face. Not that he seemed to appreciate the humor of the situation.

"Do I get along with a married nobleman who got my mother pregnant, *twice*, and then let her manage the best she could?" he asked slowly. "No, you could certainly say that we don't get along."

"You should talk to him," Natalia said, not really caring if she was meddling with things that were none of her business. She thought Carl-Erik seemed nice.

"If you say so," he said tersely.

"Not that I'm really much of an expert at relationships," she said with a rueful half smile at her own understatement. "So I guess I could be totally wrong."

A smile spread across his stern face, and she loved that she could still make him smile.

"Is he a bad person?" she asked.

"I don't actually know," David said. "I'm sorry, but I don't really want to talk about it."

"Okay," she said.

"Thanks," he said.

And then they got lost in each other's eyes.

"Sorry for slapping your face," she said softly. She had wanted to say that.

"I'm the one who should be apologizing. I deserved it."

She assumed she ought to cherish his apology, but it felt strangely depressing for a man to apologize for having kissed her. She wondered how David *actually* felt about her. After all, he had kissed her on Friday, but it had been a power display. Which he now apparently regretted.

But then today he'd offered her a job. Did he want to be friends, or something else? She wished she dared to ask, but the truth was that she wasn't asking because she wasn't up to hearing the answer. Maybe this was what they were doomed to—hurting each other and apologizing, over and over again. Maybe it would be better if they never saw each other again.

She looked away. Although it was actually a little more complicated than that. She was going to *have* to tell him sometime, certain things anyway. Because that's what people did, right? Told the man you'd slept with that, *whoops, turns out I wasn't sterile after all, and now I'm quite pregnant. And, yes, actually, I'm planning to keep it, thank you very much.* Because she'd decided she was going to have this baby. Actually she'd known that the whole time. Nothing and no one could make her terminate this pregnancy. It was *her* baby, and she would fight for it like a tigress. Well, hers and David's, of course, she added to herself. Because David could go on and on about never wanting to have kids, but this was every bit as much his doing as hers.

She drew a circle with her finger on the glossy table. Soon, one of these weeks or months, she would get it together enough to tell him.

Oh, for God's sake, just tell him now, she ordered herself sternly. *Do it fast, like ripping off a Band-Aid.* "*I'm pregnant*"—*just say it now.*

"Um, David, there's something I have to . . ." she began at the exact same moment that he said, "Natalia, I was wondering . . ." and then there was a knock on the door at *exactly* the same moment, and they both fell awkwardly silent.

Or maybe relieved.

Malin opened the door a crack and peeked in. She looked stressed out and hot.

"Sorry to bother you," she said apologetically, balancing an enormous stack of papers in her arms. She nodded quickly at Natalia and then looked at David. "Are you coming? Your board is waiting for you." She gave Natalia an embarrassed glance but stubbornly stayed. "I'm sorry . . ."

"I'm coming, Malin," David said. He stood up. "Sorry," he told Natalia as he straightened his jacket and pulled his hand through his hair. The private David disappeared, replaced by a business leader.

Natalia quickly stood up as well. "It's fine," she said. "I have to go. I didn't mean to keep you."

"You were about to say something," he said.

"It was nothing. I'll go, so you can have your meeting."

"Thanks," he said.

"Bye," Natalia said finally.

David took a step toward her. Natalia stiffened, and then she plastered on a smile, hoping to God that her true feelings somehow didn't show. That he couldn't see that all she wanted to do was bawl her heart out. David halted, and the mood was uncomfortably tense. Natalia cleared her throat and smiled again, calmly and effectively this time—at least she hoped so—and quickly extended her hand so David wouldn't get it into his head to hug her, because then she would surely fall apart, and she quite simply didn't want to do that. She'd fallen apart enough already for a whole lifetime.

Some emotion flickered in David's beautiful gray-blue eyes—she saw it but didn't know what it was—and he held out his hand too.

And then they shook hands, like two colleagues parting ways, and maybe it was forever.

Cool, impersonal, and definitive.

Despite that, it felt like she was dying here in this conference room.

She released his hand. Felt Malin watching.

Turn around and go, Natalia.

Now.

She had no choice. She ordered herself to do what was right and proper and expected. David and Malin were watching her, surely eager to get on with their meeting.

So Natalia left.

On her high heels and with as much dignity as she could muster, she walked out of the room and out of David Hammar's life.

Good-bye, she thought, and then closed the door behind her.

Good-bye.

61

The conference center was still packed with people all heading out the doors at the same time. There were hundreds of people, forming lines and crowding.

Carl-Erik Tessin was trying to get his bearings in the sea of people. A door opened a little ways off, and he saw Natalia De la Grip come out and hurry past, looking very tense. He'd liked her when they'd met at Båstad, which was unexpected given who her family was.

Daughter of Gustaf and sister of Peter, two men he had every reason to loathe.

And then Carl-Erik spotted Gustaf De la Grip. He towered above the crowd, like a bird of prey or a vulture, with his sharp features and cold eyes.

Carl-Erik took a step forward, tensing.

This was it. The time had come to confront the past. He *had* to risk it. Now or never, he repeated to himself like a mantra.

"Gustaf!" he called. His voice carried surprisingly well over the crowd, and Gustaf turned around.

Carl-Erik's whole body stiffened as Gustaf looked to see who had called his name, but he forced himself not to step away. Gustaf looked him over. Carl-Erik approached. He tried not to lean too much on his walking stick, didn't want to show weakness.

"Are you speaking to me?" Gustaf asked disdainfully once they were facing each other.

Carl-Erik tried to take a breath to calm himself. But he was jumpy. Gustaf had always been able to strike fear into him just by looking at him. Even though it had been fifty years since their days at Skogbacka, even though they were old men, the memories lingered in his body and maybe in his soul.

Carl-Erik had been sent to the boarding school when he was ten. His parents had believed in harsh discipline, and they'd sent him away, even though he was quaking with fear. Carl-Erik was so home-sick he cried at night, and he'd been scared of everything during the day—the teachers, the staff, and the older children. He'd taken so many beatings, and Gustaf De la Grip had been his worst tormentor. The things people wrote about in the newspapers these days, about harassment and hazing at the boarding schools, were just the tip of the iceberg. Anyone who'd gone to boarding school knew. Carl-Erik's hand squeezed his cane. "Yes," he said. "I want to talk to you about David."

Gustaf scoffed, and it took Carl-Erik some effort not to immedi-ately fall back into the roll of victim. He hated conflicts. Sometimes it felt as if he'd been afraid his whole life: first of his own parents, then of Gustaf and the other students at boarding school, then of his wife, and then—like some nightmarish repetition of the past—of Gustaf again.

Even today he remembered the conversation from so many years ago. It would be exactly seventeen years on the Santa Lucia holiday this year. December thirteenth, he never forgot the date, and he had hated the holiday ever since. Helena had called him in a panic. They hadn't spoken for many years; Helena had refused to see him since the day she'd realized he was never going to be brave enough to leave his wife. And she had forbidden Carl-Erik to have any contact with David or Carolina. He'd sent letters but never heard anything back. The years since then had been desolate, cold, and lonely, but he'd done what he'd done his whole life: given in.

And then Helena had called late that night, the panic audible in her voice and the words tumbling out of her as she told him about Carolina being raped, David being assaulted, and the threat against all three of them. She must have been beside herself to have called, he realized today. She'd punished him for so many years by refusing to take his calls, but she'd called when the children were in danger. Helena was a proud woman—David got that from her, Carl-Erik thought—and it must have really cost her something to make that phone call. He'd taken the call in the middle of a formal dinner with counts and barons and his wife's parents. With his heart thumping, he'd answered when the mother of his two out-of-wedlock children, and the only woman he'd ever loved, had called to ask for help.

And then he'd done what remained the most shameful thing in his whole life: he'd let her down. Sure, he'd given her money for Carolina's treatment for a few paltry years, but otherwise his failure had been complete.

Not anymore, he thought, straightening his back and looking Gustaf in the eye, never again.

"I want to talk to you," he repeated.

"Oh? And what makes you think I'm going to listen to anything you have to say?" Gustaf said with a sneer.

"They're my children," Carl-Erik said.

"What are you going on about?"

"David and Carolina are my children," Carl-Erik said, his voice not trembling. "I am their father."

Carolina and David had paid the price for his cowardice for all these years, and they had both suffered abysmally. And yet they'd turned out so well. He was so proud of them. The least he could do was to fight an overdue battle with Gustaf, to try to make up for his past failings.

"All of this is your own fault," he continued.

"You can't seriously mean that?" Gustaf said.

"David is my son. What you and Peter and that headmaster did to him and to Carolina . . . At some point you have to take responsibility."

Gustaf took a step closer. "Keep quiet, for fuck's sake."

Carl-Erik blinked. It had always been so easy for him to smooth things over, to take a step back, be the diplomat. He'd always thought that made him a likable person, but the fact was that it just meant he was a coward. When he thought about how David, his son, had taken up the fight in there, it made him stand tall.

"You should be aware that I know why David is doing what he's doing," Carl-Erik said. "And he has my full support."

Gustaf's eyes narrowed. "What do you mean by that?"

"I will make sure he has the support he needs. And I will not put up with your attacking him, not again." On some level Carl-Erik saw that David hardly needed his support. David was strong in a way he had never been. But he was not insignificant, not in the circles Gustaf moved in.

"Is that a threat? Are you threatening me?" Gustaf took a step toward him, but for the first time in his life Carl-Erik did not back down. He couldn't change the past. He would always have to live with that. But he could fight for the future, a future for *all* his children.

He glanced coldly at Gustaf. "It's not a threat. It's information," he said.

Gustaf stared.

And then, for the first time ever, Gustaf backed down.

It was a small victory. But, damn, did it feel good.

62

David ran backward down the grassy playing field. He didn't take his eyes off the soccer ball.

People were shouting all over the bare-bones soccer field in an underprivileged neighborhood outside Stockholm.

"Over here!"

"Pass it!"

"Would you *pass* already?!"

Michel, who was playing wholeheartedly, passed the ball to a gangly teenager who quickly dribbled it toward the opposing team's goal. Tufts of grass flew as Michel ran and shouted and gesticulated every bit as enthusiastically as the other players. Kids of various sizes and body types followed him loudly.

Michel would have made a great soccer player, David thought as he concentrated on following the game. Michel was tall but graceful, and he had as much of a feel for the ball as any professional player. If his family hadn't decided to send him to college, Michel could have played for one of the best teams. David was plenty good, but he was refereeing the game, which ended their practice.

He and Michel were out here every week, year-round, and he genuinely loved it—the kids, the joy of the game, and the competition. He despised most of the sports rich people indulged in—golf, hunting, and sailing. He skied occasionally, and he was an adequate if not very enthusiastic tennis player. But he liked playing soccer with his and Michel's kids best, outside the city, away from Stureplan and the financial sector. Here they were just David and Michel, and the sum of their worth was determined by how well they moved the ball.

After the game, everyone helped gather up all the balls and cones. They chatted with the kids, asked how their parents were, heard about their siblings and cousins and girlfriends, and then finally waved as they biked off home to their apartment buildings.

"That kid is totally out of control," Michel said, nodding toward a big, tall teenager who was swearing at his little brother. "He cusses and hits."

"He's young," David said dismissively. He liked the boy, knew that he was being beaten at home, and hoped he would make it to adulthood intact. David wished he could do more. Maybe they could start some sort of mentoring program . . .

"Is that some kind of excuse for acting like an asshole?" Michel dribbled a ball over and stuffed it into the cloth sack. "That he's young and stupid?"

"Maybe not an excuse," David said. "But it makes sense. Everyone makes mistakes when they're young."

"Mistakes?" Michel scoffed, collecting the last ball. He tossed it to David. "A mess of idiotic screwups more like."

"But didn't you screw up a bunch when you were young?" David asked with a laugh.

Michel shook his head gloomily. "Not as much as I would have liked."

"Oh, he's just a teenager," David maintained, not quite getting what Michel was all worked up about. He picked up a plastic cone. "Give him a chance. A guy that young shouldn't have to be out of the game for good just because he did a few dumb things when he was young, right? Keep your eye on him. He acts tough, but he's just a big kid."

"You think he could change?" Michel said.

"I think it's important that people's lives aren't ruined by things they did when they were young and stupid. Forgiveness has to be possible. Why are you taking this so personally?"

Michel kicked a ball hard to David with a somber look. "On a scale of one to ten, how dumb are you actually?"

David caught the ball. "What do you mean?"

Michel shook his head and handed him a bottle of water. "You have to figure out some things on your own," he said, as they set out for their cars.

Michel got out his key chain and unlocked his car with a sound-less click. David studied their shiny cars, the baby-blue Bentley and Michel's menacingly black BMW, status symbols of how well they'd done. Their flashy cars stood out here on the playing field below the projects like Hollywood wives at a bowling alley. It was a miracle that nobody had messed with them.

"I'm going," Michel said, opening his door and tossing in his bag and the sack of soccer balls.

David didn't ask where Michel was going—Michel had made it clear that he didn't want to discuss his relationship with Åsa—but David was sure that Michel was going to see her now as he hur-ried off.

For some reason it really irked him.

A while later, David pulled onto the highway.

Soccer usually cleared his mind, but not today. He just felt hot and irritable.

He glanced at the time and decided to go home. No one else was still at the office. It was seven-thirty on a Friday night, and even Malin had gone home this afternoon, saying that no one should call her unless it was a matter of life and death.

Preferably not even then.

David and Michel had been snapping at each other all week. He didn't really know why their relationship was so strained. Maybe all the work on Investum had been more taxing than they wanted to admit. Maybe Michel's relationship with Åsa was causing tension be-tween them.

Maybe, maybe, maybe.

Rima Campbell, on the other hand, was a real find. She was already running the company with a firm, expert hand. Hammar Cap-ital wasn't really needed anymore, not for day-to-day operations. Maybe that's what was wrong.

But there was something more, something else bothering him. David knew it. As he zoomed along the highway, he sank back into the same thoughts that had been bothering him all week, thoughts of revenge. Strangely enough, he had never seen himself as a particularly vengeful person. Hard-nosed and goal-oriented, yes. Vengeful, no.

He was sure there were some people who probably wouldn't agree.

Natalia, for example.

He pulled off toward downtown and continued on toward Kungsholmen and home. It was hot and muggy the way it got in late summer. Norr Mälarstrand Boulevard was crawling with people just hanging out, making the most of the last few weeks of summer.

He parked and took the elevator up. He tossed his keys and bag aside, grabbed a beer from the fridge, and then went up to his rooftop terrace.

He drank out of the bottle and looked out at the roofs and the sky. It was light out, and the evenings were still warm, but fall was coming even though no one really wanted to admit it yet.

All the buzz in the press had calmed down. Now he was being described as a new-school finance man: a smart, fair man, a visionary.

He sighed.

If there was one thing he did not feel, it was *smart*.

He looked out at the city.

He'd *shaken hands* with Natalia when they'd said good-bye on Monday. That was possibly the stupidest thing he'd ever done, shaking hands with the woman he loved and then letting her disappear from his life.

They hadn't been in touch since then.

Of course not, why would they be?

He lay awake now at night, staring at his ceiling and wondering what Natalia was up to. Summer wasn't over. She was probably off on a well-deserved vacation, licking her wounds, maybe, with some well-heeled patrician guy who would treat her the way she really deserved to be treated, maybe even that stuffed-shirt Jonas Jägerhed, who navigated all the social codes of the upper class so deftly.

David tried to control the nagging uneasy feelings that welled up in him whenever he thought like this. Natalia with another man. But didn't she deserve that? A man who would treat her like a princess, not destroy her family empire, force her father to disown her, and in-

·directly contribute to her getting fired. No, Natalia De la Grip could probably do with a little laugh right now, he thought.

He sighed again, deeply.

Maybe he should call her. But what would he say? She had every reason to hate him. The things he'd done to her this summer . . .

He'd been so angry for so long. And he'd always thought it was a straightforward emotion, that there was only one way to deal with it, but of course everything was so much more complicated than that.

He leaned over the railing, following the peaks of the rooflines off into the distance with his eyes.

There had been so many possible paths for him to take over the years, so many options. And he'd always chosen decisively, without hesitation. He'd chosen revenge and that had always felt right, given him satisfaction, but this last week had made him question more and more if he hadn't taken a wrong turn somewhere along the way.

He glanced out at the sky and wondered.

There was something rattling around in his head, something Michel had said. But what was it?

He picked up his phone and called.

"What?" Michel answered tersely.

"I was thinking about what you said," David said. "If Carolina could let go, then I need to as well. That's what you meant, right? When we were talking about kids being allowed to make mistakes? Obviously what happened at Skogbacka was more than just a youthful mistake, but you have to move on, right? Not forgive, maybe, but still see the mechanisms that made people act the way they did?"

He fell silent.

His mind was racing so fast that he couldn't keep up. They'd been so young back at Skogbacka, he and Peter and the others. The hazing had been ghastly. The humiliation and the brutality—they had acted like animals. It was entrenched at schools like that, it was practically *expected.* It was inhuman. But was it unforgivable?

Could you forgive something like that?

Should you forgive it?

He didn't believe in forgiveness. But maybe he'd chosen an approach that had forced him to remain stuck in the past. Did he want to stay there?

"Hello?" he said. "Michel? Are you still there?"

Michel exhaled heavily, sort of muffled. "David, I have to hang up. I thought it was something important. I'm really busy right now."

Michel was gone.

David set down his phone. He stared straight ahead. All the platitudes he'd ever heard about revenge—which he'd thought were just platitudes—swam around in his head.

What had happened at Skogbacka, the physical abuse and the rape, that had been . . . He actually didn't have any words. It had quite simply been the worst thing that had happened in his life: His memory of Carolina when they'd found her, knowing that the rape was revenge for his not falling into line. The guilt, which had almost destroyed him. The hatred. That was what had come to define his life. He'd been someone out for revenge, someone who liked the feeling of getting even. That's what had made him who he was today. A man who for the first time didn't like himself. A man who had destroyed the woman he loved.

He pulled a hand over his face, wondered if he ought to get himself another beer, take a shower, read a book—do *something*—but he just stood there.

Caro had moved on and he *hadn't*.

She'd been mad at him all week. It felt weird having Carolina mad at him. She had coolly congratulated him on his takeover. Then she'd chewed him out because she was tired of carrying the burden of knowing he was taking revenge on her behalf, and she'd told him to take his controlling nature and shove it. She had refused to talk to him about Peter De la Grip, and then she'd had coffee with Carl-Erik before going back to Denmark and her *boyfriend*.

But she was right. It had never occurred to him before that his not being able to let go of what had happened was a burden for her. He would stop now, quit being controlling and quit living Caro's life for her.

Weird how hard but also nice it felt not to carry the responsibility for another person on his shoulders anymore. Of course, he should have realized it a long time ago. Carolina had said it—she was an adult.

He stared out at the view.

No, he wasn't particularly smart.

After his talk with Peter, a completely different question had been bothering him: had his takeover of Investum been about more than he'd thought?

Damn it, this was hard to think about.

Strangely enough, he related to Peter, to his struggle to earn his father's approval. What was this takeover about—if not that David wanted to show his own biological father what he was worth? How had he never realized that? He had seen Peter's internal struggle and suddenly realized that it was the same battle he was waging.

And he was so sick of living in the past, so tired of being ruled by old demons. Carolina was right. Natalia was right. Nothing good came from revenge, not in the long term anyway. The short-term triumph and relief were all too quickly replaced by emptiness. If Carolina could move on, then he really ought to be able to as well. Eyes on the future, quit mucking around in the past. Become a better man and person. Find some other purpose in life.

And *if* he could let go . . .

David took a long, shaky breath.

If he could put what had happened behind him, if he could maybe not *forgive* Peter and the others but at least understand. If— and this was almost the biggest if—if he could forgive himself and come to terms with the teenager he'd been, then . . .

David stood up from the railing.

If he could do all that, then he could try to win back Natalia.

Suddenly it was so clear. He wanted Natalia, for real, not as a date or a fling. He loved her in a way he'd never loved anyone before, maybe hadn't even been able to love. His desire for revenge had drowned out everything else. There hadn't been room for other people, and that had left him alone, even though he'd never felt lonely. But when Natalia came into his life, it was like discovering a new dimension of existence. He *wanted* her. And he wanted her to want him, for real, as a man, as *her* man.

He reached for the phone and called Michel again.

"What?" Michel asked, testily.

"I'm never going to be able to forget what happened," David said, filled with a completely new emotion. Natalia wasn't going to make this easy for him. He'd hurt her, over and over again, tricked her. "But I accept that it happened," he said slowly. "It feels completely

unbelievable, but I'm thinking about letting go of what happened
back at Skogbacka. If Carolina can do it, then so can I."

"David?"

"What?" David almost laughed from the euphoria he felt. It was
time now, for him to become the man he wanted to be.

"I'm turning off my phone now."

63

"And how is it that you have time for me today?" Natalia asked, trying to keep the bite out of her voice. "Why aren't you with Michel?"

The question was justified. Åsa had spent every night all week with her lover/boyfriend. Not that she and Åsa usually hung out every night, but her friend had basically been invisible since the shareholders' meeting on Monday. Natalia had never had very many friends, and the takeover of Investum had definitely shaken up her social circle. She couldn't even bear to speculate about what would happen when the murky details of her true parentage became public knowledge. Swedish aristocrats weren't exactly known for fraternizing with disowned illegitimate children.

Basically, she was lonely.

"Michel is having Sunday dinner with his family," Åsa replied.

Wine for her and mineral water for Natalia sat on the table. She pulled the bottle of chardonnay, dripping with condensation, out of the wine cooler and filled her glass before the waiter reached the table.

"Apparently they do that every Sunday," Åsa continued. "But I'm really not ready to meet his mother and father and sisters. And his uncle and cousins." She watched Natalia with wine-glazed eyes. "I think he has about seventy living relatives." She pulled her finger through the droplets on the side of her glass and leaned back in the rattan chair. She stretched her legs and looked at her electric-blue

Italian shoes. Even though she was decidedly tipsy, Åsa looked sexier than Natalia had ever seen her. A white dress, blue shoes, and being in love definitely suited her.

"Who the hell has that many relatives?" Åsa continued, muttering. "It's practically a commune."

Natalia smiled. Åsa had been alone for so long. Seventy relatives was exactly what she needed, even if Åsa would rather buy her clothes from catalogs than have to admit it.

Natalia leaned back as well, allowing herself to relax on the thick cushions and the shiny woven rattan. Even though it was still early, the outdoor seating was packed with tourists, a few city dwellers, and people like her and Åsa, friends chatting over a glass of wine.

Or, in Natalia's case, mineral water.

"How are you feeling?" Åsa asked.

Natalia shrugged. "Hard to say. I assume okay. But the pregnancy is fine and totally normal. The baby is due in March."

"And your family?"

"I don't know." She brought her hand up to her throat automatically, but put it down again. She'd removed her strand of pearls with the family crest. "It feels weird," she continued, because it really did, as if a part of her, the De la Grip part, were being erased. "Like I don't know who I really am." She put her hand on her stomach instead, a gesture she found herself doing more and more and which she liked. It was the two of them now, her and the tiny fetus in there. She wasn't showing yet, but her clothes were fitting tighter, and this new protective instinct that came in waves surprised her with its strength every time.

In a way she'd already become a mother.

She still hadn't heard a peep from her own mother. They'd hardly spoken at the shareholders' meeting, and after that it had been dead quiet. Natalia had called. And called. But there was nothing more she could do. You couldn't force someone to love you unconditionally, not even a parent. This wasn't the first time her mother had given her the silent treatment. The question was whether it would wear off or if it was permanent this time. She had a hard time imagining her mother never wanting to see her again, never wanting to meet her grandchild, but there was a lot she had trouble imagining, and it had all happened anyway, so you never knew.

A long time ago, when Natalia was ten and Alex nine, their mom had gotten angry. Natalia couldn't even remember why anymore. It had been summer, and her mother had left home in a snit. Their father was away as usual and Peter, too. Natalia had been a little scared, but her ten-year-old self had assumed her mother would come back, maybe not for Natalia but at least for Alexander, her favorite child. But her mother didn't come, not that whole night, and Natalia had been scared to death. Alex had been so scared that he got sick. She wondered if that's where that sense had originated from, that sense that she was unimportant and unworthy when it really mattered.

Her mother came home the next morning, and Natalia knew that was the moment she had learned that her mother's needs came first. But strangely enough, as an adult she still hadn't thought her mother would do this, freeze her out cold now that she was expecting a child. She should have known better.

She wondered if Alex remembered that night. That through some unspoken agreement they'd decided not to call anyone. Natalia had lain down in his bed and comforted him even though she was terrified herself. Strange that she had almost forgotten the whole thing. She lamented her mother and the sense that the woman always loved herself most. She lamented a great many things. Still, new realities popped up that you had to deal with, and old ones resurfaced—for example, she still had no idea who her birth father was and obviously hadn't been able to ask her mother about it either. Her brothers were half brothers, secrets that others had known but not her. But still, in the middle of all this . . .

"What?" Åsa asked.

"I feel free," Natalia said. "Free from expectations, free from needing to act a certain way to fit in. Free, plain and simple."

Åsa shook her head. "This is the strangest summer I've ever experienced," she said, watching a couple of girls walking along with their arms around each other. "I mean, I thought *my* life was dramatic. And now there are dead sisters who aren't dead and secret fathers turning up right and left. Deceit and drama." She shook her head so her curls bounced. "And what Peter did at the shareholders' meeting. I'm never going to forget that. It was like a TV show or something."

"Yeah," Natalia agreed. The financial papers were still full of column after column of analyses and speculations.

"Have you heard anything else from Peter?" Åsa asked.

"No," Natalia replied. "He's just disappeared. Alex—who, by the way, is the only person in the family I'm still in touch with—thinks he's traveling. I actually have no idea." She made a face. "But Louise, on the other hand, sent out a group e-mail saying she was thinking about getting a divorce."

"I got that, too," Åsa said. "What about your mom? Have you talked to her?"

Natalia shook her head. "No."

"She's always done stuff like this, though, hasn't she?" Åsa asked, concerned.

"Yes," Natalia said hastily, because she didn't want to talk any longer about her collapsing family.

"You'll manage, but your father needs me," was the last thing her mother had said to her at the shareholders' meeting, and they hadn't spoken since, not even once. Alexander had told her in a text message that her parents had packed up and taken off to the estate in France. If Alex hadn't been in touch, she wouldn't have even known that. She would have suspected, of course, if for no other reason than what the papers said. The storm of criticism had been merciless.

She hadn't seen it herself, but apparently someone had leaked a movie to YouTube. A movie that showed still images of Gustaf De la Grip in various contexts all edited together into a montage. But it wasn't the pictures that had caused the scandal, it was the *sound*, because the soundtrack to the YouTube movie was composed of real clips from Gustaf's outburst after the shareholders' meeting. Anyone who wanted to could listen to Gustaf De la Grip's racial slurs over and over again. The movie spread at a speed that gave the word "viral" a new meaning. It had even been translated, Alex said. Natalia hadn't seen it, of course, but she believed him.

Gustaf had bowed out of all his positions in the Swedish finance world, effective immediately. He'd hurriedly retired and then apparently fled the country, she guessed. He would never recover from this. He was done both in the finance world and in his own noble social circles—circles where you could say whatever you wanted about women, even in public, but never, never anything racist. There wouldn't be any more hunting or fancy dinners with the king, no invitations or honorary duties. He'd brought about his own downfall, and it was going to be quite a tumble.

She knew that Gustaf had only himself to blame, but she couldn't help but feel a little sorry for both him and her mother. Neither of them was particularly well equipped for what had happened. The whole thing was so stupid. Stupid but unavoidable.

"How's everything with Michel?" Natalia asked instead, because thinking about her family was really getting her down. She'd had a big family, and now suddenly she had none. "With the two of you, I mean?"

"Good. We don't discuss the future at all, which is nice. I'm not so good at the future. But *he's* good." Åsa grinned and squirmed on her seat cushion. "Very good. I mean really, very, very . . ."

"Thanks," Natalia interrupted her quickly. "I get it. I don't need any details."

She was happy for Åsa of course. But also a little envious.

She sipped her water pensively.

She wished she'd dared to be honest with David when they'd seen each other on Monday. But that would've been hard since she wasn't even being honest with herself. She didn't have the guts to stand up for what she wanted. This was her life's trauma and weakness, the fear that she wasn't worth loving for who she was. Why else would her mother have such an easy time leaving her? And Jonas? She quite simply wasn't a woman people chose to fight for. She was easy to leave. Maybe there was something about her that wasn't worth loving, a shortcoming she wasn't aware of but that other people could perceive?

She shook her head, refusing to sink into self-pity.

"Natalia, honey," Åsa said, putting a hand on hers. Her signature heirloom gold chain sparkled. "You *have* to tell him about the baby, you realize that, don't you?"

"Yeah, I guess so," Natalia sighed, not at all convinced that that was what she had to do. "But did you know David's like you?" she continued. "He doesn't want kids." She looked at Åsa, raised an eyebrow, and said, "If someone came to you and said you were going to be a parent, would *you* be happy?"

Åsa looked guilty. "Maybe not super happy," she admitted, but then she waved her hand demonstratively at Natalia's belly. "But this is different."

Natalia shook her head. It wasn't different at all, and she didn't have the least desire to be rejected by David one more time.

Åsa raised her bottle out of the wine cooler and saw that it was empty. "Oh, what the hell." She motioned to the waiter to bring another. "I don't need to go back to work tomorrow," she said wryly. "The office is a shambles. Hammar Capital's people swept in like a biblical plague of frogs. Heads are rolling pretty much nonstop. I can't take the drama, so I'm taking some vacation time. I guess I'll have to resign, but I like Rima, and I promised to stay as long as she needs me."

Natalia nodded in agreement. You couldn't have a company lawyer who was involved with someone on the board of directors. "What are you going to do instead?"

Åsa shrugged. "I'm thinking about doing something totally new, but first Michel and I are going to get away somewhere."

She lapsed into a monologue about Michel's general awesomeness, and Natalia permitted herself to drift off for a moment. She'd never seen Åsa so happy, and naturally she was thrilled for her, but it was also a little hard. Åsa beamed like a sun most of the time now, and sometimes all that beaming got to be a bit much.

Natalia nodded, smiled, and let herself slowly drift off, listening to the babble in the restaurant, to Åsa's happy voice, and thinking that maybe, maybe, she would get through all this. It's not like people should feel sorry for her. To the contrary, life had given her more than most people.

She had always thought that she'd earned most of her success, but the fact was that it had all really just been luck. She'd had the good luck to be born into wealth, had received a good education, security, and a nice life. She was grateful for it. And surely it was too much to hope for more than she already had.

She didn't need the love of her parents or a man to survive. She would manage. And someday, eventually, it would stop hurting. You could get used to anything.

And then she looked up, and there he stood.

His dark hair looked fresh from the shower. His eyes were serious, his lips pursed; he wore jeans and a white T-shirt, had sunglasses in his hand, a stainless-steel watch on his arm, nothing more.

So freaking handsome.

Her scalp started tingling as if someone were sticking tiny nails into it. Her mouth went dry. The nausea she had managed to hold in check so far, thanks to the shade, water, and ice cubes, came surging up.

David.

Shit.

64

David stood perfectly still. He couldn't take his eyes off Natalia. She was sitting under an umbrella in the patio seating area and watching him with those intelligent eyes of hers.

Maybe it was fate that they were meeting like this. Maybe it was coincidence.

Or maybe he'd known exactly where she would be.

She was surrounded by that light that always seemed to emanate from her, wearing black linen slacks and a blouse that left her arms totally bare, black sandals, and those long, long legs. Everything, every last thing about her was perfect.

Perfect, and also something else.

David couldn't quite put his finger on what was different about Natalia, but something was. Her posture, maybe? Or the fact that she was dressed all in black? It was a dramatic color and it suited her. Made her look wild and strong.

David started walking toward her. Only then did he notice Åsa, blind as he was to her and to everyone else when Natalia was around.

Åsa fired him a sour look, raised a hand, and waved her fingers lazily at him.

"Hi," David said once he made it over to them.

Natalia raised her head and looked at him. Her golden eyes, serious and unfathomable, looked right at him, not backing down, and he was struck by a strangely unreal feeling, as if the whole world had tipped a few degrees. It was all or nothing now. Åsa said hello, but David hardly noticed her, vaguely aware that he was being rude, but unable to do anything but look at Natalia. She was drumming a finger on the table. Her nails were dark and glossy, almost black actually, and he got the sense that she wasn't planning on making this easy for him.

Good, he had so much adrenaline in his body that it was booming in his ears. He needed a real battle, one that he was planning to win.

Åsa leaned back in her wicker chair. She put an arm on her armrest and in a downright nasty tone said, "Mr. Hammar. Out for a little Sunday stroll?"

"Among other things," he said, his eyes still locked on Natalia. At no point had losing ground to Åsa Bjelke entered his plans. "I'd like to speak to Natalia," he said. "Alone."

Åsa stared at him. This was a woman to whom princes and the press bowed. She wasn't used to anything else. "You're kidding, right?" she said.

David temporarily glanced at her. He was essentially her boss, *owned* her, and he didn't have the patience to be distracted from what he was planning. "Do I *look* as if I'm kidding?"

Åsa scrutinized him. But she was wise, bit her tongue, picked up her purse with an exaggerated sigh, and asked Natalia, "Is it okay if I go?" She glared at David. "And leave you alone with him?"

Natalia nodded. "Yeah. Thanks," she said, and added, "Sorry."

Åsa rolled her eyes. "*You* don't have anything to apologize for."

Åsa stood up, elegant as always, and squeezed her way past David. She stared him squarely in the eye and—with the help of her curves, her deadpan expression, and expensive perfume—managed to communicate very clearly that he might, technically speaking, be her boss, but he ought to be very careful. "Adios," she said and left, sashaying out, with the eyes of every man in the place on her.

Except for David's.

Because David saw only Natalia.

Natalia made a quick gesture toward the empty chair, like a queen granting an audience. David exhaled. The noise around them returned, and he vaguely noted the clinking of glasses and the murmur of conversation.

"Have a seat," Natalia said, and then added tartly, "It's not taken."

He sat down, waved to a waiter, and ordered more mineral water for them both.

"How are you doing?" he asked.

She gave a faint smile, poked at a drip of water sliding through the condensation on the glass. "Well, you know," she said. "Not much has been happening."

He laughed at her obvious untruth, and even more importantly at the fact that she was joking at all. A sense of humor was good. "How are things with your family?" he asked.

She became serious. "Well, they've been better."

"I'm sorry," he said and meant it. Naturally he knew all about the YouTube movie, about her parents fleeing the country, and her family's general collapse, because no one could have missed that.

David hadn't confronted his managing director, but he knew Rima Campbell's sons were very active on social media, and he remembered how strategically her phone had been placed during the now-famous meeting. If she'd recorded Gustaf's outburst and if her sons had then made a movie out of it that crushed Gustaf for good, about that he could only speculate. In his eyes justice had been done, and the old patriarch had brought about his own downfall.

David had never wanted to hurt Natalia in any way, and yet that was precisely what he'd done. Regardless of how things went today, he would have to start thinking about his future in the financial sector. He couldn't have any more things like this on his conscience. "I'm really sorry."

"Thanks," she said simply. "And you? How's it going with Investum?"

"It's going well. You haven't changed your mind?"

She slowly shook her head. "No, I'm done with Investum," she said. "Totally done."

Her hand lay on the table. Glossy dark nails and light skin. David looked up and around the patio, tried to collect his thoughts and steel himself for the storm of feelings she roused in him. How could he ever have been so dumb—so *idiotic*—as to think he could remain unaffected when it came to this woman? Everything about her drew him in. The hair on her arms stood up, and his did as well. He saw and felt it.

"I've been thinking about what you said," David began. "About my . . ."—he cleared his throat awkwardly—". . . father."

She cocked her head and said, "Yes?"

"My dad," David said and stopped again. Fuck, it was going to take a while before he felt comfortable having an official, alive-and-kicking father.

"Carl-Erik and I have talked," he began again. "Several times. There's going to be a piece about us in a magazine, where I presume we'll come out—as father and son. We agree now. He's my father. He's a widower, and I even met his daughters. We had coffee together."

Meeting the two legitimate daughters had actually been unexpectedly pain-free.

She smiled. "Your half sisters?"

"Exactly."

"How were they?"

"Sweet. They laughed a lot. They're a lot like Carolina. She is thrilled, by the way."

Natalia watched him. "That sounds nice," she said, and something glistened at the corners of her eyes. He identified it quickly. Natalia was moved. He hoped that was good.

"Apparently we own a castle in Skåne—my family does, I mean," he said.

She laughed. "I can just picture you as lord of the manor."

"You can?" he asked skeptically. Personally he had a hard time seeing himself as someone who lived in a castle. He wasn't even sure he liked the outdoors.

But Natalia nodded, and he thought that for the sake of this woman he could learn to like grass and animals and woods. If it made her happy, he would do it, because that was all he wanted—for Natalia to be happy.

Of course, he'd bailed out Gyllgarn for her, the yellow castle she loved as if it were a person. Regardless of what happened between them, she would get it back. It was owned by a trust now, and there were some practical details left to work out, but essentially Natalia would get to decide about everything that pertained to Gyllgarn. He was lucky he'd been able to arrange it, he thought. Otherwise he would have been forced to stage yet another takeover.

"I was thinking . . . ," he began, approaching his goal.

"Yes?" Her voice was calm, cool. She was a businesswoman who was used to tough negotiations, an intrepid talent who got back up, over and over again. He couldn't afford any mistakes if he was going to win her.

"If you don't want me here because of who I am, because of what I've done, then I'll respect that," he said.

Her hands were completely still on her knee. She glanced down at them, and her dark eyelashes fluttered. She was immobile, and David's brain reminded him over and over again: *Don't lose her, whatever you do.*

For a bit he'd thought he had a chance. She'd seemed happy and a little breathless, but now she seemed less open. He kept going, his heart pounding like a sledgehammer against the inside of his ribs. This was the hardest thing he'd ever done. It felt as if there wouldn't be any more chances besides this one, and he had so desperately little to offer.

"I can't undo anything," he said quietly. "And maybe I've already messed everything up." He put his hand on the table where hers had just been.

"I want to apologize," he said. "For everything I've done to you, for tricking you, for saying things, for doing things—to you and to your family."

"Thanks," she said, but he couldn't read from that short word how she was feeling.

"I can't take back anything I've said or done," he continued. "And a lot of what we experienced together, I would never want to take back. The time I spent with you, Natalia . . ." Here he had to stop and breathe.

She glanced up at him.

"When we saw each other that first time . . . I can't explain it, but I've never felt the way I felt about you with anyone else. I know I behaved badly. I *know* that, but you have to believe me when I say that I never intended to hurt you. And what we shared—that wasn't part of some plan on my part, quite the opposite. It was the most authentic, genuine thing I've ever been part of."

Her eyelashes fluttered again.

"I don't know what to think," she said. "You have a dangerous reputation."

"I know. Some of it's true, of course. But I've never intentionally hurt someone—it's all just been business."

"All of it?"

"Yes, even Investum. In the end it was just business."

"But the other people?"

"I actively sought them out and took revenge on them for messing with my family," he said. "But just by beating them at business deals, not through violence, not through humiliation. I can't take back what I've done, but I accept responsibility for it."

"My dad said you slept with someone's wife, and I read that you tore down someone's house. That sounds awfully personal, not like something that was just business."

"I agree, but it's not true either. I wound up in bed with a divorced woman, and I let that worm-eaten house be torn down. I'm not a saint, but I'm not some revenge-crazed demon, either."

"Not anymore, you mean," she said.

He shook his head. "Not ever," he said, and that was the truth. He'd acted with a heavy hand, bordering on ruthless, but he'd never crossed the line. He'd never been so thankful for that as he was now. He planned never to lie to Natalia again; he'd made himself that promise.

"I don't know how you feel about me," he continued. "But I want you to know something. I need to say this."

She glanced up at him and said, "What?"

"I love you," he said.

She swallowed. "You do?" she whispered.

"Yes," he replied, simply.

Her hands didn't move, but at least she was still sitting in the chair.

"But you hate my family," she said.

And David felt triumph within.

Natalia was raising obstacles. That was good. He was used to overcoming obstacles. That was his area of expertise.

"I'm tired of hating," he said. "You were right all along. Revenge fossilizes you. I don't want to fossilize. I love you," he said again. There shouldn't be any doubt whatsoever that he really meant it.

"But it would never work," she said. "I want to be able to see my mother, my brothers. How do you think that . . ."

"I would never stop you from seeing your family. I would drive you there. And I would sit and smile and chat and be however polite you wanted. Or I could wait in the car. I would do whatever you wanted."

He raised his hand, placed it on top of hers. They sat that way for a little while before she cautiously turned her hand so they were palm to palm. He squeezed her hand gently, trying to convey through hand pressure and skin contact just how much she meant to him, just how hard he would try not to hurt her again. "I know how important your family is to you," he said.

"I don't know," she said hesitantly.

She had doubts, but she hadn't said no.

He leaned forward, took hold of her other hand as well, and pulled both to him. "What don't you know?" he asked softly. "Tell me. Give me a chance to earn your trust."

She looked him right in the eyes. She was so close that David could see those golden flecks in her irises. If she just leaned forward a tiny bit, he could kiss her.

"I'm pregnant," she said steadily, her voice not trembling in the least.

David stopped.

Well, he hadn't seen *that* ball coming.

"I'm sorry?"

Natalia pulled her hands back and placed them on her knee again.

"I'm pregnant," she said calmly and added, as if there could be any misunderstanding, "with your child."

David blinked, slightly dazed.

"How far along are you?" he finally asked. He didn't actually have any idea about weeks and all that business, but the question seemed as good as any.

"Eight weeks. And I'm planning to keep it," she said, belligerence coloring her voice, giving it strength and resonance.

Something started to come loose and break apart inside David, and he knew it would just keep going.

This was what he'd seen, this strength. Natalia was going to be a magnificent mother.

"But you said you couldn't get pregnant," he reminded her.

"Yes," she said slowly. "But apparently nature is unreliable in this regard." She tilted her head slightly. "How do you feel? Are you mad?"

Mad? David didn't really know how to describe the feelings that welled up inside him, but *mad* didn't come close.

"You should have told me sooner," he said. "I should have known. And you shouldn't have had to be alone with this."

She smiled wanly.

And he knew. There was a now for them, and there would be a later. There was a later for him and Natalia, and that meant he could lift mountains if he wanted to.

Something spread through his body.

A feeling he hadn't known he could feel.

Happiness.

"I want to have kids," Natalia said, as if to remove any potential doubt about what she wanted. But David had no doubt.

He smiled. "Obviously this matter is already settled," he said and decisively took her hand again. He squeezed it, and this time she squeezed back.

"I very much want to have this child," he said.

"Okay," she said. Her voice was a little dopey-sounding, as if she was having trouble catching up. He decided to take advantage of that.

"Was there anything else?" he asked.

"Huh?" She looked at him, confused, and squeezed his hand, hard. Her eyes were enormous.

"Is there anything else stopping us?" he asked.

"Stopping us?"

"From becoming a couple."

She looked at him with that look that always found its way inside him, and David didn't dare breathe.

Natalia didn't say anything. She furrowed her brow and looked away.

"Natalia?"

"Yes?"

"Do you love me?"

She looked back at him again.

"Yes," she said simply. "I love you."

David exhaled an enormous breath. He felt himself dissolving into a smile, a joyous grin that spread across his whole face and might never go away.

Natalia loved him—thank goodness. He squeezed her hand and planned not to ever let it go.

She sniffled. "And now I think I'm probably going to start crying," she continued. "I hardly ever used to cry, before, but now I do it all the time. Hormones, you know."

"Okay," David said, his voice trembling a little.

"Yes," she said, her voice not trembling at all.

He lifted her hand and kissed it for a long time. Natalia put a hand on his cheek, and he breathed in the scent of her. There wasn't anyone else, just the two of them. He leaned over and her lips met his. It was a new kiss, a for-real kiss about serious things and the future.

And everything was perfect.

65

"Hi, sorry you had to wait, but I'll see you now. Come on in."

Natalia stood up, straightened her purse over her shoulder, and followed the assistant into a brightly colored office. She'd never been here before, but she recognized the room number from several magazine articles. Its occupant often posed for photos here.

Meg Sandberg, with her bright-red hair and purple jacket, smiled and shook her hand. "I'm glad you could come. Are you done considering?"

Natalia nodded.

"And?"

"I'm very flattered by your offer. I have tremendous faith in my abilities, but what made up my mind is that I'd have you as a mentor." Natalia smiled at Meg and added, "I've always admired you."

"I'm so pleased. You should know that you were my first choice for this position."

"Yes, so I heard."

"When the headhunters said you were interested, there was no one else I wanted."

"Yes, you made an offer very quickly," Natalia said.

"Working for me is going to be different from working for J-O or for Gustaf."

"I know."

"Well then, welcome aboard."

And so it was decided. Natalia had a new job.

She was the new major accounts manager at Nordbank, one of the two largest banks in Sweden. Without asking anyone for advice, without hesitating, and without knowing whether she might be suffering from delusions of grandeur, she'd accepted this unbelievably prestigious, demanding position. Because it was a really high-level job, she thought, as Meg shook her hand again and smiled at her with those bright-red lips. A significant step up, considering how young she still was. Not to mention that she'd be part of the bank's managerial team, responsible for almost a fifth of the bank's earnings, with fifteen hundred employees reporting to her, and would answer directly to this fantastic boss, managing director Meg Sandberg. Basically, it was a job a lot of people would kill for.

"I'm looking forward to an inspiring collaboration," Meg said.

"Same here."

"Then I'll see you in two weeks. What will you be doing in the meantime?" Meg asked as she walked Natalia to the door.

Natalia smiled. "I'm getting married." She glanced at her watch. "In just a few hours, actually."

Later that same day Natalia stepped out of the shower, dried herself, and rubbed on lotion before pulling on her new French underwear. She carefully undid the cotton fabric that the hairdresser had wrapped around her head to protect her freshly styled hair.

"Do you want to see it?" she asked Åsa, who was sipping champagne and lounging in an armchair. Åsa had already changed, and she looked even more stunning than usual, in a knee-length Elie Saab dress in cool colors. Lebanese things suited Åsa, Natalia thought to herself, in more ways than one. They'd spent the last few hours getting their hair and makeup done before returning to the suite David had reserved for her, the finest suite the Grand Hôtel had, complete with complimentary champagne, a Jacuzzi, and a 360-degree view of Stockholm.

Natalia carefully opened the protective cover that surrounded her wedding dress. She held the dress up so Åsa could admire the craftsmanship.

"It's amazing," Åsa said breathlessly and without any hint of sarcasm.

"Like a dream," Natalia agreed.

The lines were clean and timeless. The dressmaker's studio had worked hard to get it ready in just four weeks. Small covered buttons, details in the finest Solstiss lace, and a masterful cut made it a world-class work of art.

"Any princess in the world would want to wear that," Åsa said. "And the shoes," she continued, staring covetously at the accompanying shoebox. "Lord almighty, those would be exactly my size if I cut off a couple toes." She moaned at the slender, high-heeled creations. "I'm *dying* of jealousy."

Natalia hung the dress up on a hanger over a door frame.

Åsa refilled her champagne while Natalia stood in front of a mirror and started touching up her lip gloss.

Suddenly they were enveloped in silence.

"I'm doing the right thing, aren't I?" Natalia asked. She bit her lower lip. She hadn't planned to say anything, but now the words were out there.

Åsa sat up. "What?"

Natalia stared into the mirror, and her own serious face stared back. Was she doing the right thing? It had happened so fast. David absolutely wanted to get married before the baby came, and given his sensitive history, she understood. And she was vain enough that she preferred to get married before she was a blimp, so it was going to happen like this: the wedding at the Grand Hôtel with just their closest friends present, dinner, and then a brief honeymoon. She and David were flying to Nice tomorrow. They would rent a car and then spend ten days in the French Riviera. Maybe it was cheesy, but she'd always dreamed of doing that, and September was the perfect time. But she and David had only known each other for two and a half months. What if she was making the mistake of her life?

"*Now* you get wedding jitters!" Åsa said, sipping champagne. "Whatever happened to 'Åsa, I've never been so sure about anything in my entire life'? Because that's all you've been saying the last few weeks." She leaned back again, and the pale colors in her dress shimmered in the autumn sun. "Although I'm glad you're having a little bit of cold feet. Marriage is actually a ghastly idea. I'm certainly never going to get married."

"Don't say that," Natalia said, stopping, her hand in midair. "Not now. You're against marriage? Am I making a mistake? Åsa?" She wondered if she were experiencing some sort of hysteria.

"Probably. But you learn from your mistakes. Or so I hear."

"Ugh, I can't focus," Natalia said, going back to studying herself somberly in the mirror. She fluffed up her hair and straightened her new underwear before putting on the dress. "You're not much support."

"I know, but I love you," said Åsa, getting up. "And I really want what's best for you," she continued, holding up the dress while Natalia carefully stepped into it. It was a short dress that came down to her knees, simple lines, but still very definitely a wedding dress.

"But?"

"No buts. This *is* what's best, that's what I mean. It doesn't get any better than this." Åsa started buttoning the small buttons down Natalia's spine. "I've never seen two people love and respect each other as much as you two do." Åsa wobbled a little, and Natalia heard fabric stretched dangerously tight.

"Are you drunk?"

"A little. Now stand still."

Natalia stood still while Åsa buttoned the tiny buttons, muttering to herself.

"My mom hasn't answered any of my messages," Natalia said over her shoulder as Åsa concentrated on the last button. "She's not coming."

"That's really sad."

Natalia nodded. It stung.

"And I assume there hasn't been any word about your biological father?"

"No."

She was going to have to deal with that, Natalia thought, but there were so many things changing right now, she could hardly keep up.

"I got the job," she said instead, turning to look in the mirror and playing a little bit with a loose strand of hair.

Åsa sank back down into the armchair again. She filled her glass and raised it as if for a toast. At this rate Natalia's maid of honor was going to be soused.

"Congratulations," Åsa said. "At least a dozen men are going to be seriously pissed off that you got that specific job. I love it when you outdo those finance boys. You're a real role model."

Natalia nodded, pleased.

It had been unsettling to shake hands with the powerful Meg, who had the energy of a blowtorch. And a little bizarre that she'd said yes so quickly. Afterward, she'd gone straight to the bathroom and thrown up.

Although of course that could have been because of the pregnancy.

"I'm starting right after we get home and working for as long as I can," she said, studying her wedding hairdo. The stylist had left some loose strands hanging and wound the rest of Natalia's hair in a loose knot. A minimal headpiece with a veil, hardly more than a whisper of white, rested at an angle in her shiny locks. It was flat with a small veil over half her forehead. "The baby's supposed to come in March. We'll split the parental leave fifty-fifty."

"Well, if it's good enough for the crown princess and her husband, who am I to think it sounds bourgeois?" Åsa said.

Natalia smiled. She was ready. "What do you think?" she said, turning around. The dress was slim and opulent-looking, the shoes adult and glamorous. A new era was starting now, and she wanted that to show.

"You look amazing," Åsa said. "But I want you to promise me something now." A stubborn look came over her face. "Promise you won't say no."

"What are you talking about?"

"Do you promise?" Åsa got up and came over to her.

"Okay . . . ," Natalia said, skeptical. She loved Åsa, but you never knew what Åsa was going to come up with next.

Åsa took off her gold bracelet, the one she always wore, the one that was her most treasured possession from her mother, and held it out. "I want you to have this," she said.

Natalia knew that Åsa slept with the bracelet on. If you Googled "sentimental value" you would get a picture of Åsa's mom's gold bracelet. "But . . . ," Natalia said and then stopped. Because what could she say, actually?

"You're my family," Åsa said. "Without you there wouldn't be anything, nothing would have worked. I want you to have this. It was my mom's and now if you have a daughter, she can inherit it. Will you promise me that?"

Natalia nodded and swallowed with a lump in her throat, holding out her arm. Åsa clasped the bracelet around her wrist. It was still warm from Åsa's body heat, and Natalia blinked rapidly to stop her tears. Åsa's eyes were also suspiciously damp-looking.

There was a knock on the door, and they both turned toward it, relieved at the interruption. They were never going to be very good at big emotional moments, she and Åsa, but they didn't need to be.

The door opened. David stood in the doorway and did what he always did—just looked at her. Maybe it wasn't super polite, but it was terribly flattering.

And he looked so good that Natalia stopped breathing.

"Wow," she said, admiring him and his broad shoulders in the dark-gray three-piece suit that fit like it had been sewn onto him, a lighter vest, and a white boutonniere.

David's eyes misted up as he came over to her. "I don't know what to say." His voice was unsteady as he visually feasted on her. "You look incredible."

"*You* look incredible," Natalia said quietly and tried not to eat him up with her eyes.

Åsa made some sort of retching sound.

David smiled. "Do you two want to see the ring?"

The two women nodded eagerly. Everything had happened so fast that Natalia hadn't even gotten an engagement ring yet. Now she was curious, because David had asked if he could pick out the combined engagement and wedding ring himself. He opened the box.

Natalia and Åsa gaped.

It was a modern ring, square and bold, with clean lines. A yellow stone, yellow like daffodils and sunshine and much too big to be a diamond, sparkled in the middle, surrounded by white stones.

"It's a yellow diamond," David explained.

"A diamond?" Natalia said, dumbfounded. It was as large as the nail on her index finger.

"Conflict free," he added, looking exceedingly satisfied. "Because

I know that's important to you. I won an auction and practically snatched it out from under a king's nose."

He grinned. "It's possible that I may be unwelcome in a certain Arabian monarchy for the rest of my life."

"Okay," Natalia said, actually almost speechless. She hadn't known that rings or stones like this even existed.

"Respect," Åsa said.

"Natalia?" David asked.

"Yes?"

"Give me back the ring. You'll have to wait for the ceremony."

"I'm not sure I can part with it," she said, but reluctantly set it back in the palm of his hand.

David stuffed the ring back in the box and then put it in his pocket.

"I have to take care of one last thing," he said. "Are you going with her?" he asked Åsa, who waved her hand in response. "I'll see you out there," he said, kissing Natalia on the cheek and leaving.

"Isn't he wonderful?" Natalia asked.

Åsa shrugged a silk-clad shoulder. "If you like super-gorgeous, super in-love billionaires, I guess." She smiled. "You make a really beautiful couple. You look like you just stepped right out of an old movie. Come on, just one glass of champagne would be fine for the baby. I read that in *Vogue*."

When Natalia and Åsa came down to the nineteenth-century salon, which the hotel's florist had filled with roses, the justice of the peace was waiting for them, along with Michel and David's family. Count Carl-Erik Tessin, serious in his conservative suit, pulled Natalia into an embrace. The three blond women at his side, Carolina and her two half sisters, laughed and hugged her.

Natalia smiled but squeezed her bridal bouquet of orange blossoms and orchids harder than necessary. She was happy, of course, but she wished someone from her family had come to the wedding. And then David walked into the room and had yet another guest with him.

Alexander.

Her brother came over to her. She saw a bruise on his chin, but he was all smiles, brushing aside her worried questions and giving her a firm hug.

"I didn't even know you were in town," she said, half-squished in his embrace.

"I wasn't," he said dryly. "But your future husband can be very persuasive. Especially since he apparently has some kind of mercenary and a helicopter at his disposal."

"You came by helicopter?"

"We landed just outside of Stockholm's Old Town twenty minutes ago," he said, muttering something that might have been "the fucking psychopath."

"David did it for me," Natalia said with a laugh. "Now be nice."

"I'm always nice," Alex said. He scanned the room, and his eyes lingered on Carolina. "Is that her?" he asked softly.

Natalia nodded.

"Are you ready?" David asked. Alexander released her and moved over to join the other guests.

David reached out his hand and grazed her shoulder, brushed aside a lock of hair, as if he couldn't help touching her. He held out his arm, and Natalia put her hand into the crook of his elbow. Together they turned to face the justice of the peace.

She was so grateful that she'd said yes to that original lunch invitation, she thought. That she had dared. It reminded her of something Åsa had said, but she couldn't quite remember what. She heard music from far away. She looked at the guests, feeling so incredibly thankful.

And then, somewhere in the middle of the wedding ceremony, Natalia remembered what Åsa had said on that day in June when it had all begun.

A life without risk is no life at all.

Natalia peered at the handsome, solemn man who would soon be her husband, and she couldn't help but smile.

Her life—summed up in a cliché from a paper coffee cup.

The justice of the peace concluded the ceremony, smiled at them both, and pronounced them man and wife. And then, before she knew what was happening, David swept her up in an enormous hug. It was a tight hug that turned into a hard kiss which in turn became so passionate that the guests started whistling and applauding. And Natalia let herself be swept away, let her husband kiss her until she was breathless, and knew that this was right. It was the two of them forever now, because this was the love of her life, until death did them part, in sickness and in health. And she thought that sometimes life *was* a cliché. How did the saying go?

When life showers you with blessings, smile.

Epilogue

One week later

Isobel Sørensen was at the airport.
Again.

Sometimes she was struck by a strange, unreal feeling, as if she were at the same airport over and over again all the time, without ever leaving. Other times, like today, she felt like she'd been on enough flights to last a whole lifetime.

She stopped to study the departures board and then sensed someone next to her, at exactly the right distance to avoid being pushy, and yet close enough that she would know he wanted to be noticed.

"What a coincidence. Are you going to New York too?" he asked.

Isobel felt a surge of irritation. Even without turning around, she knew who it was. She recognized that arrogant upper-class voice.

Alexander De la Grip.

"I just went to my sister's wedding," he continued, carrying on his conversation without seeming to care that she was ignoring him.

She thought about walking away, just leaving him there to try to hit on her without her. She didn't owe him any politeness. But she'd liked his sister, the unexpectedly pregnant Natalia, and she was tired of walking, and she had a lot of time to kill before her flight, so she just stood there.

"Love," he continued what by now would have to be described as a monologue. He put so much scorn into that word that Isobel found herself smiling despite herself.

"Love makes people do worse things than even religion," he stated.

Isobel had no objections to that. Love, religion, fanaticism—they were depressingly similar, so she was inclined to agree with him. Weird. She would never have thought she could have anything in common with a man like this jet-set prince.

She'd browsed several magazines on the plane here. There had been pictures of him in at least two of them. He'd been surrounded by women, eyes glazed from alcohol and maybe something more. He should watch out, she'd thought with a grain of cynical schaden-freude. She'd seen people die of liver failure, and it wasn't very pretty.

On the other hand, death was *never* pretty. It was nasty, sad, and horrifically unfair, no matter what anyone said.

Alexander had stopped talking, but Isobel could sense that he was still standing there behind her. She assumed he was on her flight to New York. She studied the departures board. It was leaving in exactly sixty-four minutes. He would surely be sitting in first class with its chilled champagne, warm washcloths, and obsequious flight atten-dants. There were no words for how much she despised men like him. Even if she had to admit to herself that he was one of the hand-somest men she'd ever seen. Handsome in that way that attracted both women and men, young and old. Apart from his eyes, that was. She'd noticed when he'd run into her the last time, in Båstad. She tried to remember where she'd seen eyes like that before.

"Love really messes life up," he interrupted her thoughts. "Did you know it's a modern invention? Love, I mean."

Even though that sounded familiar, she didn't say anything. She didn't share his need to hear herself talk all the time.

"So, are you going to New York?" he asked, clearly unaffected by her reticence. "Then we can keep each other company. Can I buy you a drink beforehand? They have a decent chardonnay here, actually."

Isobel shook her head.

Because now she remembered where she'd seen eyes like Alexan-der De la Grip's. Actually she saw them all the time. She turned around quickly, gasping a little for breath at having his dazzling good looks so close.

"I'm not going to New York," she said curtly. She looked into those blue eyes, eyes that were in no way angelic. "I'm going to Africa." She started to walk away. She felt him staring at her back, and she sped up.

Isobel met so many people through her work who had survived war and torture, people who had seen horrors that no one should have to see. And even if the wounds healed and were no longer outwardly visible, you always saw it in their eyes if you knew how to look.

She sped up even more. That was what she'd seen before, what she'd seen in Alexander's eyes.

People who'd been in hell and survived usually had that same look in their eyes.

Author's Thanks

I've published three previous historical novels, and it was with some relief that I looked forward to writing a book set in our own time. Anyone who's ever written a historical book will know what I mean. Not having to think about unfamiliar manners and customs, not having to go to a museum or call a historian every time I had a question about clothing, traditions, or food felt like a luxury. It felt like a luxury for about ten minutes.

Because I chose to situate the protagonists of *All In* in Sweden's financial elite, and I can honestly say that I've never done so much research, conducted so many interviews, and read so many technical books in my entire life as an author.

All In could never have been written without the generosity of people who understand the complexities of the financial sector so much better than I ever will. I want to thank you from the bottom of my heart, those of you from finance and beyond, who volunteered your time, knowledge, and expertise. You know who you are—everything that turned out right was thanks to you. The things I got wrong were entirely my own shortcomings.

I also want to extend a special thank-you to some friends who played a role in the creation of this book: Åsa Hellberg, Carina Hedberg, Petra Ahrnstedt, and Trude Lövstuhagen. You were all wonderful support, especially you, Petra. Thank you!

A big thank you to my publisher, Karin Linge Nordh, my editor, Kerstin Ödeen, and of course to the rest of the amazing—*amazing*—gang at Forum Publishing. It's a pleasure to get to work with you.

Thank you of course to my wonderful, wonderful children.

And finally thanks to my literary agent, Anna Frankl, at Nordin Agency, who in addition to selling my books abroad also has an unerring sense of when I am in desperate need of being treated to a fancy lunch.

Simona Ahrnstedt, Stockholm, 2014